Puck One Night Stands

CHICAGO RACKETEERS

EMMA FOXX

Cover by Qamber Designs

About The Book

One dating disaster, one Kiss Cam catastrophe, and a trio of hockey team hotties who are used to scoring big…

I don't do casual hookups, so I have no idea what to expect when I meet not one, but *three* hot guys who are into me.

I'm an introverted, failing-book-shop-owning, romance-writer wanna be.

But after my dating disaster at a hockey game—all caught on the jumbotron—I somehow have the attention of three men.

Nathan Armstrong is the hot, older, sophisticated billionaire owner of the team.

Why does this man want a night with me? I'm baffled…but I'm not saying no.

I should also say no to the romantic, suave, brilliant team doctor, Michael Hughes.

And the team's new hot-shot all-star player Crew McNeill.

But I don't.

And I'm loving every minute. Especially the minutes they decide we should *all* spend together. Golden Retriever Crew is all in, bossy, broody Nathan is reluctant (to say the least), and sexy, confident Michael knows what we all need. They're all here, promising to make every one of my fantasies come true.

And they do. Night after headboard-banging night.

But it can't last.

Good thing I was okay with a short-term fling because as soon as the fans find out what we're doing, our lives–and my heart–are going to be all pucked up.

CHAPTER 1

Nathan

"I'M NOT DOING THIS. It's ridiculous."

"You're doing it. You know it's a good idea."

"Someone else can do it. It doesn't have to be me."

"It doesn't have to be you. But it should be you. Quit whining."

I frown at the older woman next to me as the elevator from the top floor of our building hits the ground floor, and the doors swish open. "You look like such a sweet woman," I tell her. "But I don't get an ounce of compassion or coddling."

She snorts as she steps off the elevator into the lobby that is now teeming with people. "I used up all of my compassion in nineteen eighty-eight. You're too late."

"No," I say, my hand on her back as I guide her through the crowd of people dressed in black and silver and hyped up for tonight's game. "I distinctly remember you being nice when I was a kid."

"I was faking it. You have to be a real asshole to be mean to a kid," she says, giving me a grin.

I chuckle. I've known Valerie for thirty-four years, ever since my grandfather hired her as his personal secretary. She's one of the few people who can make me chuckle. Or who can get away with telling me to quit whining.

We step out into the fading sunlight. The Racketeers play at seven tonight, and the crowd is getting thick outside the arena. I guide her through the crowd and then hand her off to Bill, one of the security guards. "Take Val to her car, please." She doesn't typically stay this late on a game night, and I don't like that she'll be out in all this traffic, but while the fans are all coming in, she'll be going out so it should be fine.

"Evenin' Val," Bill greets her.

"Hi Bill," she says with a smile. But before she heads off in the direction of the employee lot, she turns back. "You," she says pointing at me. "Go do the promotion."

"I don't want to." It's not whining, it's just a fact. I'm not a people person. I might even go so far as to say I only truly like about three people on the planet, and Val is one of them.

"I don't know why we have to go over this every time," she says with a sigh. "It's part of your job. You have twelve VIP tickets to hand out as a surprise to fans." She waves her hand around at the people milling about. "How hard can that be? You're going to make twelve peoples' nights. That's so nice."

I roll my eyes.

She shakes her head. "Go. Do it. And yes, you have to smile."

"Dammit, this just keeps getting worse and worse. I'm leaving before you tell me I have to actually talk to them too," I say.

"Nathan William Armstrong," Valerie says. "You find twelve people who love this team, you walk up to them, smile, say something nice, and give them those fucking VIP tickets, or I'm not bringing you any tortellini soup on Monday."

I groan. Valerie has a big family gathering this coming weekend and her family knows how to eat and, more importantly, cook. She always brings me leftovers the Monday after their get togethers.

I give her a long-suffering look. "Fine."

Then I notice someone standing a few feet behind Valerie and Bill.

Someone with long red hair, and a sweet curvy ass.

She seems to be alone. Or waiting for someone, I amend, as she looks at her phone.

"Fine," I repeat, this time with a brighter tone. And even an almost-smile.

Valerie blinks at me. "Okay. Well, that's better."

Valerie and Bill move off, and I approach the redhead. She turns slightly, giving me more of a side view.

Great breasts to go with her sweet ass…yep, this handing out surprise VIP tickets suddenly seems like one of the best ideas our PR department has come up with in a long time.

"Excuse me."

She turns to face me fully, and I actually feel the entire universe pause for a moment of collective appreciation as her curious green eyes lock on mine.

Damn. She's… adorable. Round face with a sprinkle of freckles just across the bridge of her nose. Long lashes on those emerald eyes. Full pink lips.

She's looking at me inquisitively. "Yes?" she asks.

Her voice strokes over me, and I feel my blood start pumping harder.

What the fuck is that? I've definitely felt immediate attraction before, but this feels different. Do I know her? Have we met somewhere before? I doubt it. I don't think I could forget those eyes or that fiery red hair. But damn, there's something about looking at her that makes me think I could do this, just this, for hours.

Though my fingers are itching to do more than look. I want to touch. I want to run my hands through her hair. I want to see if her cheek is as soft as it looks. I want to glide my thumb across her lower lip and feel her warm breath as she breathes out…

"Can I help you?" she asks, clearly confused about why I'm just standing here like a dumbass staring at her and not speaking.

I've never felt the word flummoxed before but…this must be exactly what that word means.

I pull my shit together. "Yes." I shake my head. "Actually, I'm going to help you."

"You are?" Her lips curl slightly as if she's amused.

"First row, a VIP ticket for tonight's game." I pull one of the tickets out of my inside suit jacket pocket and hold it up.

"Oh." She frowns and glances toward the cars pulling up at the curb, dropping people off for the game. Then she looks back up at me. "I, um, have tickets. I mean, my friend does. I'm waiting for her to go in. But we've already got tickets."

"Not tickets as good as these," I tell her. "It's a special promotion. We're upgrading twelve fans tonight. I'll upgrade your friend too." I reach into my pocket.

"Well, we're… I mean, it's not… there are four of us, actually," she tells me.

Okay, even better. The faster I get rid of these damned things, the sooner I can go back upstairs. I pull four tickets out and hold them out. "Done."

She looks from me to the tickets and then back to me. "Really? Are you sure?"

"I am." I want to know exactly where she's sitting. That will make it easier to find her after the game. Why and for what I'm not exactly sure, but I've got three periods of hockey to figure that out.

"There are probably some kids you should give these to, not me," she says, still not accepting the tickets. "I'm sure they'd be thrilled."

This may be an actual first. This woman is rejecting upgraded seats? It makes her intriguing beyond her natural beauty.

"I have a whole bunch more. If I promise to find some kids to give the rest to, will you take these?"

She reaches out tentatively. "Well, okay then."

I make sure our fingers connect, and I don't let go of the tickets immediately. "What's your name?"

She meets my gaze. "Danielle."

"Hi, Danielle. I'm Nathan."

"It's nice to meet you, Nathan."

Damn, I like the way she says my name. "My pleasure, Danielle."

Her smile grows, and I let the tickets slide from my fingers. "I hope you enjoy the game."

"Thank you."

Just then a red Honda Civic pulls up at the curb and a guy in blue jeans, a plaid shirt, and wearing a blue baseball cap spills out of the backseat.

"Dani!" he exclaims, righting himself just before tripping on the curb.

He bounds over to her and wraps her in a huge hug.

I can smell the beer on him from three feet away.

She grimaces. "Hey, Ben."

"Sorry I'm a little late. I met some of the guys after work," he tells her as he lets her go.

Obviously, the meeting was to pound a six-pack of beer. He actually sways a little on his feet.

"That's okay. I'm still waiting for Luna and Kyle too."

"Yeah, Kyle texted. They're almost here."

"Great."

I know I'm scowling while taking this all in. Maybe this guy is her brother. Her drunk brother who she doesn't like hugging. Because it was clear she did not enjoy that hug.

"I'm so glad you finally said yes to them setting us up," Ben says, looping an arm around her. He looks her up and down. "Damn, you look hot."

She tugs her black cardigan sweater back up onto her shoulder, where Ben's arm pulled it down. But the move doesn't quite pull the V-neck of her T-shirt up enough to cover the swell of the tops of her breasts.

I really fucking hate Ben.

I also really fucking hate that I just gave Ben a VIP ticket to the game to sit next to Danielle.

I catch her eye. "Are you okay?" I ask, my voice sounding harsher than I intend. But fuck this guy who thinks he can show up loaded and ruin Danielle's night.

She nods but mouths, thank you in return.

I nod as she turns back to Ben, who belches loudly and doesn't apologize.

I'm definitely not letting her out of my sight tonight.

As if I was going to anyway.

I turn and make my way through the crowd. I shove two VIP tickets at two middle school aged boys that I notice decked out in fan gear. I think they almost pass out from excitement. I get rid of the other six by giving them to a family standing in line at the concession stand.

There. I did my duty. I even smiled. I think. Maybe. Kind of.

Smile or no smile, I gave them to kids as promised to Danielle.

Val can get off my ass.

Now I can sit in my owner's box and concentrate on finding out more about Danielle.

Is that over the top? Yes. Is that out of character for me? Not exactly. But for a woman? Yes, definitely.

I don't care. I don't have to explain myself to anyone.

I head up to talk to the media people. Then I track down Wade, the kid who works as the mascot, Sammy the Malamute.

After all of my plans are in place, I finally take a deep breath. There's only a few minutes until game time. I need to get up to my box and make sure Danielle got to her seats.

I round the corner and someone plows into me.

Beer soaks my dress shirt and pants, even splashing up into my face.

What the fuck?

I wipe the suds out of my eyes. And find myself staring at the shocked face of none other than Ben the Loser.

I look to his left.

Danielle is standing there, staring at me in horror.

But the front of her oatmeal colored t-shirt is soaked as well.

Ben, on the other hand, is completely dry.

Of course, he is.

"Oh, shit!" he finally exclaims. "Damn, man. Sorry!"

I wait for a beat. Is he going to apologize to Danielle? Is he even going to look in her direction?

I don't say a word to him, but I reach for her hand. I tug her toward me, then turn and start in the opposite direction. My chest is damp, and my hatred of Ben has solidified, but I also think the idiot just did me a favor. Danielle's hand is small and warm in mine, as she trips along behind me for three steps before she catches up.

I hear a confused Ben say, "Where are you going?"

"Um...I don't..." She looks up at me. "Um, where are we going?"

"We need new shirts."

"But..." She clearly doesn't know what to say to that. She glances behind her, but doesn't pull away.

I continue striding down the hall until I get to the storage room. I shove my free hand into my pocket, pull out my keys, unlock the door, and shove it open. The motion sensor light flickers on and I tug Danielle through the door, letting it bump shut behind us.

She's breathing fast, but I don't think it's from the walk.

"I'm really sorry," she says nervously, glancing around the room.

"Why?" I ask, crossing the room to the Racketeers hockey T-shirt shelves. I need to keep moving. And not look at her.

The t-shirt she's wearing is a beige color. It's not white. It didn't become see-through when it got wet, but it's plastered against her like a second skin. Because, of course, Ben got the large beers. Two of them. That or he was carrying one for her. But she has a bottle of water in her hand, so I'm guessing both of those were good ol' Benny's.

"For getting beer all over your clearly very expensive suit."

I grab a white t-shirt with our mascot emblazoned on it for her. I also pull out one for myself, a solid black with a small logo on the upper right hand side of the shirt. With my suit jacket back on, it won't even be noticeable.

Am I the only guy walking around the level where the concessions are, and where the fans are coming up the ramps and into the stands, in a suit? Maybe. But it's important for the administration to be out and about when the fans are in the arena, to see how our employees interact with them, to see how they react to various experiences like the mascot meet-and-greet, the *Feeling Pucky?* contest, and the Stick It to Cancer fundraiser.

Or so our PR department keeps telling me.

"*You* didn't get beer on my very expensive suit," I tell her as I cross back to stand in front of her. "Or on your shirt."

I hand her the T-shirt and let my gaze glance over her wet shirt.

I'd been right about the breasts. Very nice.

Her cheeks are pink, and I want to touch them again. Hell, I want to touch all of her. Instead, I yank on my tie, unknotting it, then slide it from my collar. I toss it down on the clothing rack.

She watches the entire process raptly.

"So you and Ben…" I trail off, hoping she'll fill in the blank.

Her eyes are on my fingers as I start unbuttoning my shirt.

"Um, nothing," she says absently. "He's roommates with my roommate's date for tonight."

Perfect.

"He's a dick," I point out.

She nods. But I don't think she's really hearing what I'm saying. I'm almost done with my buttons and her eyes are glued to my chest.

I shrug out of my dress shirt, and I watch as her mouth drops open slightly.

Every single second I've spent in the gym is now one hundred percent worth it. She's staring at my bare chest with wide eyes, visibly swallowing. Her cheeks bloom with color, and her arm holding the T-shirt goes slack.

I grin.

She doesn't see it. She hasn't looked up for nearly a full minute.

Only when the black cotton covers my torso does she finally blink. But she doesn't say a word.

"You should change too," I tell her.

She looks up and meets my gaze in confusion. "What? Oh." She looks down at the shirt I gave her. "Right. Yeah." Then she glances around. "Here?"

I shrug. "No one will come in here."

She looks at me again. "Um."

Well, damn. I thought maybe she'd be distracted enough to just start stripping without thinking about it. "I'll turn around." But I'm not leaving.

She glances back at the door, clearly debating. Then she turns back to me. "Okay." Her voice is softer. And she's looking at me with wide eyes and pink cheeks.

I hope she never ever fucking looks at Ben like that.

If I have anything to say about it, she won't.

She won't ever look at anyone else like that.

Yeah, that's over the top for sure.

I turn away and hear clothing rustling. I'm not even trying not to envision her peeling off the wet shirt, and then pulling the dry T-shirt on. It's all I can think about.

What kind of bra does she wear? How many hooks are there? What color is it? White or nude? She doesn't seem like the expensive lacy lingerie type, but more practical.

But I want to buy her expensive lacy lingerie.

Jesus, what is happening to me?

This girl is not my type. I tend to hook up with busy, independent women my age who don't want anything from me. No ties, no commitment, no sharing of our pasts…or futures. Women who aren't looking for soft things like cuddles and hugs.

Danielle exudes cuddles and hugs.

I wouldn't even call what I do dating, and when I run through the list of women I have fucked in the last five years, I doubt very much if any of them have a cardigan in their entire closet.

And none of them like hockey.

But Danielle is going to be sitting right behind the glass tonight at one of the Racketeers biggest games.

And my eyes will be on her all night.

"Okay, I'm done."

I turn back to find her in the Racketeers tee, her cardigan back in place, her wet shirt in hand.

"Do you need to have this replaced?" I ask, taking it from her.

She frowns. "What do you mean? I'll just wash it."

"I'll buy you a new one. Or ten. You don't have to hold onto this one."

She shakes her head. "That's ridiculous. You don't need to replace my shirt. Or ten of them. The beer was Ben's fault."

Yes it was. Dickhead Ben. She needs to remember that.

"You're not going to sit and hold a beer-soaked shirt during the game," I tell her, tossing the T-shirt into the trashcan near the door of the room.

"Well, you're not replacing it either. You've already gotten me this T-shirt," she says, plucking the Racketeers shirt away from her stomach. "Though, it's a little small."

I study her. The shirt is snug. Very snug. It makes her breasts look amazing. "It's perfect," I tell her.

She looks up quickly and catches me staring at her chest.

Her eyes widen, but her lips curl. "Yeah?"

"Definitely. That is exactly the right size."

With both of us changed, she seems to have regained her equilibrium. She actually snorts. "Okay." Then she adds, "So, you must really love your job."

"How so?" I ask, because I suspect she thinks my job is something entirely different than what it actually is.

"Because you get to give free stuff away to fans. You make

people happy." She smiles at me. "What a great way to spend your work hours."

I blink at Danielle, caught off guard. She actually means that. Sincerity is ringing in her voice, and I instantly know that she is way too good for me. Too genuine, too pure, too caring.

Which makes me want her even more.

"I've always thought of my job as more of a numbers game." Payroll versus advertising and team revenue.

"It's more than T-shirts and tickets," she says. "It's escapism. It gives people hope, something to root for, a common bond with other humans. Hockey makes people happy."

Put so simply by her, it feels like a lightbulb going off. I know that fans love hockey, but hearing this interesting woman phrase it like she has, floors me a little. "You're right."

I don't say anything else.

Damn it. I'm fucking flummoxed again.

She starts for the door.

That spurs me into action. "Let me walk you to your seat."

She gives a laugh. "No. I can find my way. God knows what might happen if you get too close to Ben again."

I have a list of about six things I'd like to have happen to Ben. "Fine. I'll see you around, Danielle."

She looks back quickly, her hand on the doorknob. "You think so?"

"I guarantee it."

CHAPTER 2

Dani

I KNEW I LIKED HOCKEY, but I didn't realize until just now how much I actually *love* hockey.

The pregame show I got with the hot suit guy taking off his shirt right in front of me in the storeroom, the free T-shirt he ogled me in, and now front row seats all made even the first two periods in the arena pretty amazing.

Despite my dud date. Ben is definitely drunk, definitely not as funny as he thinks he is, and he doesn't know much about hockey. And he won't shut up while I try to watch.

All of which really sucks. I *want* to date. I *want* to fall in love. I wanted to find *the one.*

Okay, that's what I tell my mother. And myself when I'm being less than totally honest.

I *do* want to date. But I'm less focused on *love* and more interested in some hot, make-me-want-to-get-naked-right-now chemistry. *That* would be a nice start. I'd love to meet someone who can get me all hot and tingly just with a look. Who can simply touch my hand and make my heart beat faster. Who will lean over and whisper something dirty in my ear in public. Who can make my panties wet with a single naughty text.

Like the guy in the suit earlier.

Yes, he was still on my mind. I'd felt my pulse speed up when I'd first turned around and met his gaze when he'd been offering me the tickets. And watching him take his shirt off? Hot? Tingly? Wet panties? Check, check, and freaking check.

"So you guys wanna go to the sports bar around the corner after the game?" Ben asks, his words slurring slightly.

Yeah, that someone is not going to be Ben.

"I really don't," I tell him honestly.

Looks like another night with my romance novels and my vibrator.

I glance back at the ice. I might have to download a hockey romance tonight though.

I've now seen two periods of the game between the Chicago Racketeers and the Minnesota Beavers, and I am all in on being one of the Racketeers biggest fans.

Or maybe I'm just going to be one of Crew McNeill's biggest fans.

The Chicago Racketeers are having a great season, so I've been told. And it's because of Crew, the team's high scorer so far this season, my best friend's younger brother. So I've been told.

Crew was just traded to the Racketeers. He played for the Seattle Storm for the past two seasons, but he's always wanted to return to his home team. His family is thrilled and, according to Luna, he's got very high hopes for this season and beyond in Chicago.

He's definitely playing like a man on a mission tonight. He's already scored both of the goals for the Racketeers.

"What is Crew's position again?" I ask Luna, who is sitting next to me right behind the glass at the game.

My best friend grins at me. She knows everything about hockey and tolerates the fact that I know almost nothing about the game. I know their uniform shirts are called jerseys, the black thing they hit is called a puck, and the sticks they use are called, well, hockey sticks.

She's been my ride or die since we were assigned roommates

our freshman year at Columbia College in Chicago and likes me because…I'm not always sure why, because we're pretty different. But I love the silvery-haired, crystal-loving, aura-reading girl who always has my back.

Before I left for college, my mother told me to find the loudest person in the room and talk to her. That she would pave the way for an introverted person like me, and for once, my mother's advice had actually worked. I didn't even have to go looking for her, because the minute my brand new roommate opened her mouth, I knew I'd found her. Luna told me the universe had assigned us to Room 204 because our energies needed each other. Our astrological signs aligned and my earth sign grounded her air.

I still don't know how I feel about all of that, but she's amazing, and I love her like a sister.

"He's the center," Luna tells me.

She points, but I know exactly where Crew is. I haven't been able to stop watching him. I've known this guy as long as I've known Luna. He's her high-energy, charming but annoying little brother. At least that's what I've always thought.

Tonight I've been thinking very different thoughts about Crew McNeill.

He's no longer a skinny high school kid eating everything in sight. It's been three years since I've seen him in person. He seems taller and broader, though, of course, he's wearing skates and pads so some of that might be deceptive. He's also moving so fast it's hard to really tell. But there's something about him that just seems bigger. He moves with confidence, determination, and grace.

"He's really good," I say unnecessarily.

But Luna just laughs. She's very proud of her baby brother. "I know. He's worked his ass off, and he's thrilled to be able to show it off in front of his home crowd."

"I'm so happy for him," I say. Or maybe I kind of murmur it, because I'm enthralled. That's the perfect word. I can't believe how these guys move on the ice. It's so fast, yet controlled. Aggressive, but somehow graceful.

Why haven't I been watching hockey constantly? "These are great seats," I add. "Can you believe that guy just handed them to me?"

We're right behind the player box. I can almost reach out and touch some of them.

"Hey, do you want a beer or something?" Ben asks.

I look at him and wish, again, that he'd just stop talking.

He's reasonably attractive. He has dark hair and he's wearing a plaid shirt and glasses. A little nerdy, but then I am too. He's much more my type than a hockey player. Or so I thought. Luna's been out with his roommate Kyle twice, and they thought this would be a great set-up.

It should have been.

But then the hot suit guy took his shirt off and now Crew is being a hockey star and...

Not that I'm thinking about Crew as my type. *But he could be,* a little voice in my head whispers. *Temporarily, at least.*

I almost laugh at that. I'm not really a temporarily type of girl. But that's exactly the kind of thing the heroines in my romances think. I tend to write women in my short, serial fiction that are very different from myself. Confident, sexy women who know what they want and aren't afraid to go after it. Even with men who are the brothers of their best friends, and who have puck bunnies in every city throwing their panties at them.

"Dani? Beer?" Ben asks.

Right. I'm on a date. I should really probably pay attention to him for a little while. Though really the last thing Ben needs is more beer.

"Sure, thanks," I say and force a smile.

I turn to Luna and raise my eyebrows at her. I'm asking for help, but I don't even know why. I should at least be making an effort with Ben, but mostly I just want him to disappear so I can allow myself to be enthralled by Crew without interruption. But the horn sounds ending the period and the players are leaving the ice for the locker room anyway.

Luna turns to her date sitting on her right. "I'd like a beer too, Kyle. Go with Ben and grab one for me, will you? Thanks."

Kyle straightens up immediately. "Of course. What kind of beer?"

He's practically falling all over himself to please Luna. Luna is the type of woman that men fall over themselves for all the time. She's gorgeous, fun, adventurous, and always a bit of a surprise. Even to those of us who know her and love her.

Why are we friends again? But I smile as I think it.

The guys go to the concession stand and are back before the intermission ends.

"They really do some price gouging on these beers," Ben says with a frown as he hands me a plastic cup.

I feel compelled to offer to pay for it. "I can send you money for it," I say, wanting to be polite.

"No, it's fine. Totally fine." He shakes his head but I don't think it's fine. That is obvious when he adds, "These aren't even cold. Unbelievable."

We manage to make small talk, and I keep my attention on Ben for several minutes consecutively. Look at me being a great date. He probably can't even tell I'm barely registering his story about his cat's jumping skills.

The team skates back onto the ice, thankfully, just as Ben and I seem to be running out of conversation topics. So, we have about ten minutes of stuff to chat about. Fantastic. I mean, I like cats, but really?

As the team does a couple of laps getting ready for the third period, the jumbotron flashes with the Kiss Cam.

I grin. I love those. I do love love. I love watching couples in love grin up at the camera, then grin at one another, and not hesitate to show off their devotion by leaning in and kissing. It's so sweet.

The only way a Kiss Cam can get better is if someone drops to one knee and proposes. Gah. That's the best.

"Ooh, maybe we'll see a proposal tonight," I say to no one in particular.

I know Luna rolls her eyes without even looking at her, but she's also smiling affectionately about my romantic streak.

Ben just takes another drink of beer.

A couple in their fifties are first. They do the typical grin, lean, kiss.

Then another couple flashes on the screen.

Oh.

Shit.

That's me and Ben.

Um...I turn to him. He hasn't even noticed. He's actually looking in the opposite direction, his beer to his lips again.

"Ben," I hiss, smiling because my face is four hundred times its usual size and my hair suddenly doesn't look as good as it did in my bathroom mirror at home. Smooth auburn waves now look like ginger frizz. Funny how a gigantic screen can bring out all the flaws.

"Yeah?" he asks, not looking at me.

"Kiss me," I say, quickly.

"Huh?" He does turn to me now. But he's grinning. "You want me to kiss you?"

"Kiss. Cam," I say between clenched teeth and awkwardly smiling lips.

He leans in and I'm hit by the smell of beer. *I don't want to kiss him* is my first thought. I really don't. Not even for my one and only chance on the Kiss Cam.

But I close my eyes and pucker up.

The next thing I feel is Ben shift, and the brush of what feels like...fur?

My eyelids pop open and all I see for a second is what looks like a black and silver shag carpet. But I look up and realize that

Sammy the Malamute, the Racketeers mascot, is standing just on the other side of Ben.

He's miming with his paws clenched into fists that he wants to fight Ben.

What's going on?

Ben has a beer in one hand, but he's holding his other up in surrender. He's kind of smiling but also looks very confused.

Sammy points at me, then at his mouth.

He's a dog, who's dressed like a thirties gangster, wearing a vest and tie and a fedora. So, I guess I could kiss him? Kind of? Pretend for the camera? Obviously this is some kind of set-up for laughs.

Fine, I'll play along. It'll save me from Ben's beer breath. And from giving him any ideas about any kissing that might happen later after the game.

Sammy reaches out and grabs my hand in his furry paw. I take it, grateful to be saved by a man in a full body dog costume. How often do you get to say that?

He pulls me to my feet and I shove my beer into Ben's hand, starting to climb over his skinny legs. The crowd watching the jumbotron is screaming their approval.

Hell, I'm screaming my approval. Internally, of course. I'm not really an out loud screamer.

But this is great. If I have to be on a Kiss Cam with a stranger, this is how I want it to go.

It could be an epic save. It would be an epic save. Except stepping over Ben's knees proves to be more awkward and difficult than I expect. My knees bump against Ben's and my feet tangle with his. He is now juggling two beers and trying desperately to keep them from spilling. One cup tips precariously. So do I.

Sammy's paw is too big around his real hand to have a good grip on me. Ben is close but his hand has too good a grip on the beer. There's no one to save me as I pitch forward, landing face down across Ben's lap, ass in the air, and I, of course, smack my forehead on the empty seat next to Ben.

If my head didn't instantly hurt and this wasn't humiliating—and he wasn't more concerned about the beer he's holding and we were both different people—this would be the perfect position for Ben to spank me.

Why did I think that? Again, that's something my fictional girls are into. I've never been spanked.

Then it gets worse. I feel something wet soak into the seat of my cutest high-waisted jeans.

Oh my God, Ben just spilled beer on my ass. And contrary to his earlier complaint, it is cold.

The previously cheering crowd now gasps collectively.

Yeah, there are a lot of things that look really bad on a jumbotron. A wet ass is one of them, I can assume. Since I'm face-down staring at the concrete floor under our seats and the disgusting collection of popcorn kernels, chewed up gum wads, and spilled beer, I can't confirm it myself.

"Holy shit, dude," Sammy says. "That looked gnarly. Are you okay?"

I'm not sure that's the voice I would have imagined for a mobster Malamute. He sounds like a teen surfer. In Chicago. In October.

I grip my throbbing head. Am I okay? I'm not really sure, to be totally honest.

Maybe it's the mild concussion that makes the next few moments chaotic and disorienting. I think I hear Ben say, "Dammit." Maybe that's concern over my fall. More likely he's lamenting his spilled beer.

I definitely hear Luna say, "Dani! Oh my God! Are you okay? Get her up you dumbass!" I don't know if that's directed at Ben or Sammy. Or both.

Then I hear a deep, velvety voice say, "Let me through."

I also hear another deep male voice say, "Jesus, Dani, I was gonna come talk to you after the game. You didn't have to bust your head open to get my attention."

Crew.

That's Crew's voice. Why isn't he on the ice? Before I can process that fact, two big hands grasp me by my hips and haul me upright in one smooth motion.

My head swims and I think about throwing up for a second. But a non-kiss on the Kiss Cam, a fall, and a concussion are my limit for public humiliation.

Then I turn and face the man who just pulled me out of Ben's lap. It isn't Crew. It's a total stranger.

With the most gorgeous brown eyes I've ever seen in my life.

He's cupping my face, staring into my eyes with a mix of concern and something that looks a little like...surprise? Why is he surprised? I don't know this man. But damn, I kind of want to.

He's at least six inches taller than I am, but he's leaning in to look at me. His thumbs stroke over my jaw, and I feel tingles shoot down my neck and arms. Who is this gorgeous man, and why is he touching me? Why isn't he touching me more? I think I want him to touch me more.

"Can you tell me how you feel?" Brown Eyes asks, his voice low.

"Woozy." I realize I'm gripping the lapels of his suit jacket. But I don't think it's because I'm woozy. I think I want him to keep standing close to me.

The corner of his mouth curls. "That seems about right. Are you in a lot of pain?" Those gentle but strong fingers are shifting my carefully constructed waves off of my forehead, probing along the hairline.

"My head hurts a little but not terribly."

The light touch drifts over my flushed skin, over my temples and lands on my cheeks, intriguingly close to my lips.

"Do you know where you are?" he asks.

I nod, then wince. "At the Racketeers game watching Crew McNeill. Number seventeen. He just got drafted from Seattle. I'm here with his sister, Luna. He's already scored twice."

The guy studying me laughs, and I hear Ben behind me say, "Why am I here again?"

But I also hear Crew say, "Hey, Doc, she okay?"

Doc?

The guy holding me nods. He drops his hands from my cheeks so quickly I sway forward on my feet a little.

He steadies me with a grip on my elbow. "I think she'll be fine."

"Then hand her over."

Suddenly people are moving and Crew is pushing in to stand in front of me. Then his hands are cupping my face. This is a lot of face cupping for a woman like me. I would like to be face cupped more often.

"Hey, Dani." He's grinning at me.

He might be a lot bigger than I remember, but I know that grin. His shoulder pads have nudged Ben further back from me, and his long unruly hair is poking out from under his helmet. His green eyes are pinned on me.

"Hey, Crew." Is my voice breathless because I have a concussion?

He leans in a little. "What's your date's name?"

"Um…" No, I'm breathless because Crew McNeill is not just Luna's little brother anymore. "I don't remember."

His grin grows. "That's the right answer."

Then he kisses me.

I definitely have a concussion because Crew McNeill is in the stands kissing me, and all of the people who have been watching this mini-soap opera unfold suddenly roar their approval as one.

It's loud and the vibrations ripple through me and my heart starts pounding.

I throw my arms around his neck and kiss him right back. Like I've never been kissed before. Like people kiss in the rom-com movies I gobble up like the macarons I inhale while I watch them. Like people kiss in all the deliciously dirty romance novels I read. Like people kiss in the steamy short stories I write.

Okay, not quite like that. We're fully clothed.

But now that I've kissed him, I want to kiss him like all of those stories that are in my head.

Hello even wetter panties.

Yes, *this* is what I want. Tingles, and heat, and dirty thoughts, and big hands on me. And now it's happened with *three* guys in one night. Within one *hour*.

And holy crap. One of them is Crew McNeill.

Someone clears his throat behind me.

You'd think that would be my date, what's-his-name. But it's the tall man with the medium brown skin and big hands and gorgeous eyes that Crew called "Doc".

"Don't you have somewhere you need to be, McNeill?" he asks.

Crew finally pulls back.

I realize his hands have left my face and are now resting on my ass. My beer-soaked ass.

He grins at me as he squeezes that ass, then lifts his hand, runs a thumb over his bottom lip and says, "Had to be sure the girl got a proper kiss for the Kiss Cam."

"Yeah, yeah, you're a real gentleman," "Doc" says dryly.

"Part of my job is fan relations," Crew says, his eyes not leaving mine.

"Not sure that's what they mean by that." Doc's big hand reaches across my shoulder and shoves Crew. "Get back on the ice."

Crew laughs and starts to back up. "See you after the game, Dani."

He doesn't phrase it as a question.

I just nod. I mean, what woman would say no to that?

I watch him step back out onto the ice and skate toward the middle of the rink. It isn't until that moment that I realize the game has been delayed because of all of this. Because of Crew's kiss. Our kiss. I turn wide eyes to Luna.

She's staring at me with a huge grin. *What the hell was that?* She mouths.

That was a dream come true. But I just shake my head.

"Are you okay? Really?" the man behind me asks.

I turn to look at him and nod. "I think so."

"Can I check in with you after the game before you go home? Just to be sure?"

I must give him a puzzled look as I say, "Sure. I guess so."

"I'm the team physician. Michael Hughes." He holds out a hand and I take it.

He doesn't shake my hand though, he just gives me a little squeeze.

Another big, hot hand. I actually sigh happily.

"I'd love to see you before you leave," he says.

Damn, I really love his eyes.

See both of these men after the game? Um… yes.

"So, I guess I'll just catch an Uber," Ben says from behind Michael.

The doctor's body is completely blocking me from my date. And he doesn't move even after Ben speaks.

"Yeah, you should do that," Luna says.

"I've got her," Michael adds.

Dr. Michael Hughes has me.

My stomach does a flip. I think I'm fine with Dr. Michael Hughes having me.

Wade (Sammy the Malamute)

I pull the earpiece out of my ear with a grimace.

I don't know if it's that I'm a little high or if it's that Mr. Armstrong is yelling so loud that it's not transmitting properly, but I can't understand a thing he's saying besides the word "fuck" repeatedly.

I don't know what the hell is going on.

I do know that taking three edibles before coming to work was probably a bad idea.

I also know that Mr. Armstrong is a scary motherfucker.

CHAPTER 3

Nathan

"WHAT THE FUCK JUST HAPPENED?" I ask no one in particular as I stand in the owner's box overlooking the arena. Wade isn't answering on the earpiece anymore, and I have no one else to ask immediately about the chaotic scene I just witnessed.

We're in the first home series of a new season and my new star center, who cost me a fortune in a trade with Seattle, just left the ice to kiss Danielle.

That was not how this was supposed to go.

What the hell?

I'd put her in that front row. I'd told the media booth to pan over those seats often as they did the scans of the crowd for the jumbotron throughout the game. I knew where she was sitting, but couldn't see her well from clear up here, and I wanted to make sure everything was going okay with her date with Dumbass Ben.

Okay, I also wanted to keep looking at her.

The guys in the media booth had given me a funny look, but I'd dropped the order and left. I don't care what they think. No one would question me out loud. They can talk about my crazy requests behind my back, as long as they do what I say.

But how had, 'pan over that section periodically, especially the redhead' turned into 'put the redhead and her dickhead date on the Kiss Cam'?

I'd also put a device in the ear of Wade, the kid who dresses up as Sammy the mascot, so I could talk to him when he took the VIP ticket down to Danielle after the second period. I wanted him to personally deliver the note and gift from me, but I'd also wanted to dictate what he should say to her. And I'd wanted to hear her response.

He certainly wasn't supposed to try to kiss her.

Not that her kissing the stuffed dog head would have been a real kiss but still… what had Wade been thinking? Sure, his job is to ham it up, make the crowd laugh, and sometimes he has to think on his feet during fan interactions.

But how the fuck had my very clear order to Wade– do not let that man kiss her– when I'd seen Ben leaning in, turn into her falling, smacking her head, Michael Hughes climbing into the stands, and then Crew Fucking McNeill kissing her?

I swear under my breath and resist throwing my phone against the wall since I'm not alone in the box.

Is she hurt? Is she in pain? I'm going to hurt someone if so.

The game starts again, but the camera pans back over Danielle and her friends. Her cheeks are still pink and her friend, the beautiful woman with the silver hair next to her, says something that makes them both laugh.

I stop and stare. I want to see Danielle in person again.

I probably shouldn't want that. She looks young. Too young. Forty-one year old men shouldn't feel jealous of hot shot jocks that can pull shit like jumping into the stands to kiss a girl like her while an arena full of fans cheer and snap photos and take videos.

But I do. Feel jealous, that is.

I also definitely want to see her again.

The fans ate up that entire stunt Crew pulled and I should love that. People will be posting about it and talking for days.

Instead of being pleased, however, I want to pull my impulsive new center into my office and chew his ass.

How dare he come off the ice and plant a kiss on some random fan like that?

I would be justified in disciplining him.

But looking at the redhead, I get it.

This girl…I am so damned grateful for that jumbotron that allows me to study her fully. And the fact that I own the footage and can go back and watch all of it over again just so I can see all of her facial expressions. Surprise, pleasure, embarrassment, delight.

I can't really blame Crew for abandoning everything for a chance to kiss Danielle.

Who is probably now going to sue the team both for the concussion from being dropped on her head by Sammy the Malamute and for sexual assault by one of my players.

Of course it's number seventeen. None of my other players would pull that shit. He's an expensive player who is supposed to save the season, not thrust the team into scandal.

Crew McNeill plays aggressively and sometimes impulsively, but always gets results. This is not the result I'm looking for. Since my grandfather officially retired five years earlier, I've been solely in charge of all the major decisions as co-owner. At forty one, I've been involved in the team since I graduated with my MBA, but I've technically been co-owner since I was twelve, when my father passed away.

This team means everything to me. I want a championship for my grandfather before he no longer can comprehend what it means. He watches the games on his big screen from his private room at the exclusive nursing home where he has incredibly expensive around-the-clock care. But no matter how much money I give that place, the doctors, even the research teams, can't stave off the Alzheimer's that is stealing him away. Some day, my grandfather–the man who took me in and raised me after my parents died–will no longer know the team or the sport that has brought him so much joy and pride. He won't know me. Or that I was the one who took care of his team for him.

This season has to be the one. For him.

That's why I took the chance on Crew McNeill. I am not going to let my newest punk ass player fuck everything up.

Yanking on the neck of my T-shirt, suddenly feeling strangled by it in the private box, I pull out my phone and text Michael, our team physician. Who, for some fucking reason, was also in the stands with the redhead.

Did I mention she's adorable?

Even facedown with her ass in the air.

Yes, I know how that sounds. No, I'm not sorry.

Is Danielle

I delete that.

Michael does not need to know that I know her name.

Is that girl okay?

He doesn't answer right away, which gives me time to pace back and forth in my Italian leather shoes and glance obsessively at the jumbotron, hoping the camera crew will pan back around and land on her adorable face again.

It's ridiculous how much I love seeing her in that Racketeers t-shirt. It's ridiculous how I can still feel how it felt to have her gaze on my bare chest and abs.

It's ridiculous how much I hate that asshole Ben.

She's fucking adorable and I want her.

Adorable is not my type. The word is not even in my vernacular. I'm not an "adorable" kind of guy. Until now, apparently.

I gravitate toward type A career women who want sex occasionally just to work off some pent-up stress and let their hair down, and are happy to do so with a guy who feels the same way. No emotion or strings involved. Women who don't attach and who understand that I have zero intention of falling in love with any of them. Women who don't ask me about my personal life or my feelings, and I don't ask them about theirs.

Why the hell am I thinking about love and that I don't give or receive any? Or that I'd like to wipe all memory of Crew McNeill's kiss from her lips with my own mouth. With a man's kiss– possessive and dominating and powerful... Jesus.

My phone vibrates in my hand and, grateful for the distraction, I immediately open the text from Michael.

Seems fine, but I'm checking in with her after the game.

Good, I really need to be sure she's fine. If she's hurt or in any kind of pain, I will fix it. I text back.

Tell me her status immediately when you know.

But I need to talk to Danielle again, myself. I need to make sure she's alright myself.

I also need to be sure that she got my gift. And accepted it. I want her at the next game beside me. Fuck that loser Ben. I want her watching the Racketeers in this box with me. Far from Crew McNeill's reach.

Michael texts me.

Why?

I scowl at Michael's response. I want to say 'because I fucking said so'. Why can't anyone just do what I tell them to tonight?

I take a deep breath and respond. Because I'd like to... Fuck, I can't tell Michael what I'd like to do to Danielle.

Make sure she doesn't sue us.

I wouldn't worry about that. She doesn't seem upset. She's quite...

I wait for him to complete that sentence but it takes several seconds.

Adorable.

I've known Michael Hughes for three years. We're not exactly friends, but I respect him and am damned glad he's the one in charge of the health of my team. And we've interacted enough for me to know that he also does not use the word 'adorable' on a regular basis.

Dammit. He sees it too. I instantly hate that.

Just report in after you see her.

There's a long pause with no response from Michael and I pace the length of the box twice.

Crew McNeill shoots down the ice with the puck. I move closer to the window, scowling. That little shit is going to score again.

Why am I irritated by that? He's playing for my team for fuck's sake.

At the last minute, the Beaver's defense knocks the puck away from him and I let out a breath.

I'm really messed up right now.

Finally Michael texts back.

Will do.

I slide my phone into my pocket, then shove a hand through my hair.

My heart is pounding, my gut is tight, I'm pacing, my hair is mussed.

How did this night get so out of control so fast?

I blame my PR people for thinking I needed to personally hand out VIP tickets tonight.

No, I blame Sammy the Malamute. How hard is it to deliver a simple envelope with a note and a game ticket for fuck's sake?

No, I blame Ben, the plaid-wearing drunk. Who does he think he is to be on a date with Danielle?

No, I blame pretty-boy-hockey-wonder Crew McNeill.

Yes, this is definitely Crew's fault.

Because adorable redheads probably *are* his type.

Crew

I grin down at the text from my sister.

> I took Dani to the back hallway outside the locker rooms. The doctor wants to check in with her one more time before she goes home. Can you make sure they meet up?

Danielle Larkin is waiting outside my locker room. And I will definitely make sure she's taken care of. I rush through my shower and getting back into my suit, eager to see Dani again after that kiss.

"You're already leaving?" Alexei, the Racketeers defenseman

asks. He claps me on the shoulder, hard. "Great game tonight. We should celebrate."

Usually I'm all for joking around, laughing and talking with my new teammates after a game. Especially after a win. Especially after a win where I was the only scorer. I like to stick around for the accolades. I had a damn good game.

Fuck, I'm glad to be home.

"Got somewhere I need to be," I tell him.

I pull my bag up onto my shoulder and hit the door. There are several wives and girlfriends waiting but I find the cute redhead immediately.

"Hi, Crew!"

"Great game Crew!"

A few of the wives greet me and I smile and wave. I don't know all their names yet, but my teammates have been great about making me feel included and I really need to figure out who belongs to who. I want to be a part of this team in every way.

But right now, I have a mission.

Dani.

She looks nervous. Or confused.

I head straight for her with a big smile. I haven't seen Dani in a few years, but I remember that long red hair and those big green eyes. She has an adorable little nose and creamy skin with freckles dusting lightly over her cheeks. And the curves in all the right places. My sister's best friend has always been cute, and I've been in love with her since I was sixteen and I met her moving Luna's crap into their dorm room.

And now I've kissed her. In front of an entire arena full of people. When I've just started playing for the Racketeers. Plus, there might have been a slight start of game delay due to my lips landing on Dani's. Maybe not my smartest move.

Sure it was spontaneous, but I have no regrets about that kiss.

That's also not going to be the last time it happens.

Though I'd like this time to be slightly more private so I can really explore the way she tastes.

"Hey, Dani," I greet as I stop in front of her. "How's your head?"

I'd been skating a few laps for warmup after intermission when I saw Sammy, our mascot, heading in her direction. Then she was up on the Kiss Cam, and suddenly Sammy was pulling her up, apparently to kiss her himself, and then, the next thing I knew, she'd face planted into the seat next to her date. It had all happened so fast, I was on my way to her side before I'd really registered what was going on.

But then, given the chance to rectify the no-kiss on the Kiss Cam situation, I'd stepped up.

I'm not sorry.

She tips her head up and blinks at me. I reach out and smooth her fiery red hair back off of her forehead. Her hair is silky. I suddenly want to wrap it around my fingers and tug her to me, but I don't. I study her skin first. She has a tiny bump marring her perfect flesh, and I brush my fingertip over it gently. "You have a goose egg."

"Oh, um…" She wets her lips. "I'm fine. Really."

Then her gaze tracks over me. Slowly. Twice.

I'm in a suit now. It's dark gray and I'm wearing a light gray button down shirt underneath. We always dress up before and after the games and she clearly likes what she sees. I get a lot of attention from women. I don't think that's ego talking, that's just fact. But I especially like having Dani's attention.

"What do you think?" I ask, dropping my hand from her and down over the front of my jacket.

"You… um…" She finally drags her gaze back to mine. "Look nice."

I grin. "You too."

Her eyes widen a little. 'I do?"

"Definitely." I now let my gaze track over her from head to toe. She practically invited me to. I like what I see. She's all soft curves and a narrow waist. "Very nice."

When I look at her face again, she's blushing. Her pale skin flushes a very pretty pink and I want to see what other parts of her body are that sweet pink color. And what other parts I can make flush like that. I step closer.

"It's been a while," I say.

She nods and I watch her swallow hard. "Three years. Since Luna's and my graduation party."

I grin. She knows exactly the last time we saw each other? I like that. A lot. "How have you been?"

"Fine."

That seems to be her favorite word.

She doesn't look fine. She looks flustered and fuckable. "Did you enjoy the game?"

Her gaze drops to my mouth and I grin. *Yeah, that was my favorite part too, honey.*

"I…did. You're really fantastic."

"I am," I agree. What? It's true. They don't pay me the big bucks for being pretty. Though I am that as well, if I'm being totally honest. Guys would kill for my flow.

"Congratulations on everything. I'm really proud of you, Crew. You've achieved a lot for being only twenty-two."

Ah. She's pointing out I'm younger than her. But it's only two years. That doesn't matter at all. And I intend to show her that I'm not the kid she remembers. "I'm glad you were here tonight."

"You are?"

"I haven't been on the Kiss Cam before," I tell her. Though I'm definitely going home tonight and watching the video of me and Dani on YouTube. There's no doubt in my mind someone has already uploaded it and I want to see how it looks. How we look.

Again those pretty green eyes widen. "Me either." Her voice is soft now.

"How do you feel about non-Kiss Cam kisses, Dani?" I ask her, my voice a little husky as I lean in and brace one hand on the wall next to her head.

"I love lots of kinds of kisses," she says. She's breathing faster now.

I wonder for a second if she realizes how that sounds. And how fucking hot that just made me.

I let my bag drop to the floor, cup her face, and lean in. "Well, I love giving lots of kinds of kisses," I tell her, my lips hovering just above hers. "I think we're going to get along really well."

Then I settle my mouth on hers.

She sighs softly and my cock hardens.

Damn, I don't remember the last time a woman affected me like this. This quickly. This easily. She hasn't done or said anything graphic but I'm hot and hard, and my body is aching to lift her up and press her against this wall suddenly.

At first her hands just rest on my chest but as I ease my tongue over her lower lip, she slides them up to my shoulders, and then when I cup the back of her head, tip her head back, and deepen the kiss, she moves them to the back of my head. She's tangling her fingers in my hair and, damn, for a second she really grips my hair hard as she goes up on tiptoe, pressing closer into me.

That's all the permission I need. I walk her back a step so she's against the wall, ready to give her all the kisses she can handle.

I've just leaned in when I hear a voice behind me.

"Ms. Larkin, I believe we have an appointment."

Well, shit. That's the doc's voice. I'm only mildly annoyed by the distraction. It was inevitable, given where we are, and I have no intention of letting this be the last time I kiss her so I lift my head. I look down at Dani.

She's breathing hard, looking a little dazed, and her lips are nice and pink and shiny now.

I look over my shoulder at Michael Hughes. "Hey, Doc."

"Crew." His tone and expression say that he's not exactly surprised to find me here, but he's not buying me a celebratory beer either.

"What kind of appointment do you have with my girl?"

Hughes raises an eyebrow. "Your girl?"

I look down at Dani. Okay, that slipped out. But fuck, why not? Dani's been making me smile, and giving me semi-hard-ons for years. Whereas my sister likes to give me crap, Dani has always been sweet and supportive.

"Dani and I go way back," I tell Michael.

"Hmm," he says, not overly impressed. His gaze settles on Dani. "I wanted to check in with you. Shall we go to my office?"

She blinks at him. So do I. His office?

"Can't you just do it here?" I ask.

"My office would be the easiest place to fully assess her," Michael says.

I have to admit, he seems unfazed by the fact that I practically had her pinned against the wall and was kissing the hell out of her.

"Assess me?" Dani asks, seeming surprised.

Michael steps forward. "I just want to be sure your head is all right. I won't be able to rest until I know you're fine."

I loop an arm around her waist, suddenly feeling a jab of protectiveness. "Is there a chance she has a concussion?" I hadn't been close enough to see her fall so I didn't realize she might have a worse injury than I'd realized. I know about concussion all too well. You don't play a game like hockey for most of your life without having your brain banged around in your skull a few times.

"There is," Michael says calmly.

Calmly? She could have a concussion? Well, shit. Why didn't that occur to me before? If so, why is he saying things calmly? Shouldn't he maybe even be alarmed? What the fuck are we doing standing around here talking? Fuck I was about to lift her up and dry hump her against a brick wall and she's actually injured?

I gently push Dani toward Michael. "Fuck, Doc, check her out. Make sure she's alright."

Michael nods. "I plan to." He looks at Dani and his expression softens.

That doesn't seem like a professional vibe, but what do I know? Maybe that's how he looks when he's in concerned doctor mode. I wouldn't know. When he's working on hockey players he's mostly in annoyed doctor mode.

"Right this way, Ms. Larkin," Michael says.

"You can call me Dani," she tells him, stepping up beside him.

I want him to put his arm around her. What if she gets dizzy and stumbles?

So I step up on her other side and put my arm around her waist again, hugging her up against my side.

"Excuse me, are you Danielle?"

The three of us all turn to face the security guard.

Dani nods. "I'm Danielle Larkin."

"Mr. Armstrong sent me to find you. He'd like to see you in his office."

Mr. Armstrong wants to see her? In his office? What is it with all these guys wanting Dani in their offices tonight?

"Why?" I ask bluntly, my arm tightening around Dani. I expected Nathan would have some words for me about the kiss with Dani, but none of that was her fault.

"He didn't say," the guard says. "Just that I was to escort her upstairs."

"He probably wants to smooth things over. I'm sure a fan getting injured in the arena is a concern," Michael says.

Sure. Okay, that makes sense. Though I'd expect Nathan to send someone from the public relations office. He isn't exactly a social, make-people-feel-warm-and-fuzzy guy. I'd think he'd want to send one of the bubbly women who go out to charity events or one of the funny, charming younger guys who handle the social media accounts.

I don't want to let her out of my sight before I can kiss her again at least once—maybe twelve times—so I guess I'm going with her. Though I'd love to avoid my team's owner after pulling the kiss cam stunt tonight.

Then again, I did score three times. He can't deny that making me a Racketeer was one of his best moves yet.

"Who's Mr. Armstrong?" Dani asks.

I look down at her. "He's the owner of the Racketeers."

"The owner?" Her eyes widen, and she starts to shake her head. "Oh, no. I don't want to meet him."

I laugh. "Why not? Maybe he's going to give you season tickets."

She frowns. "Why would he do that?"

"Because he saw you try to climb me like a tree in the stands and then the way I played, and he wants you to be here to inspire me?" I say with a grin.

She blushes again, and I feel like I just scored another goal. God, she's pretty when she blushes.

"He wants to check in and make sure you're all right after your…accident," Michael says. "He texted me to get a report. Now I guess he wants to see for himself that you're fine."

"He doesn't trust you?" she asks.

Michael gives her a half-smile. "Mr. Armstrong very much thinks he always knows best."

Dani sighs. "Can you come along?" she asks Michael. "You can do the assessment up there in front of him and then everyone will realize I'm okay."

"Of course, I'd be happy to take you upstairs." Michael glances at the security guard. "Okay with you, Ken?"

The guy nods. "Sure thing, Dr. Hughes."

"This way," Michael says to Dani.

I turn her toward the elevators, my arm still around her.

"Where exactly are you going?" Hughes asks me as we all start walking.

"With Dani," I say simply.

"You weren't invited."

"Too bad." Then I shrug. "Nathan loves me."

Hughes just scoffs at that.

Okay, Nathan Armstrong doesn't love me. But he loves what I do for his team and he pays me very well for it.

And these two men are not going to meet with my girl without me.

CHAPTER 4

Michael

THE ELEVATOR DOOR closes with a soft thump in front of me. I'm standing next to Dani, who is moving restlessly. I glance down at her and she's shifting on her feet, rubbing her hands over her arms, biting her lip. She's watching Crew, who is smiling at her in reassurance.

I don't usually refer to grown women as adorable but she truly is. There is something about her, a combination of sweet and sensual that instantly appealed to me. This is a woman with layers, and I want to peel them all back, one by one until I reach her soft core.

I move closer to her, almost imperceptibly. My arm brushes against hers and she turns, startled, staring up at me with a puzzled expression. Her mouth parts and her tongue sneaks out and wets her bottom lip nervously. She tucks her wavy hair behind one ear and leans my way, into my touch, so her arm is aligned with mine.

Heat shoots through me like a bolt of lightning.

She can sense it too. What I'm feeling. What I felt the moment I looked into her eyes in the stands after she'd hit her head. There's a pull between her and me, like an electromagnetic field, drawing us together. It seems to be confusing her, given that she was just kissing Crew.

It doesn't confuse me. It just turns me on.

The air in the elevator feels thick with sexual tension. Given I'm a good eight inches taller than her, I can see the swell of her breasts peeking out above the V of her Racketeers T-shirt. The shirt is snug against her curves, but the cardigan has slipped down on her left shoulder, dragging the T-shirt with it, and exposing more of her breast than she seems to be aware of. I reach out and shift the sweater back onto her shoulder so the shirt underneath slips back into place.

She jumps a little, then looks down at her chest. She whips her head around to stare at me, cheeks pink. "Thank you," she murmurs.

"Of course." And just like that, I have every intention of getting her number before I leave this arena tonight.

It's been a few months since I've been on a date, and about a year since I was exclusively seeing one woman, and even though Dani isn't my usual type, it feels right to ask her out. I tend to date women in the medical profession because they understand the demands of my career. Which has turned out to be a terrible strategy because none of them seem to care much about pursuing anything serious, and they definitely don't want a man taking care of them. I don't sense that from this woman at all. She has a vulnerability about her that makes me want to wrap my arms around her and tell her everything will be okay. I'm a natural nurturer. It's why I was drawn to medicine. But taking care of rowdy hockey players isn't the same thing at all. I want a soft, sweet woman to take care of. In all ways.

The elevator arrives on the top floor and swooshes open. I put my arm across the elevator door and wait for Dani to exit first.

Crew immediately follows her like an eager puppy, his hand on the small of her back.

Crew's obvious infatuation with her doesn't bother me. I don't need to compete. I know who I am and I know what I'm worth.

Dani can make her own choice once she's presented with it. Or hell, she doesn't have to choose. If she wants to go out for beer and pizza with a young, cocky hockey player and then let me take her for candlelight dinners with champagne, she can have both initially.

Let her explore her options, try us both on for size.

I follow them to Nathan's office and Crew doesn't even pause to knock.

"Hey, Nate!" Crew greets as he ushers Dani across the threshold.

I can practically hear Nathan's teeth grinding. No one calls him Nate. Especially not his players. Crew McNeill is damned lucky he's good.

Fine, he's really good. He's one of the best. He could be one of the best to ever play if he stays focused, stays healthy, and takes it seriously.

All of those are up in the air, of course. He's twenty-two, full of himself, and plays as if every night is going to be his last on the ice. He puts it all out there. Which is amazing. And scary as fuck.

"Mr. McNeill," Nathan greets coolly as I enter behind them. "I didn't realize I would have the pleasure of seeing you in person tonight."

He says 'pleasure' in a tone that indicates it's anything but.

"You're welcome," Crew tells him. "You can congratulate and thank me for the game in person this way." Crew escorts Dani to one of the chairs in front of Nathan's enormous walnut desk and then takes the one next to her.

Nathan is actually standing at the floor-to-ceiling windows overlooking downtown Chicago.

He meets my gaze and I give him a commiserating eye roll, then nod. Yes, Crew is a pain in the ass. But yes, he's worth it. So far.

"Dr. Hughes. You're here too," he states. Not because anyone is unaware of my presence, but that's his way of pointing out that he wasn't expecting me and isn't exactly pleased.

So he wanted to see Dani alone.

Interesting.

I was surprised when he'd texted to check in, but the PR angle of checking on a fan who was injured in a stunt with the mascot did ring true.

Now I'm not at all sure that was what is behind his desire to see her.

"Nathan, this is Danielle Larkin," I say, moving to stand beside her. "Dani, this is Nathan Armstrong. The owner of the Racketeers."

I look down at Dani and find her blushing. And this isn't the sweet little pink stain I saw in the stands when I first held her face in my hands. Or the darker pink flush of desire on her cheeks after Crew kissed her—either time. This is a bright red blush of mortification.

What is going on?

Nathan is already moving around his desk toward her. "Miss Larkin," he greets. "It's nice to see you again." He holds out his hand to her. "I assume Ben is getting home somehow? Alone?"

I lift a brow. He's seen her before? Who the hell is Ben? And he definitely emphasized the Miss. He actually glances down at her ring finger checking for a rock. Now that's totally unexpected.

"Uber. Yes, alone," she says, her voice a mere whisper.

Surprised, I look down at her from my position next to the chair she's in. She's suddenly acting shy. And she's not looking directly at Nathan, but at the view behind him. But she takes his hand, reluctantly it seems to me.

"I'm glad you didn't get beer on this shirt," he says. "But I'm happy to replace these jeans." He lingers with her hand in his, far beyond the point of politeness, and his gaze tracks down her body.

She swallows hard. Twice. "That's not necessary, Mr. Armstrong."

She then removes her hand from his and crosses her arms over her chest as if she needs protection. She's eyeing Nathan warily, and I don't blame her. He's coming off as very intense right now. I put my own hand on her shoulder to reassure her. Crew drops a palm onto her knee.

"Are you sure? It looked like they got really wet."

I can't believe he just said that. Given that Dani's eyebrows shoot up, she can't believe it either. "I… no. I mean. Yes. I'm sure."

I don't care how they met, he's flustering her.

"Nathan," I say, putting an edge to my voice. "Miss Larkin made herself clear."

He gets the message, sitting back a little.

I don't think Nathan is a bad guy at all, he's just used to compliance from those around him. Sometimes he just needs to be reminded to back the fuck off.

"My apologies," he said. "I just want to make sure you're unharmed and satisfied with your Racketeers experience."

"You didn't tell me you were the team owner," she says. Her tone is almost accusatory.

So they have met. But she didn't know who he was. This is interesting. I have no idea how that scenario could have played out. It's not like Nathan is generally accessible or that a woman like Danielle would have an opportunity to meet him. Certainly not where his identity wasn't known.

It's clear Nathan is interested in her, but instead of feeling jealous or competitive, I feel protective of her. Given the way she is reacting right now, I doubt she would be a good fit for a man like Nathan. He's too domineering.

At any rate, I shift a little closer to her. "You two have met?" I ask, more to reassure her with my presence than because I care how they met.

Dani glances up at me and nods. "He upgraded my tickets. That's how I wound up that close to the ice."

I'm still not entirely sure how that happened but it doesn't matter. They met.

Nathan props a hip on the edge of his desk directly in front of Dani rather than taking a seat in the huge leather chair behind his desk like he normally would. Like any professional would.

"What did you think of me?" he asks.

He's also completely ignoring Crew. Crew scoots his chair even closer to Dani. The arms of their chairs are touching and he's leaning into her personal space.

"That you worked in PR," she answers. "You didn't correct me. You didn't tell me your last name either but I guess I didn't notice because I was distracted by your…the tickets."

Nathan gives her a knowing look that I don't understand at all. What's that about?

"If you would have read my note, you would have known who I was," Nathan tells her.

She frowns. "What note?"

"The note with my gift."

"You sent her a gift?" Crew asks.

Nathan doesn't even glance at him.

"What gift?" Dani asks, looking truly confused.

Fuck, I'm really confused here too.

"The VIP ticket to join me in the owner's box for a game."

She swallows hard again. "Oh. I didn't get it."

"I know. I'll replace it. Wade…" Nathan pauses and draws a breath in through his nose, sounding like he's struggling to control his temper. "Sammy the mascot, was bringing that down to you when…everything happened."

"Oh," Dani says again. And then nothing more.

Crew's hand tightens on her knee and now Nathan's gaze drops to that hand. He scowls.

Dani puts a hand on her chest, over her heart, and it's not just her cheeks that are red now. The flush is creeping down her throat to her chest.

Dani is being crowded from every angle. It's a miracle she can even breathe. The tension in this room is so fucking thick I think we're all having trouble taking a deep breath. Jesus. Everyone is being so fucking obvious. I glance at my own hand on her shoulder. Including me. I force myself to pull back, giving her space. One of us has to be the voice of reason here.

"I don't think Dani has any lingering signs of a serious concussion," I say, getting to the point of this meeting. Or what I thought was the point, anyway. Now I'm not so sure. "She seems fully coherent." I look down at her. "She might have a bit of a headache tomorrow. I'll give you my number," I tell her directly. "You can call me any time with any questions or if anything comes up that you're concerned about."

When she looks up at me, she does meet my gaze directly and she smiles. I feel my chest tighten. She's so damned pretty.

"Thank you, Dr. Hughes. That's really nice of you."

"Michael," I say. "And I insist. In fact, I'd like your number too. I want to check in tomorrow and then again in a few days. Just to be sure you're not having any residual symptoms."

Crew pipes up. "I'll be seeing her. I'll let you know if anything comes up."

I look at him. He'll be seeing her?

He clearly reads the question in my gaze. He leans back in his chair, but drapes an arm over the back of Dani's. "Dani and my sister are besties. They live together. And they're business partners. It's no problem at all for me to see how Dani is first thing in the morning. Or to tuck her into bed at night."

Real subtle. I don't roll my eyes because I'm not getting into a dick measuring contest with this kid. "And where did you get your medical degree from?" I ask him. "Are you sure you know what to look out for and be concerned about?"

Okay, maybe I am going to get into a dick measuring contest with this kid.

It's hard to ruffle him though. He grins. "I'll be concerned if she calls me by some other dude's name or something. Unless of course it's, 'Oh God'. I get that a lot."

There is no end to this guy's ego.

Dani gasps softly and she spins to look at Crew.

His cocky grin softens to something more affectionate and he reaches up to tuck a strand of hair behind her ear. "You can also call out, "more" and "harder". That won't worry me at all. I'll be more worried if you don't."

None of this bothers me, actually.

And it's still not going to stop me from getting her number or asking her out.

"I didn't realize Miss Larkin is your girlfriend," Nathan says. His voice is practically a growl.

I snap my gaze to his. He's staring at Dani, confirming my earlier suspicions. As if there were any doubts.

Nathan definitely wants her too.

Fucking fantastic.

Of course, there's no way Nathan thinks she's adorable. Adorable isn't a Nathan word at all.

"She's not," Crew says, not taking his gaze off Dani. "Yet."

Nathan makes another growling sound and stands, and I immediately jump in instinctively.

"Dani, can I offer you a ride home?" I ask. "I know your friend said you were going to take an Uber, but I'd like to be sure you're still feeling well when you're dropped off. You really shouldn't be alone."

Crew shakes his head. "I've got her."

"I need to be sure she's medically stable."

"You just said a minute ago she's fine."

"I said she *seems* fine right now, but I want to keep monitoring her."

"And I said I'd let you know if anything changes."

We stare each other down. I'm a patient man. I can outlast him. His urge to make a move will be too great.

But it only lasts a second.

"You need to stay behind," Nathan commands. He's looking at Crew and he's not happy. He looks like he could chew glass and like it. "We need to discuss you leaving the ice, holding up the start of play for ninety-seven seconds, and your impulse control."

"Oh, that wasn't Crew's fault at all," Dani says, suddenly

leaning forward in her chair. Toward Nathan. But she looks genuinely worried. "Crew and Michael both came up to check on me. Crew was just goofing around and trying to make the whole thing less embarrassing for me. I was the one…" She stops. Swallows. Glances at Crew. Then says, her voice softer, "I was the one who really made that kiss too much and kept him up in the stands."

Crew shifts forward and opens his mouth, but Dani's hand goes to his leg just above his knee and she squeezes. He shuts up. I think more out of surprise than anything, but it works.

"Please don't be mad at Crew, Mr. Armstrong," she says.

Nathan is staring at her as if he can't believe what he's hearing. "My name is Nathan," he growls softly. "Not Mr. Armstrong."

"Nathan," she says. "Please don't fine him or bench him or whatever. It was all my fault."

"The fuck it was–" But Crew is cut off by Dani squeezing his leg again.

"Crew and I are old friends," she goes on. "It's true that I live with his sister. I haven't seen him in a while and we just reverted back to our old teasing ways. I *promise* it won't happen again."

"Dani," Crew says, his voice low and tight.

Clearly he doesn't want to make that promise.

She glances at him. "You are *so* happy to be back here in Chicago, playing for Nathan's team," she says. It's clear she's giving Crew a you'd-better-go-along-with-this look. "We'll behave in the future because I really do want to watch you play again in person. I don't want Mr. Armstrong to banish me from the arena."

"It's *Nathan,*" Nathan says, clearly irritated and not sure what exactly to do or say. "I would never banish you from the arena." He sounds perplexed.

Crew is also staring at her like he isn't sure if he should argue with her or kiss her. He looks like he wants to do both. But finally he just nods. "We'll *try* to behave," he says.

I have to hide my smile. This woman has two of the cockiest, always-get-their-way, always-win men just staring at her and nodding.

She is something.

I hold my hand out to Dani. "Let me take you home."

I wonder if she's aware that there are three men essentially trying to claim her. Probably not. She doesn't seem like a woman used to being romanced and seduced.

Or claimed.

That's truly the best word. I'm not sure any of us has anything as sweet as romance or even seduction on our minds at this very moment.

Words like *mine* are what's going through our heads.

After a heartbeat, she takes my hand and lets me pull her to her feet. She pauses and looks back at Crew. "It was wonderful to see you again."

He gives her a grin. "Same. And we'll see each other again soon."

She just nods. Then turns her attention to Nathan. "It was nice to meet you. Don't worry about my little tumble. I'm fine, honestly."

Nathan gives her a single nod. "It was a pleasure to meet you, Danielle."

I think I feel a little shiver go through her. That's…interesting.

I don't let go of her hand as I start for the door.

I don't intend to let go of her until I have to.

Crew

Michael escorts Dani out of Nathan's office.

Nathan glares at their backs like a man obsessed.

I'm pretty sure he is. And I'm pretty sure I know what–or rather who–he's obsessed with.

Dani.

Both Michael and Nathan want Dani.

Just when I've figured out *I* want Dani.

Huh. This could be fun.

The door shuts behind them and Nathan immediately focuses on me.

"What the fuck were you thinking, McNeill?"

I sigh. "I just reacted. The fans loved it."

"You delayed the game. I should fine you."

I almost say 'Dani asked you not to'. I think just maybe that would actually matter to him. Which is very interesting. Nathan Armstrong is not someone well-known for letting other people's feelings and opinions matter. Instead, I frown. "It was a minute delay. And the fans loved it."

"Do you know what that costs us from the network when we delay the team? By a minute and thirty seven seconds? A fuck ton, that's how much it costs us."

Of course he's a guy who counts every single fucking second. "The fans loved it," I repeat.

He scowls. "That's all you care about?"

"No. We also won. And I scored all the goals. I also care very much about those two things."

Nathan is still sitting on the front of his desk. I know he perched there earlier to be closer to Dani, but I have to admit it's a power position. He's higher than I am sitting in the chair in front of him. I'm caged in with the two arms of the chair. He's bracing his hands on either side of him on the desk, his feet braced on the floor, knees spread.

The guy might be a rich asshole who's nearly twenty years my senior, but he's built solid and I know that if he wanted to make this physical, I'd be hurting tomorrow.

"But hockey is what you care about most," he says after several seconds of silence. "Hockey is your true love."

I nod. But there's a strange feeling of trepidation niggling at the back of my neck. "Racketeers hockey," I clarify. After all, this guy is my boss. But it's true that I am now playing for the team. The one I grew up wanting to play for. I'm wearing the jersey that was in every one of my daydreams when I was a kid out on the ice, pretending I was competing for the Stanley Cup.

Nathan gives me a single nod. I gave the right answer.

"Do you have Danielle's phone number?" he asks. It should seem out of the blue, but it doesn't. We're both very aware of the subject of this particular meeting. And it's not the ninety-seven seconds I cost the team. It's the *reason* I cost the team ninety-seven seconds.

"I..." I don't want to answer this. I have this weird feeling that giving her number to Nathan Armstrong is going to impact my life in ways I don't even understand. That's very woo-woo for me. That sounds a lot more like my sister. But I definitely feel like I'm at a fork in a road I didn't even know I was on. "I can get it," I finally say. I can text Luna and have it within minutes.

He gives me another nod. "Get it."

I hesitate. Then I take a deep breath. "I don't think that's a good idea." I meet his gaze directly as I say it.

He lifts a brow. "I didn't ask for your opinion on it."

No, he didn't. "Dani is an old friend," I say. "I can tell her you want it and let her decide if she wants you to have it." I'm not sure I even want to do that, but fuck, I can't make decisions for Dani.

"Get me her number, Crew," Nathan says firmly. "Right now."

I lean back in my chair and cross my arms. Nathan Armstrong could fire me. But he won't.

Probably.

I'm valuable to him. To this team. To his chances of having a championship. I know he inherited the team from his grandfather. I'll bet he wants to make grandpa proud.

I'm his key to that.

"No," I say.

He actually looks surprised for a moment. I'm guessing that's a word Nathan doesn't hear much. But I wonder if he's surprised it's coming from me. I'm well known as an easy-going, if cocky, fun-loving, good guy. I can be mean on the ice as needed, but I'm a crowd pleaser, great for PR, great for big fan events, great with kids. I'm not an enforcer. I don't start fights. I'll fight back if someone swings first. If someone goes after my goalie, I'll absolutely be in the pile. But my trash talk is more about how fucking good I am and how they all want to be me, rather than about anybody's mama.

But Nathan wants something I want and I'm okay with sharing, but I'm not okay with him having her all to himself. And he needs to know it.

"I own you," he finally says.

"You do," I agree with a nod.

We stare at each other for a long period. Then he says, "What do you want?"

I cock a brow. "You'll negotiate for her number?"

He doesn't seem happy about it, but he says, "I will."

Nathan Armstrong is the youngest owner in the league. He's also known as the biggest asshole. But he's willing to negotiate with his newest, young, hot shot player, who he's pissed at, for a woman's phone number.

That means he does really want her.

Huh.

I'm open to anything where people are having a good time, feeling good, and no one's getting hurt. Especially people I care about.

I care about Dani.

But I want to make her my girlfriend. I'm pretty sure my forty-something year old boss, the billionaire owner of my hockey team, is not thinking quite the same thing about her.

That's fine. They can have fun, if that's what Dani wants. But he has to understand that I'm in this for real.

Still, Dani really is the only one who can actually tell him no.

I pull my phone out and text Luna.

Ask Dani if I can have her number.

I pause and sigh. Then text again.

And if I can give it to Nathan Armstrong too.

Then I look up at Nathan. "Here's the deal," I say. "I want to date her. I'm serious. I want a chance at a relationship with her. So, if she sits in the owner's box with you for a game, she wears my jersey. You will not hurt her. And no means no. About anything."

He narrows his eyes. "Absolutely not on the jersey."

A text from Luna pings my phone.

She said yes *smiling emoji* You better be good to her, Crew.

Then she adds a phone number. My heart thumps hard and I can't help but smile.

But then I look up at Armstrong. I wiggle my phone. "That's the deal," I tell Nathan.

There are probably twenty-six other ways he could go about

getting her number. But after five ticks, he scowls, and says, "Fine."

Okay. We have an agreement. I hand over Dani's phone number to the asshole billionaire owner of the Chicago Racketeers.

Then plan to take her one of my jerseys first thing tomorrow.

CHAPTER 5
Dani

TINGLES. Heat. Wet panties. Dirty thoughts.

And high hopes.

That's what I've got now.

I have three men who all seem interested in me and even though I'm not sure *why* exactly, and I'm *way* in over my head with sophisticated, experienced guys like this, I really like it.

As Michael pulls me toward the door, his hand warm and strong, I give Crew a parting glance, and he gives me a wink. Then I glance at Nathan Armstrong. I quickly look away when I find him watching me.

Nathan, the guy who stripped off his shirt right in front of me, is the Racketeers owner? I knew he was wearing a really expensive suit. But this guy is a billionaire. A really hot, really sexy billionaire.

I expected the team owner to be older. I'd envisioned a man in his seventies with a shock of white hair and a pocketful of Werther's Originals.

That is not this man.

He's closer to forty than seventy and he has dark hair with a hint of silver in his trim beard. His eyes are steely gray and he's tall, lean, and muscular. He's still wearing the T-shirt he put on in the storage closet, but those suit pants are clearly custom tailored.

I don't know what's in the guy's pockets but it's not caramels.

When he leaned against his desk, his feet were on either side of mine, boxing me in. I had a view of his slim fitting tight suit pants and his crotch. Talk about hard candy.

With Crew's hand on my thigh, Michael's on my shoulder, and a smoldering stone-faced billionaire a few feet in front of me, my entire body had just about burst into flames.

This is what I want. The full attention of multiple guys. Multiple hot guys who know what they're doing. And who can tell me *what to do.*

I'm no seductress. I mostly know what I've read in books. But the books I read are very hot.

I mean, I've touched a penis. I'm not a virgin. But I'm a virgin in all the things I *really* want to do.

These guys seem like they could help me out.

I can't help that thought as it flits through my mind.

The door glides closed behind us right as I hear Nathan demand, "What the fucking hell were you thinking, McNeill?"

It's a frustrated yell. A roar. A sign of a serious ass-chewing to come.

Dammit. I really tried to help Crew out.

But why would I think a man like Nathan Armstrong would listen to me?

I glance up at Michael. "That doesn't sound good."

"Nothing he doesn't deserve. He'll be fine," he reassures me as he hits the button for the elevator.

I feel responsible for Crew getting reprimanded. It was my fault he left the ice. "But he's new here."

We step into the open elevator and it starts down.

Michael chuckles. "He's the number three scorer in the league. Nathan will yell at him, maybe punish him in some way, but by next week it will be forgotten. Things like that don't stick to guys like Crew. He's too talented."

"I kissed him back," I blurt out. "I made it worse."

"And the crowd loved it." Michael smiles at me.

That smile eases the tightness in my chest. If Michael thinks Crew will be okay, I'm inclined to believe him. Even though I don't know him. He has a very calming presence.

"Here, put your number and your address in my phone." He hands it to me.

I do as he suggests and then hand it back to him. He's an easy man to both be around and to look at. He makes me feel instantly at ease. Like he has control of every situation. He's also ridiculously good-looking.

He has an amazing jawline, a strong nose, a mesmerizing smile, and he smells absolutely divine. I've never wanted to sniff a man as much as I do right now.

Crew smelled like soap from his post-game shower.

Nathan smelled like expensive cologne and money, if that's even possible.

Michael smells like an old library with a roaring fire blazing in it. Like leather and paper and a hint of smoky sandalwood. It's both soothing and sexy.

"You live in Lincoln Park?" he asks, reading my address on his phone. "You're not too far from me. I'm in Bucktown."

I do that Midwestern thing where I launch into an explanation of how and why I live in a neighborhood with skyrocketing rent prices. Or maybe it's just something I've picked up from my parents, who live in a small town in Indiana and seem to experience actual physical pain when they spend any money whatsoever. "I live with Luna, Crew's sister. Their parents bought the building, otherwise I'd never be able to afford it. We have a bookshop and bakery on the first floor and we live upstairs. It's called Books and Buns." I smile, as I always do when I think of our little shop. It's a dream come true for both of us. The bookstore makes no money, and that makes me feel bad, but I can't help continuing to believe that it will, someday, somehow. "Luna's dad thought the neighborhood was a good investment and that we'd get more foot traffic for the businesses. And that it would be safe for two single girls."

Okay, that was a lot to dump on him. I pause for a breath as we exit the elevator and adjust my sweater. It's fallen off my shoulder again. Maybe it stretched out when I fell across Ben's lap.

Michael leads me to a black luxury SUV with his hand on my lower back. I love the way he touches me. It doesn't feel like he's pushing himself into my personal space, but it feels protective at the same time. He unlocks the vehicle and gives me a hand up. Once I'm settled on the seat, he reaches across me to fasten the seatbelt.

That's ridiculous. I don't need help putting a seatbelt on. If any other guy I've dated did that, I would be offended and think he was being a dick. But with Michael it feels like he's taking care of me.

As he maneuvers us through traffic, he asks me questions about how Luna and I met, about the bookstore, about what I like to read, and more seemingly small talk. But I watch him through it all. And everything he does, from changing lanes, to choosing a radio station, is done with an air of competence that is so damned sexy.

"What about you?" I ask. "What made you become a doctor?"

He glances over at me with a smile. "I have five younger brothers and sisters who were always getting into scrapes. I liked being the big brother who could fix it, give them a hug and a Band-Aid and a pep talk."

Just like I'd suspected. He enjoys taking care of others. That is so appealing to me, the idea of getting a hug when you're hurting.

"That's a big family. I'm an only child. I've always fantasized about having a huge family, the kind where you get a lake house in Wisconsin all together and spend every week in the summer there fishing and swimming and roasting s'mores." Even the thought of a future like that makes me sigh with delight. "It can be lonely as an only child."

"I've always wanted a lake house too where I get to man the grill. I love to cook. Where did you grow up? I'm from Decatur. My mom is a professor at Millikin University."

"Franklin, Indiana. Typical small-town life. I spent a lot of time reading."

"I was a bookworm too," Michael says. "I enjoyed sports, but I was just mediocre at it. My favorite thing about it really was being part of a team."

It's easy to see how Michael wound up the Racketeers physician then. "You must love your job."

"I really do."

We pull up in front of Books and Buns and I'm not surprised that there's a parking spot. Michael Hughes seems like the kind of guy who can always find a parking spot when he needs one.

"Thank you for the ride."

"My pleasure." He gives me a smile that makes heat pool in my lower belly. "Hang on," he says as I reach for the handle of the door.

He gets out and jogs around the front of the SUV. He opens my door for me and offers me a hand down and I almost swoon. Is this because he's an older man? Is it because he's a doctor and hangs out with a more sophisticated crowd than most of the guys I date? Did his mother just engrain manners in him from a young age? I don't know the answers to that, but spending too much time with this man is going to ruin me for dating guys my age who pull up, grin at me and say things like, "I'm coming in, right?"

Michael walks me to the door that leads up to the apartment above Books and Buns. There's a staircase inside that goes up to the second floor, but we have this exterior entrance as well.

"Thanks again," I say, turning to face him. Suddenly I don't want him to leave. But "Do you want to come up?" seems really forward.

"Do you have a boyfriend?" he asks.

I blink a couple of times. I wasn't expecting that. Wow, men who work for the Racketeers are all very direct.

"I don't." For the first time in a while, I'm glad that's the answer to that question.

Michael seems pleased to hear it. He nods, then his thumbs move over his phone. A moment later, my phone dings with a text. I look down.

"Now you have my number. Use it any time," he says.

A ribbon of heat swirls through my stomach. "Okay."

He dips his knees so he can look more directly into my face. "I mean it. I'd really like to hear from you."

"To be sure I don't have a concussion?"

"To hear your voice," he says, his own voice a low, smooth rumble that ripples down my spine. "*And* to be sure that you're okay."

I could look into this man's eyes for hours. It's not just the color, but there's a warmth there that makes me just want to sink in. I step a little closer. Did I mention how great he smells? "To make sure my head is okay?"

"To be sure *you're* okay."

That was how he said it before but I think I just wanted to hear it again. That sounds different somehow than just a concussion check. "Why wouldn't I be okay?"

"I want to hear from you even if you are. I'd love to hear that you've had a great day and things are going well and you're happy."

Oh, my God. Who is this guy?

"I'd also like to be a part of making your day great, if you'd let me. Can I take you out sometime?"

Is there a single woman in the entire world that would say no to that? A handsome doctor who smells like a library wants to take me out? Um, yes.

"I'd like that."

"Are you going to be dating Crew?"

I blink again. Am I going to be dating Crew? God, I hope so. But I'd also love to date Michael. So, I…have no idea. I must look confused because Michael says, "He mentioned to Nathan that you're not his girlfriend *yet*. He seemed to think that might change."

"Oh. He was probably just messing around," I say. "I've known him forever. It's not like that between us." But my thoughts are racing. Could it be like that now? I've never thought for one second about dating Crew McNeill before now, but that kiss… Correction, those kisses. The first one was pretty great. But the one where he was backing me up against the wall in the hallway? I want more of those.

"I don't think Crew agrees," Michael says, confirming that the chemistry I felt wasn't in my head.

"Well, he hasn't asked," I say with a little shrug.

"What if he does?"

"What if he does?" I ask in return.

"I would still want to take you out."

I smile. *Yes.* "I would still say yes to your invitation." I am not going to lose the opportunity to go out with Michael on any concern that Crew might object to the doctor and me dating. I'll cross that bridge if and when I get to it.

He smiles too and I swear I feel my knees wobble. "Then how about this weekend?"

"Okay." I like a man who doesn't make me guess if he's interested in me or not. It feels exciting but also reassuring.

"Okay." Michael doesn't go anywhere. He's still standing on the sidewalk in front of me.

Is he going to kiss me too? I would really like that. I haven't kissed anyone in a long time. Well, before Crew kissed me earlier, that is. I haven't had a great kiss in a really, really long time. Again, before Crew kissed me. I certainly haven't kissed two guys in the same night…ever. Not ever. But I could write a short story about that and my fans on the online forum would eat it up.

"Text me," I tell him.

"I'll *call* you," he says.

Right. Men like Michael Hughes call women they're taking out. That's classy. I love it.

I nod and then turn toward the door that leads up to the apartment I share with Luna. But just then my phone vibrates. I pull it out of my pocket and see it's Luna.

Hey, are you okay?

Yes, just got here.

Oh, good. Is it okay if I give my brother your number? He also wants to share it with Nathan Armstrong?????

I stare at the message. They both want my number? Michael has it now too.

I swallow hard, but type.

Sure. I'm sure Mr. Armstrong just wants to be sure I don't sue the Racketeers for my fall.

eyeroll I've heard he's a dick. Oh, also...Kyle's here. Maybe give me a half hour?

I laugh, even as I have to resist the urge to defend Nathan. I have no reason to believe he's *not* a dick. But I don't like having Luna call him that for some reason.

"Everything alright?" Michael asks.

I look up quickly. "Yeah, Luna has company, so I'm just going to hang out in the bookstore for a bit." I feel my cheeks heat as I say that. It's stupid. I'm not talking about sex with Michael. I'm talking about other people having sex. But I'm telling Michael and I'm very attracted to him, and I can't help but think that I would love to be the one getting naked upstairs. With Michael. I'm a little jealous of Luna. Not because of Kyle. But because I haven't had sex in ages, and now it's all I can think about because three hot guys have suddenly appeared in my life in one night. Three hot guys I can't seem to say no to and who all seem interested in me. Unless I did bump my head extra hard.

"By yourself?" Michael asks.

I have to think for a second about what he's talking about. Because my brain is still on the topic of sex. And yes, I do have sex by myself sometimes. And tonight I'm going to while thinking about him. And Crew. And Nathan Armstrong.

My cheeks get hotter.

"Um, what?" I ask, unable to retrieve what he's talking about.

"You're going to hang out in the bookstore by yourself?"

"Oh, yes. For a little bit." I start texting Luna.

Hey, yes, I'm fine. No problem. I'll be down in the bookshop.

I hit send, chew my bottom lip, then text again.

Also, I got kissed tonight.

What????? Omg!!!! Wait, NOT BEN RIGHT???!!!
Was it the hot doc???!

My cheeks grow even hotter.

No, not Ben. It was

God, do I tell her it was Crew? I have to. Luna is my best friend. I can't keep this from her.

It was your brother.

Oh. Yeah, I saw that, remember.

She's obviously not as excited about this as I am.

No. Another one. After the game.

There is a long pause. The three dots pop up, disappear, then pop up again.

Um...I'm sorry?

I stare at her response. Then laugh.

Trust me. Nothing to be sorry about. It was really good.

Um...wow. Okay. Well...okay. No wonder he wanted your number. At least he has great taste in women.

Aw, see? This is why she's my best friend. She just doesn't get worked up about much.

I was hoping it was the hot doctor though, I'll be honest. What happened when you talked to him?

He's amazing. He's actually here with me now. He brought me home.

!!!!!!!! Girl, take him inside the shop and feed that man some cookies!

What? Really?

Yes! Keep him around. Fill him up with butter, sugar, and chocolate, and then kiss him!!

I look back up. Michael is still patiently waiting on the sidewalk. "Luna said she won't be long, but would you... maybe would you like to come into the shop with me? I can offer you a cookie."

That sounds wrong. I hear it immediately.

The corner of his mouth turns up ever so slightly but Michael is too well-mannered to comment on it. He just says, "I'd love to eat a cookie."

Oh, God.

CHAPTER 6

Michael

I'VE ALWAYS HAD a sweet tooth and I'm craving some sugar now, but I am not thinking about baked goods.

All I want to taste is Dani.

Watching Crew kiss her made me want to stake my own claim, to press my lips to hers and see if I can make her sigh and lean into me. But I'm a patient guy and her roommate, Luna, has just given me a door to walk through. Literally.

I glance up at the sign affixed to the brick building over the door. Books and Buns. It's adorable, like Dani. It makes me smile to see the colorful logo, the pastry perched on a stack of books.

Dani digs in her bag for her keys and I glance around the area, making sure there's no one sketchy. It's a nice neighborhood, but it's late and it pays to be cautious. Even if I wasn't wildly attracted to her, I still wouldn't want her hanging out in the shop by herself. The minute she throws the lights on anyone walking by would be able to see she's in there alone.

"Two of my favorite things right here," I say.

"Hmm?" Her head jerks up and she simultaneously drops her keys.

We both immediately drop down to pick up the fallen keys. We end up face-to-face, only inches between us. She freezes.

"Let me get those," I murmur, so close to her the exhalation of her held breath dances across my lips.

She's not pulling away as I scoop up her keys, my eyes never leaving hers. She's giving me a look that is sweet and filled with longing. She wants me to kiss her.

So I do. Just a light quick brush of my mouth over hers, a barely there whisper of a kiss that instantly makes me hard, and leaves us both wanting more.

Which is exactly what I want.

I stand up and reach my hand out to help her up. She takes it, her fingers trembling slightly.

"Books and baked goods," I tell her. "Two of my favorite things."

"Oh! Right. You like to read." She smooths her hair back and tugs at the hemline of the tight Racketeers T-shirt she's wearing.

It looks like it got shrunk in the wash now that I really assess it. It doesn't seem her style and she has been tugging at it all night. I do appreciate the plunging V neck though.

"Which key?" I hold the keychain up for her. It's an orange fuzzy pom-pom and there are three keys on it.

"The square one."

"I do love to read," I say, as I insert the key into the lock. "Fiction, nonfiction, classics. Thrillers, biographies, fantasy. Just about anything."

"I love to read too. Obviously. Mostly genre fiction."

"I don't have as much free time as I'd like but being on the road with the team actually works to my advantage with my reading time. I usually read in my hotel room right before bed."

"I read in bed too," she says as I turn the lock and push the door open. "Romance."

I stand back to let her enter first. "Romance books? That is one thing I can't say I've read. Are they like rom-com movies? I enjoy most of those."

"Some." She flicks the lights on. "Some are funny, some are

very steamy, some are emotional. Some even feature aliens and monsters."

"Now I am definitely curious. Two aliens falling in love? Interesting."

"It's usually a human with an alien or a monster."

"Even better." I close the door behind me and lock it. "You'll have to recommend a title for me to read."

"Oh, well, I'd have to think about it. You need starter monster romance, not the hard core stuff."

I'm not exactly sure what that means, but I'm willing to find out. I'll start a monster romance book club with her if it means I can spend more time with Dani getting to know her better.

"Which kind do you prefer?"

"The steamy ones," she says with a shrug. "I guess I'm living vicariously."

If that guy she was with at the game is any indication, I can see why. It also reminds me that I need to take it slow with Dani, allow our attraction to slowly heat up to a boiling point. She deserves that. She deserves to be romanced. I sense a sweetness, maybe even a little submissiveness in her, that makes me hot and hard. The caretaker in me fucking loves that. The things I could teach her…

"Me too," I tell her with a grin. "It's been a lonely six months or so. I'm not leaving here tonight without buying one of your favorites to take on the road with me."

She laughs softly. "I'll do my best to pick out one you'll like."

I take in the shop. It's cozy and charming. Immediately in front of me in a painted mural on the wall that reads, "Lead me not into temptation. Unless it's a bookstore bakery."

"I love the place," I say, sincerely.

The aesthetic is warm and bohemian, with colorful rugs, exposed brick, and lots of plants. The book shelves are small and approachable, with rust and mustard colored velvet overstuffed chairs and ottomans scattered about. The bakery area is small, with only a few tables and cane back wooden chairs, with two glass cases that are currently empty. The Buns part of the Books and Buns logo is on a wooden sign affixed to a teal wall.

"Thanks. The cookies and pastries are all in the fridge." Dani moves towards the cases. "When Luna does her displays, with all the various shades of brown in the baked goods, the wall behind it is a great contrasting backdrop. It photographs well for social media. She does croissants, cookies, pain au chocolat, and eclairs."

"All the classic French baked goods."

"Yes." She glances back at me with a smile. "There should be a few left over from today. What's your preference?"

Her.

She's my preference.

"What are you having?"

"I want an eclair if there are any left. I love pastry cream."

Now there's an image to keep me up at night. Her sweet plump pink lips covered in cream… The thought morphs into a visual of her mouth wrapped around my dick, sliding me in and out of her wet warmth…

I clear my throat.

"Come on. Let's raid Luna's fridge." Shyly, she reaches out for my hand.

I take it, feeling that tingle of electricity shoot through my fingertips at her touch. I understand the science of attraction. I'm a damn doctor. But this feels almost unexplainable.

She leads me into the back and I let her take control of the situation. She already had Crew panting after her and Nathan basically marking his territory earlier. She doesn't need me doing the same.

It's not a competition but I do have one thing they both severely lack. Patience.

I can take my time getting where I want to go.

Even if the idea of Dani sliding her tongue through the cream of an eclair makes me want to groan. This is about her, not me. And where we can go together, not just immediate gratification.

Dani lets go of my hand to tug the fridge door open and I

shove it in my pocket so I'm not tempted to press her against the wall and kiss her until she's forgotten what an eclair is.

She pulls out an eclair in plastic wrap. "There's only one. We'll have to share it. But there's a cookie too." She holds an enormous sugar cookie up in her other hand. "Unless you want one more than the other. You deserve first pick for being so attentive to me tonight."

God, she's nice. She fits in this environment, surrounded by books and sugary sweetness. She's a redheaded ray of sunshine. "I think we should share."

"I do too." She smiles up at me. "Can I ask you something?"

"Anything." It doesn't even give me a tremor of alarm. I have no hidden skeletons in my closet. I'm not that guy. I've lived my life straightforwardly.

"How old are you?"

Even easier than I was expecting. "Thirty-five. And here I thought you were going to ask me my deepest darkest secrets or something."

"Those too," she says playfully, reaching for a couple of porcelain plates.

"I'm an open book," I say, holding my arms out. "Easy to read. No secrets here."

At times, that has actually worked against me. I've had women complain that they couldn't understand me, that they didn't trust I wasn't hiding something. Apparently, if you're open and honest, that's suspicious.

"I'm a fast reader," she says. She eyes me and gives a nod, like she believes she can trust me, which she can. "Can I show you something?"

"Of course," I say without hesitation. That could mean anything, but I don't get the impression Dani has any deep dark secrets either. I don't think she's secretly a webcam girl, has an incarcerated boyfriend, or a penchant for poisoning lovers.

If I had to guess, it's something like a medical test result for a loved one she wants me to take a look at.

"Great. I'm going to make a latte. Do you want one too? Then we can go sit down and I'll show you what I'm talking about."

"I'd love one." I reach out for the plates with the cookie and the eclair. "Let me get those."

A few minutes later we're sitting at one of the bistro tables in front of the pastry cases and Dani is cutting the eclair in half. It oozes cream onto the plate. I reach out and swipe my finger through it and put it in my mouth. It's perfection. The taste and texture are exactly as they should be and I make a sound of approval. Dani's eyes darken as she watches me. She picks up one half of the eclair and flicks her tongue over the chocolate glaze spread on top.

"Good, aren't they?" she asks, when I take the other half and bite it.

"Amazing."

"I think one bite is all I need," she says, putting the remainder of the pastry back on her plate.

"Just one bite and you're satisfied?"

"I don't know about satisfied so much as on sugar overload. Besides, I want a bite of the cookie too."

"Right. The cookie." I reach out and break off a piece. I raise it to her lips and wait for them to part. I ease the cookie into her mouth, letting two of my fingers follow.

She takes the cookie into her cheek and her tongue flicks over my index finger, a damp slide along my skin, tugging at my senses. It's a hot tease of what she could do to my dick and I clamp down on the urge to pump my fingers in and out of her mouth, hard.

Instead, I drag them back out, swiping a crumb off of the corner of her mouth and easing it gently back between her lips. She's breathing harder now, her chest rising up and down rapidly in the tight Racketeers T-shirt.

I slowly pull back, and lick the tip of my fingers that were just in her mouth. She watches the movement, her pupils dilating. God I love this building tension between us. Rather than wrapping my hand around the back of her neck and pulling her into a kiss, I relax into the chair, spreading my legs apart and easing them out in front of me. "What did you want to show me?" I ask, lifting the cup of coffee to my lips.

"Oh! Right. Um." She presses her lips together and pulls out her phone. She nods once, like she's reassuring herself she's doing the right thing. "I know you said you don't read romance novels, but you like to read, so you know good writing. I… I have been writing my own serialized romance story and putting it up on an app called Habanero where people read it for free and critique it."

"You wrote a fiction story? That's so cool, Dani. I'd love to be creative like that. I can only consume any form of art, not create it." It's true. I went to medical school for a reason. My brain is attracted to logic. Find a problem, fix it.

"Well, I thought it was cool too. I mean, I've always wanted to be a writer. It's a dream, my one true passion. Not just to sell books, but to sell *my* books. But on the platform they all think it sucks." Dani isn't looking at me as she says all of this, but is scrolling through her phone. She finds what she's looking for, swipes a few times, and then turns the screen to me. "Will you read it and tell me what I'm doing wrong?"

For a second, I'm surprised. Then I'm honored. "Of course I'd love to read it, though I'm not sure how much help I can be. Like I said, I can consume books but I can't create them. My professor in college told me I have the creativity of a Vulcan."

She laughs. "What? That's clearly not true at all and I've only known you for a few hours."

"Thank you. I agree. I understand emotion. I just can't paint a masterpiece, do any sort of crafting, or write an essay that doesn't sound like AI. So I'd love to read what you write, but I don't know anything about editing."

"I'd still just like your opinion. Everyone has been, well, harsh, and I've been just too embarrassed to show it to Luna or my family or other friends, because what if they tell me to give up? That this isn't my future because I'm lousy at it? When it's all I've ever wanted to do?" She's looking at me with pleading eyes.

Well, hell.

This story could suck big donkey dick and I'm going to reassure her. No one has the right to squash anyone else's dream. I'll have to use my calmest bedside manner skills.

"I'd love to," I say, taking the phone from her hand.

She clearly means right now.

"Just right here," she says, pointing to the screen. "It's the fourth scene. The hero and heroine's first kiss. She's been kidnapped by the mafia and one of the bodyguards has fallen in love with her and has released her from the cage she's being held in."

What the fuck? I didn't see that shit coming. My sweet sunshine has a dark side? It takes all of my professional-mode skills to not react.

"Okay. Got it." I nod. "I've seen every mob movie ever made. I'm on it."

She smiles in relief. "Thank you, Michael. I really appreciate this." She shoves her chair back and stands. "I won't read over your shoulder. I'll be over by the travel section."

When I start to read the chapter, it's clear Dani doesn't actually have a dark side. At all. Not one teeny tiny fucking little bit. She wants to write this particular type of story for a reason only she knows, but her heart isn't in it. She glosses over everything brutal with almost zero description and describes in great detail a very sweet and tender friendship blossoming between a one-handed bodyguard and a shy, glasses-wearing bookworm whose father owes the mafia so much money the only way he can repay them is to offer his daughter's virginity.

The bodyguard doesn't sound like a badass bodyguard.

We're in his point of view and he thinks things like her wheat-colored hair flows dramatically over the high peaks of her creamy globes.

The only creamy globes I've ever seen are the milk glass pendant lights in my parents' laundry room.

Beyond those developmental concerns, Dani writes well. She has evocative descriptions, fantastic pacing, and great character development. Aside from the bodyguard's internal dialogue.

The woman in the story is perfect. Her reactions are appropriate, her emotions feel real to me, I can sense her longing for the one-handed bodyguard, whose name is Sturgeon.

I assume there is a dramatic backstory that came earlier or will come later as to why he's missing a limb and that the heroine, Divine, will save him emotionally at the same time he saves her physically. Dani has built all that in enough to make me believe it.

Their conversation leading up to the kiss is filled with angst and raw emotion and makes me feel bad for both of them. They're in a hell of a mess, what with the mafia boss's lieutenant getting out of prison soon and wanting to marry her to exact revenge on his betrayer and all.

But the kiss is a little flat. Even though I don't read the genre and don't know what readers expect, I can assume they want a little more than this.

She'd waited her whole life for this. Her first kiss. His lips took charge of her mouth, and she found herself swept away on a river of passion.

A rat ran over her foot, startling her out of Sturgeon's embrace.

Huh. I take a huge bite of the cookie on the plate and collect my thoughts. I'm not even going to address the fact that Sturgeon sounds like Charlotte Bronte. Maybe it's intentional. Maybe there's a plot twist where Sturgeon is actually a poet.

A text pops up from Luna on Dani's phone while I'm rereading the chapter again to make sure my first reaction was correct.

You can come upstairs whenever. Kyle left.

Flicking the text away, I go back over the kiss. I think Dani is shying away from it. Scrolling through the comments posted below her chapter, the readers agree and make that brutally clear.

OMG all that build up and then one sentence???? She blue balled us!

Ugh. So disappointed.

Sturgeon sounds like a pussy.

I think this author has soooo much potential but that kiss was like my ex. Done before it really started. Girl, get an editor and keep writing! Don't give up!

I stand up and walk toward Dani. I have the perfect way to encourage her. I'll sweep her ass away on her own river of passion and show her it's all in the damn details.

CHAPTER 7

Dani

FLIPPING BLINDLY through a book on Paris, my bucket list travel destination, I bite my lip and try not to glance back to see if Michael is done reading. I feel like the eclair is churning in my stomach, sour and thick. I've never let anyone I know read what I've written and while I haven't enjoyed having strangers online trash my story, I can deal with that. They're strangers.

But if Michael tells me it's horrible, that's going to hurt. Which is why I haven't let Luna read it. I don't want her to give me a look of pity and say, "Oh, sweetie, it's good," when she's clearly lying her ass off.

Michael moves up behind me. I immediately sense his presence and whirl around to beg him to go easy on me. I open my mouth to speak but he doesn't allow me to say anything.

His hands are on my cheeks, thumbs caressing my skin. "You're an amazing writer, Dani," he murmurs. "You have great pacing and characterization and evocative descriptions and emotions."

"I do?"

He nods. "Just one critique. That was not a first kiss, Cookie." His thumb brushes over my lower lip. "That was a footnote."

My skin feels warm where he's touching me and I'm almost

overcome with relief that he seems genuine in his compliments. I don't even mind the critique because he's right. One hundred percent right. The kiss made me panic. I couldn't think of any way to describe it that didn't seem ridiculous. Kissing is nice enough. But I've never been destroyed by a kiss like they are in the novels I read. Or the way I want Divine to feel in the story I'm writing.

I've never felt caught up, carried away to the point where I've forgotten where I am or what my name is.

Until Crew earlier tonight, that is.

"Really?" I whisper. "You think I'm a good writer?"

"Not good. Amazing," he corrects, his deep brown eyes sweeping over my lips. The pad of his thumb rubs over my mouth in a teasing, tantalizing circle. "But that kiss, Dani. You have to give them more."

"I don't know how," I admit.

His eyes are hot as he studies my face, seemingly taking in every detail. His thumb brushes over my lower lip in a tantalizing circle almost as if he is in awe. As if this moment is one he wants to imprint on his memory. I want to do the same. Remember this anticipation, remember Michael's gaze.

"How about some inspiration?" he asks.

Then he lowers his head.

Our mouths meet and I feel like I've touched a live wire. Electricity licks along every nerve ending sending currents of heat and need to my core. He kisses me softly, pressing, then retreating, then pressing again for longer, then retreating. For several seconds, he just kisses me sweetly, one hand cupping my face. He nips my bottom lip, then licks the tip of his tongue over the spot.

God, I want more. More of...everything. I want to truly taste him. I wanted his mouth everywhere.

"More," I whisper against his mouth.

He lifts his head. Again he studies my eyes.

What does he see in there? Desire for sure. But does he see that it's easy for me to trust him, to allow myself to be swept along by our passion?

He must. "I want to give you everything," he says.

Heat spikes in my inner thighs. I reach up to wrap my fingers around his wrist, squeezing. I nod. "Yes. Give it to me."

He gives a soft groan and kisses me again. But this time, he drags his mouth from my lips to my jaw. He kisses along the curve to my ear. "I don't even know if you know what that means."

"If I don't, it doesn't matter. I trust you," I say breathlessly.

"Fuck," is his muttered response as he kisses down the length of my throat.

My entire body lights up. It feels as those presses of his lips settle between my legs and my clit throbs as he licks over my collar bone. I want his tongue there. Between my legs.

"You taste so fucking good," he says against my skin. He kisses back up to my mouth, this time pressing harder when he takes me, sliding his tongue over my lower lip. When I sigh, he strokes his tongue along mine. "So fucking sweet, Cookie."

My nipples tighten, my panties get wetter, and I feel my back arch. I need more.

"Michael. Please."

This time his groan is more of a low growl from his throat. He backs me up against the bookcase, and presses into me with his whole body.

His whole, hard, hot body. He looks down at me again, his expression both aroused and bemused. "This is just a kissing scene, remember?"

Damn it. I wish it was a he-gives-me-an-orgasm-scene. "Right. Inspiration."

"Use all five of your senses, Dani. Tell the reader how I feel to you." He sweeps his tongue inside my mouth and presses his hard thighs against mine.

"Hard," I breathe when he pulls back. "You feel hot and hard."

Michael gives a soft moan. "What do you hear?"

I tilt my head, giving him access to my neck. He lavishes kisses on me.

I understand his sensual little writing exercise. "The sound of our breathing, the desire in our voices. You smell like leather and God, it's so sexy, Michael."

"You smell like coffee and a light floral perfume," he murmurs. "And you taste like sugar and temptation. I want to taste you all over. See if the rest of you is as hot and greedy as your mouth."

"I want that." Goosebumps trip down my neck and tighten my nipples. His hand trails over that same path, as if he knows. His calloused finger drags over the sensitive skin of my neck then cups my breast, sliding his thumb over my nipple, making my pussy clench.

"Yes, I definitely want to kiss and taste you here," he says, circling the hard tip. He returns to my mouth, kissing me again as he plays with my nipple.

The pressure is both a relief and torment.

His tongue strokes mine as he kisses me deeply, the motion making my clit throb.

His hand slides down my side to my hip. He squeezes, then moves to cup me through my jeans, his big hand hot against my pussy. I know he can feel how hot I am. I shift my knees apart so he could touch more of me.

"And oh, yes, I will taste you here," he growls against my mouth. "Deep and long. Take care of you until you scream."

Without meaning to, I rock against his hand. I need more pressure right there, right now. "Please, yes," I beg.

He lifted his head, breathing hard…

I'm clinging to the book rack behind me, weak in the knees, and fighting for air.

Until I've forgotten where I am or what my name is.

But I'm going to remember every detail of this kiss forever.

"We forgot the final sense," he says, breathing hard. "What we see. You look beautiful, Dani. Flushed and pretty and perfect."

He looks like my every fantasy sprung to life. But before I can say that he sucks in a breath and points toward the stairs.

"Now go upstairs and write that. In full detail. Write every single thing I did and said and every single thing you felt when I did it to you."

Breathless, my panties wet, my nipples standing at attention beneath the absurdly tight T-shirt Nathan gave me, I nod. "Okay."

"Right now, Dani. While it's fresh in your mind." Michael tugs me forward and spins me in the direction of the stairs. His hand drifts from my lower back to my ass, giving it a quick squeeze as he pushes me. "Go. I'll call you tomorrow."

I glance back. "But… I have to lock up after you."

"I'll handle it. I still have your keys. I'll bring them back to you tomorrow."

I debate for less than one second. I trust Michael. Besides, what is he going to steal, a Jack Reacher novel? A coffee mug? The empty bank bag?

"Thanks!" I say breathlessly. "You're the best, Michael. The absolute best."

At my words, he starts a little and the look he gives me is so intense, I pause. I suddenly want him to fuck me in the bookshop, bent over a velvet chair, staring down a row of hardcover gold foil-edged Shakespeare books.

That's how good that kiss was.

And I think maybe he's thinking that same thing.

But then he shakes his head a little, as if he's clearing his throat. "Go," he says, pointing again at the stairs. "Make magic happen."

"Goodnight." I blow him a kiss and run before I can change my mind. I pound up the stairs and throw open the door to my apartment.

"Can't talk!" I say, blowing past Luna who is watching TV lying on the couch, a blanket pulled up to her chin.

She doesn't answer and I realize she's actually asleep, much to my relief. I don't want to talk. I want to write. My fingers are itching with the urge to hit the keyboard and my thoughts are swirling.

I crack my knuckles and let it all flow out of me.

Twenty minutes later, I stop and lift my hands off the keyboard, staring at my screen. I just typed all of that without stopping once. It just spilled out of me.

But…that's it. That was the kiss with Michael. My blood is pumping, my whole body is hot. Even hotter now that I relived it and wrote it all out.

I read it over again, finding myself squeezing my thighs together. God, my readers are going to love this.

But now I have to end this scene.

Argh! I really just want to call Michael and demand he come back here and help give me an ending.

I pick up my phone and text him.

I wrote the scene.

He responds immediately. It's like he was waiting to hear from me and it makes me warm and melty.

How do you feel about it?

I debate how to answer that. I'm happy with it. My readers will love it and I feel like I broke through a barrier I've been dealing with. There's nothing flat about this kissing scene.

But he also left me here all riled up.

Hot and bothered.

He texts back just one word.

Perfect

Perfect?! That's perfect?

And mad at you because you left me like this.

He just sends me a winky face emoji.

So I send him a screenshot of my favorite vibrator.

His response takes a little longer this time.

Thank you.

I frown at the two words.

For what?

I was going to go to bed with images of me going down on you against that book rack. But I have something else to add to the scenario now.

I stare at that response for a very long time.

I don't respond. I have no idea how to respond to that.

I go back to Divine and Sturgeon.

"Soon, my love, soon," Sturgeon said, brushing her hair back from her face.

"Please, now. I need you."

"The anticipation will make it that much sweeter. Trust me."

My readers will hate being left hanging there.

Which is great.

That means they'll come back for the next installment.

Oh…crap.

That means I'll have to write the next installment. Which means it will have to be really good. And involve more than even this kiss.

Well, I hope Dr. Hughes meant it when he said he's willing to help me with this.

With a wicked grin, I shut my computer down for the night.

But I don't fall asleep before pulling out my favorite vibrator.

The only surprise is that it's not just Michael Hughes that appears in my dirty fantasy. Crew McNeill is also there.

And a certain broody, bossy billionaire.

I might be in trouble.

CHAPTER 8

Dani

"OKAY, WHAT IS GOING ON?" Luna demands of me as she whips a mostly empty coffee mug away from our only customer, a regular named Harold who is still doing his crossword puzzle, his plate empty. He devoured his pain au chocolat well over an hour ago.

He's just lingering now, like he does every weekday. He's in his seventies and is bored since his dog, Patsy, passed away six months ago.

"Hey," he protests. "I was still drinking that."

"It was cold dregs, Harold," Luna tells him. "Time to go home and feed your cat. It's almost eleven."

It's more like ten thirty. Harold leaves every day at eleven on the nose to saunter home. But Luna is having none of it today.

His bushy gray eyebrows lift. "Got a hot date or something?"

"Girl talk," she tells him grimly. She jabs a finger at me. "This one has some explaining to do."

"Me?" I ask, innocently, putting a hand to my chest. I can already feel my face heating up. Damn Irish skin. "I have no idea what you're talking about."

Then I yawn, and I'm forced to cover my mouth with my hand, embarrassed.

I was up late last night between the writing, the texting with Michael, the self-love, and the repeated tossing and turning afterward as I replayed in my head over and over both Crew and Michael's kisses. And Nathan's whatever-the-hell that was in his office. Plus, Nathan's bare chest and abs. Those are emblazoned on my brain like a brand.

I slept in the shirt he gave me. While I used my vibrator and thought about Crew, Michael, and Nathan, all doing deliciously dirty things to me. All at once. Together. It took a while, obviously.

Yet, in spite of getting almost no sleep, I'm bouncing with energy. I've been bustling around the shop all morning, dusting and rearranging shelves, and running my hand over every velvet chair with a happy sigh, and grinning with every pass by the pastry cases. The cookies and eclairs taunt me with hot reminders of Michael's finger in my mouth, of those hot grinding kisses, of his reassurance that I'm a good writer.

Earlier, I did an impromptu dance with the Swiffer around the bookrack Michael pressed me against. That's how giddy I am.

"Your aura is red," Luna says pointedly. "Your aura is never red."

That alarms me. "Is that bad?" I ask. Maybe that's why three different men flirted aggressively with me last night and two kissed me. Maybe this is a fluke. A full moon phenomenon, or the planets aligning, or my body is throwing off sexual energy in an attempt to stave off my biological clock.

Which is ridiculous. I'm twenty-four.

But I'm pretty sure I'll be devastated if all this virile male attention evaporates as quickly as it appeared.

"Red means energetic and fiery," she says. "Bye, Harold. See you Monday."

Poor Harold stands up, but he doesn't look offended. He eyes me. "You do look a little red. Maybe you have a fever. I'm outta here. I can't get sick. I'm immunocompromised."

He's gone as fast as he can with a bad hip. I shake my head at

Luna. "You are out of your mind. He's basically our best customer."

"Harold will be back. He loves my cappuccinos." Luna comes over to me and puts her hands on my arms, giving me a shake. It makes all her bangle bracelets clatter and her chandelier earrings sway riotously. "What happened last night? I'm dying here. Tell me everything."

"Is a red aura a bad thing?" I ask cautiously. "You seem really agitated about it."

"No, not at all." She waves that off. "And I'm only agitated because I'm so happy you're finally getting out there again! You deserve it. You *need* it. You know how much I fucking hate Brandon Fredricks and what he did to you. That asshole kept you from dating for two and a half years! And you haven't gotten laid in even longer! Last night is like a breakthrough!"

I shudder at the mention of my ex. I met Brandon in my sophomore sociology class. He was cute and we had instant chemistry. And he was bossy. That's what I thought I wanted.

That is *what you want,* I correct myself. *But you want* good *bossy. Caring bossy. Not controlling Brandon bossy.*

I'd realized through reading spicier and spicier romance that I wanted to be bossed around in the bedroom. What I hadn't quite figured out yet when I'd met Brandon was that not every likes-to-be-in-control guy was good at bedroom bossy.

Brandon wasn't a loving, caring, sexually dominant man who would understand the trust and respect it took to truly have a woman be submissive to him sexually.

He was just an asshole.

I hate when you wear skirts like that. You don't need to show everything off to all the other guys, Dani.

I don't ever want to see you talking to Marcus or Landon again, do you hear me?

Where were you last night when I tried to call you? You need to pick up when I call, Dani.

An asshole who also shamed me about my fantasies. Like wanting to be a romance writer.

And like my suggestion of using toys together.

I don't do it for you? You think I need help? Thanks a lot, that's a real turn-on.

Or like my fantasy of him binding my hands and blindfolding me.

What the hell is wrong with you? You want me to force you? How do you think that makes me feel? You should want to do this. Why can't we just do it like normal people?

And definitely like my ultimate fantasy of being with more than one man at a time.

No real man wants to share. Jesus, Dani.

I could still remember the look of shock and disgust on his face.

Sure, maybe at some crazy sex party with some slut they're all just messing with, but why would you think I'd want to be with some girl who'd pass herself around like that? There's no way I could watch some other guy fuck you! Holy shit. What guy could? He'd gotten out of bed and stomped to the door.

I'd tried to explain that this desire didn't mean I didn't love him. I'd tried to explain that sex with multiple partners wasn't dirty or wrong, but he wasn't listening. I'd instantly realized things were over between us.

I was hurt and angry for about a month.

And then…a little part of me started to wonder if he was right. If there was something wrong with me. If all of that really just belonged in books. And I started to feel humiliated.

"Tell me about every delicious second you spent with Hot Doc," Luna urges.

I take a deep breath and focus on the woman who was my biggest supporter during that time. I told her everything Brandon said, and Luna had been ready to go to his house and take a butcher knife to his dick.

She gave me pep talks. She assured me that sexual fantasies

are normal and that it was all Brandon's problem, not mine. She insisted that I would definitely have a chance to have an amazing sexual experience with multiple guys. I just needed to find the right guys.

But I've barely dated in the past three years, and I haven't had sex at all. Not even with one guy.

Unless you count my imagination and dreams. Because *those* are insanely hot.

"Here. Just read about it. Just replace Sturgeon with Michael and Divine with me." I find the doc on the app on my phone. I uploaded it this morning and I already have forty views and one positive comment.

Now THAT'S more like it!!!! Kiss me, Sturgeon!!

Michael's advice and ahem, inspiration, clearly worked.

The bell rings over the door. Luna takes my phone as I turn and see a delivery man. We're not expecting any packages, but I go over and greet him with a bright smile. "Hi!"

He's not having it. He just shoves a box at me and says, "Sign here."

"Sure!" Surprised at how heavy the small box is, I juggle it, take the stylus and sign my name with a flourish on his electronic box. I glance at the label and see it's for me.

Curious, I glance over at the return address. It's from Frosty's, my favorite ice cream shop in Franklin, Indiana, my hometown. What on earth? I definitely didn't order anything from them.

Using scissors behind the cash register, I slice open the box and find packs of dry ice in it. Beneath that is a pint of my favorite flavor, Nutty Buddy. My first confused thought is my parents sent it, but there is no way. The shipping rate on this was hefty, and that is not something they would ever endorse. They would tell me to walk around the corner and grab a scoop at the neighborhood shop.

There's a small white envelope, so I pull it out and remove the card.

Danielle,

I want to see you tonight.

Nathan Armstrong

It's not a question. It's a command. From Nathan, the billionaire. My whole body is suddenly so flushed with intense heat, it's a wonder I don't melt the ice cream pint I'm holding into a puddle of sticky liquid.

Now there is a guy who could do bossy in the bedroom right.

A tiny corner of my brain flashes back to Rina, the girl who lived down the hall from Luna and me our junior year of college. One night we'd gotten drunk and started talking about men, sex, and fantasies. I'd admitted that I thought I was a submissive and would love to meet a true dom, someone who could boss me around in bed while also cherishing me and taking care of me. Rina had whirled on me and launched into a ten minute long rant about how being submissive in *any* way to a man set the feminist movement back fifty years and why would I ever let a man tell me what to do and didn't I think that having agency over my own body and life was important?

I'd started crying, Luna had started arguing with her, Rina had stomped out, and…yeah, I was still thinking about *that* almost two years later too. Twice I'd brought up my fantasies and twice someone I cared about stomped out.

Ugh. I *know* that I'm not setting any movements back. I want to be independent and make my own decisions in every other way. But when it comes to sex, I find the idea of a man who *knows* me, who knows my body and who makes my pleasure his number one goal, who wants to worship me and ensure that I'm getting exactly what I need so fucking…

"Dani!"

I jump and spin at Luna's exclamation. I clutch the ice cream to my chest. "What?"

"This is amazing! Holy shit! This is what happened with Hot Doc?"

Oh, right, the kiss. I nod. "Exactly what happened. Except the last line. He pulled back and made me go upstairs and write. He didn't say that part about anticipation making things sweeter. I added that part." I pause. "But I guess I do believe that."

Luna just stares at me. Then slowly her mouth curls into a grin. "Oh. My. God."

"I know." And I do. I know. I'm already all worked up again and thinking about my vibrator.

"What's that?" Luna notices the pint of ice cream.

I look down. "Ice cream. From Nathan. From Indiana."

"What the hell are you talking about? Who's Nathan from Indiana?" She gives me a confused look.

I shake my head. "No. Nathan from the Racketeers."

She frowns. "I have no idea what you're talking about."

Oh, right. Luna doesn't know about Nathan or the visit to his office or anything that happened after she left me in that hallway outside the Racketeers locker room.

I take a deep breath. "The guy who gave us the VIP tickets and my T-shirt last night was actually Nathan Armstrong. The–"

"Nathan Armstrong?" Luna interrupts. "As in the owner of the Racketeers? The one who wanted your phone number from Crew?"

I nod.

"Why is Nathan Fucking Armstrong sending you ice cream?" Now she crosses her arms and looks at me like, 'Young lady, you better start talking faster.'

"He saw me fall and wanted to be sure I was okay. So he asked a security guard to bring me up to his office." I tell her the rest of the story about all of us meeting in Nathan's office, and how Crew had to stay behind, and how Michael brought me home. Then I gesture toward the box with the dry ice. "And now he sent me my favorite ice cream from home."

"You've told him where you're from and what your favorite ice cream is while you were in his office?"

I shake my head. "No. I have no idea how he knows that."

Luna's eyes suddenly widen. She looks down at my phone and her fingers start flying over the screen. Then she stops, nods, and holds it up for me to see.

It's a photo of her and me on social media. We're in Franklin, at the ice cream shop, grinning with huge bowls of ice cream in front of us. The caption says "my best friend and my favorite ice cream! Perfect day!"

My eyes widen right along with Luna's.

She scrolls up three photos and shows me again. This time it's me eating a cone from the shop around the corner here in Chicago. The caption reads, "Not Nutty Buddy from Frosty's, but still pretty good."

I meet her gaze. Her eyebrows are arched.

"He's…sweet," I say.

"He's a stalker," she replies.

"He's a hot stalker who sends me ice cream," I say with a shrug. Then I grin.

"Oh my God." She points a finger at my nose. "You like him."

"He asked me out tonight." Actually he *told* me to go out with him, but I don't think Nathan asks people for things. He just demands them. And that makes a little shiver of heat slide through my body.

"You do. You like him. Oh, my God! Both him and the Hot Doc!"

Just then the little bell over the door to the bookshop jingles and we both turn.

It's a guy with shaggy blond hair, wearing a Racketeers polo and khakis, carrying a bright yellow gift bag.

What is this about?

"Hi, can I help you?" Luna asks. She steps in front of me.

Oh, boy, Luna is getting a little Mama Bear on me now.

"I'm looking for Dani Larkin," the guy says. "I'm supposed to deliver something to her and pick something up?"

"Who sent you?" Luna's eyes are narrowed.

"Um... Dr. Hughes," the kid says.

"I'm Dani." I step around Luna and give her an eye roll.

"Oh, hey. I'm Austin. I work for Dr. Hughes. He said to tell you that he had a patient emergency come up and he's really sorry he couldn't bring these over himself." He hands me the gift bag. I pull out the white, green, and blue tissue paper, grinning even before I know what's inside.

I love presents, what can I say? And I'm getting two today from two different very hot men who are, for whatever reason, interested in me. Best. Day. Ever.

Inside are my keys, that Michael said he would return and a mug. I pull it out. It says Future Bestselling Author. I melt. I absolutely melt. My eyes even sting a little. God, that man...

In addition, the mug is filled with candy kisses.

Oh my God.

Luna is shaking her head when I turn back. "Giirrrl..."

"I know." I clutch the mug to my chest right beside the ice cream.

"Uh," Austin says. "He also said to be sure to pick up the book you were going to pick out for him."

The romance novel. I grin. "Sure. It's right over here."

I head for the romance section and straight for my favorite spicy novel. I pull One Night In Paris from the shelf and hand it to Austin.

"Tell him..." Nope, I want to write him a note. "Just a second." I head back to the front counter, put my new mug and my ice cream down, and pull out a sticky note. I write quickly.

I hope you enjoy the ending to this one better than the one I had last night.

xo D

I stick to the inside page and hand the book to Austin. "Thank you."

"Sure thing."

As soon as the door bumps shut behind him, Luna spins to face me. "Okay, keep talking. I need to know everything."

I keep telling her about last night. I tell her more about Nathan's office and how all three of the guys acted and what they said, how Michael insisted on taking me home, the whole scene in front of the store, our talk in the bakery, him reading my story, and… well, she read about the kiss.

All I leave out is about her brother declaring that I'm not his girlfriend…yet.

"So what are you going to do–"

Luna is cut off by the bell jingling again.

She gives a little frustrated groan as we both turn to greet…

Crew.

"Hey, ladies!"

I'm speechless. I'm also immediately hot and tingly.

And I like it. A lot.

"Hey, what are you doing here?" Luna asks. "And why is your hair wet?"

"Because I just washed it in the shower," he says, giving me a she's not very bright look. "How are you today, Dani?" he asks, sauntering up to me with a charming grin. "Sleep well?"

Oh God. It's like he knows.

Which is ridiculous and impossible. He can't know anything about what I did and with who and by myself afterward.

"Fine. Great. Absolutely amazing. Like a baby," I babble. "You?"

"I didn't sleep much. I had a great game last night and I got to steal you away from both your dumb date and Sammy the Malamute. I was on a real high." He reaches out and flicks a finger over the delicate necklace in the shape of a quill I'm wearing. "That's pretty."

The tip of his finger barely brushes over my skin, but I still feel a tingling sensation fire up in my core. I'm glad I wore another low neckline today. "Thanks," I whisper.

Crew is dressed in joggers and a hoodie, his damp hair curling enticingly around his strong jawline. He's so damn cute. Yet also hot and muscular and mouthwatering. His dimples are on full display. He's carrying a bag.

"For you," he says, holding it up with a flourish.

"Oh, Jesus H. Christ," is Luna's opinion.

"You okay, sis?" Crew asks, leaning his elbow on the counter.

"I'm annoyed."

"With me?" He actually bats his eyelashes at her.

"Constantly, yes," she informs him. "And with the fact that I put out last night and have no ice cream or inspirational mugs to show for it."

Crew blinks at her. "Um… people get those things for putting out?"

She points to my ice cream and inspirational mug.

One of his eyebrows arches. "What are those?"

"Gifts," I squeak. I'm trying not to feel guilty about them. Why would I feel guilty?

"From?" he asks.

"Michael and Nathan."

His eyes narrow slightly, but he nods. "I see." He reaches into the bag he carried in and pulls out what looks like a shirt. Then he shakes it out.

It's a Racketeers hockey jersey.

With a huge number 17 on it.

And McNeill across the back.

Oh…

"Of course," Luna mutters.

I look at her. "Of course what?"

"If you're going to pee on someone to mark your territory, you want everyone to know that you did it." Luna shakes her head at her brother. But she looks amused.

I frown. "What?'

"Anyone can give you ice cream and a coffee mug. But that—" she points at the jersey, "Is his name emblazoned across your body."

Crew is grinning again. I have to assume that he agrees with her assessment.

"I assume you do want to pee on her?" Luna asks Crew.

"I don't know what kinks you're into sis," he says. "But I'm into whatever Dani wants to be into."

Luna narrows her eyes. "You want her."

"I absolutely fucking do."

"This is for me?" I ask.

I know, I know. Stupid question. Of course it's for me. But I'm still a little discombobulated by these men. I've imagined stuff like this. Read about it. Written it. But in real life it's far more potent.

"Yes." Crew bunches up the jersey and slips it on over my head.

His fingers glide through my hair and down over my breasts, making contact with my tight nipples over the shirt. He smoothes the front down repeatedly, his large palms shifting past my waistband and coming perilously close to stroking my clit through my jeans. He pats way longer and much more than is necessary and I enjoy every single second of it.

"Okay, I think that's good," Luna says. "I'm open-minded and you two dating is great, but I can't watch you pet her."

He grins at me. "Perfect." He turns me so he can see his name across my back. Then pats my ass. "That's my girl."

Luna sighs heavily.

I don't know if Crew's attention is because he wants to annoy his sister or because he's really into me, but I'm enjoying it, I can't deny.

"Gotta go to the gym." Crew kisses me softly. "I can't wait to see you in my jersey at the game tonight."

I simply nod and watch him walk out. Am I going to the game tonight? I have no idea. I don't know anything other than the fact that I'm delirious with pleasure. I feel like a goddess. The attention from these three men is heady stuff. I don't know what will come of it, if I'll be like Cinderella at the ball tonight and as of midnight this will all disappear, but I'm going to enjoy it for now.

Luna clears her throat and I pull my gaze from Crew's ass. I blush as I meet my best friend's eyes.

"Who are you and what have you done with the Danielle Larkin of the last few years?" she asks.

I laugh. "I don't know, but I'm having a really good time."

Luna finally smiles. "I can tell. And *thank God.* Also, fuck Brandon Fredricks. I love seeing you happy like this. You're glowing."

I put a hand to my cheek. "Am I?"

"You are." She put a hand on her hip. "So are you actually going to date all three of them?"

I look down at the jersey, then at the ice cream that is probably more the consistency of a milkshake now, then at the mug full of kisses. "I think I am." I look at her again. "Are you okay with me dating Crew?"

She takes a second to think about it, then nods. "I am. I really am. You're the best. He'd be lucky to date you."

I pull her in for a hug. "Thank you."

"And he definitely knows I'll kill him if he hurts you. Now I just need to let the other two know." She blows out a breath as we lean back. "This is going to be a lot of work for me. They better be worth it."

I feel a little flip in my stomach. It's strange that I can feel this so quickly, but I already think they will be.

Very worth it.

CHAPTER 9

Nathan

SHE'S NERVOUS. She's fidgeting on the seat of my town car next to me on our way to the restaurant. And talking incessantly. It's actually adorable. Of course, it is.

I don't know that there will ever be a time when Danielle Larkin won't be adorable to me.

But I don't want her to be nervous. I want her to want this date. To want to be with me.

And I really need her to stop moving. Because when she's shifting on the seat like that, all I can think about is how it would feel to have her shifting like that in my lap. Naked.

"I can't believe you found my favorite ice cream shop," she says, for the second time. "That was just so…sweet of you. I haven't had that ice cream in such a long time."

"Three months," I say.

Her gaze flies to mine. "What?"

"That was the last time you had it. July. At least that was the last time you posted about it." I shift on my seat, trying to ease some of the pressure on my cock. "I suppose you could have had it since then. When were you last home?"

"I…" She trails off. "That was…the last time."

"I'm glad you liked it."

She shifts again, crossing her legs, then uncrossing them. I finally reach out and clamp my hand down on her thigh, stilling her.

Her skin is smooth and without thinking, I let my fingers stroke over the velvety softness. "Stop wiggling," I tell her, my voice husky.

"Sorry." She's breathless. "I'm…I've never been taken on a date in a town car with a driver."

I give her a small smile. "That's why you're nervous?"

She wets her lips. "I–" She shakes her head. "No."

"Then why?"

"I'm not sure I'm nervous, exactly. I've never been out to dinner with a guy like you. I thought we were going to a hockey game."

Yes, she'd mentioned that on the phone when she'd called to thank me for the ice cream and respond to my note.

"As much as I love hockey, I can do better than beer and nachos," I tell her.

She smiles at the mention of beer. If it weren't for her asshole date and all the beer last night, I might not be sitting here with her right now, so I'm over my annoyance with Ben.

"Well, I was all ready," she says. "I have a jersey now and everything."

"You bought a jersey? I kind of liked that T-shirt." I really fucking liked that T-shirt. I'd love to see her in it again. In only that. While I fuck her.

I have to shift on the seat again.

She smiles and says, "I didn't buy it. Crew gave it to me."

My hand tightens on her thigh and I have to consciously relax it. "McNeill gave you a jersey?"

She's not smiling as brightly now. Probably because I just growled at her.

"Yes."

"A generic Racketeers jersey?" I ask, knowing full well that's not what he gave her.

"No. It's got his name and number on it."

Yeah. That's what I thought. And exactly what I would have done if I was him. Hell, the guy told me that's what he was going to do.

"Did he ask you out?" I ask her. He told me he was going to do that too.

"No. Not specifically." She looks up at me through long lashes. "But, I think he might."

I nod. "He will."

I stroke my fingers over her bare thigh again. I love the little dress she's wearing. It's black, simple. I know it's nothing outrageously expensive like what most of the women I date wear, but it's probably the nicest thing in her closet. She's also wearing heels. Hot pink ones. That she will definitely be leaving on when I fuck her later.

And I am going to fuck her later.

Unless she absolutely says no and that she doesn't want me at all, I am getting this girl naked. Tonight.

"Does that upset you?" she asks. She rests her hand on top of mine. "That Crew might ask me out?"

"Yes," I say simply.

"Why?"

"Because I want you."

She smiles up at me. "You have me. Right now. I'm here."

"I don't want anyone else to have you."

"Hmm." She runs her thumb over the back of my knuckles, studying our hands. Her hand is so much smaller and paler against mine.

"Well, I don't think you get to make that call," she says.

I lift a brow. Is that what she thinks?

I don't own her, no. Yet.

"I can make it so you don't want anyone else," I tell her.

Her smile grows and she looks up at me again. "I look forward to you trying."

Is that right?

Does my sweet Danielle want us to fight over her? I study her closely. I don't know if that's it, exactly. I think she likes me bossy, though.

I test it out with another low growl and lean in, meeting her gaze directly. I also run my hand higher up her thigh. I cup her between her legs through her panties. "Be careful, little girl," I tell her, low and gruff. "I don't play around."

Her eyes are wide and I can feel how hot she is between her thighs. She swallows. Then says, "I'm not a little girl."

I run my middle finger up and down the middle of her panties. She makes a little whimpering noise. She's wet. Excellent.

"Have you fucked him?" I ask.

"Crew?" Her voice is soft as if she's having a hard time getting enough air in her lungs.

"Yes."

"No."

"What about Hughes?" I bite out.

"No." She pauses. "But I've kissed them both."

Fuck. I shouldn't be surprised. Both of those men are intelligent. Given the chance to kiss this woman, neither of them would have passed it up.

"And I'm going to date them both."

I narrow my eyes. "We'll see."

"I know what I want," she tells me, but her attempt at sassy boldness is tempered by the pink in her cheeks and the fact that she's breathing faster. And that her gaze is locked on my mouth.

"I'll show you what you want," I tell her. She likes competitiveness? Men *trying* for her attention? She hasn't seen anything yet. Then I lean back, pulling my hand out from under her skirt. "Let's go have dinner."

We've pulled up at the curb in front of Loretta's, my favorite five-star restaurant in Chicago. It's on the top floor of a building on Michigan Avenue, so it has a fantastic view of the lake and downtown. It's almost as good as the view from my penthouse. I know the owner personally and can always get a table, but I rarely bring dates here. I don't wine and dine the women I spend time with.

I definitely have sex, pretty much whenever I want or need to, but it's not romantic. I don't need to impress the women I choose to fuck. We're both there for one reason—to get off without any strings. There doesn't need to be a lot of extras. Maybe some wine. Occasionally food. But not even much conversation.

They don't ask me a lot of questions. I don't ask them a lot of questions.

They're attracted to me because of my money, and power. They sleep with me because I can give them exactly what they want—orgasms with no demands on their time or attention outside of the bedroom.

I don't know where any of them grew up, their favorite ice cream, or even the exact address of where they work.

I already know all of that about Danielle and I had to find all of it out myself. I worked at it.

I never work at it with women.

Danielle is different in almost every way from the women I usually take to bed.

I want her with an irrational intensity. And I do want to impress her, but not with my money, or my penthouse, or my connections, or my power. I want to impress her with how happy I can make her, how well I can take care of her, and how special I can make her feel.

I don't know if it's because I met her when she was with that asshole Ben who was treating her like an afterthought, or because I witnessed her get injured, or because Crew Fucking McNeill wants her and I'm not sure that cocky little fuck knows what it means to take care of someone other than himself, but I have this absurd need to make Danielle feel like a princess.

And then fuck her brains out.

But then again, giving a woman an orgasm she can still feel the next day, is absolutely one way to take care of her.

"Oh, um, okay."

Danielle is flustered and her cheeks are pink and I'm sure that for a moment there she forgot we were on our way to dinner.

"But first, take off your panties."

Her eyes go round. "Wh–what?"

"Take your panties off." I know she heard me perfectly before, but if she needs a moment to process that command, I can be patient.

"Why?" she practically whispers.

"Because I told you to."

She might go out with McNeill and Hughes, but it's going to be a very different experience than going out with me.

She wets her lips again and then my blood pumps hot and fast when she reaches up under the skirt, wiggles that cute ass on the seat of my car again, and pulls her panties down.

Yes. Danielle does like to be bossed around.

This will work out *so* very nicely.

When they're down over her heels, she looks up. "Now what?"

I hold out my hand. She hesitantly hands them over. I tuck them in my pocket. Then I open my door and step out. I pull my suit jacket together, buttoning it, then take her hand, helping her out of the car. "Keep your knees together so you don't flash anyone," I say near her ear. "I'm the only one you're spreading your legs for tonight."

Her cheeks are bright pink as we enter the building.

Once we're in the elevator on the way up to the top floor, she moves to stand near the back wall, her ankles crossed, her fingers clasped in front of her.

But I'm having none of that. I take her elbow and pull her to stand in front of me, her ass against my hard cock. I put a hand against her stomach, pressing her into me. But we don't speak. She leans into me and after a few floors, I feel her arch her back slightly, rubbing against me.

I smile and say into her hair, "Yes, that's all for you."

She sucks in a quick breath.

I run my hand up the outside of her thigh, hiking her skirt with it. My hand rests on her upper thigh, but I don't let her dress get high enough that anyone on the security camera gets to look at her. She's all mine.

I slide my hand over her pussy, my middle finger brushing her clit.

Her head falls back against my chest. "Oh my God, Nathan."

I move my hand lower, pressing my finger just barely inside her entrance. She's so fucking hot and wet. "And this is all for me," I tell her, my voice rough. "I can't wait to feel this all over my fingers and cock, and to taste it with my tongue."

She gasps and I feel her fingers wrap around my wrist. But she does not push me away. She holds on tight, as if afraid I'll pull away.

I do pull away.

She doesn't get this right now. She has to wait, anticipate, be on edge, think about this for the next couple of hours.

We have a romantic dinner to eat before I take care of any other feasting.

Twenty minutes later we've been seated at the private table I requested with a fabulous view, a private waiter, drinks, and the special private menu. And I'm not sure Danielle has noticed any of that.

She's definitely squirming on her chair, her skin is flushed–not just her cheeks, but her throat and chest too–and she's downed two glasses of ice water.

Maybe I overdid the pre-seduction seduction.

I smile as I lift my glass of scotch. I'm not sorry.

I am a little out of my element though. And I fucking hate it. I'm always in my element. I purposefully spend time in my damned element. Until this girl. She has me feeling off-balance. Not just because I'm not a dater, or a conversationalist, but because tonight I want to be.

She's spent time now with two men who are interested in her and who she, apparently, is also interested in.

Yes, I want to take her to bed, but I also want to know more about her. I want to know what they know.

McNeill has known her for years. Danielle is his sister's best friend. They have a history, though I don't know much about it. He's still known her outside of hockey and for much longer than just since the other night at the game.

And I know Hughes. The guy is the quintessential "people person." It makes him a great doctor. He's been not just a physician to the guys on the team, but also a mentor and, at times, another coach. I know the guys go to him for advice and help with things that go beyond their physical issues.

There is no doubt in my mind that he talked to Danielle the other night when he took her home from the arena. Hell, he probably knows her favorite color, her first childhood pet's name, and all of her hopes and dreams.

Fucking hell, a little bit of me wants to know her hopes and dreams too.

Why? Why do I need to know her? Why do I care?

I have no idea. I could, obviously, take her home, fuck her, and then forget about her.

But I've been asking her questions for the past ten minutes.

I now know she's an only child, that she met Luna in college, that her degree is in English, that she knows next to nothing about hockey, and that her mom is a nurse and her dad is a teacher in her hometown of Franklin, Indiana.

But every time I ask her something about her, she also turns it around on me.

"So, my parents are pretty great," she says. "Typical mom and dad from a small town in Indiana, I guess. They don't totally understand me. They'd love it if I would have gone to college and gotten a degree in teaching, or engineering, or if I'd decided to become a cosmetologist, or an astrophysicist, or something they understood. But running a bookshop that doesn't make any money, and living with my best friend who runs a bakery seems kind of...frivolous to them."

"Your parents understand what astrophysicists do?" I ask wryly.

She laughs lightly and I want to kiss her. Not run my hand up her skirt, but just kiss her.

"Well, no, maybe not. But it's something they think other people would go "Oh, that's impressive" about."

"People know what bookshops are and do," I say, frowning. "Why isn't that something they can be happy about?"

"Probably because it's actually Luna's shop," she says, lifting a shoulder. "Luna's parents bought it for us. The bookshop also doesn't actually make any money. I don't actually write any of the books inside of it." She sighs. "I think they'd just like to see me doing something that contributes. Either to my partnership with Luna, or to the world at large." She gives me a sad smile. "I would too."

I hate that. I hate that she's sad about anything. This woman is not meant to be anything but bright and happy.

Well, maybe panting, screaming, and sweating from sex. But not sad.

"Your dad is a teacher. Surely he values books."

"Of course. But using them for something. Or writing them. Not just owning a place where they sit on shelves and occasionally selling them to other people to use. The occasional being a big deal. It's my dad. He worries about my financial security." She ducks her head. "I shouldn't have told him about loaning out my books."

"Loaning out what books?" I ask.

She shrugs. "In the bookstore." She meets my eyes. "Sometimes people come in to browse. And they fall in love with the idea of a book. Or they read a little bit and want to read the whole thing, but they can't because they can't afford it. Or a child comes in with their parent and the parent has set a limit of two books, but the kid really wants four. So I let them borrow the books and bring them back."

I look at her for two beats. "That sounds like a library."

She nods. "I know. But…I love people who love books. The most important thing is people getting to consume stories. Things that will make them happy and teach them new things and take them to new places." She sighs a happy sigh and gives me a smile that hits me right in the gut. "I just can't say no."

I sigh, frustrated with her father, a man I know almost nothing about and have never met, and with this woman…But even before I finish that thought I realize that it's not Danielle I'm frustrated with at all. It's my reactions to her. Her using her damned bookstore like a library–and being financially unstable because of it–makes me want to haul her into my lap and…cuddle her. And, of course, buy the bookstore and let her do whatever she wants with it forever.

Fuck. I'm not supposed to want to cuddle with her. That's not what this is supposed to be.

"Do you like your bookshop?" I finally ask.

"So much," she says without even hesitating. "But I do feel like maybe I'm not a part of anything that's important."

"But–"

She cuts me off. "What about you? Tell me about your family."

"It's just my grandfather." I turn it back to her. "Books are important, Danielle. Don't let someone make you feel bad about spending your time on something you're passionate about."

She waves that away. "Just your grandfather? Can I ask what happened to your parents?"

"Car accident," I say shortly. I don't talk about this. And I don't want to make this woman sad. That story is definitely sad. "You are a part of something important, Danielle."

"Sure, kind of." She leans in, resting her chin on her hand. "Tell me about your grandfather. He owned the team before you, right?"

"Right. Tell me why you chose to open a bookshop if–"

"Does your grandfather still come to games?" she asks, interrupting me.

"No."

"Why not?"

I blow out a breath. "He's not able to."

"Oh, why–"

I lean over, wrap a hand around the back of her neck, pull her in, and kiss her.

That will shut her up.

But I'm not prepared for what kissing her would do to me.

Her mouth is sweet and soft. So is the sighing sound she makes. My entire body goes hard and hot. My hand tightens around her neck and I pull her even closer. I open my mouth and taste her fully, my tongue sliding over her lips, then her tongue.

She makes a soft, needy sound and I want more of that. I'm ready to haul her up onto the table and spread her out for my meal when I hear someone clearing his throat.

Our waiter.

I pull my mouth off of hers. Maybe to fire the guy. But then I realize this interruption is a good thing. The things I have planned for this girl should not be done in a restaurant.

"I have your appetizer," he says, moving to set the plate down.

"Thank you," I tell him without looking away from Danielle.

She's breathing hard.

I let her lean back, but I drop my hand to the seat of her chair and pull it closer to mine.

"I'd really like to know more about your family," she says softly.

I look at her with a lifted brow.

"I don't talk about my family." I pick up one of the tiny portions of fig and goat cheese bruschetta and lift it to her mouth.

She gives me a look that says she knows exactly what I'm doing but she opens and I slide the hors d'oeuvre onto her tongue. She closes her mouth and chews, watching me the whole time.

After she swallows, she asks, "Are you close with your grandfather?"

She's relentless.

"Danielle," I say warningly.

She lays a hand on my arm and I tense, but she simply squeezes. "I'd like to know you better."

"There's no need for that."

"You've been asking me questions. You know a lot about me. I just want to know you too."

"You don't need to know me," I say firmly.

"I know Crew."

I stare at her. I should not react to that. I do not need her to know that she can get to me so easily. But this definitely stokes the competitive streak in me that makes me want to win the prize. Her. She's the prize and I want to win her.

And I can tell she knows it. She knows this is the way to get to me.

"What do you know about Crew?" I ask.

"I know that he skipped college to go straight to the draft. I know his parents. I know his grandfather, actually." She picks up another piece of the bruschetta, pops it in her mouth, and chews watching me. Then she licks her finger and says, "I've even been in his bedroom."

I lean in. "When?" Jealousy rips through me, hot and sharp.

She leans in as well. "About a year ago."

"You slept with McNeill a year ago?"

She smiles and shakes her head. "I slept in his childhood bedroom about a year ago when I went home with Luna to visit. He wasn't there."

I take her chin between my thumb and finger, pulling her in until our noses almost touch. "You're playing with me, little girl."

"Yeah, I know."

I'm kind of an asshole sometimes. Okay, I'm often an asshole. Yet, this sweet, caring, beautiful girl wants to know me. She'll do whatever it takes to break down my walls. She's not intimidated by me. And it makes me want her even more.

I kiss her. Partly to shut her up and partly to remind her who's in charge. But again, I'm lost in the kiss. Her mouth is hot and so fucking sweet. I drink her in, I taste every inch of her mouth. And I want so much more. I hear a moan and realize the deep, needy sound comes from me.

"Dammit, Danielle," I say against her mouth.

"You know, at some point my mouth won't be busy or full and I'm going to keep asking you questions," she whispers.

"Oh, I'm going to work very hard to keep your mouth full and busy." My body heats just thinking about that.

"I just want to know as much about you as I know about them," she whispers.

Fuck. She's got me figured out. Making me compete with McNeill and Hughes is maybe the one thing that could make me talk.

No one pushes me. No one asks me questions. Unless it's things like, 'What can I do for you, Mr. Armstrong?' or 'Can I get you another drink, Mr. Armstrong?'

I tell people what to do.

I definitely want to tell Danielle what to do.

But this girl is pushing other buttons of mine.

Still, I can't snap at her, or be mean to her, or completely shut her down.

She's too sweet for that.

And…fuck. I want her to know me, too.

I take her chin again and look her directly in the eye. "My parents were killed in a car accident when I was twelve. I was in the accident too. I was badly injured but survived. I miss them every day. I went to live with my grandparents after that. My grandmother died about ten years ago. I've run the team with my grandfather since I graduated with my MBA. I took the team over entirely eight years ago. My grandfather is now in a care facility. He has Alzheimer's and many days doesn't even know who the

Racketeers are. But for the days that he does, I'm determined to do my best with this team and give him a championship before he doesn't remember them, or me, at all."

I say it all in one big monologue, in a low, determined voice. I watch her expression go from pleased that I'm sharing, to surprise, to pity because of what I've told her.

I let her go. I pause only a beat before I ask, "What did you want to be when you grew up?"

"A writer," she answers without blinking.

"Why aren't you a writer?"

"I am a writer. I'm just not making a living from it yet."

I nod. I like that answer better than her not writing at all.

"What did you want to be when you grew up?" she asks.

I shake my head.

She sighs. "Just so you know, if we keep going with whatever this is, I'm going to eventually break down your walls."

"Who says we're going to keep going with whatever this is?" I ask.

She flinches slightly. If I wasn't staring at her I wouldn't have even seen it. But that little flinch makes my heart twinge. Dammit.

But it's true. I'm not making any promises about anything after tonight. Or about any walls coming down.

Finally she nods. "You're right. No one said that."

I bring another piece of bruschetta to her mouth. "Eat."

"I'm already getting full. This is going to be a problem."

"But it's good, isn't it?"

She complies but then says, "It's amazing. This restaurant is very impressive but I don't even know what half the things on this menu are. You know I would have been fine with Chinese takeout from your favorite neighborhood place."

That isn't surprising to me and I don't think she's just saying that. Money doesn't seem to be a priority to Danielle. It also means she's willing to go home with me.

"That would have been a fantastic idea," I say. "Let's do that."

This restaurant is designed for conversation and a slow,

leisurely meal of several courses of top-rated cuisine. That's not what I want right now.

"It's going to be a while before we eat dinner." I lift my hand and gesture to the waiter.

He immediately comes to the table. "Yes, sir?"

"When our dinners are finished, wrap them up, and deliver them to my building. Leave them with the doorman. Don't forget dessert."

"Yes, sir." He turns on his heel and leaves.

I push back from the table, stand, and hold out my hand to Danielle.

"What's happening?" she asks as I tug her to her feet.

"You know exactly what's happening."

She lets me lead her back through the restaurant, into the elevator, and out to the car without saying another damned word or asking another question.

But that's all the consent I need.

CHAPTER 10

Dani

NATHAN'S BUILDING is a high rise on the coast with valet parking, four doormen and a swanky lobby. My head is already swirling from the glass of wine I drank and the way Nathan dragged me out of the restaurant before we even ate dinner. The way he kissed me… the way he kept turning the conversation back to me. He's relentless when he wants something and it's clear that what he wants now is me.

God, this is what I want. A bossy, dominant man who is confident and knows exactly what he's doing to me, but who is also tuned in to me, who wants to take care of me at the same time he wants to do unspeakably dirty things to me.

He hasn't said that. It would seem out of character I suppose for him to say something like *I want to take care of you*, but everything Nathan does seems focused on making me happy. Whether it's his hand on my back as we walk, holding doors for me, telling me I look beautiful, feeding me, or making me so hot and needy I can barely walk on my shaking legs.

As we exit the car, I'm very aware that I'm not wearing panties. They're still tucked in Nathan's pocket and every step creates a friction that only adds to the painful ache deep in my core. I can't wait to get up to his apartment so he can make it go away in the most intense and delicious way possible.

I know he will. Nathan won't stop until I've come multiple times. That determination has been firmly etched on his face all evening in every confident and bold statement he's made.

"Good evening, Mr. Armstrong," one of the doormen says as he holds the shiny glass door open for us. "Miss." He nods his head toward me.

The doorman looks to be in his sixties and has bushy brows and a warm smile.

"Good evening, Christopher," Nathan says. "This is Danielle. Danielle, my overly formal head doorman." He turns back to Christopher. "One of these days I'm going to convince you to drop the whole Mr. Armstrong bit and just call me Nathan."

"Today is not that day, Mr. Armstrong," Christopher says with a grin. "How was your dinner?"

"Excellent. How's your wife? Is her hip still bothering her?"

They chat a bit about Dorothea's post-surgery recovery. I'm impressed that Nathan has stopped to speak with the doorman and that he seems genuinely interested in Dorothea's recovery from surgery.

There is more to Nathan than he lets on, as is evidenced by the way he tried to deflect my attention from his personal life over and over during dinner. His teen years must have been difficult, grieving the loss of his parents. I'm sure he learned the coping mechanism then that he uses now—to change the subject. He's afraid of being vulnerable, that's obvious, and I feel privileged to be someone he's confided in, in any way. Even if I had to drag it out of him. Even if his delivery was clipped and lacking in emotion.

I don't take it lightly. It makes me feel that he trusts me.

"Mr. Armstrong is a good man," Christopher tells me. "He paid for my wife's physical therapy when our insurance maxed out."

For some reason, that doesn't actually surprise me. "Really? That's very thoughtful of him."

Nathan looks a little embarrassed to have his generosity revealed though.

He's scowling at Christopher.

I wonder if he realizes what a grump he looks like half the time.

It doesn't make him any less attractive to me. If anything, now that I've learned a tiny bit more about him, his growlyness is even sexier.

I'm sure the money doesn't matter to Nathan, not really. He has billions of dollars. But he's taking a human interest in his doorman, and I find that incredibly appealing.

God, he's just so hot.

I really, really want to get naked with him as soon as possible.

"But I'm sure you already know he's a great guy or you wouldn't be here. Mr. Armstrong never brings women up to his penthouse. You must be something special."

Now that's an interesting tidbit of information.

"Is that so?" I ask, more delighted than I should be. I don't imagine for one minute Nathan is celibate, so why isn't he bringing women home? He must go to their apartments or book a hotel. I look straight at Nathan, fighting the urge to grin. "I do feel special."

The scowl has turned up a notch. It's a full-fledged glare.

As if he can intimidate the doorman into zipping his mouth shut and me into continuing to believe he's just a rich guy with an empty hole in his chest where his heart should be.

I'm not even exaggerating. I'm pleased that he's allowing me into his home. Which means I need to pump the brakes on my runaway emotions. None of this means he wants more than one night.

Who says we're going to keep going with whatever this is?

The words had been rude and had made me question if

tonight was wise. But then I realized at least he's honest. I can appreciate that. I know exactly what I'm getting.

Sex with Nathan. Tonight. Nothing more, nothing less.

I've never had a one-night stand, but damn Nathan Armstrong is an excellent choice to start with. I can't wait to see what dirty and delicious things an intense and experienced older man can do to me.

It would be so easy to get swept up into Nathan. His demanding words, his confident touch, his grand gestures. But this is not about catching feelings for Nathan, and I might need to remind myself of that once or twelve times over the next few hours.

"If I ever want to run for a political office, I'll hire you to run my campaign," Nathan tells Christopher dryly. "You lay on the bullshit pretty thick."

Now I don't know what to believe about the other women not going up to his apartment, but it doesn't matter anyway. Every woman in Chicago could have been in Nathan's bed before tonight and I'm still going to take my spot as next in line.

Surely Nathan knew he could easily seduce me. But he's chosen to pamper and spoil me tonight. Well, even before tonight. The ice cream from Franklin was over the top. But I'll just accept all of it, enjoy it, and not overanalyze it.

Christopher laughs. "Have a great night, sir."

"Oh, I absolutely intend to," Nathan says. His voice is low and edged with a hard lust that makes my cheeks, and the rest of my body, burn.

The elevator doors aren't even closed before Nathan stalks toward me.

A shiver of anticipation rolls through me as he backs me up against the wall, boxing me in with his muscular body. It always feels like the air is charged between us when he's this close to me. Or across the dinner table. Or in a car together. As if a summer storm is about to be unleashed. I watch him silently, pressing my thighs together against the yearning I feel in my bare pussy as he moves teasingly toward me, leaning in so slowly it's maddening.

Then his mouth covers mine and there is nothing slow about it. It's commanding, powerful, dominating. He kisses me with rough, urgent presses on my lips as his hands slip around to grip my ass through my dress, squeezing with enough pressure to make me gasp.

He yanks my hip up so that my dress slides toward my waist and my leg is resting on his thigh. I would be worried about security cameras and what they can see except he's pressed over me, a shield that covers my bare sex. He grinds me against his hard cock and I gasp, a surge of hot wet arousal soaking into the front of his pants.

Nathan growls, reaching a hand down to slip it in between us. He teases over my dampness and strokes my clit. A moan escapes me.

"I can't wait to fuck you, Danielle. If this elevator doesn't go any faster, I'll be forced to take you right here," he says.

I wouldn't even object. But the doors choose that moment to slide open and Nathan tugs me forward. The elevator goes directly into his apartment and as Nathan strips off his suit jacket, I peel away from him, needing to catch my breath. I head straight to the floor-to-ceiling windows.

"Wow, Nathan, this is just incredible." I take in the sweeping views of the coastline and the inky darkness of Lake Michigan beyond it. During the day, it must be breathtaking. I glance over my shoulder at the spacious and luxurious apartment with a sleek and modern gourmet kitchen. "This is an amazing apartment."

"You like it? It's yours," Nathan says, moving in beside me and shifting my hair back to kiss the back of my neck. "You can have it."

"What?" I laugh softly, bemused. He's very over-the-top sometimes and obviously not serious. "You're giving me your apartment?"

"I'll give you anything you want if you let me get you out of this dress."

I shiver when his lips shift to my earlobe and his fingers tease at the zipper of my dress. "Where will you live if this is my apartment now?" I ask.

"I have two other apartments. And a house in Florida. But I'm keeping the key to this place so I can have you whenever I want."

"You have me tonight," I whisper. He does. My body feels like warm liquid as he flicks his tongue over my ear.

"I'm going to have you every way I possibly can. Are you ready for that?" he murmurs, his hot breath tickling my neck.

"Keep your apartment. I can't afford the taxes," I tell him, leaning back, rubbing my ass against his hard body. I can feel his cock nudging me. He growls in the back of his throat, his grip hardening on my shoulders. "But get me out of this dress now. Please."

Instantly Nathan has the zipper down and the dress over my shoulders and on the floor at my ankles. I barely have time to blink before he turns me around so I'm facing him.

"Danielle," he says, gray eyes sweeping over me from head to toe, taking in my black bra and nothing else.

The way he says my full name makes me feel older, more sophisticated than I generally do. When his gaze lingers on the juncture of my thighs, completely bare, I swallow hard, desire settling like a thick wet blanket over me. I fight the urge to squirm as he rubs his jaw and shakes his head slightly.

"Jesus. You're so fucking gorgeous. Take your bra off for me and show me your pretty tits."

The words are demanding, rough. I would never have thought that would be my style of seduction but with Nathan it excites me. I find myself arching my back, putting a hand on my hip to give him a better view.

I'm not uncomfortable being naked, but I'm not sure I've ever felt the power of my body as much as I do right now standing before him in nothing but my sky high heels. His appreciation is palpable. His eyes are dark with desire and he's gripping his hands in tight fists, like he's resisting the urge to touch me.

I reach behind me and unclasp my bra, easing it down over my shoulders. Nathan starts undoing the buttons of his shirt cuffs as he watches me. I remove the bra entirely and spin it on one finger. "What should I do with this?" I ask, a little nervous, more than I'd be with Michael or Crew I think, but mostly turned on to be fully exposed to his gaze.

I desperately want him to tell me what to do. To take the lead. To be demanding. How do I make sure he knows that?

It's not an issue with Nathan. Demanding and in-charge are as natural for him as breathing. "Look at me while you slowly let your bra drop to the floor. Then leave those fucking shoes on and walk over to the wet bar. Sit on a stool there and wait for me with your legs crossed. I want to be the one who spreads you wide open for my tongue."

Hell, yes. I shiver and do as he says without hesitation, dropping the bra and walking toward the bar that lines one wall of the living area. I feel his eyes on me, an intense gaze that makes my skin heat. I take a deep breath as I walk in my heels, putting a sway in my hips to showcase my ass for his pleasure.

"What else do you want?" I ask, over my shoulder. I want to hear it all. I want him to say everything out loud and graphically.

"Danielle," he murmurs, giving a rough and low laugh. "I just want you. Every single sexy inch of you."

Turning to take a seat on the stool, I take in a view even better than the one through the windows. It's Nathan shirtless, his bare chest just as enticing as I remember it from the night before in the storage closet. I cross my legs tightly the way he demanded, wanting to run my hands over those rock solid abs and slip my hand down past his waistband. I can see his erection pressed against the fabric of his pants, straining, and my mouth waters.

Once he's directly in front of me, he kisses me, gently this time, his fingers trailing down over my shoulders, before taking a teasing path over the curves of my breasts, making the smallest hint of contact with my nipples. It makes me ache for more.

"How experienced are you sexually?" he asks, nuzzling into my neck. "Tell me everything. It will help me know how much you can take. Because I want it all, but I want this to be incredible for you."

Oh, God. That's such a terrible subject. I wish I could just start from scratch with Nathan.

"Um, I've had sex," I tell him, head lolling back, wanting to give him better access to my skin. "But it's been a while." I arch my back as well, to entice him to do more with my nipples than the barely there back and forth rhythmic tease he is doing now. The ache deep inside my pussy is throbbing painfully and I squeeze my thighs even tighter, wanting, needing him to touch me, but sensing not to ask.

Nathan knows how to make this amazing for me and I need to let him.

"How long?"

"Three years."

He sucks in a quick breath and his head lifts. I look up. He looks even more turned on.

"Have you been with a few men or many men?"

His mouth returns to the front of my throat and he starts kissing down to the swell of my breasts and I blank on how to answer. He flicks his tongue casually over my nipple, like he's done this a million times before. Like he owns my nipple. Like he owns me.

"What?" I ask. I can't remember the question. It doesn't seem as important as what he's doing to me.

"How many men have fucked you?" he asks. He sucks on one nipple, while rolling the other between his thumb and finger. Then he rubs his beard over my breast as he tugs on the opposite nipple.

I feel like fireworks are exploding from my nipples and

sending hot sparks through my body and setting my pussy on fire.

"Danielle," he prompts firmly, tugging on my nipple again.

Oh, right. Yes, I've had sex with other men. Two. Whose names seemed to have been wiped clear from my memory banks.

They weren't him.

They no longer exist.

The pressure of his fingers squeezing my nipple increases to something almost painful and yet I feel nothing but deep aching pleasure.

"A few. Two. Is two a few or does it have to be three to be considered a few? I guess two is just a couple and three is a few," I say, chattering on breathlessly, not sure where to place my arms. "But I did only two. Or they did me. Mutual doing?" My hands are fluttering, hovering over him but not touching.

"Did they make you come?"

I shake my head. Of course, I faked it with Brandon because he just got pissed when I tried to talk to him about what he could do differently to make it happen.

His eyes darken and I can tell he loves that answer.

"Do you make yourself come?"

I press my lips together but nod.

"With your fingers, or with toys, or both?"

He's still playing with my nipples and then stroking his hands down my sides, squeezing my hips, then sliding his hands back up to caress and tease my breasts.

"Both," I answer, my voice shaky.

"Can you take a thick dildo, Danielle?"

I swallow hard. "Um. Mine's... average sized?" I don't really know. "It's not the biggest in the online catalog if that's what you're asking."

His smile is slow and wicked. "Then we'll have to be sure you're very prepared."

Oh wow. If that means what I think it means...

With his hands firmly on my hips, Nathan lifts me onto the bar while kicking the stool out of the way with one smooth move. He shifts to my knees and spreads my legs without preamble. I gasp at the sudden exposure.

"So pretty," he murmurs. "All this pink softness, so open and wet just for me." He strokes over my folds with his thumbs, dragging a low moan from me. "Getting you ready is going to be such a pleasure."

Nathan bends over and studies me even closer, blowing a warm breath onto my sensitive clit. The bartop is cold beneath my bare ass and my senses feel heightened, my skin flushed. I lean back, palms flat, watching him study me intimately as he massages in teasing circles, approaching my clit but always skirting away at the last second. He puts his mouth on my inner thigh. I feel his tongue and light suction.

I want his mouth on my clit, his fingers buried inside me, but he doesn't. I'm near begging. He just kisses and licks my inner thigh, strokes and glides his fingertips along my folds endlessly, minute after minute, occasionally pressing a kiss just north of where I want him to.

The ache is unbearable. I shift restlessly, urging my hips forward, trying to force contact. "Nathan. Please."

"What, love? What do you need?" He sounds casual, like we're merely holding hands strolling down the street. Not like he's torturing me endlessly.

"Touch me," I breathe.

"I am touching you."

"More." I lift my hands to grip his head, to force him to grind his mouth down on me, but he catches both of my wrists and pins them to the counter.

"You want more?" he demands, glancing up at me.

I nod, rapidly.

"Do you want my finger or my tongue inside you? Or should I play with your clit?"

"I… I don't know." I don't. Neither of the guys I had sex with in the past did anything like this. I'm not sure they even knew I had a clit. I just know I want something. Or maybe I want everything. I'm flustered and desperate. I've never been this close to an orgasm with so little actual contact.

"Damn. No one's ever worshiped this sweet pussy correctly, have they?" he asks, sliding one finger over my clit again.

I bite my lower lip and shake my head.

"That is unacceptable," he says, circling the sensitive spot.

It sure freaking is. I let my eyes slide shut, my whole body zinging with sensation.

"Eyes on me, Danielle," Nathan says firmly.

My eyes flutter open and I look down.

He holds my gaze as he leans in and glides his tongue over my clit, before sucking the tight aching bud gently into his mouth.

I almost leap off of the countertop at the sensation.

His finger fills me, and stretches me, exploring, until he finds the spot that makes me cry out. His tongue flicks over my clit as his finger gives hard thrusts in and out.

Without thinking, my hand flies to his hair, holding on as he licks, sucks, and finger fucks me.

Then he adds a second finger, stretching me further.

"So tight," he praises. "So perfect. You taste so good. I could stay here for hours." He licks and sucks again. "When you come, I want to hear my name, Danielle. You cry out for the man who is treating this pretty cunt right for the first time."

God. *Yes.* The graphic dirty talk, his fingers, his mouth... they're all perfect. Exactly what I want. It's only another minute, at most, before an orgasm hits, my hips bucking as it rips through me without warning.

"Nathan, oh God!" My fingers grip his hair as I press even closer to his mouth as I ride the waves of pleasure. "Nathan!"

"That's right," he says, his fingers continuing to move. "That's my girl."

The intense sensations slowly start to fade and he slides his fingers out, lifting them to his mouth and sucking them clean as his gaze tracks over me. His gaze lingers on my breasts and between my legs. He looks pleased.

I'm sure I look wanton. My thighs are spread, and I can feel how wet I am. I'm flushed from head to toe, my pale skin hiding nothing, I'm certain. But his look of possessiveness keeps me from feeling even the tiniest bit of shame.

"They'll know I was here first," he says, his voice rough.

"What?" I ask, my voice soft since I haven't fully caught my breath.

He runs a fingertip over a spot on my inner thigh and I look down. There's a red spot there that I know will turn into a light bruise.

"You gave me a hickey?"

He looks proud as he nods and also runs that fingertip over my breasts. I look down and see the whisker burns on both.

"I marked you. Whoever is here next will know they're not the first."

My eyes widen. Wow. "Eventually it will fade."

He gives me a hot, possessive look. "Don't tempt me to tattoo you."

This guy is so over-the-top. And he gets so caught up in moments. He won't care about any of this tomorrow. But right now… it's kind of hot. At least according to the way my pussy clenches and the tingles dance over my entire body.

"What's next?" I ask.

His gaze locks on mine. His hands go to his belt. My heart rate picks up.

"Everything, Danielle," he says with promise.

CHAPTER 11

Nathan

FUCK SHE LOOKS good sitting on my bar, legs spread, wet and pink and hot from the orgasm I just gave her.

Of course I marked her. Of course.

The possessiveness I feel for this woman is insane, but it's real, and in the past ten minutes, I've accepted it. Embraced it, even.

She hasn't been fucked well in the past. But she might be by someone else in the future.

So I'll be the first. The first man to make her feel all the things she needs to feel, deserves to feel.

She will remember me.

I undo my belt, unbutton and unzip my pants, watching her watch me.

She wants me. She's so fucking needy right now. And I will fulfill every need she has and a few she's not aware of.

"Did the assholes you were with in the past have you suck their cocks?" I ask.

She looks away from my very obvious erection inside my dress pants. "Um ... I didn't say they were assholes."

"I did. They didn't make you come. That is not how you fuck a woman," I tell her. I grasp her around the waist and lift her off the bar, setting her on her feet in front of me. "Did you suck their cocks?"

She nods.

Of course. Guys like that always get what they want even when they're not giving their partners what they need.

"Let's erase those memories," I tell her. My voice drops lower. "On your knees."

She immediately kneels in front of me. Lust surges through me, but so does a strange sense of pride. This woman is sweet. Sunshine. Even a little innocent. But she'll do this for me.

I grip her chin and tip her head back. "You're willing to be a pretty, dirty little slut for me, Danielle?"

She sucks in a quick, surprised breath. But then she steals my breath by nodding.

I don't let on how that affects me. I tighten my grip on her face just slightly. "Say it," I command softly, but firmly. "Tell me you're my little slut. That you'll do anything to please me."

She opens her mouth, but before she can say anything, I slip my thumb inside.

She immediately sucks on it and my cock pulses painfully.

"Once you say yes, Danielle, once you give me this—this dirty, gorgeous side of you—you're mine. Know that."

Hughes and McNeill won't do this. They won't be like this with her. This is all mine.

And she loves it.

She sucks on my thumb again, and nods.

I slip my thumb out of her mouth, and she says, softly but clearly, "I'm your little slut, Nathan. I'll do anything to please you."

Jesus. My breath hisses out and I pull my cock out, fisting it tightly, pumping up and down to relieve some of the pressure. Then I hold it for her and watch her open her mouth.

The first touch of her tongue on the tip nearly sends me to my knees. She licks, her tongue swirling around the head, then sucks softly. At my groan, she sucks a little harder.

I let her play at the top for a couple of minutes, but then I press my thumb against her chin. "Open, Danielle. Take me."

She does. Promptly. Obediently.

Fuck. I might never get enough of her.

The thought hits me hard and suddenly.

She gives a little moan as I ease into her hot, wet mouth. She likes this. That is so, so good.

I cup the back of her head, holding my dick with my other hand, working to control the intense urge to thrust. She's not ready for me to actually fuck her mouth. And this is just foreplay for now anyway. But my body isn't listening.

I glide in and out, coaching her. "Tighten your lips around me, Danielle."

She does. She braces her hands on my thighs as I go deeper.

"Relax," I tell her, gathering her hair in one hand. "Breathe through your nose."

She adjusts amazingly quickly.

"That's right. That's so fucking good. Take me as deep as you can."

She leans in and I gently slide deeper.

Then I pull out. This is not how I'm going to finish and all I needed to know was that she would do this, that she'd follow my commands.

I look down at her, brushing her hair back from her face. "Need your pussy now, Danielle."

She looks at my cock, right in front of her face. "Can I touch you?"

It might kill me, but I nod.

She wraps a hand around me and slides it up and down the length, still slick from her mouth.

"Fucking hell," I mutter, locking my knees.

She doesn't even look up at me. She adds her other hand. She pumps up and down a few times, as if measuring my girth and length. Then as I'm about to pull her off, she leans in and licks the head again.

"Danielle," I grit out.

"I like doing this to you," she says, almost in wonder. "I didn't like it before, but I love your cock. I love to make you feel good. I love how you feel and sound and taste."

That's it. I lean over, scoop her up under her arms and lift.

She instinctively wraps her arms and legs around me, settling her hot pussy against my cock.

My pants are still around my damned ankles, so I shuffle us over to the couch and prop her on the back of it.

"There are so many ways I intend to fuck you tonight," I tell her. "This is just the first."

She nods her understanding. I let go of her only long enough to get rid of my shoes and clothes.

She runs her hands over my shoulders, chest, and abs while I do it. When I straighten, she leans in and kisses my chest. Then licks. "I understand the desire to mark me," she says against my skin. "I want to mark you too. Make sure anyone else who ever sees even your naked chest knows I was here like this with you."

Lust surges through me again. Fuck I want to be marked by her.

I have never felt something like that before.

I've had more sophisticated, successful, more mature women. I could have nearly any woman I could want.

But this girl has wrapped me around her finger in just over twenty-four hours.

I'm in so much trouble.

If I was even half as intelligent, not to mention hard and cynical, as I'd like to think I am, I'd get her dressed and in a car home in the next thirty seconds.

But of course I don't.

Instead, I carry her over to the floor-to-ceiling window that overlooks the lights of Chicago and the lake. I turn her to face the window.

"I hope you get wet every time you see the Chicago skyline," I tell her.

A little shiver goes through her.

"Hands up on the glass. Don't move them."

She obeys.

I move to turn off the lights behind us. Now the view is clear, and there's a reflection of us in the glass.

I run my hands down the front of her body, stopping to cup her sweet tits, play with her nipples, and stroke over her belly, before I slide one between her legs. I circle her clit. "Eyes stay open. I want you to see us moving together. I want you to always have that image. And I want you to see how goddamned beautiful you are when you come apart."

She gasps, then moans as I ease a finger into her. Then a second. Her breathing is faster now and her fingers curl against the window. Then I start to add a third. She tenses.

"You can take it," I tell her gruffly against her ear, pressing my cock against her ass. "You need to take it. I'm going to fill you so full. You're going to grip me like a fucking vise. It's going to be so damned good."

She blows out a breath and I feel her muscles relax a little. She moves her feet apart.

"That's right. Take my fingers so I can get you ready to be fucked the way you need to be fucked."

Her pussy tightens around my fingers, but it's not with nerves now. I tug on her nipple with my other hand and I feel her get wetter.

I pump my two fingers deep, thrusting in and out slowly, my thumb playing with her clit.

Then I have an even better idea.

"You play with your clit," I tell her. "And tell me what you think about when you use your toys."

She takes a shuddering breath. "Recently?" she asks.

That might have been a mistake. What if she tells me something about McNeill? Or Hughes? But I need her to relax.

"When did you last get yourself off, Danielle?" I pinch her nipple and move my fingers in and out.

"Last night."

Oh, that's a great answer. I love that she takes care of herself. And doesn't have a guy around to do it for her. "With a dildo in your cunt, or a vibrator against your clit?"

"Both," she says, breathlessly. "I have one that's both."

"Excellent." Even if it is average sized. "Finger on your clit," I command.

Her head drops forward, but her hand moves, bumping against mine where my fingers are buried in her pussy, her middle finger finding her clit. She starts circling.

"Tell me what you thought about."

"Um..." She takes a deep breath and lifts her head, looking at the window, meeting my gaze in the reflection. "I was with three guys. One was fucking my mouth, one was playing with my nipples and clit, and one was fucking my pussy."

Everything out of that sweet, dirty little mouth makes me hard.

I would have never thought a fantasy of a woman with three men would do that to me, but fuck, I don't think I've ever been this hard.

And it's because of how much it turns her on. Her pussy is practically gushing, and I can easily slide my third finger into her now.

"That is a dirty slut answer," I growl against her ear, fucking her slow and steady with three fingers.

She nods. "I know." She seems proud of herself.

I am too.

"Come on my fingers, Danielle, so I can get inside this tight pussy that I need so fucking much."

She gasps, her finger moves a little faster over her clit, but she's coming within seconds.

The hot grip on my fingers makes me almost lose it.

I quickly slide my fingers out, lift her foot to rest it on the seat of the chair that's next to us, opening her wide.

"I can't get you pregnant. And I test routinely."

"Um, you...*can't*..."

"Are you okay doing this without a condom?" I ask, harsher than I intended. I *need* to be inside her.

She meets my gaze in the mirror. "Yes." She doesn't even hesitate.

Then I bend my knees, fit my cock against her hot entrance, and push inside the sweet, slick pussy I'm going to dream about until I die.

She moans as I slowly slide home.

When I'm balls deep, I grip her hips, and put my mouth against her ear. "You are fucking perfect."

I pull out and thrust back in deep.

She whimpers. "Oh God, you feel so good."

"So." I thrust again. "Fucking" I thrust again. "Perfect." I thrust again.

She presses back into me and I know she's feeling fine. I reach up to play with a nipple as I fuck her, those gorgeous tits bouncing in the reflection.

Her eyes are on us. That's perfect too. I want her to remember this.

"You're going to come again, Danielle," I tell her. "Hard. Crying my name."

She nods. "Yes. God, yes, Nathan."

I pick up the pace, fucking her faster and deeper. And she takes it all, pushing back into me, her arms braced on the window, her expression wild and wanton.

"You're going to feel me everywhere tomorrow," I promise darkly, tweaking her nipple and then leaning in to kiss, then bite down where her neck curved into her shoulder.

"Nathan." Her fingers curl against the glass and I feel her pussy tighten around me.

"Yes, Danielle, come for me, my sweet little slut."

I fucking love that talking to her like that is what pushes her over the edge. Her pussy clamps down around me tightly and she cries out.

"Oh, yes. Oh, fuck, Nathan! Nathan!"

My name on her lips–*loudly* on her lips– makes me grip her hips and pound into her. Her skin is so pale and delicate that I might even leave little bruises there. And that thought makes my balls tighten and an orgasm roll up from what feels like the depth of my fucking soul through my body and into hers.

"Danielle!" I roar. "Fuck! Yes!"

I wrap my arms around her, clutching her to my chest as she sags, her hands sliding from the window. I just hold her, not wanting to slip out of her body yet.

We both breathe deeply and I stare at our reflection in the glass in front of us.

I want this. Her. Over and over.

That is the only thought that makes it through the daze of pleasure and possessiveness.

I have two choices as of this moment.

Keep her forever. Or never see her again after tonight.

There will be nothing in between.

CHAPTER 12

Dani

NATHAN WOKE me up twice in the night. After insisting I spend the night.

Not that it was ever posed as a question or invitation. It was "you're staying" and him giving me a shirt to sleep in, telling me there was no need for panties anyway, and taking me to bed.

And I *loved* it. Being bossed around was even better than I expected. It made me so hot, every single time.

He fucked me there with me on my back, him kneeling between my thighs, all the lights on, his sharp, dark eyes taking in every single detail.

I feel like I can hide nothing from this man.

It's scary and wonderful at the same time. He's intimidating, but he also makes me feel protected and cherished. Even when he's talking dirtier to me than anyone ever has. It's perfect.

After the first time in his bed, we showered, where he washed me from head to toe, and then he made me orgasm with his mouth again. Then he carried me to bed, put me on my hands and knees, and fucked me again.

Then in the night he pulled me on top of him and made me ride him. Not that it was anything I was going to protest. And then, just before dawn, he fucked me in the very vanilla missionary position.

Though the words he said and intensity in how he did it was anything but vanilla.

The man knows what he's doing.

Now we're in his town car, on our way to my apartment.

And he's holding my hand.

I'm definitely sore from everything last night, I get wet just thinking about it, and he called me his dirty slut several times. But he's now holding my hand. After making me a bagel with sweet cream cheese and fresh strawberries and a cappuccino from his very own extremely fancy, incredibly expensive espresso machine.

I know he doesn't intend for anything to happen between us beyond last night, but I'm so glad I had that night with him. He's made so many of my fantasies come to life. I know I'm not crazy for wanting those things. And now I know that there *are* men out there who can make them real for me.

He's treated me like I am not just a sexually naive, twenty-four year old bookshop owner who doesn't know anything about the game that's so important in his life and business.

He's made me feel sexy, interesting, and worthy of pampering and adoration.

The car pulls up in front of my building and I say, "Thank you so much for last night, Nathan."

It seems so inadequate but I don't know how to express what I'm feeling.

He lifts my hand to his mouth, but instead of kissing the back of it, he turns and presses his lips to my palm, sending zings of heat through my body. "It was very much my pleasure."

I take a deep breath and smile.

He leans in. "Are you sore?"

He's so sweet to be concerned. I nod. "Yes."

He gives me a wicked smile. "Good."

Or maybe not so sweet. "You're so dirty," I scold. But my voice is too breathless to sound anything but turned on.

His voice drops. "So are you, dirty girl. Thank you for that."

If I had panties on, they'd be wet again right now. But I don't. He kept them. So I just squeeze my thighs together.

He notices. And smirks. Then he gets out of the car and holds out a hand to help me out.

He's wearing blue jeans and a fitted black T-shirt today rather than a suit, and when he'd walked out of the bedroom, I swear I almost drooled.

The man is annoyingly handsome in everything.

And out of everything.

We walk toward the front door of the book shop. I plan to go into the shop and check on any phone messages and mail before I head upstairs. I will not say anything about seeing him, talking to him again, or…anything.

It hits me that I'm sad.

I knew this was a one night thing. No way would a man like Nathan Armstrong want to keep seeing me. We have nothing in common. I have nothing he could want long term. Sure maybe he'd want to sleep together again, but that could be really bad for my heart.

Though very good for your writing.

Well, there is that.

My next installment of my story is going to be so good. My readers are going to eat it up.

No pun intended.

Okay, maybe there's a slight pun intended.

I'm wrapped up in my thoughts about how I'm going to use last night as inspiration and don't notice that there's someone standing in the little alcove of the bookshop until he pushes away from the wall and says, "Well, good morning you two."

I focus on Crew.

Who is eyeing us with curiosity rather than any obvious anger or jealousy.

I can't say the same for Nathan when I look up at him.

His jaw is tight and he's glaring at Crew as if he'd like to punch him. Or fire him.

Crap. Nathan is kind of Crew's boss.

But I told him last night that I'd kissed Crew. And that I thought we were going to be dating. This shouldn't shock him.

"Hi, Crew," I say with a smile. "What are you doing here?"

He looks so good in blue jeans, tennis shoes, and a dark green Henley that molds to his chest, shoulders, and biceps, the color bringing out the green of his eyes.

I feel Nathan's hand on my lower back. His presence beside me suddenly feels bigger and hotter. Is that possible?

"I'm here to see you, of course." Crew gives me one of his I'm-charming-as-fuck-aren't-I? grins as we stop in front of him.

And he is. It's not really a matter of opinion. He's charming. And good-looking, and talented, and funny, and cocky as hell.

"That's sweet," I say.

"Why?" Nathan asks over the top of my words, slipping his arm around my waist and resting his hand on my hip.

Crew doesn't even look at Nathan when he says, "Because I can't let the rich, older dude she's fucking have all the fun, can I?"

My eyes go wide and I actually gasp. I'm not sure if it's because Crew just called Nathan old, or because he blatantly assumed Nathan and I slept together, or because he's right and I'm not used to talking about stuff like that out loud on the sidewalk outside my bookshop. Or anywhere else. Is it that obvious Nathan is bringing me home after banging my brains out? And if so, is there something I should do next time to make it less obvious? Is there going to be a next time? How do I feel about there being a next time? Or there not being a next time?

Clearly I'm very distractible this morning.

"Don't forget that this older dude signs your paychecks, McNeill," Nathan says.

Crew chuckles. "You're grumpy this morning. Did you pull something last night? You gotta stretch before physical exertion, man. I can show you how to make sure your hips and groin are nice and loose."

"That is absolutely never going to happen," Nathan informs him.

"I'm just thinking about Dani," Crew says. "Want her to have the best experience possible." He gives me a wink.

Why is Crew poking at Nathan? That is not a good idea. Nathan is not just his boss. He's not exactly laid back, even when he's in a good mood.

"I'm not the one who's sore from last night," Nathan says.

I look up at him quickly. He's watching me now. With a possessive, and heated look in his eyes.

"Okay, then," Crew says. "Good to know." He reaches out and takes my hand. "I'll be gentle with her then."

Nathan does make a soft growling noise at that, but he doesn't stop me when Crew tugs me forward, out of Nathan's embrace. In fact, he sighs.

It's as if he realizes he doesn't have a good reason to stop Crew.

He might be feeling a little territorial and Crew is definitely poking at him and he couldn't resist rising to the bait, but when it comes right down to it, Nathan doesn't want to keep me. He doesn't want a repeat of last night.

"Bye, Nathan," I say, giving him a smile. I'm not sure what the protocol is here. How do you thank a guy for the things Nathan did to me? I mean, I am grateful, but I think he knows. The panting, moaning, and screaming last night was a sure giveaway.

His smile is slow, sexy, and just for me. "Goodbye, Danielle." He leans in and kisses my cheek. Then whispers, "You were magnificent."

And just like that my core heats.

I like that *so* much. I want more of it. Lots more.

He leans back and the look he gives me tells me that he knows *all* of that.

Then he gives Crew a look. "She'll need to go upstairs to

change before you take her to the circus or the mall or whatever you have planned."

Oh, a dig at how young Crew is. So the competition isn't over yet.

"Is that right?" Crew looks me up and down. "She looks absolutely delicious to me."

Even as I roll my eyes at his obvious attempt to rile Nathan, I feel my heartbeat flutter at the way Crew looks at me too.

I don't know what good luck charm I accidentally rubbed a couple days ago or what good deed I did that the universe has decided to reward me for, but having all of these men giving me attention is very, very nice.

Nathan and Crew couldn't be more different but they both make me feel sexy and adored and *thank you, Universe, I'll have some more.*

"Well, she'll need some underwear on for roller skating or swinging in the park or whatever you kids are going to do."

Crew just chuckles. I wonder if anything can get under his skin.

"I do love roller skating, though, as you know, I'm better on the ice." He looks me up and down again. "But where are your panties, Dani? Do you make a habit of going without, pretty girl? Because I approve."

My cheeks are bright red I'm sure, and I shoot Nathan a frown. "No, I, um–"

"They're at my penthouse," Nathan says smoothly.

"I see. Well, I guess we do have some things beyond a love for hockey in common, boss," Crew says. "Our taste in women, for one."

Oh my God, enough of this. I turn to the bookshop door, shove the key into the lock with more force than necessary, and push the door open.

"Bye, Nathan," I call as I duck inside.

No surprise, Crew is right behind me. He's laughing as he closes the door. "Well, that was fun."

"Fun?" I ask, heading for the counter to check the mail and messages. "Antagonizing your boss and my–" But I break off when I realize that I have no idea what to call Nathan.

"Yes, fun," Crew says, thankfully not dwelling on terms for Nathan and me. He props himself against the bookcase across from the front counter. I have the expanse of wood and about four feet of floor between us and I still feel jumpy with his eyes on me. "Nathan never has anyone hassle him. I love that you're getting to him. It's good for him to have some fucking emotions for a change."

"Me?" I ask, surprised. "It's you who's getting to him."

He shakes his head. "I wouldn't be able to if it wasn't for you."

That makes my stomach swoop. But it shouldn't. Nathan just said goodbye to me. I take a breath, flip through my mail, and then turn toward the steps leading up to my apartment. "I do need to change clothes."

"I love that you just came home in the same clothes you wore last night," Crew says. "Good for you."

"Yeah?" I study him. I thought he was interested in me in a romantic…okay, a sexual…way. But he truly seems fine with the idea that I slept with another man last night.

"Yeah. You look happily rumpled. And glowy. It's very cute on you."

I don't know what to say to that, but it makes me happy. I finally just nod. "Thanks."

"And I look forward to contributing to that."

My breath catches in my chest. "Oh yeah?"

The grin he gives me makes my stomach swoop too. "Oh, yeah."

Well, I guess that answers that. "So you want to come upstairs?"

He shakes his head. "I want to take you out."

"Okay."

"Before I make you come so hard you'll see stars."

My breath rushes out. Geez. These men. I might not survive having a fling with these three hot, dirty, intense men.

But I'm going to die with a huge smile on my face.

"I, um…so, I'll just…"

"Go change your clothes," he fills in for me, with a knowing smile. "But hurry."

"Right. Yes." I start up the stairs. "Be right back."

I showered at Nathan's so in the bathroom, I simply comb my hair, brush my teeth, swipe on very light mascara and lip gloss, and spritz on some body spray. Then I cross to my closet, stripping out of my dress and bra. I first reach for a cute pair of jeans, but then decide on another dress. I mean, I don't want there to be anything in Crew's way if he wants to slip a hand near, or into, my panties.

I even contemplate putting on panties at all. For ten seconds. In the end, I do. I'm not a no-panties girl. Not really.

At least not yet.

CHAPTER 13

Crew

OF COURSE NATHAN fucked her already. I should have seen that coming.

Damn, that guy is wound tight.

But I don't mind sharing if it makes her look as happy as she looked this morning.

Yes, I've wanted her for years. Yes, I want more than a hot fling with her. But Dani's someone I truly *like* too, and damn, that's a pretty awesome combination.

So, she's fucking Nathan.

And if I was another guy I would probably hate that.

But I don't. I like that Dani is feeling sexy and wanted and worshiped, and if she wants to be worshiped by multiple men, I'm all in.

Two years ago, I had a girlfriend who had another boyfriend, and we had a hell of a good time. The three of us just clicked and if Lexi hadn't landed her dream job in New York and moved across the country, we would have definitely kept things up beyond the six months we had. Tyler went with her and I didn't hear from them much now beyond the occasional *nice game* text, but I still think fondly of them. They're the ones that showed me that a threesome could be more fun than just a wild one-night thing.

Of course, with Dani I want things to last. Long beyond six months. I'm not letting her go. So Nathan's going to have to be on board with this too, and I'm going to fucking be sure he's treating her right, but as long as he does, and she's feeling good, then I'm good.

And when things end between them, I'll still be there.

Dani is a long-term kind of girl. Maybe not for a guy like Nathan Armstrong. Jesus, being with that guy long-term would be a lot. But could *I* be a long-term guy for her? Yeah. Definitely.

I hear the steps creak and look up from the book I'm flipping through. It's a romance and I actually flipped past a sexy scene to the scene where the guy makes a big grand gesture to get the girl back after he said something stupid.

Grand gestures…now that's something I can get into. I feel like big gifts—skywriting, and enormous balloon bouquets, and getting down on one knee at center ice—is totally my wheelhouse.

"I'm ready."

My heart kicks when she comes into view. She looks so pretty. She's in a light green dress that's covered in tiny white flowers and a white sweater over the top. Her hair is loose around her shoulders. And her smile is sweet and just a little shy.

Dani Larkin and I are going on a date. A real fucking date.

Weird.

And awesome.

"You look beautiful."

"Thank you." She comes to stand in front of me.

She smells so good too. Fresh and sweet and I want to run my nose up and down her neck, into her hair, down into her cleavage… okay, so my sweet, romantic thoughts are easily derailed. Yes, I want Dani and I welcome that change in our relationship.

"What color are your panties?" I ask.

Her cheeks get lightly pink. "How do you know I'm wearing panties?" she teases.

She is. I just know she is. Will she take them off for me? Yeah, I'm pretty fucking sure she will. Will I get to keep them the way Nathan did? Yep. Pretty sure of that too.

But she's got them on now.

"I don't mind waiting to find out," I tell her. "But I'm going to guess they're white. Tiny. Cotton. But they've got little flowers on them." I lift my finger and trace it along the neckline of her dress. "Something that kind of matches this pattern. I bet they look sweet as fuck. But I also bet they get a little wet when I tell you that I can't wait to pull them aside and taste your pussy without even removing them. And if I win that bet, you have to agree to show me these panties when I ask."

Her lips fall open with surprise.

I lean in. "Did I win the bet? Are they a little wetter now?"

She simply nods.

I smile. "Excellent."

"Do you…" She clears her throat. "Do you want to see them?"

"I do," I say. Then I stop her as she moves to lift her skirt.

Damn, Dani is about to lift her skirt for me right here inside her cute little bookshop. "Later."

She wets her lips. "Okay." Her answer is almost a whisper.

"Okay." I take her hand and start for the door. "Let's go."

She lets me lead her out onto the sidewalk and she turns to lock the door. "Where are we going?"

"I have a surprise for you." I can't wait to show her what I arranged for our date.

We turn left and start down the sidewalk, our fingers linked, walking amongst the morning crowd like any other couple.

I don't date much. I hook up. A lot. I party. Also a lot. I occasionally take women out to fancy dinners, or to expensive clubs, and I guess those could feel like dates. But I don't hold their hands as we walk. I don't stop at coffee carts and buy them caramel vanilla lattes, or stop in front of every other window so they can point something out that catches their eye and makes them smile.

I do all of that with Dani…and fucking love it. Every single thing. I even get her extra whipped cream on that latte. Dani is an extra whipped cream kind of girl and I have this sudden need to make sure she has extra whatever-she-needs.

We finally arrive at our destination.

"Here we are."

Dani looks up at the sign over the door, then looks at me in confusion. "Here?"

"Yep." I tap on the glass of the door and wave at the skinny man in blue pants and a grape purple jacket. He grins and comes to let us in. "Hey, Len."

"Crew, nice to see you." He shakes my hand, then steps back to let us enter.

"Len, this is Dani. Dani, Len. He manages this gallery. His brother-in-law, Connor, is one of my teammates."

The KM Studio is a space for introspective expressions of the pressing social issues of modern times. At least that's what the website and brochures say. I'm not exactly sure what that means, but I think I get the general gist.

Put more simply, it's an art gallery.

"Wow," Dani says, looking around. "Hi, Len. This is beautiful."

"I'm happy to have you," Len says. "When Connor asked if I'd open early for Crew because his girlfriend was a huge art lover, I was delighted. Crew is our son's favorite player. Even above Connor." Len laughs. "Crew has spent a lot of one-on-one time with our son and has been so patient and generous with his time. It's my pleasure to do him a favor in return."

I feel a flush on the back of my neck. I don't need Len's thanks or a favor in return. I love spending time with his kid, Oliver.

But Dani is looking up at me with curiosity and a soft smile and I don't mind having that look trained on me from this girl.

"Ah, come on, Len. Stop. Just let us look at your pretty junk for a little while, okay?" I say, waving off his praise.

Len grins. "Sure. Take your time. Enjoy. You've got two hours before we open up."

"Thanks."

I take Dani's hand again, just wanting to touch her. She lets me intertwine our fingers and lead her into the next room.

There are framed paintings and photographs on the wall and several statues or carvings or whatever they're called on pedestals throughout the room. We wander through, stopping to look at each thing.

I pretend to study them, acknowledging that they're maybe sort of interesting, but I'm way more tuned into the woman beside me. I'm not an art connoisseur by any stretch. This is all an attempt to do something I thought Dani might enjoy. I'll admit that Nathan wasn't way off when he mentioned roller skating and the circus. I wouldn't have taken her to the circus exactly—I don't think the circus is in town—but that does sound more fun than an art gallery. But I don't mind doing things outside of my comfort zone if it will make her happy.

I can look at art. That won't hurt me. I'll go to foreign films or the symphony or whatever other high brow stuff this sexy little nerd wants to do. I just want to be with her.

"What do you do when you're spending time with Len's son?" Dani asks as we are standing in front of the fourth painting.

"Play hockey."

Of course. Hockey is my life.

"Oh. Do you coach?"

"Yeah."

"Like a youth league or something?"

I nod and look down at her. "It's a camp. For kids in wheelchairs."

Her brows rise. "Oh."

"Len's kid, Oliver, is hilarious and I've spent some extra, after-hours time with him."

Her eyes were soft. "Why is he in a wheelchair?"

"He has CP. Cerebral palsy. Len and his husband, Anthony,

adopted him as a baby, knowing that he had some problems and that he'd need a wheelchair and extra care for life. They are amazing parents and Oliver is awesome. I love spending time with him."

Now she is looking at me like she wants to kiss me.

I really like that look.

"I'd love to meet him sometime."

"I'd love to introduce you," I say sincerely. Oliver will love her. He'll tease me incessantly about having a girlfriend, but I'll welcome it in this case.

"That's a really great thing to do, Crew," she finally says.

"Thanks. But that's not why I brought you here," I say. "I didn't expect Len to tell you that."

"I'm glad he did."

I'm kind of glad he did too. I'm more than just the dumb athlete people assume I am. Which is stupid, because hockey is a game of strategy along with skill, but it's a stereotype I don't usually bother to fight. With Dani though, I want her to know there is more to me than meets the eye.

"So which is your favorite piece here?" she asks, looking around. "I'd love to see it. I'll admit I don't know a lot about art. I can tell the things I like and don't, but I don't know much about it. So teach me what you know."

I shake my head with a chuckle. "Hell if I know. I've never been here before."

She looks up at me with surprise. "What?"

"I brought you here to impress you. I figured you were into this stuff."

She laughs. "Why would you think that?"

"You're a bookworm. You're classy and sophisticated and smart."

She outright snorts now. "I'm classy and sophisticated?"

I feel myself grinning. "Aren't you?"

"Definitely not."

"So you'd rather go to the circus?"

"Or roller skate," she says, her eyes twinkling.

And I fall a little bit more in love with her.

She had fun with Nathan. He wined and dined her. And obviously fucked her well. But she puts herself in the same category as he put me.

"So we're both in an art gallery and we know nothing about art?" she asks.

"Or introspective expressions of the pressing social issues of modern times."

She lifts a brow. "Yeah. Or those."

I laugh, feeling light and happy. "Yep."

"Do you want to do something else?" she asks. Her smile is so cute. "The Children's Museum is fun. We could go there."

I laugh. That actually does sound fun. But that's not what I want to do right now. "I'm going out of town for a string of road games tomorrow."

"Okay."

"So there's something I'd really like to do today, before I leave."

"Okay."

I take both of her hands and start walking backward, heading for the corner of the room. There's a shadowy area behind a larger pedestal that holds a tall statue of…I have no idea what that's supposed to be.

I stop when we're behind the pedestal and mostly blocked from the doorway and hallway outside. Though if Len comes looking for us, he'll see plenty.

But that's what makes this fun.

"I'm ready to see how accurate my guess was."

She realizes what I'm talking about immediately. "About my panties?"

"Yep."

She gives me an adorable, sly smile. "Okay."

"But there's something else I need to know first."

"What's that?"

"How sore are you from last night?"

She blushes quick and bright. And I love it. I lift my hand and run the tip of my finger over her cheek. "I just want to be sure I don't hurt you, sweetheart."

"I'm…a little sore," she confesses, her cheeks burning. "But, not so much that I'll say no," she adds quietly.

I dip my knees and catch her mouth in a quick kiss. "You are a dream, you know that?" I say against her mouth.

She sighs happily. "I feel like I'm in a dream."

"Well, let's turn this from a dream into a fantasy, shall we?"

I start gathering her skirt up in one hand. "Show me what you put on for me."

"For you?" she asks, her hand working on the other side of the skirt.

"You knew I'd be seeing these," I say, confidently.

She pulls her bottom lip between her teeth, but she's smiling. I know I'm right.

I tug her sweater off one shoulder and kiss her neck, then down her shoulder, nudging the top of her dress over as she pulls up her skirt.

"What do you think?" she asks, breathlessly.

I pull back and look down. I have to lean to really see.

They are white, I was right about that. And tiny. But I got the little flowers wrong. Instead, they have lip prints on them.

I grin. "Oh, naughty girl. Are you trying to give me a hint?"

She laughs softly. "Why do I feel like you're not really a hint type of guy? You're more a just-blurt-it-right-out guy, right?"

"Abso-fucking-lutely." I meet her gaze. "Blurt it out, Dani. Tell me what you want."

She sucks in a little breath, but I can tell she's excited by the look in her eyes.

"I want your mouth on me first."

I love the way she said *first,* obviously indicating she wants more than that. I'd be happy with just that, honestly. But I'm not going to stop if she wants more.

I drop to my knees. "You're gonna have to hold this up out of my way."

I put her free hand on the skirt, and she obediently pulls both sides up out of my way, revealing the panties completely.

My mouth is already watering. I lean in and kiss her inner thigh. She makes a little moan. I can smell her arousal and the sweet scent of some body spray. I can also smell a more masculine scent that I assume is the soap from Nathan's shower that morning.

I feel a surge of something I can't quite name. It's not jealousy, but possibly this is fueling a bit of my competitive nature. I want to make this good for her. Better than what she had with Nathan. Or at least different. I want her to have distinct memories of being with both of us.

Yes, Nathan is a rich businessman. But I've got money too. He's about twenty years older than me, so I can imagine that being with him is different in many ways. He's an asshole too. I'm sure he's nicer to Dani than he is to me and many of the other people I've seen him interact with—at least he better fucking be—but I'm guessing there's still a bit of an edge, even with Dani. He's probably bossy as fuck. Does she like that? A part of me wants to ask her. But now is not the time.

I know for a fact that he was not fun, or lighthearted, or funny. I sincerely doubt that Nathan Armstrong has it in him to be funny.

"So, since you're not really an artsy type of girl, I'm going to assume that you've never been eaten out in an art gallery before." I give her inner thigh a little lick then a kiss.

"You would guess correctly."

"Or while at the circus, or a county fair..." I lick her again as she giggles breathlessly. "Where I would take you on a Ferris wheel, and win you a big stuffed teddy bear, and feed you cotton candy."

She says softly, "Correct, and oh, yes please to all of that."

"Well, you're going to be my treat today. I am going to eat you up like I would a bunch of cotton candy or…" I lick her again. "A big, sweet snow cone."

I switch sides and lean in to kiss her other thigh.

Then I see it.

"That territorial bastard," I mutter.

She looks down. "Oh that…"

I run my fingertip over the reddish-purple mark on her thigh. "Yeah, that. He marked you." I lean in and kiss it. "That's hot. And I don't blame him a fucking bit." I move right beside it, and kiss the pale, smooth skin. "Two can play that game," I say, before sucking gently. When she moans, I suck a little harder, then release her flesh. I look up. "I'll leave the other side for Hughes."

She sucks in a little breath. But then shakes her head. "Nathan won't see it."

I lift a brow. "Why's that?"

"I don't think Nathan and I are…doing that again."

I laugh. "You keep thinking that, sweetheart." I saw how the boss man looked at her this morning when he dropped her off. He's not done with her. And Dani was glowing. I love that this girl is getting all this attention. She deserves it.

"You think…" She trails off.

"I do." I kiss her thigh again. Then kiss my way up to the crease where her thigh becomes her pelvis, right where the elastic of her panties rests. "But don't worry. I've got you covered for whatever you need in case he doesn't." I lick along that elastic band.

She sags back against the wall. "Yes, Crew."

Fucking love hearing my name on her lips.

"You're not going to get to be loud, Dani. This is a nice sophisticated, classy place. I doubt very much if there's lots of pussy eating going on in here." I run the tip of my finger underneath that elastic, feeling her hot folds that are getting nice and wet. "Though if there was, I might become a patron after all."

She makes a sweet little purring sound as the back of my knuckle brushes over her clit. I still haven't looked at her without the white cotton between us, but I love teasing her. "I am definitely going to appreciate the beauty of the female form for a little bit right now, though," I tell her, finally pulling the panties away from her sex. "And I absolutely adore the color pink." I run my finger over the slick pinkness I've exposed and the sweet little nub of her clit.

Her breath hisses out.

"God you're beautiful." I dip my finger into her wetness and drag it up over her clit.

"I should've known you'd be a talker." Her voice is ragged as if she's having a hard time getting enough air to speak.

"You don't like talking during sex?" I circle over her clit, pressing a little harder.

"It's good. It's fine. I just want you to use your mouth for something else."

"Tell it to me bluntly, babe."

Her eyes pop open and she looks down at me. "Suck on my clit, Crew."

Heat jabs me low and hard. I did not think she'd do it. And I had no idea how fucking hot that would be.

Then I do what the lady tells me. I lean in and take her clit between my lips. I kiss her, then I suck. Hard. Then I flick my tongue over her quickly. Her gasps and moans tell me that I'm giving her exactly what she wants. So I keep going.

I add a finger and within seconds I have her shooting up and over the edge and the way she cries out my name twists my balls, my gut, even my heart into a damned knot.

I get to my feet and she immediately cups my cock through my shorts.

I capture her mouth in a deep kiss, stroking my tongue along hers, knowing she can taste herself.

"God, that was hot," I tell her.

"I want you, Crew. Will you fuck me? Please? Right now?"

"Of course." I laugh. "Are you kidding?"

"Do you have a condom?"

"Yes, ma'am."

"Okay. Here? Is that okay?"

"Jesus, Dani, quit asking me if things are okay. Yes, I will fuck you. Anywhere, anytime, however you want it."

"Oh, my God. This is so hot." She drops her voice. "We're in public."

"Not exactly. But we could get caught."

Her eyes sparkle.

I chuckle. "Christ, that turns you on, doesn't it?"

She gives me a little smile that I fucking love.

"Okay, naughty girl, let's go." I dig my wallet out of my pocket, flip it open, and find a condom. By the time I drop the wallet to the floor, she's already got me unbuttoned and unzipped. Her hot little hands wrap around my cock a moment later and I have to pause as lust streaks through me.

I brace one hand on the wall and just breathe for a second.

"You okay?"

I grit my teeth and nod. "You're just about to end up with a handful of cum if you don't stop that. I need to get inside you."

"You weren't kidding about the blunt thing."

"There's no guessing with me."

She grins. "I like that."

"Well, here's some more. I'm going to put this condom on, lift you up against the wall, and fuck you so hard you will feel this wall later. You gotta tell me if I'm going too hard."

She nods eagerly. "Okay."

I laugh. "I had no idea you'd be like this." I'm rolling the condom on as I say it.

"I didn't either." She seems delighted though.

"Drop the panties, sweetheart."

She shoves them to the floor, then hikes up her skirt. I step forward, cup her ass and lift her up against the wall. Her legs wrap around me, and my cock is right up against her sweet hot pussy.

"Dani," I grind out. "You feel so fucking good."

"Fuck me, Crew. Please."

"Gladly." I pulled my hips back slightly, position myself at her entrance, and then sink in. She's tight. So tight.

Then Dani clutches my shoulders, and her pussy tightens around me, and I am right back in the moment with only her. In the hottest, tightest pussy I've had in a very long time. With the sweetest, most adorable, surprising woman that I've ever had in my arms. Her eyes are locked on mine, and I stare into them as I thrust deep over and over.

Bluntly, I say, "You are the hottest thing ever. Jesus, how did you learn how to fuck like this?"

Her mouth curls. "You're doing all the work."

I squeeze her ass. "Good point. Next time you're on top."

"Promise there's a next time?"

"Absolutely. I'm also getting inside that adorable mouth."

Her eyes widen, as does her smile. "Okay."

She's fucking eager. She might kill me. And I can't wait.

"The one thing about having you up against the wall like this is I've got to hold onto your sweet ass. You have to reach down to play with your clit. Let's go. I wanna feel you come on my cock, sweetheart."

She immediately reaches between us and starts working her clit. It does amazing things to her pussy and pretty soon she's clamping down and squeezing me.

"Yes, fuck, Dani. That's it, girl."

She keeps going, her thighs tighten around me, and the next thing I hear is "Yes! Crew! Yes, yes!"

"My turn, sweetheart," I say, roughly. I pick up my pace, thrusting into her harder and harder until I'm coming, losing myself in her heat, her sweetness, and just how damn fun this is.

I am taking this girl on a Ferris wheel.

This girl is going to be at one of my games in my jersey.

I'm going to take her to the Eiffel Tower. And I've never wanted to go to Paris before. Ever.

I'm also going to buy her kittens, and cuddle her on the couch, and take care of her when she's sick, and throw her the best birthday party she's ever had.

And I'm going to take her home for Christmas. And even though she's been there before, this time I'm going to hold her hand and touch her and kiss her under the mistletoe and call her my girlfriend. All in front of my grandma.

Yeah, I'm officially gone for this girl.

About thirty-six hours after kissing her for the first time.

I'm probably going to want to propose in another day or two at this pace.

I finally pull back and let her feet drop to the floor.

She pulls her panties back into place and straightens her skirt as I try to decide what the hell I'm going to do about the condom. That's one thing about sex in an art gallery, it makes cleanup a little awkward.

Dani seems to realize that at the same exact moment and digs in her purse, handing me a tiny travel package of tissues. She giggles. "Here."

"This does not mean no spontaneous begging me for fucking when the need hits you in the future," I tell her.

She nods. "I'll pack some wet wipes and stuff just in case."

I reach over and grasp her chin, pulling her in for a kiss. "You do that. Because what I said stands. Any time, anywhere, anyhow."

"I won't be forgetting that."

Eventually, we feel ready to walk out of the art gallery and it occurs to me to hope that Len doesn't have security cameras in every room in the gallery.

Then it occurs to me that he absolutely has security cameras in every room of the art gallery.

Wonder what it would take to get a copy of that video. I wouldn't mind watching that. A few dozen times.

CHAPTER 14

Michael

My office. 2pm today. Be there.

THE UNEXPECTED TEXT had arrived just ten minutes before two from Nathan. I knock on the door at the designated time, curious what's on our team owner's mind. Armstrong is an efficient guy, but this is cryptic and clipped even for him.

"Come in," Nathan barks out, sounding more like a drill sergeant than a businessman.

The minute I open the door and spot McNeill in a chair with his hands laced behind his head, I realize exactly what—or rather, who— is the reason for this unexpected meeting.

Dani.

This should be interesting.

"Hey, Doc, what's up?" Crew asks me, flashing his dimples. "You got the summons too, huh?"

"Crew." I nod. I look at Nathan, who is standing behind his desk, his hands jammed deep into his suit pants pockets. His expression is stormy, determined.

"Yes, I did. Nathan, what's going on?"

"Danielle spent the night with me last night."

Okay, then. Definitely not a meeting about hockey.

And for having spent the night with sexy little Dani, he doesn't exactly look relaxed with a post-sex satisfied smirk. He looks wound even tighter than ever.

Armstrong has it even worse than I thought. The man's jealousy is off the fucking charts right now. I almost feel sorry for him. He looks like he's forming an ulcer right in front of our eyes.

"Is that what this is about?" Crew asks, sounding astonished as he drops his hands. He tugs on the strings of his Racketeers hoodie. "You already told me that this morning. Good for you, bro. I hope you had fun." He shrugs.

My thoughts exactly. Who Dani has sex with isn't really any of my business unless it's with me, which it will be soon. She's obviously enjoying all this sudden male attention and given her choice of reading material, she has a sexy side that she wants to explore. I just can't get the visual out of my head of going down on my knees in front of her and eating that sweet little pussy while her back is propped against a bookrack.

I spent an hour last night reading the romance novel she'd given me and I absolutely, one hundred percent, need to implement chapter twenty-two on her sexy little ass.

"It was…more than fun," Nathan says stubbornly. "For both of us, damn it."

I can't help it. My eyebrows shoot up. Whoa, this is really out of character for Nathan. It sounds like he has feelings for Dani. Actual, legitimate feelings.

To be honest, I'm proud of the guy. He needs someone to come in and knock down one or two of his walls. It has to be lonely as hell to be this guy, with no family other than his grandfather. It would be great for Armstrong to have someone in his corner, caring about him and putting up with his grumpy attitude.

Crew grins. "Look, I need to hit the gym. If this is going to take any longer, tell me you at least ordered us some Panera. Isn't that like standard meeting protocol? I wouldn't say no to a cherry pastry right now."

Nathan glares at him. "Is that some kind of sexual taunt?

Talking about cherries? Are you trying to say you were actually there first because that's not what Danielle told me."

"What?" McNeill's face reveals he is genuinely astonished. "No. Don't get your dick in a wad. I just like pastries, Jesus. Who doesn't like a cherry pastry?"

He looks to me for confirmation.

"I do love a cherry pastry," I agree. "Though I prefer eclairs."

I smile at the memory of watching Dani flick her tongue through the cream of an eclair. I clear my throat, shifting a little as my dick hardens. None of these guys have that visual. That's my own private moment with Dani, and I'm not sharing it because I don't need to brag and stake a claim on her the way these assholes do.

Crew nods in satisfaction and turns back to Nathan. "See? Doc agrees. Pastries rock. Nate, you don't sound like you had fun last night at all. You seem like you were blue balled if I'm being totally honest with you."

"I had a fucking amazing time," Nathan snaps, pulling his hand out of his pocket and pointing a finger at first Crew then at me. "Danielle did not blue ball me. We had sex all night. Five times."

Damn, he's trying to prove his point hard. Maybe he has a girlfriend in Canada too. I'm fighting the urge to laugh. I do believe Nathan, but he sounds ridiculous and desperate. Which would make his head explode if he knew that.

"Do you want a round of applause?" Crew claps his hands in front of Nathan in a circle. "There you go. Can I go now?" He starts to stand up.

"Sit your ass down. I've been thinking about this all day."

Of course, he had. If he'd seen Dani this morning with Crew, I'm stunned he waited this long to call us into his office.

"I've decided that I want to be with Danielle. That means the two of you need to back the fuck off."

Is that so?

I could use Panera now too. I need coffee to navigate this

alpha male mating crap. Nathan is wound tight and this conversation is now taxing my pretty impressive patience. He sounds like we're fighting over a toy in the sandbox. And he's the only one fighting.

"I don't think you get to decide that, Nathan," I say, determined to stay calm. Sometimes I wonder if the man even hears the shit that comes out of his mouth. "Dani is a grown woman. She makes her own decisions."

"I took her out first," he says. "You both moved too slow."

"You licked her first so she's yours?" Crew asks. "Or gave her a thigh hickey? Is that how it is?"

The way he says it makes me a little concerned where this is going. If I have to step in between these two, forget a cup of coffee. I'm heading straight to the pub around the corner.

"That's how it is. Don't touch her. The only one having sex with Danielle is me." Nathan is glowering at us both.

Crew leans forward, elbows on his knees. "Well, damn, I wish I had known that was the rule before I fucked her this morning. Saw your little mark and added my own."

And there it is.

I actually appreciate the guy's willingness to put Armstrong in his place. A grin slips out before I can stop it.

What I don't appreciate is that now Nathan has come around the side of his desk as if he's going to take a swing at McNeill. His top player. Who's damn near half his age.

Today is clearly a hard day in the life of a billionaire.

"McNeill," Nathan growls.

"Sorry, not sorry," Crew adds. "Guess Dani didn't get the rules either because she eagerly pulled down those little panties for me."

Nathan's jaw drops. "You little shit."

Crew looks left and right over his shoulder. "Who are you talking to?" he asks.

McNeill is truly a savant at irritating the hell out of Nathan.

I'm starting to get concerned Armstrong might actually have a stroke.

"Now, just calm down," I say, sticking my hand up in front of Nathan before he strangles Crew. "This needs to be discussed like rational adults."

"Why? Did you fuck Danielle too?" Nathan looks at me in outrage.

Rubbing my chin, I sigh. "No. But if I had that is none of your business. It's Dani's business."

"I want to be with her," Nathan says.

"No one's saying you can't be. But you don't get to decide who else is." I clap Nathan on the shoulder and give it a reassuring squeeze. "I get it. You caught feelings. That's understandable. She's adorable."

He flinches.

"But Dani picks who she dates and whether or not she wants to be exclusive," Crew chimes in. "You don't get to be all caveman and decide she's only with you because you said so."

"I'm the caveman?" Nathan scoffs.

"Yes. You're the one trying to drag her off to your cave."

"He's not wrong," I agree.

"What if she doesn't want to be exclusive?" Nathan demands. "You're both going to be okay with that?"

"Yes," Crew says with zero hesitation. "I want what she wants. I want her to be happy. I intend to date her. Long term boyfriend-girlfriend stuff. I've been crazy about her for years. But I think right now she's enjoying the attention and she deserves that. She deserves more sexual experiences. She deserves to feel special."

Nathan snorts. "You're a liar."

I trust McNeill. He looks sincere. He's an easy-going guy off the ice.

I need to back him up on this. "Crew is right. This is about Dani. Her pleasure, her happiness. She's calling the shots. She can choose any of the three of us, or she doesn't have to choose at all."

"We're just all supposed to date her around each other?"

Nathan starts pacing back and forth. "No. No way. I'll lose my mind if I have to sit at home picturing she's out with one of you two or worse, at home with you."

It's a risk to say what I'm about to say.

But Dani is worth it.

"Or we could share her." I let it drop like a missile out of a bomber jet. "Give her that option."

"Bingo," Crew says, sitting up straight. He points at me. "You're a motherfucking genius Doc. I'm in. Completely."

"Thanks, man." We fist bump.

Nathan shakes his head. "I just told you I don't want to do that. It will kill me to know she's in bed with either of you."

"By share, I mean share," I say. "Sure, we'll each have a little bit of alone time with her but mostly we'll all be together."

His face is still blank.

I spell it out. "Having sex with her at the same time. A foursome, where we all focus on her." The very thought of our sweet little Dani all spread out naked for us to worship from tip to toe makes me hot and hard. I want this for her so fucking bad because she should be showered with attention.

Crew is nodding. He looks absolutely delighted. "Exactly."

Nathan's jaw is working but he seems to have been rendered speechless.

"Listen, there are only a few options here,"I point out. "A, we all walk away from her. B, we let her pick who she wants to date. C, we all casually date her separately. Or D. We share her, together."

"Always pick option D," Crew says with a smirk.

"What makes you think Danielle would want a foursome?" Nathan asks.

"Because she gave me her favorite spicy book to read and there's a reason it's her favorite, right?" I ask. "In the book this girl has guys coming at her from all directions. It's a damn dick-fest. Two and three guys at once. She's taking it every way a woman can take it, and some I'm not even sure are actually possible, even though the heroine is a gymnast." I'm going to have to read pages forty-three to forty-five again to confirm.

I have Nathan's attention.

"Really?" he asks, and he sounds thoughtful, not furious.

"Yes. The point is, Dani loves this book. There is something about it that is appealing to her and while the plot is solid, I would assume it has more to do with the fact that the men all focus their attention on the female character. There is a heavy emphasis on double penetration." For some random reason, I bring both my hands down into a karate chop facing each other, as if that's a realistic visual aid. It isn't.

Crew whistles. "The ladies love the DP. Been there, done that."

"You have?" Nathan looks at Crew as if he thinks the younger guy is just screwing around.

"A few times for fun, but my last serious relationship was a threesome. Lasted six months. It was awesome. I'd absolutely do it again if Dani is in."

I'm glad to hear McNeill has experience with at least a threesome. So do I, though it was only once and a number of years ago. At any rate, I'm willing to jump from three to four to give Dani everything she wants.

"She told me that she gets herself off thinking about being fucked by three guys," Nathan says slowly.

I'm not surprised she'd say that given what she likes to read and write but Nathan clearly is. His brow is so furrowed there is no chance he's getting Botox. The space between his eyes is like a map of the Grand Canyon right now.

"See?" I tell him. "She admitted it to you. Right out loud. She wants three men taking her to the next level."

"I already took her to the next level," he grumbles, starting to pace again, arms crossed over his chest.

"I'm sure that was great," Crew says, moving closer to Nathan. "Every level feels amazing when you're conquering it. But there's always another level up a ladder or through a cave. Usually when you level up it comes with a treasure chest filled with coins." He claps Nathan on each shoulder and gives him a shake. "Let Dani have the treasure chest and find gold, Nate."

"We've got the keys to unlock the treasure chest for her," I add. "She can't do it herself."

Nathan shakes off Crew and goes to the window and stares out.

Long moments tick by.

McNeill and I eye each other.

He shrugs. He opens his mouth like he's going to pitch the idea again.

I hold up a hand to stop him, shaking my head.

Then suddenly Nathan turns. He squares his shoulders, and gives us a grim look.

"I'm in."

Crew gives a whoop.

"You sure?" I ask him, not sold on his response. He looks more like he's agreeing to a colonoscopy instead of group sex.

He nods curtly. "If this is what Danielle wants, I'm in. Don't fucking ask me again."

I hold my hands out to placate him. "Got it. So we all agree we'll run this by Dani and let her decide what she wants?" I give them both a stern look. "With no one pressuring her."

Crew already has his phone in his hand and is tapping out a text. He looks up at me, guilt all over his face. "What does that mean, specifically?"

"It means delete that text you're writing." I put my hands on my hips, determined if we're going to present this idea to Dani we can't overwhelm her with a bunch of egos competing for her attention. "Rule number one. Dani is the most important thing here, not you competing with Nathan or your dick or anything else."

"I'm not a fan of rules," Crew says, mildly. "But I get it. Focus on Dani. I totally agree."

"The other important thing here is the Racketeers," Nathan said. "I'm not suggesting you two sign an NDA, but you have to agree to keep any sort of arrangement we make with Danielle a secret. This won't be good for the team or anyone's career if it gets out publicly."

I nod, because he's right. "Of course. You have my word. We have to protect both Dani and the team."

"Can you keep your mouth shut?" Nathan asks Crew.

McNeill nods. "I know you think I'm a fuck up, but hockey is my life. I love this sport and I love playing for the Racketeers. I would never do anything to jeopardize the team's reputation or distract from the fact that we're going to have an amazing season."

Nathan looks reassured. "I respect that. I want a championship this year. That's why you're here and I expect you to make that happen."

"I will," Crew says, with a confidence that gives him an edge on the ice.

It's also irritating off the ice.

"We're all on the road tomorrow for the game in Texas," I say. "Does anyone have plans with Dani tonight?"

Nathan and Crew both look at each other. Nathan is practically snarling. Crew has stiffened in his chair.

But he says, "No."

Nathan relaxes. "I don't either." Though he looks like that admission cost him a huge chunk of his soul.

"Keep it that way. We can ask to see Dani together when we all get back in town. In the meantime, just stay cool. Keep talking to her the way you've been and don't pressure her or get competitive."

It's completely pointless to say. These two can't stop themselves. I wouldn't be surprised if Crew actually sent the text he was composing. Or if Nathan calls Dani the second we step out of this office. But I don't want this to descend into chaos where Dani is overwhelmed.

"Don't make her regret this before it even starts," I say.

They both give me nods.

But then Nathan says, "If we go forward with this, no one is touching my dick but Danielle. Just so we're clear on that."

I appreciate that he wants clarity. "No problem. Likewise, Armstrong. It's smart that we talk through expectations beforehand."

"I don't care if either of you touches my dick," Crew says. "It's all about how you're feeling in the moment. But I will respect your personal boundaries."

"Then we all understand each other."

Nathan looks like he doesn't understand us, himself, or anything about this. It makes me appreciate how much he really likes Dani if he's willing to subject himself to Crew on a regular basis.

"Can I go?" Crew asks, standing up. "I need to work out and go pick up the new suit I ordered. I look hot as fuck in silver."

"Yes, you can go."

Crew heads to the door and waves. The door slams shut behind him.

"I have regrets already," Nathan says, rubbing his chest like he has heartburn.

I shrug. "Dani likes McNeill. They have friendship and a connection because of Luna. Either put up with him or bow out."

"I'm not bowing out." His voice is steely.

"Neither is McNeill," I say mildly.

My phone buzzes.

I smile when I glance at the screen. It's a text from Dani.

> Hi! Would you want to read my latest scene before I upload it to Habanero?

I meet Nathan's gaze. "I'm not bowing out either."

CHAPTER 15

Michael

SITTING DOWN HARD on my sofa that evening, a glass of red wine in my hand, I sigh with relief. Today was exhausting. Not only did I have to mediate between Crew and Nathan, the Racketeers defenseman sustained a hip flexor strain in practice. Alexei is known for his aggressive skating style and he beats the hell out of his hip joints and groin muscles. He's rotating joint and soft tissues injuries every other season.

As team physician, I always feel responsible when these guys injure themselves doing something I've warned them not to do. But they're athletes and they want to win, despite that we've talked endlessly about stretching and not overextending in practice.

Stretching.

The word has an immediate visual popping into my head of Dani taking two dicks at once like Paris, the heroine in her favorite book.

Damn.

Now that's something I can't wait to try. Or watch.

Adjusting myself in my joggers, I take another sip of wine and debate if I should listen to a podcast or reread key parts of One Night In Paris.

But then a notification dings that a doc from Dani has been shared with me.

Hell, yeah. I can't wait to see what my little spicy smut writer has cooked up today after her night with Nathan. And morning with Crew. She must be feeling inspired.

In the hotel he'd gotten for them, Sturgeon knelt between Divine's thighs, all the lights on so that he could sweep his gaze over the length of her naked body. She shivered under his view, feeling stripped before him in every way.

He could see all of her, inside and out.

The hotel was luxurious, with a view of the city skyline, and Divine didn't understand how Sturgeon could afford this. He was a bodyguard. But being there with him makes her feel safe and protected for the first time since her abduction. Maybe ever. In spite of her age, it just now felt like she was fully a woman.

"Divine, spread your legs," he ordered. "Open yourself to me."

Shivering, she obeyed him immediately. Cool air hit the heat between her thighs, generated by Sturgeon's blazing gaze.

"That's it, pretty girl." His thumbs massaged my soft folds before he settled his thick cock between them. "You want me, don't you? You want all this cock deep inside you."

"Yes," she murmured. "Please. I want your cock."

He bent down and kissed me, possessively. "I'll give you everything you've ever wanted."

Then he was inside her, filling her completely, as she cried out in pleasure.

He never looked away. He never closed his eyes.

He just drilled his gaze into her while his cock did the same.

She was dripping with her arousal, soaking him. Her hips were relaxed, legs slack. She just laid back and let him dominate her with his dick, drawing them both closer and closer to completion. The sensation built and built in her core, and her eyes drifted shut.

He gripped her chin. Not hard, but commanding. "Don't close your eyes. I want to see you when you come all over my dick."

She couldn't speak or protest. She must obey. He knew how to pleasure her. She trusted that.

He eased a finger between them, teasing at her clit. "Come for me, my sweet Divine."

It was all she needed. Everything that had been held back burst forth, an explosion of ecstasy, fanning out from her pussy to every inch of her body. Her mind emptied in pure bliss as she gazed at him in wonder, screaming her approval.

"Yes, fuck, yes!"

He smiled, a sharp smile of satisfaction, before he emptied himself into her with a controlled orgasm, teeth gritted.

"Sturgeon," she whispered, overwhelmed. "Don't hold back."

He was still inside her. "I own you, Divine. I own this hotel, I own the casino. I own everything, because I'm the mafia boss, not a bodyguard."

Confused, she stared up at him, pushing her hair back off of her face. "I don't understand. You're a billionaire?"

He nodded. "And I've kidnapped you from your kidnappers. I own you now, body and soul. Tomorrow we marry."

Okay. Plot twist. I didn't see that one coming. No pun intended. I grin, shaking my head. I'm starting to really get invested in the story. Especially the scenes from Divine's point of view because even though the language is a little hyped up, it feels and sounds like Dani to me. It's like getting a peek into her brain and her desires.

This is obviously about Nathan.

Dominating and bossy.

I don't care that she's writing a thinly veiled retelling of her night with another man. I'm loving every minute of watching her blossom into her sexuality.

I can't wait to see her experiencing everything she wants to in bed with me, Nathan, and Crew. She's going to come apart for us in the best way possible.

The last line of this newest scene mentions marriage. I realize that it is technically fiction, and for whatever reason, Dani has chosen to write in the mafia subgenre, but I wonder if marriage is important to her. I hope it is. Not that I'm thinking that far ahead, but that's a mistake I've made in my dating life. I've chosen to spend time with women who aren't interested in marriage or kids and in the end, I've just been disappointed. The ultimate goal for me is a wife and a family.

I make a Facetime call to her. I know I told Crew and Nathan they couldn't make plans with her for tonight, but a phone call is regular communication. It's what I would do normally after reading a scene she's written and I don't want her second guessing what my response is or doubting her talent.

Dani accepts my call. Her face appears, a surprised smile on her face. She's obviously lying in bed. There are pillows propped up behind her. Seeing all that red hair fanned out against the backdrop of fluffy white sheets makes me hard. I want to be in that bed snuggled up against her, dusting kisses across her neck and sliding my fingers through those wavy strands of hair. I want to kiss every single freckle she has, mapping her body with my tongue as I descend between her breasts…

"Hi," she says.

Ripping my thoughts back to the present, I smile. "Hi. I didn't wake you, did I?"

"No, I can't sleep. I've just been tossing and turning."

"A lot on your mind?" I imagine being pursued by three men at once would crowd your thoughts.

"You could say that. It's been an intense few days." She shifts a little and I can see she's sleeping in that Racketeers T-shirt Nathan gave her. The one that's too small.

She's not wearing a bra, obviously, and it gives me a perfect view of her chest and her nipples. Her tight nipples. The bedding is up to her waist, making me wonder what is going on below it.

Is she wearing panties or is she naked, having spent the night touching herself?

"What normally helps you sleep? An orgasm?" I ask.

Her cheeks turn pink but she nods. "Yes."

"Were you working on one before I called?"

"Sort of. I was warming up to it by reading a little. I haven't, um, started yet." The screen tilts and a purple vibrator is on the pillow next to hers.

Damn. I grip my dick and give it a hard squeeze beneath my gray joggers. "I didn't mean to interrupt you. I just wanted to tell you I loved what you wrote. Divine is really coming into her own. We can talk tomorrow though." I'm being polite, of course. Trying to be respectful. I want to stay on this call with her and I want to walk her through getting off with that vibe.

"No, no, we can talk now. I want to talk now." She pushes herself into more of a sitting position and the shirt clings to her nipples and rides up, exposing her midriff.

"That shirt is still too small," I tell her. "But in this context I'm a huge fucking fan."

She glances down at her chest. "Oh, I forgot I had this on." Her fingers brush down the front, as if she is flicking off a piece of lint.

"You could take it off." I prop my phone up onto a vase on my coffee table. "To be fair, I'll take my shirt off first." I strip my T-shirt over my head and toss it on the couch next to me.

Her eyes widen. Her tongue flicks over her bottom lip. "Michael. Oh, my God, you're..." She reaches for a water bottle. It's a pineapple shape. She sucks on the plastic green straw eagerly.

I grin. "You thirsty?"

She nods eagerly. "Very, very thirsty. You're hiding a whole lot of hotness under those golf shirts and button ups."

That makes me grin. "I try to keep in shape."

"That's not trying, that's succeeding."

Yeah, I'm loving this. My ego is being stroked. If only I was in that bed, she could be stroking my dick at the same time. "Your latest scene is great. I wouldn't change a thing. Did Nathan inspire it?"

"A little. Does that bother you?"

"No. I want you to enjoy yourself. That doesn't mean I'm not a little jealous though. I'd like to see you coming myself, Cookie. Can you come for me if I talk you through it?"

"Now?" She sounds a little surprised, but mostly excited.

I knew my sweet girl would like a dirty phone call. She's primed and ready for all kinds of sexiness from all the reading and writing she does.

"Yes, now. Give you a little more inspiration. Take your shirt off. Give me just a glimpse. Then you can cover up. Or not. It's up to you. I just want to know that you're totally naked."

As she shifts a little, tugging her shirt up with one hand, I keep talking. "You're not wearing panties, are you? You've already readied yourself for that vibrator?"

She doesn't hesitate. "Yes. I mean, no, I'm not wearing panties. I need to set the phone down for a second."

"Sure. Should I leave my pants on or take them off?" I ask. I don't want to spring a hard dick on her if she's not into that. Some women want to feel a dick but prefer not to study it too closely. This motherfucking erection I'm sporting right now is going to fill the whole damn screen of her phone if I let it loose.

But Dani makes her feelings very clear. "Off," she demands. "Now."

I can't see her face, because the phone is obviously on her nightstand. I have a view of the ceiling but I can hear fabric rustling and her voice comes through loud and clear. "I want to see you, Michael. All of you."

"Your wish is my command, Cookie." Since my phone is propped up and I'm sitting down, it only takes a second to lift my ass and shove the joggers down to my ankles. I kick them off and I'm lightly stroking my dick when she reappears.

Dani is under the covers, reclining back against the pillows .

"I—

She's about to speak but then she sees me and her words evaporate.

I squeeze the base of my shaft harder, making my dick jump a little.

"Yes," she breathes. "Oh my God."

"Show me your breasts. Just a little bit." There's lotion in the drawer of my end table and I reach over and yank it open, fishing around for the tube, but not wanting to leave the view of the screen.

Dani tilts her head flirtatiously and lets the covers dip ever-so-slightly. I can see the swell of her breasts and nothing more. I groan. "More, baby."

"You want more?" she asks, running the back of her fingers across her fair skin, dipping down below her breasts.

I nod, filling my palm with a dollop of lotion and start to stroke. "More. Will you let me see you?"

She lifts the phone higher so that my view is from above her.

Then she eases the covers down, baring her breasts.

"Fuck, yes." She's got a gorgeous full chest, with tight raspberry-colored nipples that make me want to draw them into my mouth and suck.

Dani shocks me then by kicking the covers with her feet, revealing the whole of her naked body. I'm speechless for a split second before I recover and pump my dick harder.

"Baby. You are absolute perfection. Look at how hard you're making me." I move my phone forward and give her a close up shot before returning it to the coffee table.

"Michael," she breathes, her palm sliding down over her belly and down between her soft folds. She cries out when she makes contact with her clit. "I want you so much. Ever since you kissed me."

I watch her explore her wet pussy with her index finger with rapt fascination. I've never seen anything sexier.

"I want you too, Dani. God, so much. Why don't you fuck that vibrator and pretend it's me?" I ask, keeping my words low and hypnotic. I want her totally lost in the moment, coming to the sound of my voice.

Her lips are parted in pleasure, her eyelids heavy. Her cheeks and her chest are pink from arousal. She nods and her hand disappears from view before reappearing with the vibrator.

Dani doesn't play around. It's immediately between her legs, easing into her pussy. I almost lose it in my hand as I watch the toy sink inside her wet body.

"That's it, baby. Put it right there, right where you need it, making you feel so good. Do you like to just play a little or do you like it deep?"

"Both." She's breathing heavier now, her wrist starting to move faster as she pistons the vibe in and out of her sweet pussy. "I like watching you stroking your cock."

I've matched her rhythm so that I'm going up and down the length of my dick in time to her pushing the vibrator. It's a hot, tortured tease just watching her and not being able to touch a single inch of her, making me throb with need, thighs tense, as I strain to hold back.

"Is the speed on your little toy right?" I ask. "Or do you need more? Less?"

"More," she says eagerly. Her fingers tease around trying to find the button, which is just another form of torture for me.

I want my fingers there, exploring. I want my tongue there. I pause, holding the base of my dick with an iron grip. I'm close. Too close.

But then Dani finds the button and cranks up the speed. I can hear it fire up a few notches, whining a little in her quiet bedroom.

"Michael."

"Is that good? Is that going to make you come?"

She nods and then she's there, shaking her way through an orgasm. She maintains eye contact with me the whole time, and that's all it takes for me to follow. I give two more hard pumps and then I'm pouring over into my palm, murmuring her name over and over in a chant.

A few long seconds later, she yanks the covers back up over herself, like she's just realized what she's been doing. She blows out a breath and shoves her hair back off her damp forehead.

"Wow. I've never done that before."

"No?" Fuck, I love that. I love being her first for something. I love that she felt comfortable being vulnerable like that with me. "I want to make you do it again when I'm there, when I can lean over and taste all that sweet cream."

She takes a shaky breath. "Oh my God. That would be so hot."

"I'd make you clean me up too, Cookie," I tell her, my voice low and gruff.

Her gaze drops to where my hand is coated in my cum.

"I'd like that," she says huskily.

"Yeah, you would," I tell her. "You'd be a good girl and get me hard again. Then I'd fuck you nice and slow and deep, making sure you know that I consider that purple friend of yours a part of the team, but never a replacement for what I can do to you."

She blows out a breath. "Can you come over right now?"

I chuckle low. I don't mind that she's written a sex scene with Nathan as inspiration, but I love the idea that I'll be a part of her naughty imagination going forward too. Again, we're all playing for the same team. "Trust me, I'd love to but not tonight. We're leaving early tomorrow and if I come over there will be no sleeping for either of us." Besides, I did promise the guys I wouldn't see her if they didn't. "But I'll be thinking about you."

She nods. "I'll be thinking about you too."

"Good. And Cookie?"

"Yeah?"

"No using that vibrator again until I'm there with you."

Her eyes widen. "What? But...that's so long from now."

I smile. I love that she wants this and is so eager. "Only a few days. Waiting will make it sweeter."

She pouts and damn, she's so sexy and adorable at the same time.

"Can I use my fingers?"

"Promise to call out my name nice and loud and sweet like you did tonight?"

She pulls her bottom lip between her teeth and nods.

"Okay, then you can use your fingers and think about me."

"Okay." She hesitates, then says, "Will you be using your hand and thinking about me?"

"Like I have every night since we met," I tell her.

Her lips part in surprise, but her eyes are sparkling with a combination of pleasure and mischief. She likes that.

"Be sure you call out my name nice and loud and sweet," she teases.

"There's no one else's name," I tell her honestly. "Only yours."

She suddenly looks a little shy, but again very pleased.

Yeah, this girl needs to get used to not just hearing hot and dirty things from me, but lots of sweet, heartfelt, true emotions too. Because she really is the only woman I think of.

"'Night, Cookie. Sweet dreams."

"'Night, Michael. You too."

"Oh, they will be now."

CHAPTER 16

Dani

I HAVE a lot of energy to start the day. I didn't see any of the guys last night since they were all getting ready for the road trip to Texas, so I actually went to bed early.

Not that I slept early. I was actually up late. I was writing. Then reading. Then hoping one of the guys–or two…or three of the guys–would show up to surprise me. Or ask me to come over. When that didn't happen, my imagination kept me up until Michael video called me.

That had been a very relaxing phone call. I'm warm just thinking about it.

I did hear from all three of them. Yesterday and now again this morning. Michael had texted first.

> I'm going to miss you. Can't wait to see you when I'm back

Then from Nathan came a command.

> I want to see you when I get back. I'll send a car.

Crew had texted late at night.

I can still taste you and can't wait to taste you again

This morning he'd been the first to text and ask how I was.

Sore and sleepy. I've been...busy lately

I'd added a winky emoji and an eggplant emoji.

Michael had greeted me shortly after that.

Good morning, beautiful. I loved the new pages and discussing them last night with you. ;) You're amazing.

I was still floating from that.

Nathan had also texted this morning.

We will not be going out. Plan accordingly.

I laughed and texted back.

I assume I don't need to pack panties.

Correct

.

Yes, he gets right to the point and he's dirty, but even his messages make me float.

I love having attention from these men. It's all different kinds of attention and I'm soaking it up like it's sunshine and I'm a newly budded flower.

I end up going through the rest of the inventory I need to do, dusting my entire bookshop, doing some website updates, and sending out a newsletter to my customers. All before two o'clock. At two I sit down behind the front counter, drag in a deep breath, and feel a strange exhaustion sweep over me.

Okay, it isn't that strange. I know exactly where it's coming from. Yes, in part, it's because I haven't slept much the last few nights. Between staying up late writing after Michael took me home, my night with Nathan, followed by my big afternoon with Crew, my body is running on adrenaline, and caffeine.

But it isn't just the lack of sleep. My body feels like it's buzzing. Just the thought of any of the men and my body heats and endorphins flood my system. And I feel like I'm constantly thinking about one of them.

Or all of them.

From the amazing way Michael kissed me, to all of the dirty things Nathan said and did, to the nymphomaniac who took over my body in the art gallery with Crew.

I would almost call what I'm feeling... giddiness. This is so unlike me.

I love it.

I love this new side of Dani. Danielle. Cookie. I love that they all call me something different. I love that they all treat me differently.

Michael is so sweet and romantic. Nathan was so bossy and dirty. Crew is so playful and fun. I'm different with each one of them, too. It's like they each tap into a different part of my personality. And I like all of these sides. I love being romanced. Michael makes me feel sweet and adored. But I also love being wanton and being able to say all the filthy things I want with Nathan. He makes me feel empowered in a way I've never felt before. And it's so fun to tease and flirt with a guy like Crew. I would have never thought I had it in me to draw or keep the attention of a guy like that, but he makes me feel like all those sexy, fun, confident girls in high school and college I wanted to be.

And I love that I don't have to choose between them.

I can tell Nathan doesn't love the idea that I'm seeing the other men, but I've been honest and told him that's what was happening, and he certainly hadn't pulled away. That gave me a thrill.

Even if he didn't embrace the idea enthusiastically, he is still obviously willing to go along with it to be with me.

And Crew had taken me out *after* knowing I'd been with Nathan.

Michael had talked me through a hot session of phone sex, also knowing that the scene I'd written had been inspired by Nathan.

They all know about one another and they are all still texting me, thinking about me, wanting to see me.

I really can have them all. At least one at a time.

My heart starts racing thinking about bringing up the idea of having them all at once. I really think Crew and Michael will at least consider it. Nathan is the only one I'm not sure of. But if he says no...I'll be disappointed, for sure. But I'll still have two hot, sweet men who make my heart pound and my panties wet. Two will still be a fantasy come true.

But three would be even better

Yeah, yeah, I tell my wanton inner voice. But I grin. Men are like cookies...why have one, or even two, if you could have three.

I have to admit at the moment, though, knowing they're all out of town, and that none of them can suddenly show up and surprise me, lets me relax a little.

I'm sore, I'm tired, and I need an early bedtime tonight.

I grin even as I blush thinking about those sore muscles. Those muscles haven't been worked out like that in... ever.

I also want to get some more writing done.

I already dictated some notes this morning as I was blow drying my hair because I didn't want to lose them. These three guys are giving me plenty of fodder for my Habanero writing. This is going to be some of the best I've ever done.

Will I still be able to write this well when I'm no longer seeing these guys?

I'd already thought Nathan and I were done. But I guess I get one more date. There is no way a forty-year-old billionaire is going to keep seeing me, though. There is no way he's going to make a twenty-four-year-old his actual girlfriend.

Crew and I might see each other a couple more times. I hope we do. He is so much fun, and brings out a playful side of me that I didn't realize I have.

But Crew McNeill can have any woman. He literally has women throwing themselves at him every single night. There is no way he was going to find me interesting for anything long term.

He's on the road tonight, in fact. He'll have tons of offers in just a few hours.

My heart squeezes as the thought occurs to me. I don't know what he'll do about those offers, and honestly it's none of my business. We aren't in a committed relationship. Hell, I had sex with another guy the night before Crew took me out. If Crew takes another woman to bed tonight, I can't say a thing about it.

But the stab of jealousy is real. I can admit it. I'm such a hypocrite.

Then there's Michael Hughes. I sigh happily thinking of him. Michael is boyfriend material. For sure. He's someone I could see myself dating seriously. He's eleven years older than me and sure, this might just be sex for him too, but it doesn't feel that way. He's not quite as gruff and bossy as Nathan, but he does give me lots of delicious I-want-to-take-care-of-you-in-*every*-way vibes that I want to wallow in.

The little bell above my shop door jingles as a pretty woman with long dark curls steps inside.

I stand and paste on a smile, pushing thoughts of my suddenly very full social life to the back of my mind.

"Hi, I'm looking for Danielle Larkin," the woman says.

"I'm Danielle."

"Oh, hi!" Her smile is warm. "This is for you." She comes forward and hands me a gift bag and a single rose.

A week ago, I would have been very confused by this. Today

I'm actually delighted to find that the only question here is, which of the three guys is the rose from?

I know I'm smiling like an idiot.

But two seconds later I realize I know exactly who it's from.

Speak of the devil. This is from Michael. The red rose is the giveaway without even looking in the package.

I know my guys—yes, my guys. I'm already thinking about them as mine. That's going to be a problem when it all ends. I know that. I know my heart is going to be a little broken. But for right now my entire body feels warm and mushy. Including my heart.

Michael is absolutely a single red rose kind of guy.

It's way too traditional for Nathan. He would come up with something far more over-the-top and exotic. If nothing else, there would be six dozen roses, not just one. And Crew would never send flowers. That's way too old-fashioned and predictable. He's more the type to send balloons. Or a giant frosted cookie. Or a singing telegram.

Actually, he's more the type to show up with the balloons and do the singing himself.

I take the rose, smiling as I lift it to my nose. "Thank you."

The woman nods. "Of course. Do you have a message in return by chance?"

I give her a puzzled look. "I'll just text him later."

Her face falls in disappointment. "Dang. I was hoping for some info. I've never seen him like this."

I can't help but laugh. "You know Michael personally?"

She smiles. "Yes. My husband is actually one of the trainers in the Racketeers' athletic department. I don't normally do this kind of thing, of course, but he couldn't figure out a way to get this particular gift to you. They were getting everything ready to get on the plane to leave and he was talking about how he just had to get a special gift to someone before he left. I volunteered because I thought it was romantic." She laughs and gestures to the bag. "I mean, I think it's sweet he's trying to take care of you. And I assumed because of the rose that you're not just a friend or a cousin or something."

My eyes widen. I didn't realize that Michael was talking about me. I shake my head. "No, not a cousin."

She must've read my surprise, because she quickly reassures me. "He didn't say anything specific. Just that he really wanted you to know that he was thinking about you while he was gone. But he wasn't sure how to get this combination of things to you. I don't know what it means, but it was important to him."

Curious, I now dig through the bag. I pull out the little note that's tucked inside first. It's a plain piece of paper, like something he just swiped off his desk, but he'd taped it shut so no one would read it.

I can't have you sore when I get back. Take a long soak and then I'll kiss it better when I see you.

Whoa. We haven't had sex yet. But I feel connected to him anyway. As much as I do to Nathan and Crew. Sharing my stories with him has felt intimate in a whole different way than what I've done with Nathan and Crew. Michael is more... sensual. He's romantic. Things are going slower with him, but that feels right. Somehow I know that sex with Michael will feel more like making love. It will be long, and hot, but he will be very into lots of different sensations, lots of touching, drawing things out.

I know my cheeks are blazing hot, but I smile as I pull out bath salts, bubble bath, two candles, and an eye mask. Everything I need for a relaxing bath.

Of course my hot doctor is literally taking care of my body, even over the distance.

Even though he didn't cause any of the pain.

Wait a second... how does he know...

I put a hand over my mouth.

Was Crew running his mouth? He'd better not be talking about me in the Racketeers locker room!

I look up at the woman. "Um… thank you."

"I hope your ankle…or whatever… feels better soon," she says.

Oh, my God. I nod. "I'm sure it will. And I'll definitely text him. I really appreciate you going to the trouble of getting this to me."

"Well, Michael is a special guy. He means a lot to the guys on the team. He's more than just a doctor, you know? He's kind of a mentor. Definitely someone everyone looks up to. And not just the players. Everybody in that department. He's been so great to my husband. So, anytime we see anything that makes him happy, everybody piles on."

My stomach flips at the idea that I might be something that so obviously makes Michael happy. They haven't even seen me with him. But evidently the idea of me makes him happy. It is a very odd feeling that strangers can know this, but I love the idea that Michael could actually have feelings like that for me.

It's going to be really hard going all these days without seeing the guys. And I want to see all of them. Equally.

There is no way I could choose between these guys.

"What are some other things that make Michael that happy that you all notice?" I ask her.

Her eyes brighten and I can tell she genuinely likes Michael. Which, of course, makes me like her. "Oh, he discovered this new microbrewery in town, and he was talking about it one day and the guys all got together and bought him like three cases of the beer." She laughs. "And then there's this movie theater where they show classic movies. He was talking about it one day and how much he loves going there, and all the guys got together and bought him a gift certificate. I don't think he'll have to buy a movie ticket for the next two years."

I grin. I love that Michael is surrounded by people who care about him like that. And I love that he openly enjoys things so much that the people around him notice. He is such a good guy. And now I miss him even more than I did before.

"Well, again, I really appreciate the trouble you went to."

She shakes her head and waves her hand as if it was no big deal. "I hope I see you around. Hopefully Michael will bring you to some team's family functions."

Yeah. That would be awesome. Except that there are two other people on the team that would also maybe want me to be with them. Or who could, at least, make it awkward if I'm there with Michael.

Ugh, this could be complicated.

A little of that giddy, happy cloud I was floating on seems to diffuse.

I force a smile and nod. "Yeah, maybe."

We say goodbye and she makes her way out of the store.

I whip out my phone and text Crew.

You better not be talking about me in the locker room, McNeill!

He doesn't respond. Dammit. He's probably on the plane. Or in a team meeting. Or warming up. Hell, I don't know what a day on the road to an away game is like.

I spin on my heel and yell, "Luna!"

Late morning is usually a little quieter for her as well. It's after the initial morning coffee and pastry rush, but before people come in for their afternoon pick-me-up.

She looks up as I storm into the bakery. "What's going on?"

I hold up the bath items and rose. "I got a gift."

"Yeah, yeah." She bends back over the pastry she's adding chocolate swirls to. "Quit rubbing it in."

"Rubbing what in?" I drop the items on the counter next to her.

"You have three boyfriends, and they're all texting you constantly because they can't even spend twenty-four hours away from you now. I don't know how you went from my awkward nerdy little friend who has been sexually repressed since those fucking assholes in college clipped your wings to this femme fatale who now has three hot, rich men drooling over her, but…" She looks up and gives me a grin. "I really like it. Being absolutely adored and sexually worshiped looks good on you."

I quickly glance around the bakery to see if anyone overheard. We are blissfully alone. "Sexually worshiped? Who said that?"

"Your face. The glow about you. The fact that you're walking about six inches off the floor," Luna teases. "And yes, I hate you for it. I'm also so jealous. But I love everything about it. You totally deserve this."

I lean onto the counter, and pin her with a serious stare. "And you swear you don't care that one of them is your brother?"

"I absolutely don't. I'm thrilled that he is smart enough to want to date a woman like you."

I shake my head. "I don't know if I would go so far as to say we're dating. You know as well as I do that Crew's going to get tired of this. We're having fun now, and I hope that we do it for a little bit longer, but there's no way we're going to get serious."

"Why not?" Luna frowns. "Is Crew not someone you would be serious with?"

I think about that for a moment. She's my best friend. She deserves the truth, especially when it's about her brother. I swallow. "Actually, I think I could be serious about Crew. He makes me laugh. He makes me happy. He makes me feel different… lighter, sexier, fun. He makes me look at things differently. And he just has this way about him of making everything more colorful, and more laid-back. But I know he's a hard worker. I know the things that he's serious about always get his full attention and full energy."

Luna looks relieved. Which also makes me feel relieved. I would hate it if this was weird between us.

"Good. Because eventually Crew is going to get serious about someone. You are absolutely the type of girl that could happen with. He's known you forever. And he's finally settling down in other ways. Sure, early in his career, he was a playboy and having fun and going out and playing the part of the goodtime guy. But now he's back in Chicago, I think he wants to stay here. He wants to make this his home, his team. And I think that he wants the city, and the team management, to see him as serious and to keep him here. I mean, he's always going to be a good time, that's just his personality. But I think that he would like this to be a long-term gig. Settling down with someone here makes sense."

All of that makes my heart beat faster. Crew is a great guy. And if he wanted to get serious, and really was going to stay in Chicago, then I can't help but think that I would love to be the girl that he got serious with. I love his family, I love this city, I love…him.

Oh, God. Is that possible?

But, could I be falling in love with him? I've known him for a long time. I like him, I trust him, I want him.

That could all add up to falling for him.

"You don't think he's talking about me in the locker room do you?" I ask Luna.

She frowns. But she hesitates, thinking about it. Which I appreciate. Then she shakes her head. "No. Other girls? A hot hook-up? Maybe. But you? No way."

And that feels right. I agree. But then how did Michael find out I was sore?

Of course, Luna's mention of the Racketeers' management, along with me being sore, makes me think of Nathan.

"Well, I can't imagine being serious with Nathan. I mean, he's a lot older than me, he's a billionaire, there's no way he's gonna want to get serious with a woman who is so much younger who can't even make her own business work. But, we had one really hot night and I do not regret it. I would do that again in a heartbeat."

"I am so happy for you and still waiting for details," Luna

says, holding her hand up. I give her a high five and we both laugh.

"Dirty. Bossy. Dirty. And five times," I tell her.

She stares at me. "Oh my God."

I nod. "Right?"

"Who is that from? I mean, I kind of wanted it to be from my brother. I want to think that he's cool enough to send you a rose afterwards, but that feels billionaire-ish." Luna laughs. "Of course, my brother is a millionaire. I keep forgetting that. But a rose doesn't seem like Crew's style."

I laugh. "Exactly what I thought. But it's not really Nathan's style either."

"No?"

I lift the rose to my nose and pull in a long breath. "This is from Michael."

Now it's Luna's turn to lean onto the counter. She pops both elbows on the counter and then rests her chin on her hands. "Yes. Tell me about the hot doctor."

"Well, we haven't slept together. Yet. But we had really hot phone sex and I know we *will* sleep together. He's kind of more the type for me to date, actually. I can see myself getting serious with him. He's older than me too. But he's romantic. Sophisticated. I mean, he's very sexy. But he's a little less intense than Nathan. And I swear, just the kiss he gave me the other night was almost enough to set me on fire."

"This is amazing," Luna said. She fans herself with her hand. "If I'm not getting any, at least I'm in the front row for this."

"What happened to Kyle?"

Luna shrugs. "We mutually ghosted each other. It just didn't feel right."

"I'm sorry." The door in the bookshop jingles again as someone comes in. "Hang on," I tell her. "I'll be right back."

I poke my head around the archway that separates our two businesses. "Hi, can I help you?"

It's a guy in a T-shirt and jeans, wearing a ball cap, he's carrying a paper bag. "Yeah, I have your delivery."

"I didn't order anything."

He looks down at his phone. "This is the address. Dani Larkin?"

"Yes."

"Then this is for you." He thrusts the package at me and turns and leaves.

I frown. The package is a plain white bag. I open it as I return to the bakery. But I freeze halfway across the floor.

Oh, no, he didn't.

But he did. And I know who this gift is from too.

This is definitely from Crew.

"What is it?" Luna asks.

"Um." I look up. "I'm not sure I should show you."

She straightens and props a hand on her hip. "Now you have to."

"It's from your brother."

She rolls her eyes. "Is it something dumb?"

Hmm. No. I would not call this 'dumb'. "It's…" Finally, I just blow out a breath and cross to the counter. I set it down and pull out the two items. The first is cotton candy flavored lube. Which of course makes me think about when he said he'd like to take me to the circus or a county fair. Crew can even make lube playful and fun.

The second is a set of three dildos. Each one bigger than the last. And the package says they can specifically be used for… ahem…stretching.

"Oh." Luna says. "Yeah, okay. Not dumb. Also probably didn't need to see that."

I just shake my head and pull the note out.

Be sure you have that lube with you.
I love eating cotton candy.

And stretch while I'm gone.
Only good pain, sweetheart.

A winky emoji and a tongue emoji are at the bottom of his note.

He's so…much. But I'm laughing even as I look up at his sister. Who he had to know would be here when this delivery arrived.

She holds up her hand. "Please don't read that out loud."

Before I can respond to that, the door of the bookshop opens again, the bell tinkling.

I sigh. "Hang on."

There are two women standing just inside the shop door. "Hi, can I help you?"

"Yeah, we're here for Danielle," one of the women says with a big smile.

I'm starting to feel overwhelmed. "That's me."

"We're here for your massage," the shorter, blonder of the two says.

I stare at them. "My… what?"

"Mr. Armstrong sent us," she explains. "We're here to give you an in-home spa treatment. Starting with a full-body massage. He said you have some muscle soreness. You'll also be having a manicure, pedicure, and facial."

"And I'm here to give the same treatment to your friend Luna," the taller blonde says. "Are you ready?"

"Yes!"

Luna has come into the shop behind me. She gives me a big grin. "I was Team Crew before because you being my sister-in-law would rock but I could pretty easily become Team Nathan if this is how he rolls."

I roll my eyes. "If I told these three men that I love giraffes Crew would buy me a huge, cute, stuffed giraffe and take me to the zoo. Michael would find some amazing book for us to read about a romantic safari. Probably a spicy one. And Nathan would have me on an airplane to Africa."

Luna links her arm with mine. "Okay, honestly? I'm Team All Three of Them because you deserve it."

I think about that as I lock up the bookshop and bakery while Luna leads the two masseuses up to our apartment for our spa treatments.

I think maybe I'm Team All Three of Them too.

My phone chimes with a message and I pull it out.

It's from Crew.

Of course not I'm not talking about you in the locker room, sweetheart.

Then how did Michael know I'm sore today?

Oh, well, I talked to Michael. And Nathan. But not in the locker room.

I stare at the message.

Oh.

My.

God.

You what????????

We talked about you. In Nathan's office. And on the plane.

I stare at the message. They were talking about me. My first reaction is shock. But then I realize there's no way I should feel shocked. All of these guys are very sexually confident and open. Nathan and Crew already had a confrontation about all of this. And they know Michael took me home from the game that first night. I can imagine Michael being mature and...actually, I can easily picture Michael being a mediator between the other two.

But the "in Nathan's office" finally sinks in.

Nathan called you all in for a meeting?

That also doesn't seem all that shocking. If Nathan wanted to see me again. I honestly hadn't thought that was the case.

Yep. And it's all good. But we're all concerned about you being sore. Well, not Nathan. He seemed proud. He's an asshole. You should dump him. Just date me and Hughes.

I read that message over three times.

It also doesn't surprise me that Crew would have told them I was sore. That seems…almost sweet. Or something? Like he would have gone to the other guys who care about me and would have said, "Guys, she's sore. We need to take care of her," and then they all did that in their own way.

I press a hand to my stomach. That should seem so weird. Three men talking about me. Talking about how I was sore from sex. From sex with two of them. But they all got concerned and then sent things over to take care of me. One in a sweet way, and one in a playful, funny way. But both things that would actually help. And one just being smug that he made me still feel him two days later.

My body heats thinking all of that through.

I am so in over my head here.

Hey, I'm just kidding. You don't have to dump Nathan

Crew is evidently taking my long silence as annoyance.

Though fuck he's wound tight. But we all want to see you when we get back. So you're welcome for the stretching program.

He adds another winky face and then three eggplant emojis.

My heart starts pounding and my palms start sweating.

Wait…What. The. Hell??

Three eggplant emojis…

"Are you okay?" Luna asks.

I look up. She's standing on the stairs.

"Um. I'm…"

"You look upset. Or confused." She tips her head. "Or…stunned?"

I nod. "All of those."

"What's going on?"

"The guys are talking about me. Together."

Her eyes widen. "They're fighting over you? That's amazing."

But I shake my head. "I don't think so."

"So, one of them is telling the others to back off?"

That would be Nathan if it was anyone.

The thought hits me out of the blue. But then I shake my head as I think about Crew's message. "I think they're talking about… how to work this out. How to all date me." Then I frown. "Without me."

Crew texts again.

> You better rest up over the next couple of days, because when we're back, you're not going to be getting much sleep.

When we're back. Yeah, they've definitely been talking about me.

Behind my back.

"This could get complicated," Luna says. "Who are you going to choose?"

That's the question.

Or is it?

Who would I choose?

How could I possibly choose between them?

I shake my head. "I don't think I can," I tell her.

"What do you mean?"

"I think that—" I take a breath. "I think it's all of them. Or none of them."

"Wow."

"Yeah. I need to have a talk with my guys."

CHAPTER 17

Nathan

OUR PLANE TOUCHES down in Chicago around four-thirty. It's been three days since I've seen Danielle and I'm beyond restless. I've texted her twice, but I'm not really the type to have long text conversations. I'm also not a talk-for-hours on the phone, so I haven't called. I've jacked off multiple times to thoughts of her though.

And I miss her.

So fucking bad I ache with it.

Not just her body, but her sweet smile, her blushes, her sassiness, just…her.

Dammit.

That wasn't supposed to happen. She could have just been a fun one-night thing. Even a fling for a few weeks. But I can already feel that she's more than that.

For a man who never lets there be strings attached to my sexual relationships, there have been strings with this girl since the moment I laid eyes on her.

The possessiveness I feel for her when I know she's been with McNeill and Hughes is unprecedented. The way I tried to stake my claim with them before we left for the road trip was insane.

And now, my guts are twisted thinking about how we move forward.

These men are not bowing out and Danielle clearly doesn't want them to.

So...I'm left with a choice.

Let her go. Or find a way to make this work with two other men in her life.

Actually, there's no choice.

I want her.

McNeill and Hughes are now a part of my life in a very non-professional way. And I have no idea how that's going to look. Or how I will feel as we go forward.

I pull my phone from my inside jacket pocket the moment the plane's wheels touch the runway.

Hughes is seated in the seat across the aisle from me. He also has his phone in hand. He looks over. "You better check your messages before you send your car for her."

He knows exactly what I was about to do.

I also don't know if I'll get used to that. The man can read me—seemingly can read most people—with an uncanny accuracy. I've never had anyone around who notices or predicts my thoughts and reactions so easily. I've never had anyone pay that much attention to me. Now I have both him and Danielle.

I don't respond to him, but I do open my texts. I have easily a dozen. Most are business. But there's one from Danielle. I feel my heart kick against my ribs just at the sight of her name.

What the hell? I've never had a woman affect me like this.

I want to see you. Five-thirty. The Moonlight Bistro.

I start to respond. I don't want to go out. I need to see her. In private. I told her as much the other day. But I pause and look over at Hughes, understanding dawning. "She texted you too?"

He nods. "Moonlight Bistro. Five-thirty."

My stomach knots. Fuck.

I pivot in my seat. "McNeill!" I bark.

Crew's head pops up over the seats. "Yeah, Boss?" He smirks.

Jesus, he drives me nuts. It's like having this very private, very personal connection through Danielle makes him even cockier and more sarcastic with me.

"Up here. Now." I'm still actually his boss, though, and in public, especially around the team, we will act our parts.

He undoes his seatbelt and ambles down the aisle toward me even though the plane is still taxiing on the runway. We get a frown from our flight attendants, but this is a private flight so we bend the rules.

He drops into the seat next to me. "What's up?"

"Did you get a text?" Hughes asks, his voice low.

"Yep. Five-thirty date." He grins.

"Not just you," Hughes says.

McNeill's grin dims slightly. "Oh yeah?"

I hold up my phone. "We've all been summoned."

He nods thoughtfully. "Our girl has something to say."

"To all of us. At once," Hughes agrees.

Well…fuck.

We're off the plane, bags gathered, walking toward the airport entrance thirty minutes later.

"My car is at the curb," I say. McNeill and Hughes have both stuck close. I suppose we're all feeling a little edgy. Danielle wants to see all of us, at the same place and time.

"I parked my car in the garage," Hughes says, gesturing toward the covered parking garage.

"I'll have someone bring it to you," I say. I text one of my assistants who is still getting his bags inside.

Hughes starts to protest.

"We're all going to the same place to see Danielle. We need to formulate a plan," I tell him.

"A plan?"

"To talk her out of dumping our asses," McNeill says.

Hughes looks at him, then at me. "Do you think that's what this is?"

I press my lips together, but nod. "It could be. We've possibly overwhelmed her."

Hughes seems to think that over for a second. Then he blows out a breath. "Dammit."

He digs his keys out of his pocket. Brad, my young assistant, comes huffing up to the curb just then. "Yes, Mr. Armstrong?"

"Take Dr. Hughes's keys and drive his car to his apartment. Then take a car home. You can put it on your expense report."

He takes the keys and starts for the garage.

McNeill shakes his head. "It's good to be the boss."

"Remember that," I tell him. Then I point at the car. "Get in."

I'd love to be the boss in this group.

But I have a feeling the real boss of us is Danielle.

We drive for about five minutes, all of us seemingly lost in thought, before Hughes says, "Maybe I shouldn't have had phone sex with her the other night."

McNeill whips around to face him. "When?"

"The night before we left." Hughes actually looks apologetic.

"You told us not to do anything with her!" McNeill says, his tone accusatory.

"When did I say not to do anything?" Hughes asks.

"You said not to see her or..." McNeill frowns. "Something. You basically said we should leave her alone."

"I said not to do anything you wouldn't normally do. Dani and I talk on the phone. That wasn't unusual. It just got...a little out of hand."

McNeill narrows his eyes. "Or a little *in* hand, right Doc? What the hell?"

"I didn't call her for phone sex," Hughes says. "We were talking about her writing and one thing led to another."

"Her writing?"

"Yes, her writing," Hughes says. He sounds frustrated which is a sure sign we're all short-tempered. He's always the cool one. "She's a writer. She's working on getting published and I'm helping her."

"I...didn't know that," McNeill says with a frown.

I didn't either.

"Anyway," Hughes says. "It's been a lot in a short amount of time. We're all pretty intense guys. Maybe we just need to give her some space and time."

"No," I respond immediately.

"She might be about to dump us," McNeill says. He's leaning back in the seat, one ankle crossed over the other, looking completely relaxed. But his expression is serious. "We need to do something."

He's actually concerned about this meeting with Danielle.

He cares about her.

The thought shouldn't be a shock. It's not. He's known her for a long time and they clearly have some chemistry. But Crew McNeill comes off as a cocky, do-whatever-he-wants, always-lands-on-his-feet Golden Boy. I know he cares about hockey. I know he cares about the Racketeers and playing for his hometown team. The ice is the only place I see intensity and anything other than smiles and nonchalance.

Until now.

Until Danielle.

"I agree with McNeill," I say, the words surprising me as much as they clearly do the other men. "We need to convince her not to walk away. But I don't think backing off is the right thing. We need to show her that we're all serious about her. About this." I look at both of the other men, meeting their gazes directly. "If we are serious about her."

"I am," Hughes says, easily.

"Me too," McNeill says.

"I mean serious," I tell him. "No other women. No partying. Committed."

He nods. "I'll propose tonight if you want me to."

Jesus, I do not want that.

At least…I don't think I do.

I frown. What would I do if Crew got down on one knee in front of Danielle?

Suddenly I don't think I'd punch him.

I might…just get down on my knee next to him.

What?

I scrub a hand over my face.

This is all fucking with my head. But I do want them to be serious about her.

Danielle deserves to have commitment, people who are dedicated to her happiness, to protecting her, to making her happy.

And, as strange as it is, these men seem to be all of those things…and I like them for that.

McNeill had no reason to stand up to me the other day in my office. I'm more powerful than he is. I'm his fucking boss. I could have fired him on the spot. But he didn't back down. He said he wanted her and he faced me straight on, honestly, without flinching, risking his position on the team—the team I know means everything to him—to say it to me.

Is it fucking weird that there are three of us who want to be involved with her? Yes. But why am I suddenly feeling relieved that I'm not walking into that bar to see Danielle alone?

With McNeill and Hughes with me, I have a really, really good deal for her.

"Then we all go in there, we tell her how we feel, that we want her, and—" I take a deep breath and say something I almost never say. "—we let her call the shots."

I never let other people take charge. I never turn things over to other people.

But Danielle has me wrapped around her little finger. Already. And I'm ready to do whatever it takes to be with her.

Hughes nods. "Okay. We let her call the shots."

"Unless her call is walking away," McNeill adds. "That's not happening."

Yeah, McNeill and I are definitely on the same side here.

My life is just getting more and more strange.

We finally pull up in front of the bar. I instruct my driver to wait. If things go my way, we'll be needing the car to take us to my apartment soon.

Hughes is the first through the door. McNeill holds the door for me and stops me before I step inside.

"We've got this, right?" he asks.

I nod. "We do. If we do it together." And I realize I mean that. The three of us have something special to offer Danielle. All of us. Together. Something I think she wants and needs.

McNeill claps me on the shoulder. "Okay. Lead the way, Boss."

And again, I realize that I'm probably the boss for only about another minute.

The Moonlight Bistro is a bar but it's a sophisticated place that specializes in martinis. The interior decor is black and silver, with a marble floor, and a twenty-foot arched ceiling with a skylight in the center where a frosted glass "moon" hangs. There are high glass-topped tables with black leather stools throughout the room in front of a stage with a black baby grand piano. Around the perimeter of the room are black leather booths with high backs that promise seclusion and private conversations.

The hostess leads us to one of the booths where Danielle is already seated. With a half-empty pale pink martini in front of her.

She looks up as we approach and straightens when she sees us. Her mouth curves into a gorgeous smile and my stomach unknots slightly. She doesn't look upset. Or like she's about to break up with three boyfriends.

"Hi," she says, slightly breathless as the hostess leaves us.

Michael slides into the booth next to her, draping an arm over her shoulders, leaving McNeill and I to sit together opposite them.

Hughes leans over and kisses her cheek, then nuzzles her neck. "Missed you," he says softly.

She's blushing prettily, but smiling up at him when he pulls back. "Missed you too."

I want to kiss her so badly, my hands clench into fists to keep from reaching across the table. But I realize that I don't actually feel jealous watching Hughes kiss her. I love the way she's smiling at him. She looks so genuinely happy. Clearly she's very comfortable with him. She leans into him, not bothered at all by the way his big hand rests on her shoulder.

"Give me some of that." McNeill doesn't care that there's a table in between them. He leans over, hooks his index finger in the front of her blouse, urging her up out of her seat.

She giggles, but leans over the table, meeting him partway as Hughes sweeps her glass out of the way before they knock it over.

McNeill cups the back of her head and his kiss isn't sweet. Or quick. He seals his mouth over hers and is clearly French kissing her deeply.

When he lets her go, she looks slightly dazed and the tip of her tongue darts out, running over her lower lip.

"Hi," he says huskily.

"Hi," she returns, smiling.

He lets her go and Michael tucks her up against him again.

Her gaze flickers to me. "Hi, Nathan."

"Danielle." I let my gaze travel over her face, her freshly kissed lips, down her throat and the pink flush there, to the upper swells of her breasts in the scoop neck blouse she's wearing. "You look gorgeous."

"Th-thank you." She stutters over the words, and presses a hand to her chest.

I lift a brow. She seems nervous around me. She's smiling, but it's not the bright, happy smile she gave Michael, or the playful grin she gave Crew.

I reach across the table, palm up. She knows what to do without any words and that pleases me. She puts her hand in mine. I run my thumb over the back of her knuckles, then lift her hand to my mouth. I brush my lips over her knuckles, then turn her palm up and kiss the center. "I'm so happy to see you."

She dips her head, but she's smiling now. A more genuine smile. "I'm glad to see you too."

"Thanks for the sweet pussy pics before the game," Crew says. "My new favorite good luck charm."

Danielle's eyes go wide as she looks at him. "You got pictures from someone before your game?" she asks. Then she glances around and lowers her voice. "It wasn't me."

"No, I didn't. But that would have been nice," he tells her, one brow arched. "Were you too busy studying all the dick pics Doc sent you to even think about me and my needs?"

She blushes again but laughs. "I didn't realize you were in need of a good luck charm from me. You could have asked."

He's watching her with amusement, but also clear affection and I feel a warmth in my chest that surprises me.

"First, it is noted that you'll send pics if I ask," Crew says. "Second, I guess I didn't need them, since I scored three times, but maybe that was from actually being *in* your magic pussy." His voice drops to a lower, rougher tone. "So we need to keep that in the routine. Third, I notice you aren't denying studying certain photos from our hot Doc to the point of distraction."

Danielle gives Michael a shy, but adorably sexy look. "It was a video," she says, her eyes locked on Hughes' gaze. "And I'm not going to deny it was distracting."

"You did not record it," Hughes says, his voice gruff. "Did you?"

Danielle lifts a hand and taps her temple. "It's all saved right up here."

He laughs and hugs her tighter, bringing his mouth closer to her ear. "Same, Cookie. And I've replayed it too. More than once."

She's fucking glowing. These men make her happy. She's flirting and teasing with them, clearly feeling adored.

Because they do, quite obviously, adore her.

Crew is still his cocky, laid-back self. Michael is still composed and polished. But they're both so noticeably happy to be here with her and her with them.

And clearly Crew and Michael are friends. They like each other. They're comfortable there together. With Dani.

Every dynamic at this table makes me…want to be a part of it.

But Dani's having a hard time making eye contact with me. I'm definitely more intense than either of the other two, and with all of us here together, it seems evident that she's less comfortable with me.

I hate that. But I love what they do for her. They offer her something different from what I do. And from what each other does. And she's basking in all of it.

"So what did you want to talk to us about?" Michael asks. "Or did you just want to be wined and dined by your three favorite men?" He looks across the table at both McNeill and me. "We're all yours."

McNeill stretches and tucks both hands behind his head. "Yep. Just tell us what you want sweetheart."

I nod when her eyes find mine. "Anything."

She nods. Then reaches for her martini. She lifts it to her lips, takes a huge gulp, swallows, and sets the glass down.

"Okay. Well, I did want to talk to you. And I thought seeing all three of you together would be best, and easiest, so you all hear the same thing from me and I don't have to have this conversation more than once." She looks at each of us. "And so we can all talk about it together."

Michael hugs her even closer. "That's a great idea."

She looks up at him and smiles. His praise seems to calm her.

"We've all been thinking about you non-stop, Dani," Crew tells her, abandoning his laid-back posture and leaning in. He reaches out and takes her hand between both of his. "Give us a chance to give you everything you want."

She smiles at him and I see even more tension leave her. "Okay."

He looks eager. "Okay? You'll let us all give you what you want?"

She swallows, but then looks at me. Our gazes lock as she says, "That's what I want. All of you. With me. At the same time."

Heat and lust rock through me.

I brace for the jealousy, the possessiveness, the *hell no* to follow.

But it doesn't happen. I'm shocked, but it's true.

Looking at her cuddled up against Michael, her hand sandwiched between Crew's two hands, looking at me hopefully, I realize there is only one answer I can give.

She takes a breath before I can respond and says, "I want you all. I have feelings for you all. I can't choose. I don't want to. So I either want all of you, or…none of you. And when I say all of you, yes, I want to go to dinner, and watch TV, and talk about my day, and make breakfast together. I love the surprise gifts, and the texting, and the phone calls, and missing you while you're gone, and being excited to see you when you get back. I want to talk about books." She looks up at Michael. "And I want to go to the circus and county fairs, and art museums." She shoots Crew a little smile. Then she looks at me. "I want to learn all about hockey and go to every home game." Then she focuses on the nearly empty martini glass. "But I also want the sex. With all of you. Maybe sometimes one at a time. But also…" She wets her lips and I see Michael squeeze her shoulder while Crew squeezes her hand in encouragement. "Together. All of us."

Michael watches her for a few seconds, but she just sits quietly, not looking at any of us. Michael drags his gaze first to Crew, then to me.

Finally, he says, "If everyone is in and willing and we talk it all out, this can work. The time I did it, it was a lot of fun."

Danielle looks up at him quickly. Her mouth is open in a little O.

He reaches out and lifts her chin with his finger, closing her mouth. "Yes, I've done this before."

"You are full of surprises," she tells him.

He leans in, their noses almost touching. "You have no idea." He drags his finger along her jaw. "But I look forward to showing you."

And fuck…I want to see it. I'm shocked as the thought hits me, but I want to watch Michael light Danielle up. He already does with just a finger against her face. I can only imagine what he can do given free reign over her whole body.

Crew gives a low whistle, also watching them. "Damn. I am in," he says. He looks at each of us. "Probably no surprise, but I'm fine with letting everyone know what I think and how I'm feeling about things." He turns his attention back on Danielle. "And Dani, sweetheart, right now, I feel like giving you about a dozen orgasms before the sun comes up tomorrow and making you feel like a fucking goddess."

She sucks in a little breath.

"But making breakfast together and a trip to the circus…or another art museum is definitely also on my list." He gives her a wink.

She grins at him.

Then she looks at me.

And I would give this woman the goddamned moon.

Even if it means having two other men help me pull it down and carry it to her.

So I say the only thing I can. "The car is right outside and my apartment is the closest."

CHAPTER 18

Crew

THE RIDE back to Nate's is brief, Dani tucked between me and Doc, Nathan across from us. He is just watching as we take turns dusting kisses on her neck, hands stroking over her thighs, her waist, her nipples. Just little light touches, a whisper here and there, ramping her up. Pregame warmup.

She's wearing the scoop-necked blouse, with a short skirt, and boots that only cover her ankles, leaving her legs bare.

"Good girl wearing a skirt. You're ready for us, aren't you, pretty girl?" I say against her neck.

She moans softly and nods as I stroke my fingertips lightly along her inner thigh.

Dani is breathing hard by the time we pull up outside Nathan's building and we've barely even gotten started. I don't want to kiss her lips until we're upstairs. I want to draw out her anticipation, make her tremble with need, with desire. Hughes seems to be damn near psychic because he seems to be instinctively in agreement with me.

I have no idea what Nate is thinking or feeling and it makes me want to include him. I'm a team player. I've spent my whole life working in tandem with other guys for a common goal, literally. So when we all get out of the car, I step back so Nathan can move in next to her, but to my surprise, he doesn't.

Maybe this whole situation is weirding him out more than he wants to admit.

But if he isn't going to hold her hand or wrap an arm around her, then I sure in the hell am. She needs to be touched. I put my arm over her shoulder and draw Dani closer to me. I murmur in her ear, "You good?"

She nods and looks up at me. "A little nervous but mostly excited."

"Just let me know if anything is too much or you're not comfortable. This is about what you need and want. We're all here for you, sweetheart."

Hughes is in step with us on her other side. "Exactly. We'll check in with you, but you can speak up at any time. Let us know where you're at." He slips her hand into his, lacing their fingers together. He raises her hand to his mouth and lightly kisses her knuckles.

"I trust you both," she says, looking back and forth between us.

Nathan makes a sound in the back of his throat. I wait for him to say something, but he doesn't.

The elevator opens right into his penthouse apartment and that's all the green light I need. I tug Dani through the doors and yank her against my chest. She gives a soft laugh that I cut off with a kiss.

"Mm, cotton candy." I sweep my tongue between Dani's lips, swirling around. "I like your taste in martinis."

"I was just thinking about the gift you sent," she says, tilting her head back to offer me her neck.

"Doc, come taste our girl," I say, turning to Michael.

"Can't wait," he says, shifting in next to Dani.

I shift my mouth lower, dropping kisses over her chest, tugging down the front of her shirt so I can flick my tongue across her flesh. Michael moves in, taking her mouth in a kiss that has her moaning softly under her breath. The sound gives me a kick of lust and I want more. I want to taste her pussy again.

"What do you think, Doc?" I ask him conversationally as I drop down in a squat. "Like cotton candy, right?"

"Just as sweet," he agrees.

His hand is on her chin, tipping her head toward him and she's kissing him while her fingers seek me out, burying in my hair. I ease up her skirt and brush my lips over the front of her panties. "Your pussy is going to be even sweeter, Dani." I press a kiss onto the cotton, and she's already dampened them. "Damn, so wet."

But before I can ease them down and flick my tongue over her, she's eased back.

It's Nathan. He's tugging her away from me and Michael, turning her and taking her in a hard kiss. She gives a soft cry and I'm not sure if it's pleasure or disappointment at being yanked away.

I give Michael a look and he nods.

"Armstrong, you need to sit this first part out," Michael informs him, wrapping a hand around Dani's upper arm.

"What?" The boss's expression is stormy.

But we're having none of his bullshit. This is about Dani, not his jealousy. If he can't get over it, he'll ruin it for all of us. That's not going to happen. Besides, I almost feel sorry for the guy. He's never had to work for a damn thing. It's about time he learned a little patience and how to wait his turn. It will be good for him. Make him a better boyfriend to Dani.

"You've never seen Dani with other men. You need to watch for a few minutes, adjust to it, appreciate how much fun she's having," Michael says.

"You're making her uncomfortable," I point out. Dani is stiff in his hold, her shoulders almost to her ears.

"Is that true?" Nathan demands, gazing down at her and sounding appalled.

"A little," she admits. "Not uncomfortable," she rushes to add. "A little nervous. I just don't want anyone to be upset."

I'm pleased to see his gaze soften as he studies her face. He cups her cheek. "I'm..." He shakes his head. "Fuck, I don't know."

"Are you turned on?" she asks, staring up at him. Michael is still holding her arm, but he's not pulling her away.

I'm still on my knees. Which is exactly where I intend to stay for this woman, for as long as I need to.

"I...am," he admits. He smooths his thumb over her cheek. "Are you?"

"So much," she breathes.

"Nathan," Michael says, low and firm. "Step back. We've got her."

Dani's eyes are still on Nathan's as she nods. And he lets go of her as Michael does pull her away from him now.

I grin up at her as she looks down at me. "We sure do," I tell her with a wink.

She smiles, her fingers tangling in my hair again. "I know."

Michael pulls her hair back with one hand, putting his mouth against her bared neck, but gathering her skirt up with his other hand. "Now where were you, McNeill?"

Oh, fuck, that's hot. He holds her skirt up for me and I drag my nose and mouth up her inner thigh. She's trembling. "Right about here," I say, pressing my mouth against the front of her panties.

"That's what I thought," Michael says. "Here." He moves Dani's hands to the skirt, making her hold it up. She does without question. Then he takes one thigh and lifts it, propping her foot on the short bench that sits underneath the coat rack in Nate's entryway. "Open up, sweet girl."

That's fucking perfect. I slip a finger under the edge of her panties, running the back of my knuckle over her wet folds. She gasps and grabs the outside of Michael's thigh for balance, gripping his dress pants in her fist tightly.

"We've got you," he murmurs. "Just let us take care of you."

She leans back into him so he can support her weight. Our gazes collide as I pull her panties to the side and run my knuckle over her clit. I love everything about this.

"Keep that skirt up so Nate and Doc can see everything," I tell Dani.

She hikes the skirt higher and I grin my approval, then I lean in and take a long lick.

She gasps loudly.

Michael groans and pulls her shirt up and one bra cup down. He takes her nipple between his thumb and finger, rolling it and then tugging gently. She bucks against my mouth.

"Oh yeah, do that again Doc. That makes her pussy even wetter." I tease the entrance to her pussy with my finger, easing in just to the first knuckle.

He squeezes her nipple and I feel the flutter around my finger. "Our girl likes that," I tell him. "Suck on her there, while I suck on her down here." I circle her clit.

"Let's move a bit," Michael says. He shifts so he's sitting on the bench with Dani on his lap. He pulls her little boots off, then sweeps her panties down her legs and off. He tosses them to Nathan.

I watch as Nate catches them. His expression is hard to read. He's definitely turned on. And...conflicted. He looks like he wants to rip Dani out of Michael's arms, but he also looks very into what's happening. His cock is evident behind the dress pants he's wearing and he's tossed his jacket and rolled the sleeves of his dress shirt up on his forearms.

His jaw is tight but he's watching every single movement Dani makes. And every single thing done to Dani.

Then I focus on our girl. Michael turns her on his lap, dropping one of her feet to the floor, propping the other on the bench, spreading her open and again hikes her skirt up. Now her pussy is fully exposed to all of us.

She looks completely wanton.

Her hair is spilling over Michael's lap. She's breathing hard. Her face, throat, and chest are flushed a pretty pink that matches the pink between her legs where I intend to spend the next several minutes.

Michael then pulls her blouse up over her head and tosses it to the side. He unhooks her bra and then fills his big hands with her gorgeous tits. He leans over and takes a nipple in his mouth, licking, then sucking. She arches up with a, "Michael!", her arm sliding up to loop around his neck so she can pull him closer.

He palms her other breast. "I've needed these in my hands and mouth since our phone call," he tells her, sucking hard again.

Fuck, watching them is so hot. I press my hand against my aching cock.

"McNeill," Michael says, lifting his head. "Get to work." He inclines his head toward Dani's pussy.

I immediately move into position at the end of the bench. I cup her ass, putting my hands between her sweet cheeks and the wood, lifting her as I lower my head. I lick her twice, then suck on her clit.

She's moaning and lifting to get closer to my mouth. I look up and watch Michael playing with her nipples, moving between kissing them, and kissing her mouth.

"So fucking pretty, Cookie," he tells her. He slides his hand down, over her breast, over her ribs, over her stomach, brushing close to where I'm licking. "Let us hear you. Let us know what you need."

"More," she begs. "God. Everything. More."

I lick and suck again, harder now.

"Yes!"

"Tell him, Dani," Michael says, his voice firm. "Tell Crew what you want."

"I want…" Her head thrashes back and forth in his lap. "More. I need…filled up."

Michael strokes his hand back and forth over her belly. "We're gonna fill you up so good, Cookie. You think you can take us all?"

She nods. "Yes. God, yes. I want that."

"Make her come, Crew," Michael says. "She needs to be hot and wet and soft for us."

I fuck her with my tongue and she cries out.

"That's it, sweet girl," Michael says soothingly. He's playing with a nipple again, squeezing and tugging. "Come on his tongue. Give him all that sweetness."

I ease two fingers into her and her pussy immediately squeezes hard. "Oh, yes, Dani, like that. Fuck my fingers, honey." I circle her clit with my tongue, moving my fingers in and out.

She's gasping. "I'm so close. Crew! Yes! Oh, my God! Michael!"

I'm feeling pretty fucking fantastic right now, giving this girl her first orgasm of the night, right in front of the two other men. Hey, I'm cool with sharing and being a team player, but I do like being the star, after all.

I pick up the pace of my thrusts. "God, I could eat this pussy all night," I tell her, licking over her clit. "But I can't wait to feel all of this sweet cum on my cock and I gotta make sure you can take all of us all night, don't I?" I add another finger, stretching her as I finger fuck her. "You're gonna take us so good. You're such a sweetheart. You're gonna let us use this pretty body all night. We're gonna absolutely ruin you, Dani girl."

I lean in and suck hard on her clit as Michael lowers his head and takes her nipple in his mouth again.

And then she's coming apart. Her fingers are gripping my hair, her thighs are squeezing my head, her pussy has my fingers in a vise as she cries out, "Yes, yes, oh fuck yes!"

Michael seals his mouth over hers, kissing her as her body shakes and she starts to come down from the peak. I lean back, wiping the back of my hand over my mouth, watching them.

Then I look over at Nathan.

Oh that guy is messed up. He's so turned on, but he has no idea what to do about it.

I've spent the night in a holding cell next to a clown and a guy dressed up like Taylor Swift. I've woken up in a sleazy hotel in Miami next to two dudes and three girls. Two of whom were dressed up like Taylor Swift—the girls, not the dudes. I've hopped a plane to Vegas with two girls and come home with four girls. None of whom were dressed up like Taylor Swift. But I did have Taylor Swift's phone number for a while.

And *this* night is shaping up to be the most interesting of my life.

CHAPTER 19

Michael

I'VE FINALLY GOT my hands on Dani's naked body. But as I gather her in my arms and stand up from the bench where Crew just made her come hard with his mouth—okay, I like to think I had a little to do with it too—Nathan takes a step toward me.

"My turn. Couch," he says shortly.

I lift a brow. "Nope."

Nathan Armstrong is the boss when we're in the Racketeers arena. Not here. Even though this is his apartment, he's not in charge of this.

Dani is. If she stops this, or changes this, or chooses only one of us, it will devastate us. And we'll do anything for her, anything to make this work. She has us wrapped around her little finger. And we all know it.

Even Armstrong. If he fucking slows down and thinks for a second.

He's already unbuttoning his shirt. He stops and turns back to me. "Excuse me?"

"I said no. Bedroom. All of us." I hold Dani to my chest and start down the hallway that I assume leads to the bedroom.

"Hughes," Nathan grits out between teeth that are clamped so tightly I'm surprised his jaw hasn't cracked.

I look down at Dani. She's watching me with wide eyes. And a little smile.

"How're you doing?"

"I'm really, really good," she says with a light laugh. "But he's…"

"Fine," I tell her, loud enough that Nathan can also hear. "He's fine."

"But he wants–" she starts.

"You, Cookie," I say. "I know. And he's going to have you. With us." I glance over my shoulder at Nathan. Sure enough, he's right on my heels. Crew's behind him, grinning.

"Okay," she says. The look she gives me hits me hard in the chest. "I trust you."

I give her a little squeeze. I will never let anything happen to her. Not even Nathan Armstrong.

"Which way?" I ask Armstrong when I'm in the hallway and there are three doors to choose from.

"Oh, you need me now?" he asks, but he pushes past me and opens the door at the end of the hall.

Dani giggles softly, pressing her face against my chest and I grin. She's not afraid of Nathan. He's a growly asshole, but she likes him and wants him to be a part of this. As long as he doesn't try to leave me or Crew out, this is going to be fine.

I follow him into the master bedroom and…holy shit.

I was too distracted by Danielle to really study much of the penthouse when we were out in the main area, but I take a moment to appreciate this room. I knew the guy was loaded, but damn. I have a great apartment in a leafy neighborhood, but I've chosen to live modestly on the second floor of a renovated brownstone in Bucktown. It has nice finishes, but it's on the small side because I travel with the team and don't need all that space. Plus, I grew up in a small house crowded with siblings. Too much space makes me feel too alone.

But Nathan's place is amazing.

"This view is great," Crew says, looking out the window that gives us a breathtaking view of the lights of downtown in the foreground and then the dark expanse of the lake beyond.

"Let's make the view gorgeous," Nathan says, gesturing to me to put Dani on the bed.

I smile. Nice. That was very nice.

I lay her on the dark gray duvet. Nathan is already shrugging out of his shirt. His eyes on her and nothing else.

I don't blame him. Her red hair and pale skin against the dark gray is a gorgeous contrast. She seems to not know what to do though. Her legs are moving restlessly and her hands are gripping the duvet. She looks from him to me to Crew.

Crew approaches the bed with a grin. He reaches over his head to grab the back of his shirt and tugs it up and off. He throws it to the side and starts on the fly of his jeans. "You feelin' like the main course of the banquet, spread out on the table for us all to feast on, Dani girl?" he asks. "Cuz you're not."

He leans his knee on the mattress, making it dip.

"No?" she asks with a laugh.

"Nah, you're dessert. All the sweet stuff." He reaches out, running a hand up her thigh closest to him. "And I'm definitely gonna be ruining my dinner, fillin' up on you." He leans over and puts his mouth against hers. "Or filling you up."

She laughs, the sound light and sweet and I feel myself smiling just from the sound of it.

Crew and his playfulness is a great contrast to Nathan's broody seriousness. I look at my boss, expecting a scowl and more teeth grinding.

I'm surprised to see him watching Crew and Dani kiss and tease with an expression that's more bemused than angry. He drops his shirt on the floor next to the bed.

"My turn," he says.

His tone is firm, but it lacks the harshness of earlier.

Crew looks up. His hand is full of one of Dani's breasts. He brushes his thumb over her nipple. "Be my guest," he says. But he doesn't move. She's on her back, he's at her side, leaning over, his mouth hovering over hers.

That leaves plenty of room—plenty of Dani—for Nathan.

Nathan doesn't say anything to that, but he moves in, joining her on the bed on her other side. He cups her face, turning her toward him so he can kiss her. But Crew continues playing with her nipple.

Her fingers thread into Nathan's hair and she sighs into his mouth. He rests his hand on her belly as he kisses her deeply. Her thighs part and she makes a soft whimpering sound.

I shrug out of my shirt too, then palm my cock. But I'm happy watching right now. She's so gorgeous like this. Spread out, being worshiped, totally in control whether she realizes it at this moment or not.

She has all of our balls in the palm of her hand, figuratively anyway. And I suspect she's got our hearts there too. She's got mine anyway.

"Nathan," she murmurs against his mouth. "Touch me." She rests her hand on his, on her stomach, then slides it down between her legs.

He cups her there. Then slides one finger into her.

I move to the foot of the bed and wrap a hand around her ankle. "Let me see, Cookie." I move her legs apart and she happily spreads them further for me.

For us.

Nathan is thrusting his finger deep, slowly, over and over.

"She's so wet for us, isn't she?" Crew says. He brushes her hair back from her face and presses a kiss to her forehead. He's kneeling by the bed now.

"So fucking wet," Nathan agrees.

"Such a good girl," Crew says, licking over her nipple. "Getting so wet for our cocks. Coming so sweet and easy for us." Then he sucks on her nipple.

She gasps and arches closer to Nathan's hand. "More, please." She looks at me.

I shake my head. "I think Nathan wants your pussy first, Cookie."

"You need my cock, Danielle?" Nathan asks her, circling his thumb over her clit. "You need to be fucked?"

"Y-y-yes," she says raggedly as shivers shake her body.

"Take my cock out," he says.

She reaches for his pants immediately. She undoes his belt, then unbuttons and unzips his pants. She has her hand wrapped around his cock a moment later. She seems almost relieved as she strokes him.

"Where are your condoms, boss?" Crew asks.

Nathan pauses. He wraps his hand around Dani's on his cock, stopping her movements. "Don't have any. Don't need them. I just got tested."

Crew focuses on Dani. "You on the pill, sweetheart?"

She bites her lip and nods.

"Cool. I test regularly too." Crew looks over at me. "Guessing the Doc is good to go?"

I nod. "Yeah." My cock is so hard thinking about fucking Dani without a condom, I can't get much more out than that.

Dani is looking at Nathan though. "Is that all?"

He shakes his head. "Later."

"But..."

He presses a finger to her lips. "You're safe." He pauses, watching her eyes. "Do you trust me?"

I hold my breath. This is a big moment. I can sense it. Earlier, Dani told Crew and I that she trusted us. It was unprompted. We didn't ask for it, she just gave it.

Nathan needs to hear this from her. Just like in the foyer when Crew told him he was making Dani uncomfortable, Nathan is realizing that he's very intense with her. And that maybe he needs to fucking relax.

That he has her without acting like a caveman.

"I trust you," she says softly. "Completely."

He seems relieved. He nods. "Good." Then he stands up,

shucks out of his clothes entirely, and moves to kneel between Dani's thighs. He just watches her for a long moment.

I'm actually shocked he's completely naked in front of two other men.

Who are not.

Finally, he looks at Crew, then me. "Do we need to draw stick figure diagrams, or does everyone know where they need to be?"

Crew snorts then grabs his side. "Jesus, Nate. Warn a guy before you get unexpectedly funny. I might pull something. And I need to be in top shape for our girl." He gives Dani a wink. "Though I promise, even at less than 100% you're gonna be walkin' funny tomorrow."

She slaps his arm as she laughs. "Crew!"

He shrugs and stands, shedding his clothes. "Girl, as long as you can stand up straight, we're doin' something wrong and we'll have to keep you in this bed workin' on it. Just warnin' you."

She covers her eyes as she blushes hard and laughs.

Which makes me laugh. "You're spread out, bare naked, with three men drooling over you, but you're blushing about *that*?" I start unbuttoning and unzipping my pants too. "What did you think was gonna happen in here tonight?"

She's grinning as she uncovers her eyes and looks at me. "Well, you know very well what I read about. I didn't want to let my expectations get too high. That's all fiction, right?"

I drop my pants and boxers, kicking them out of the way, and approach the side of the bed opposite of Crew. I'm smiling but I don't have to try to add the heat to my tone when I say, "It's fantasy, Cookie. And we're going to blow all your expectations right out of the water."

Her eyes are hooded when she licks her lips and asks, "Promise?"

I stroke my hand down her arm, linking our fingers. "Promise."

Nathan's hands go to her waist and he pulls her toward him. "Need you, Danielle," he says simply.

Her eyes are on him as she nods. "Please."

He slowly eases her onto his cock. The sight of her pussy stretching around him, the sound of the hitch in her breathing, and the way her eyes slip shut all make me fist my cock, squeezing.

Crew leans in and takes her mouth, the kiss slow and deep.

Nathan's gritting his teeth as he pauses, balls deep. He circles his thumb over her clit, easing out, then thrusting in again nice and slow.

Dani whimpers and swivels her hips, as if she's trying to get closer. She doesn't have much leverage. Her legs are spread wide, her thighs resting over Nathan's as he kneels between them. He's controlling the pace with his hands on her waist, and his own hips.

Crew has his fingers in her hair, holding her head still as he kisses her and plays with her nipples lazily. She's at their mercy.

And I don't think she likes it.

I watch, just waiting to see what she'll do.

She finally pulls away from Crew, frowning up at Nathan. "What are you doing?"

His jaw is tight. "Fucking you."

"No you're not."

His eyes snap to hers. "What?"

"You've fucked me before," she says. "It wasn't like this. I want that."

He frowns. "I thought I was upsetting you being like that."

Her eyes widen. "I thought *you* were upset. I thought you might punch Crew in the face or fire Michael! I'm *not* nervous about how you are with me."

He's stopped moving. He's staring at her.

She reaches out and grasps his wrist. "I want all of you because you're different. You make me feel different things. You treat me differently but in all ways I love. You bring out different sides of me." She wiggles her ass, moving on his cock and Nathan's nostrils flare. "I want you to share me because it's so good for me, so hot, because you know that together, it will be the best I've ever had. But I don't just want three guys. I want *you three.* I want to feel every inch of you, Nathan, and I want to know that you are here with me, in me. You, Nathan. I want you to fuck me the way *you* fuck me."

I know my eyes widen. I see Crew grin.

"That's our girl," he says. "Tell us what you want."

Nathan's body is frozen, but his gaze is hot as he stares down at Dani.

Then suddenly he moves. He leans in, bracing his hands on either side of her head as Crew jerks back out of the way.

"Tell me how you want me to fuck you, Danielle," Nathan practically growls.

She puts her hands up to his face, holding him as she says, "Like I'm your dirty slut."

Crew sucks in a breath, then whistles. "Holy shit, Nate. You get dirty slut Dani? Let's *go*."

Nathan is still staring at her. They're nearly nose to nose. But finally he says, "Yeah. I get dirty slut, Dani."

Then he scoops under her ass and rolls to his back, taking her with him. She's now on top, facing him, her thighs on either side of his hips. He's still buried deep. Then he lifts his hand and brings it down on her ass, giving her a hard spank.

She gasps, then moans as a bright pink handprint shows on her sweet, creamy skin.

"*Yes*, Nathan," she says, wiggling against him, taking him deeper.

"Don't ever tell me I make you nervous without being very clear about how I'm scaring you. I want to know exactly how you're feeling," he says. "Do you understand?"

She nods.

He spanks her again.

"Yes!" she cries out, but she also moves over his cock as if she's trying to get some relief from a different kind of pain.

"I want to know everything I make you feel whether it's bad," he slaps her ass again, not hard, but enough to make her gasp and the pink get brighter. "Or good." He gives her one more smack.

She rotates her hips. "Yes. Yes. I promise."

"What do you want right now, Danielle?" Nathan asks gruffly, kneading her hot pink ass.

"For you to fuck me the way you fuck me." She pauses. "With them."

He gives her a single nod and then presses her down harder on his cock. She moans. He looks at Crew. "You heard her."

"Yes, sir." Crew is grinning. He reaches for his jeans and pulls out a small plastic bottle. He holds it up for Dani.

She laughs, though it sounds breathless. "You got yourself some too?"

"I couldn't risk that you'd forget it," he says. He leans in and kisses her. "When you suck my cock, it's only right that it tastes like cotton candy too."

Then he opens the bottle and pours some of the lube into his hand. He strokes his cock as he moves in behind her.

He looks at me. "Unless you want second position?"

I look at Dani, Nathan, and at Crew getting behind her, clearly ready to take her ass. Heat floods through me and I shake my head. "I'm good over here, for now."

"Well, you better come closer than that," Dani says, crooking her finger at me.

I lift a brow. "And why's that?"

"Because you've teased me with that gorgeous cock long enough. I have one more place to put one." She taps her bottom lip.

"You want it to taste like cotton candy?" Crew asks her, stroking his hand up and down her back, then over her ass cheeks. "Jesus, Nate, you heated her up good back here."

"I like the idea of you looking at my handprint on her while you fuck her from behind," Nate says, squeezing her hips.

Crew chuckles. "Well done."

Dani looks down at Nathan in surprise. Then smiles. "It's

going to be awhile before we can totally get rid of that possessiveness, huh?"

He squeezes her again. And does not smile. "Never going to happen."

I decide not to point out that she's about to take a guy in the ass while giving another a blow job right in front of Nathan.

He's come a long way already.

Dani looks up at me with those gorgeous green eyes. "And no, I just need Michael to taste like Michael."

Crew pinches her butt. "But you want me to taste like candy?"

She laughs and swats at him. "You said that, not me. You're the one all into my pussy tasting like candy too."

He strokes his hands up her sides, then around to cup her breasts. "Nah, sweet girl, you are delicious, as is." He tweaks her nipples. "But when we go to the circus, I'm getting real cotton candy and we're going to do very inappropriate things with it. Just because."

"McNeill," Nate grinds out from under Dani.

"Yeah, boss?"

"Get in there, or I'm going to fuck her without you."

Crew laughs. "Damn. Impatient much?"

"Yes," Nathan says.

Crew strokes his hand over his cock, then runs his hand down Dani's ass again, then up between her cheeks, spreading lube. "You ready for me sweet girl? You gonna take me in this tight little hole?" He presses a kiss to her shoulder as he eases a finger into her. "You gonna take me and Nate at the same time? You gonna be a good girl and fuck two big cocks at once?"

She's trembling and she moans as he moves his finger. "Yes," she pants. "Yes. I want to. I...hope so."

"You haven't done this before, Cookie?" I ask, resting my hand on the back of her head. I turn her to look at me so I can see her eyes. "Dani, have you done this before?"

She wet her lips. "I want you all at once. I want this, Michael. I just...it's new. But I want to do it for the first time with you," she adds quickly. She looks down at Nathan and reaches back to grab Crew's arm. "Only with you three. You're the only ones I would."

I stroke her hair and share a look with Crew, then Nathan. They're now both totally serious.

"Okay," I say soothingly. Fuck. I know they're feeling what I am—a mix of lust so strong it's nearly buckling my spine, along with a streak of protectiveness that makes me want to just wrap her in bubble wrap and never let her out of this bed, along with a possessiveness that insists we be the ones to give her this fantasy and take her to this place. "Okay. We've got you," I tell her, stroking my hand over her head. "We've got you."

CHAPTER 20

Dani

I'M a mess of emotions and sensations. And nothing is really happening.

Okay, that's not totally true. I'm in bed, naked, with three gorgeous, huge, naked men. One of them is inside me. One of them is touching me in previously uncharted territory. And one of them is acting like my personal coach.

I want to laugh. I'm about to experience double penetration sex for the first time in my life and one of the most gorgeous, sophisticated men I've ever met—someone I really respect—is coaching me through it and assuring me it will be okay.

But I'm not going to laugh because Crew just eased a second finger into me and I can barely breathe.

In a good way.

I'm so full. Every one of my nerve endings feels like it's on fire.

And I want more.

It's like I'm reaching for something and I'm almost there but need just a little more of a boost.

Yeah, from Crew's dick.

Okay, maybe I will laugh.

Nathan's fingers dig into my hips. "Danielle," he says tightly. "You're killing me."

I look down at him. "Why?"

"I'm barely hanging on and you're laughing?"

That makes me want to laugh harder for some reason.

"The poor billionaire who's got his cock buried balls deep in the hottest, tightest, sweetest redhead he's ever met is feeling bad about life?" Crew asks. His voice sounds tight.

His words make me want to laugh too. I love when he teases Nathan.

"Shut the fuck up, McNeill," Nathan tells him.

Crew moves his fingers and I gasp.

"I'm hurtin' way more than you are, buddy," Crew mutters.

"Oh, the poor millionaire, super star hockey player who's about to fuck the hottest, tightest, sweetest redhead he's ever met in the ass is feeling bad about life?" Michael asks dryly.

Now I do laugh.

They all stop what they're doing and stare at me.

I shake my head. "Sorry. Nerves. Adrenaline. Endorphins," I stammer. Love. I left that one off, but I'm pretty sure that's part of what I'm feeling too.

I love these guys.

Each of them. Or at least, I'm on my way there with each of them.

And together. I love them when they're together. Crew poking at Nathan. Nathan being all growly but also listening to them try to teach him how to be a better boyfriend. Michael being the voice of reason.

I give a happy sigh and relax against Nathan's chest, just letting all the happy sensation flood through me.

I also love how they all want to make me feel good.

I love that very much.

"Okay, sweet girl, you ready?" Crew asks.

Nathan puts his mouth against my ear. "You going to be a pretty, dirty little slut for all of us?"

That causes a flood of heat to wash through me and I know he feels the way my pussy tightens around his cock.

There's a rumble in his chest. "I thought so." He squeezes the back of my neck. "Take him good, Danielle."

Crew squeezes my ass and I feel the head of his cock. "Relax, sweet girl. Let me in."

Michael strokes my back. "God you look gorgeous, Dani."

I want this so much. I make my body relax and I feel Crew press harder.

"That's it," he croons. "That's my girl."

He works his way in, all of my guys, touching me, stroking me, telling me how beautiful and hot, and tight and amazing I am.

When he's fully inside me, Crew takes a deep breath. "Goddamn, Dani. Think of those Christmas vacations at my mom's house where we could've been doin' this. Why didn't you grab me and kiss me sooner?"

And again, I laugh. Even though I've never felt anything like this–physically or emotionally–before. "You kissed me at that game, McNeill."

He strokes my ass, then pulls out slightly before pressing back in. My whole body lights on fire.

"Yeah I fucking did," he says tightly. "I'm the dumbass that wasn't fucking this perfect body years ago."

"McNeill," Nathan bites out. "Stop talking."

Crew strokes in and out again. "Why's that?"

"Because it reminds me that you're here."

Crew barks out a laugh, I grin and lift my head. Nathan doesn't look mad though. He's maybe even, possibly, almost smiling.

"But he didn't fuck me years ago," I say. "No reason to be jealous."

"Right," Nathan says dryly. "No reason at all."

Then he starts moving.

And Oh. My. God.

I am unable to form words. Or thoughts. Or do anything but hang on.

Literally.

I clutch at Nathan's shoulders and just let them take over.

Until I feel Crew gripping my hair and turning my head. I open my eyes to find Michael stroking his cock.

"You've got three gorgeous holes, sweet girl, and three men who need you bad," Crew says.

And that's all he has to say. I reach for Michael, bringing him to my mouth.

I think he might have been about to protest, but as soon as I lick over the head of his cock, his head falls back, his fingers replace Crew's in my hair, and he lets me suck him in deep.

"Good girl," Crew praises. "That's our sweet, dirty, beautiful, very good girl."

For several glorious minutes—or maybe it's hours, or days, or years, I don't even know—my three men fuck me. Nathan pounds up into my pussy, Crew thrusts in rhythm with Nathan from behind, and Michael fucks my mouth.

I'm just here for them. I just want to feel them come. I want them to fill me up.

I don't even think I'm capable of another orgasm because my pleasure feels too widespread, too chaotic, to condense into one simple climax.

But I'm wrong.

Suddenly, seemingly out of the blue, I feel the pressure and pleasure winding tight, deep in my pussy and then it releases. I cry out around Michael's cock.

He pulls me off of his dick so I can breathe and I'm panting and gasping and nearly sobbing.

"Fuck, Danielle, goddammit," Nathan grinds out. He's holding me so tight and suddenly I feel him explode, filling me up.

I turn back to Michael, taking him into my mouth again, desperate to make him come.

Again, it seems like he hesitates for just a moment, before beginning to thrust.

"Dani, God, yes. Fuck."

"Jesus, Dani," Crew is panting behind me. "You're fucking everything." Then he pulls out and comes, hard and hot, on the curve of my ass.

Michael is right behind him. His fingers tighten in my hair. "I'm coming. Pull back, baby."

But I grasp his thigh, holding him still.

"Fuck."

He comes in my mouth and I swallow as much as I can. Some drips from the corners of my mouth, but Michael quickly pulls his cock away and leans in to kiss me in a dirty, messy, hot kiss that I swear, makes my pussy even wetter.

Crew pulls away from me with a groaned, "Holy fuck." He flops onto the floor as if he can't even take a step.

Michael lets me go and sinks back onto the pillows behind him, breathing hard.

And I collapse onto Nathan's chest.

His hands stroke up and down my back and he just holds me.

Holy fuck is right.

I can't sleep. My whole body is still tingling and I keep replaying the night. I've had solo sex with Nathan and Crew and it was amazing, but this? This is the most sexually and emotionally satisfied I've ever been in my entire life. My guys were everywhere, all over and in me and it was perfect.

I sigh contentedly and snuggle up closer against Michael, who fell asleep spooning me. Nathan is asleep on my opposite side, snoring lightly, one hand possessively on my hip. It wasn't discussed, but he managed to secure the solo spot on the outside of the bed. It is his bed, so I suppose that's fair. Crew is so easy-going that he took the other outside spot next to Michael.

But it's Crew I hear now ease out of bed and quietly pad across the floor to the bedroom door. He's not going to the ensuite bathroom but out into the main living area. I listen for a minute but I can't hear any of his movements. Since I can't sleep either, I decide to go check on him but I'm trapped between my other two guys.

There's only two options—down or up. I try to shimmy lower, but realize I'll never make it to the foot of the bed without suffocating, which would be an absurd ending to the greatest night of my life. I can't even imagine Luna explaining that kind of death to my parents.

How did she die, Luna?

Oh, well, Mr. and Mrs. Larkin, she suffocated in a big bed with three hot men after they fucked her brains out.

I go up, inching toward the headboard on my back. Nathan's hand slips off of me and he rolls over onto his opposite side.

Michael's voice rumbles in my ear, sleepy and sexy. "You okay, Cookie?"

"I need to use the bathroom."

"Just roll over me. You'll never get anywhere going that way." His big arm slides under my back and he hauls me over on top of his muscular chest.

His eyes are still closed. He looks sleepy and delicious. I give him a soft kiss on the cheek.

"Mm," he says. "That was sweet."

I roll off of him and squeeze his hand before exiting the bed. "Go back to sleep," I whisper.

A glance at Nathan shows he's still out like a light. He looks softer in his sleep, more vulnerable. I'm tempted to kiss him as well, but I feel like he'd bolt awake if I did and he needs the rest. He really put himself out there tonight for me. For all of us. A wave of tenderness rushes over me. He's more complicated than Crew and Michael, but that makes it even more special that he's willing to share me with them.

I'm falling in love with him.

With all of them.

Is that even possible? Maybe it's just endorphins from all the sex, but it doesn't feel like that's it. This is deeper, more profound. I already suspected my feelings for Crew were morphing into love, but now I'm starting to feel the same for Nathan and Michael, although in different ways.

I grab a chenille throw off of the club chair in the corner of the bedroom and wrap it around myself. The plush fabric feels both comforting in the chilly air and sensual against my bare skin. All my nerve endings are on hyperdrive now after all that attention.

Crew is in the kitchen in his boxers, standing there with his hands on his hips.

"Hey," I say. "Can't sleep?"

He turns and gives me a warm smile. "Hi, beautiful. I'm hungry. Sex makes me ravenous and baby, that was the best sex ever."

"I agree."

His hair keeps flopping into his eyes and when I reach him, I gently push it back. "You need a haircut." Then I give him a kiss. "What are you going to eat?" I ask.

He moans and pulls back. "You, once I have real food. But I can't figure Nathan's kitchen out. There are no pulls or knobs on anything and it's like one solid wall. Does he even have a fridge? Is this all just fake, a prop kitchen?"

I laugh softly. I had those same thoughts when I spent the night with Nathan before. "This is the fridge." I tap the largest cabinet. "And the drawers all open like this." I press a corner and it pops out.

His eyebrows go up. "Whoa. That's like kitchen magic. What do you think Nate has in the fridge? Five bucks says it's just bottles of Perrier water and jars of caviar."

"I'm not taking that bet. What's in your fridge? Old takeout boxes?"

He nods. "One hundred percent. Plus beer and condiments because they don't go bad. I'm on the road all the time, as you know."

"Condiments go bad."

"No, they don't. You can keep ketchup packs for like twelve years."

"Crew, no, you can't!" I hope he's kidding.

He pulls the fridge open. "Well, well. Nate's both normal and an adult. Look at this." He pushes the door open wider.

It's clean and filled with organizational containers that hold fresh vegetables, cured meats, various cheeses, protein shakes, and yes, Perrier water. But there's also yogurt, brown paper packages from either the deli or the butcher, and a bakery box. Three bakery boxes, actually. Two are tucked behind the first. And they all have the Books and Buns logo on them.

"These are Luna's pastries," I say, flipping the box open and spotting her signature au pain chocolat. "Why does Nathan have so many?"

"I think Boss Man is a bigger softie than he wants us to know. He's probably just trying to be supportive," Crew says. "Either that or he's throwing a party, but he still chose Books and Buns out of the zillion bakeries in Chicago."

My heart squeezes.

Crew takes out the eggs, spinach, and some goat cheese. "Are you hungry?"

I shake my head. "No, thanks. But I'll keep you company."

He sets everything down on the island and turns to me. Only the pendants over the island are on and they're casting a soft glow on him. His expression is serious as he closes the space between us and cups my cheeks and gives me a whisper of a kiss.

"I'm in love with you, Dani," he murmurs. "I've been half in love with you since I was sixteen and now I'm all the way there."

"Crew," I whisper, wrapping my arms around his neck, my emotions on overload. "God, I love you too. Is that crazy?"

I'm treated to one of his signature grins. "Crazy good, that's what it is." He gives my ass a playful tap. "There's more where that came from."

I laugh lightly, feeling weightless and giddy. "I'm looking forward to it. To all of it."

Crew makes his eggs and we chat about hockey as he eats,

about the team's prospects for a championship, and I see his passion for his sport, his career. For me. He's happy and so I am.

Before we crawl back into bed, he peels the throw blanket off of me and teases his fingers over my nipples, earning a low moan from me. He puts a finger to his lips and jerks his head in the direction of the bed.

"Goodnight," he murmurs in my ear. "I love you, I love you, I love you."

I shiver in the dark. "I love you too."

"In you go," he says, giving me another pat on the ass.

As Crew gets back in bed, I approach the bed from Nathan's side and kiss him. He stirs and opens his eyes.

"Scoot over," I whisper.

To my surprise, he obeys, though he reaches for me and pulls me up against his chest in a strong but gentle embrace.

It feels perfect.

Like everything I need is right here, right now in this king sized bed.

With my guys.

CHAPTER 21

Dani

I WAKE up in the morning in bed alone. I'm very surprised by that, to be honest.

I stretch, and note additional soreness. And smile.

Dang, last night was fun.

I want to do it again. And again. And again.

But I'm alone and I need at least one of my hot boyfriends to do anything like what we did last night. I lay staring at the ceiling. Are they my boyfriends now? Hmm…I might need to discuss that with Luna.

But my bladder and my stomach both insist I get out of bed and take care of them first.

I head into Nathan's bathroom, pee, wash my face, brush my teeth, run a brush through my hair, and contemplate what I'm going to wear.

It only takes me ten seconds to realize that of course I'm going to wear one of Nathan's dress shirts. And no panties.

I pad down the hall toward the kitchen, hoping at least one of them is still here.

I'm delighted to hear all three voices before I turn the corner.

I hang back for a moment, just listening to how they are together when they don't know I'm there.

"So, is Dani going to be calling you daddy? And, more importantly, do we all have to call you daddy?" Crew asks.

"Why would she call me daddy?" Nathan asks, his tone sardonic.

"Well, you know, because we all have to ask you for permission for things," Crew says.

I know him well enough to know that he's grinning. I cover my mouth.

"Gee, I thought maybe that was a jab at his age," Michael comments in his smooth, deep voice.

"His age?" Crew asks. "What about his age?"

"Nathan is a little older than the rest of us," Michael says.

I can picture his smile as well and my own grows.

"No kidding?" Crew says. "I had no idea. He's so…laid-back. Fun. Easy-going. Not at all buttoned-up and old-man-ish."

I giggle softly, also imagining Nathan's face.

"McNeill?" Nathan asks.

"Yeah, boss?"

"You may call me Mr. Armstrong."

"Even in bed?"

"Especially in bed."

My stomach swoops. I'm grinning like an idiot, but also that sounds like Nathan is open to more of last night.

"Damn, that's kinda hot," Crew says.

"Besides, if anyone gets the label daddy, it's Hughes, because he corrals us all."

That is true.

"And we're going to put down some other rules," Nathan says.

"Don't even say that you always get her pussy first," Crew says. "That's not fair."

Nathan clears his throat and I feel another swoop.

"I was going to say that you have to clear out by seven the next morning."

Crew laughs. "No way. No morning sex with our girl without me."

Our girl. I love when they call me that.

"No one's having morning sex today," Michael says. "We worked her over pretty good last night. This morning is for us to be sweet, romantic. Pancakes, coffee, kissing her goodbye, showing her we like her for more than her body."

"Agreed," Nathan says.

I can hear Crew's sigh from here. "Fine."

Hmm… that is very sweet.

But also, no morning sex?

"And out by seven on a weekday," Nathan repeats. "We do have jobs, McNeill, including Danielle."

"Today's a weekday," I say as I come around the corner and head toward the kitchen. "Do I need to get out of your hair?"

I'm disappointed but it's not unreasonable.

Nathan turns and spots me wearing his dress shirt and nothing else. His nostrils flare and he shakes his head. "I didn't mean today. Can I get you a coffee?"

Not today implies the future and that makes me feel giddy as hell. I want to jog in place with my arms out while I squeal in glee that I might have another night like last night. But I make an attempt at playing it cool.

I nod. "Yes. Please."

Nathan is wearing a robe, open over his boxer briefs, which should look ridiculous but actually looks sexy as hell. I've never seen a man other than my father wear a robe in real life, but Nathan looks nothing like my neurotic and thrifty dad in his ratty fleece. This robe looks like it costs more than my rent, and Nathan looks rumpled, and sleepy, and sophisticated, and commanding all at once. Like when he was fucking me last night, gripping my hips so hard I'm sure I have faint bruises this morning.

Michael tells Nathan, "She likes both cream and sugar."

He remembers how I take my coffee because of course he does.

Michael is amazing at keeping track of all the little details. Currently, he's ladling pancake mix onto a griddle. He's dressed in his clothes from the night before, but his shirt is unbuttoned, giving me a fantastic view of his chest. I refuse to blush thinking of how he came in my mouth and I swallowed with enthusiasm.

Maybe I blush a little. It was just so hot.

"That smells delicious," I say, taking a deep breath as I approach the kitchen island.

Crew is in his underwear with a morning erection I'd like to get my hands on. They've decided on no morning sex, but I know who is the weak link here. I saunter over to Crew and wrap my arms around his neck. He makes a sound of appreciation in the back of his throat and squeezes my ass enthusiastically with both hands.

"Good morning." I kiss him, teasing my tongue between his lips.

He groans and sets me back with willpower he must use in playing hockey. "Good morning, sweetheart. I like you for more than your body."

That makes me laugh. "I know that."

"You're not supposed to actually say that," Nathan tells him. "You're supposed to just show her."

"Oh, like you do?" Crew rolls his eyes. "Where's that coffee, Boss?"

Nathan asked if I wanted coffee but has made exactly no move to get me any. He's just standing there watching me and Crew with his own erection tenting his boxer briefs.

Nathan swears and goes over to the absurdly complicated coffee, latte, and espresso maker. It looks so elaborate it probably also makes tea, smoothies, and ice cream. It might even turn water into wine from the looks of it.

"Sorry," he says. "I'm getting it."

I'm more amused than annoyed. He was enjoying watching me with Crew.

Michael flips the pancakes. "How did you sleep?" he asks me.

"Like I had three incredibly sexy guys fucking me all night."

Crew groans again. Nathan pauses in fiddling with the buttons on the machine, his shoulders stiffening.

"What does that mean specifically?" Michael asks, giving me a slow smile as he divides pancakes across four plates.

"It means totally satisfied," I say, stretching a little as I lean across the island to be closer to him. I am well aware that Nathan's shirt is riding up and Crew can see a peek of ass cheek. "I didn't even dream because I didn't need to. All my dreams came true last night."

"That's the best thing I've heard since you coming last night. Multiple times. I do love you screaming our names, Dani." Michael moves around the island and hands me a plate. "Eat." He brushes over my lips with a soft kiss. He tastes like blueberries.

I sigh in contentment and take a seat. "Wow. This looks amazing. I would have been happy with a cup of coffee and one of those pastries Nathan has in the fridge."

"They're lemon blueberry pancakes. I'm no chef, but I enjoy spending time in the kitchen. It relaxes me. And I really like having other people to cook for."

Nathan finally hands me a cup of coffee but he doesn't say anything. He doesn't eat his pancakes either. He mostly just stabs at the stack with his fork.

It occurs to me as the rest of us eat and chat that we're in Nathan's apartment, interrupting his morning routine. When we're obviously all done eating, except for Nathan, I decide to take the lead and give him his space. "Well, Crew, Michael, we should probably head out after we clean up."

Nathan doesn't even protest. He also says, "I have a housekeeper. You don't have to clean up."

That makes me frown. "It takes two seconds to put a plate in the dishwasher." I can tell something is weighing on him. Or maybe it isn't. Maybe he just wants to be alone.

Crew spends just as much time slapping my butt with the dish towel as he does cleaning up, but we manage to get the kitchen put back together with Michael while Nathan is in the shower. He did dump his uneaten pancakes in the trash and put his plate in the dishwasher though.

Baby steps.

That seems to be the way it is with Nathan.

I never imagined he would be sharing his bed with these guys and yet he didn't even complain when I asked him to scoot over. I don't want to push him so far out of his comfort zone that he bails because this whole arrangement works because it's all of them. I can't imagine losing Nathan in my trio of guys. It would change the entire dynamic, and I'm happy with it exactly the way it was last night.

That's why when he comes back out, fully dressed in a suit for work looking like, well, a billion dollars, I'm dressed and ready to go when Michael and Crew give casual goodbyes to him.

"Danielle, can you stay for a minute?" Nathan asks. "I wanted to explain something."

I exchange looks with Crew and Michael but they don't seem to have any more clue than I do what it might be about.

"Of course."

"Later, Nate," Crew says with a wave. Then he slaps my ass and gives me a resounding smack on the top of my head. "Talk to you soon, sweetheart."

Michael kisses my cheek. "Have a wonderful day. Bye, Nathan, thanks for hosting."

"Don't say that again. It sounds... untoward," Nathan says with a frown.

"I don't even know what that means," Crew says, hitting the elevator button.

Michael just shakes his head with a grin. "Got it. Nothing untoward."

Then they're gone and I'm alone with Nathan. I look at him

expectantly. "You don't eat breakfast?" I ask, when he doesn't immediately speak.

"What?" He looks up from where he's been studiously adjusting his jacket sleeve. "No. I usually just drink a protein shake. I don't like to chew in the morning."

That makes me want to snicker. Nathan doesn't like a lot of things. But I can tell from his expression he needs me to be serious right now.

I just wait for him to offer up a reason he wanted me to hang back.

Finally he clears his throat, crosses his arms over his chest, and meets my gaze. "You asked about condoms. I don't need them because I can't have children. I can't get you pregnant."

My eyebrows shoot up. That's an important piece of information about him and he just announced it like he got us a table for two at eight. "How do you know that?" I ask carefully, wanting to know more.

"I told you my parents died when I was twelve in a car accident and I was injured too. I won't go into details but infertility was one of the results."

"Oh, Nathan," I say before I can prevent it from slipping out. I can't even envision what kind of injury would result in that. "That's terrible. You must have been in so much emotional and physical pain."

He winces. "Yes."

"I'm so sorry." The man without family beyond his ailing grandfather can't even have his own. All the money in the world can't buy him a biological child.

But he just shrugs. "I was so young I'd never even given much thought to having kids. The chance was gone before I knew I wanted it, you know? I think it would have been harder if I was older."

"That's a lot of loss all at once." I reach out and take his hand. "Come here. Come sit down with me. Unless you have to get to the office?"

The corner of his mouth turns up ever so slightly. "I'm the boss, remember? I don't answer to anyone."

I lean in closer and closer on tiptoes, expecting him to pull back. But he holds his ground until we're practically nose to nose. I grab his tie and give him a soft kiss. "Hey, guess what, Nathan Armstrong? From now on you have to answer to me. And you don't have to shoulder burdens all by yourself, do you understand that?" I tug the tie to emphasize my point. "I'm your lover but I'm your friend, too, you know."

His head shifts from side to side. "No," he says, his voice low and raw. "I didn't know that."

"Well, now you do."

Nathan

Danielle is smiling up at me, confidently and sweetly, as if what she just said isn't the equivalent of an atomic bomb being dropped on me. I stare down at her, taking in every faint freckle dotting her creamy skin, the slight upturn of her adorable button nose, the tempting cupid's bow of her perfect lips, and the messy tousle of her auburn hair, untamed still after our night of group sex.

I let two other guys fuck her in front of me. Hell, at the same time. And I was more turned on than anything else, which is a total mind fuck. I never would have dreamed I'd get into watching a woman I love be pleasured by other men. Yet, all I could think was that I could squash my jealousy and personal desires because Danielle takes priority over me.

I want to give her everything and if that means sharing her with Crew and Michael, both of whom I actually like, in spite of all my grumbling, I will.

But now she is being the generous one. Giving me something I didn't even know I needed or wanted.

Friendship.

And love.

The emerald green of her eyes are shining with an emotion I can't quite grasp, or believe, or want to acknowledge. Love.

I don't want to be wrong.

Because I'm not really all that lovable. I can admit that. I'm a bossy, grumpy asshole who is lacking a sensitivity chip. A woman hasn't told me she loved me since I was twenty-five, and when my college girlfriend broke up with me, her departure speech included such gems as "loving you is slow torture," and "being in love with you is the equivalent of jumping into a shark tank covered in bait."

I'm not wrong about how I feel.

But I don't want to be wrong about how Danielle feels, so I don't say a goddamn word. I just stand there like a stone statue.

"How often do you see your grandfather?" she asks.

Swallowing the damn golf ball size lump in my throat I force myself to speak. I'm fantastic at pulling my shit together and faking that I'm fucking fine but it's hard to fake anything with her. Maybe I don't need to. Isn't that what she just implied?

"At least twice a week. I try to go as often as I can but sometimes the team schedule makes it difficult."

"Can I go with you next time and meet him?"

My heart starts to beat unnaturally fast. "What? Why?" I ask, both secretly thrilled and terrified all at once.

Being vulnerable around Danielle scares me, like tarantulas

and a losing hockey season, but at the same time, I love that she doesn't seem turned off by my rusty insides.

"Because he's important to you. And you're important to me."

Fuck, just like that I'm done. Sunk. It's over. I'm in love with Danielle and there's no stopping it now.

"You're important to me too," I say. My voice is gruff and I hate that. I force myself to smooth it over. "I'd love to take you to meet my grandfather. He'll be shocked that I managed to score myself a nice woman."

She smiles. "I can't wait because I want to ask him what you were like as a kid. Did you wear a suit as an eight-year-old?"

I give a crack of laughter, relieved to lean on humor, but also, happy. Just fucking happy to be around her. "Smart ass. No, I did not."

"I bet you were the guy all the girls wanted as a teenager. The aloof and devastatingly handsome hockey heir."

I brush her hair back and shake my head, amused. "Hardly. I was a little bit shy, actually."

Danielle laughs out loud. "Bullshit."

"It's true. I took a freshman to my senior prom because I didn't have the balls to ask any of the girls in my class. I just charged up to this cute girl on the volleyball team and demanded, "Go to prom with me," and she blinked and said, "Okay."

"So nothing has actually changed," Danielle says. Her eyes are twinkling and she slaps my shoulder in delight. "You're shy? Is that what all this big bad brooding boss act is?"

Well, fuck. That is not what I meant. "No, no, fuck no. Don't you dare tell that to McNeill and Hughes." I should be horrified. But I'm laughing because being around Danielle makes me lighter, amused, less defensive. It's easy to share with Danielle. It's easy to be myself, no walls up, not guarded, not painfully aware that everyone wants something from the rich guy.

I'm just Nathan with her—hell, maybe even Nate—and I like that.

"Or what?" she asks playfully. "What are you going to do to me?"

I give her ass a smack and it's not a mere tap. It has some power behind it. "You will be punished."

Danielle gasps with pleasure. "I can't wait."

God, this woman is everything.

CHAPTER 22

Crew

IT OCCURS to me after my morning workout that we need some additional ground rules. And yes, I'm aware of how weird it is that I'm the one thinking like that.

But Michael and I left Dani with Nathan at his apartment this morning. And he's the big boss, which means he doesn't have to report to work at any specific time. So he can do whatever he wants.

With Dani.

And even if it isn't sex, I'm wishing I could be there with her. With them. Doing whatever. Did they just talk? Do the crossword? Go for a walk? Get Nathan something else to eat because he's apparently too good for lemon blueberry pancakes—which fucking rocked by the way? Whatever they did, I would have wanted to do it too. With them. Yes, even including Nathan.

And yes, all of that thinking did make my workout pretty shitty. Distractions like that are going to be a problem.

I knock on the doorframe of Michael's office at the arena. He looks up from his desk.

"Hey, come on in." He puts his pen down and sits back. "What's up?"

I look behind me. There's no one in the hallway but I close the door anyway.

Hughes's eyebrows arch. "Everything okay?"

"I'm just thinking, how do we date Dani?" I ask, crossing my arms and leaning back against the door.

He doesn't seem surprised that Dani is the topic of conversation rather than hockey. "Together," is his simple answer.

"Together. We take her out to dinner together? To the movies? All four of us?"

He takes a breath. "I think, for now, while we're figuring this all out, we need to all spend time together. And stay in. I don't think you or Nathan really needs the publicity a poly relationship will bring so early on."

I nod. "So nothing one on one with her?"

"I think eventually we'll get to that. It's unrealistic to think that we'll all four always be around to do things together. And there's no reason that she can't have time with each of us alone. But we need to get comfortable with our group dynamic first."

"What about Dani and Nathan this morning then?"

"It was his apartment. Makes sense we'd be the first to leave."

"Then next time I need to invite you all over to my place and kick you guys out the next morning?" I ask.

Michael shakes his head. "I think we need to have a consistent place that is...ours. The place where we all spend time together." He's frowning now.

"What?" I ask.

"We need to be sure Nathan is okay with it being his place," Michael says. "Obviously it could be your apartment. Mine too, for that matter, though you both have bigger places."

I think about that. I wouldn't mind all of us gathering at my place but... Jesus, it will sound stupid out loud but Nathan's place just seems more obvious. It's more grown-up. Mine is a bachelor pad. I don't think I even have enough towels for all of us. I definitely don't have enough forks. Unless plastic ones count.

"Nathan's place feels right," I say. "Which is weird because it also feels kind of cold. But…" I trail off, thinking about our time there.

"But what?" Michael prompts.

"When we're all there, it doesn't." I shrug. "Last night was hot as hell, of course. But even this morning when we were all having breakfast it felt…good. And I don't think Armstrong hated it."

Michael nods, seemingly thinking that over. "I think you're right. In fact, if any place becomes ours, I think it should be Nathan's. I think he needs his apartment to become a home most."

Damn, that hits me in the chest in an unexpected way. "Is it stupid that I think he'd agree? Deep down and not out loud of course."

Hughes smiles. "Not stupid. I think we're thawing him out. Dani's sunshine for sure is melting some of his ice."

He's completely right. Of course, that girl and her warm smiles and big heart and passion—in the bedroom and just for all the things, and people, she loves—could melt the polar ice caps. Armstrong has no fucking chance of resisting her. I'm just not sure he knows that yet.

I pull my phone out and start typing. "Okay. We need to all get on the same page here."

"Who are you calling?"

"No one. Group text." I look up as Michael's phone pings with a text notification.

> #17 to Cookie & Co.: More rules: No one-on-one dates. We all get together at Nathan's. Michael cooks. No panties allowed for girls @ home.

Hughes grins. "We're Cookie & Co?"

"I like your nickname for her," I say with a shrug. "Okay if I borrow it for this?" I don't think anyone but Michael should call her that out loud. It feels like it's his.

He actually seems pleased. "Sure. And you called Nathan's place home," he points out.

I did. I typed it without thinking. "You think that's okay?"

"Guess we'll see." His thumbs start moving over his phone.

Doc to Cookie & Co.: Let me know of any food allergies or things you won't eat. No panty rule seconded.

I grin.

Another text pings both our phones.

I'm shocked as hell to see it's Nathan.

Boss to Cookie & Co.: No panties thirded.

I start laughing. He gave himself a nickname in the group. I mean, I call him boss all the time and it definitely fits, but I love that he's leaning into this. He's definitely thawing. "I guess we're all on the same page," I say to Hughes.

Michael is grinning as well. "It's a really great page."

I couldn't agree more.

I turn and pull Hughes' office door open just as another text comes in.

It says it's from Cookie to Cookie & Co. It's just a photo of panties piled up on a bed.

The quilt on the bed is very girly. Very Dani. As are those panties. There's pinks and peaches and lavenders and pale blues. There's lace and bows, flowers, and hearts.

I groan and look at Michael. He looks equally amused and turned on.

My phone dings again.

Cookie to Cookie & Co.: My packing just got a lot easier. Thanks.

"She's…" I start.

"Adorable," Hughes fills in.

I laugh. "Yeah."

CHAPTER 23

Nathan

"YOU COULD AT LEAST TRY to smile."

I glance over at Valerie, my grandfather's former secretary. She's wearing a navy cocktail dress and she's not smiling any more than I am.

"Look in the mirror," I tell her dryly. "We're a couple of old grumps standing on the sideline."

We're at the Stick It To Cancer charity event and while it's a great cause and I should be mingling and thanking donors, I'm gripping a glass of scotch. The various players, coaches, and team sponsors are laughing and chatting.

While I'm over here, missing Danielle and wishing I was at home with her.

I'm comfortable in this Armani tux. But I suck at faking friendly.

"Stanford loved these events," she muses. "You'd never find him propping up a wall."

As if I need the reminder. "I know. He was great at this. It makes his absence even harder."

My grandfather had been a classic networker. He could work a room like nobody's business, remembering the smallest details about every person at the event all while making everyone feel at ease and included.

My father had been good at this as well. From what I've been told, his style was a little different. Less jovial, more dedicated seriousness, an emphasis on the charities and the work that was being done.

Me? I get the job done.

But I'm better behind a desk or at the computer, managing logistics and money, not people.

"Rumor has it you took a friend with you to visit him this week," Valerie says, sipping a glass of red wine. "A female friend."

I frown at her. "Are you stalking me? That's creepy, Val."

"Get over yourself. The nursing facility tells me what visitors Stanford has, just like they do you."

"I didn't actually think you were stalking me, but your defensiveness suggests maybe I should consider it," I tease her.

She rolls her eyes. "Who is the girl?"

"None of your business. She's a friend." Friend, girlfriend, love of my life…

Not that I've told Danielle how I feel because I haven't. But having her meet my grandfather was a big step for me. I'd had sweaty palms and a racing heart and I wasn't even sure why. She had been sweet and supportive and had held me in her arms afterward when she saw how hard it was for me to witness him slip into confusion right before our eyes.

Danielle is the comfort I didn't even know I needed. She's there, every day, reliably, with that soft smile, sometimes sassy comebacks, and an open and generous heart.

Two other guys are always there too. Guys who would be just as good at this whole schmoozing thing as my grandfather and father. Guys my grandfather would like. Guys *I* like.

McNeill and Hughes.

They started out as my competition and somewhere along the way they morphed into something like fraternity brothers. I like their company. Crew's barbs, Michael's reminders to cool my heels, are starting to feel very familiar. Enjoyable. Something I look forward to, in fact.

Yes, it's about Danielle. I love her.

But it's also about bonus friendships with these guys that I never expected to have.

"You have a friend? Honey, I'm so proud of you," Valerie says, patting my arm mockingly.

To my surprise, her teasing stings a little. Fuck. A lot.

In the past she's taken jabs at me and it's never bothered me. It's her form of affection and I know that. So why the fuck does it hurt now?

"Harsh," I tell her. "But don't be proud of me yet. I'm sure I'll fuck it up somehow." That's a huge fear of mine. That I'll be the one to come up short in our Cookie & Co. foursome family and they won't need me. Or want me.

That thought has me shoving myself off the wall, taking down the half-filled glass of scotch in one fiery swallow and heading into the fray. I've spent most of my life lonely. For the first time in forever I have something good in my life, relationships and people that I care about, and I don't want to lose that.

Crew is actually laughing and animatedly telling a story, surrounded by his teammates. He gets along with everyone, everywhere he goes. He's a media darling, he's a favorite among the other players, and he makes Danielle laugh.

He doesn't need another friend. He has a million.

Yet even now as I'm walking past, he spots me and calls out, "Boss! Get over here! I need you to hear this story."

The other players part for me like I'm fucking Moses and they're the Red Sea. That's what happens when you're the billionaire boss. It's amazing power and it sure as hell has its perks, but it has a downside. No one really likes you. Or you're never sure if they do.

But then there's McNeill.

Call me crazy, but I think he actually likes hanging out with me in the same way I enjoy chilling with him. We're total opposites and it's fun to give each other a hard time.

"If this story involves being arrested or waking up with a stolen zoo animal, I don't want to hear it," I tell him, with a smile I don't even have to force.

He claps my shoulder. He's lost his jacket and tie already and looks a little drunk. "I've never stolen a single zoo animal. No, listen, this is about that time in Boston when that ref called a high stick on me, which was total bullshit and was just targeting because he hates me. I stole his whistle and put it in my—

Jesus. I throw my hand up. "Stop talking. I don't want to hear this."

Alexei , our defenseman, lets out a snort. "You did not!"

McNeill nods. "I did," he says solemnly. "In my pants, rolled it all over my sweaty balls."

"That's way better than where I thought you were going with that," Jack Hayes, our right wing, says.

"I can't believe you're telling Mr. Armstrong this," goalie Blake Wilder comments. "Like, seriously, dude. Boundaries."

"He thinks I'm hilarious." Crew throws his arm around me and hugs me to his side. "He loves me."

He's definitely drunk. At least a little buzzed. He's being way too open for this environment.

But his obvious affection for me makes me feel good.

All of this makes it harder and harder to keep our arrangement a secret.

Crew has given me the perfect opener to get us both out of the event at the same time, which is winding up anyway, without arousing suspicion.

I have no doubt that Danielle has spent a pleasant evening at her own apartment alone or hanging out with Luna, but we all made plans to meet up at my place after the charity event and I'm looking forward to it. After these events get me wound up tight and left with feelings of dissatisfaction and loneliness, I usually go home and drink alone while watching an espionage movie. I like how car chases and explosions fill my apartment with sound.

Which is as pathetic as it sounds.

But now I don't have to go home alone to a place that rivals an echo chamber.

Instead, Michael and Danielle and Crew will all be there, and we'll catch up on each others' week, hang out, and end up in my bed, taking turns worshiping our Danielle until she's shaking and screaming out in pleasure.

The thought makes me impatient.

Michael is picking up Danielle right about now, so it's time to get the hell out of here.

"Are you drunk?" I ask Crew, giving him a look that I hope he interprets correctly as me wanting him to exaggerate how much alcohol he's had.

He does, giving me a wink no one else can see before saying in a booming and jovial voice, "I'm not fucking drunk. Lighten up, Nate."

"Whoa, McNeill, uh, take it down a notch," Blake says. He rubs the back of his head and looks nervously between us. "Maybe lay off the tequila."

"Lay off my jock," Crew tells him. He goes to point his finger at the goalie and stumbles. He knocks into Blake's beer, causing it to splash over the edge of the glass.

"Oh, shit," Alexei says.

Blake, who is older, a rule-follower, and in control of himself the majority of the time, appears to be fighting the urge to take a swing at Crew. His nostrils are flaring as he shakes beer off of his hand.

"Go home, McNeill," he says tightly. "Before you embarrass yourself and the Racketeers. This is for fucking cancer research."

That's my cue.

"I completely agree," I say, nudging Crew. "Come on. I'll take you down and get you a car."

Crew shakes me off and raises his hands. "Okay, okay. It's

cool. I'm cool." He points to Blake. "You're cool." He pivots and gestures between himself and Alexei. "We're cool. Everyone's so damn cool and we're going to win a motherfucking championship."

His goofy drunk act actually seems to readily win the guys back around. They're all shaking their heads and are in various stages of smiling, from resisting the urge to full grins. Everyone loves Crew.

Even I have to admit he's hard to stay annoyed with and I've worked really hard at it.

The minute we're in the elevator he turns to me. "How'd I do?"

"Not bad," I said. "Though you could have skipped spilling Wilder's beer all over him."

"That was actually an accident."

I snort. "You're a handful."

He puts his hand on his dick. "That's what Dani says."

Was I just thinking I like this idiot? I roll my eyes. "Say that in front of her. It will only serve to make me look better."

"Hey, I got us out of here tonight by being fake drunk. I took one for the team. Don't be mean."

"You're not drunk at all?" I ask. I thought he was at least a little buzzed. That means he included me in his circle of teammates sober, which makes me feel… interesting. Grateful isn't the right word. Pleased, I guess. That's what I am. Pleased.

"Hell, no, I'm not drunk. We have plans tonight with Dani. Do you think I'm going to risk whiskey dick or being sloppy all over her? Nope, no way." The elevator opens. "I just have hella acting skills. Unlike you."

I pull my phone out to order my car from the valet with the app. "I don't need to act."

He steps out of the elevator and grins at me. "Maybe you should try it."

The valet pulls my Lamborghini around. I don't drive it as often as I'd like because it's hard to open it up in the city, but it works well for events like this one. Anyone seeing me arriving appreciates the flash of a sports car.

"Can I drive?" Crew asks, as the valet hands me my keys.

"Over my dead body."

"You know, you're like a much, much older brother to me," Crew says as he opens the passenger door and I go around to the driver's side.

I pause and tell him over the roof, "You're like the younger half-brother I never wanted from my father's second marriage."

He grins. "That's sweet. See? You're warming up to me."

I play my role and roll my eyes because that's what he expects and wants, but in reality, I am.

I'm warming up to all of this.

Some people are fortunate to be born into a family filled with love and laughter.

Others create theirs.

My grandfather and I had our own little two man family unit, with some side characters like Valerie and my grandfather's cousins. Small, but mighty, and I've been missing that more than I realized until these last few weeks.

When me and McNeill step out of the elevator into my penthouse we find Dani and Michael in the kitchen, talking and making popcorn, music playing over the integrated speakers around the room. I'm struck by how different this is from my usual post-cocktail party evenings.

The room feels toasty warm, vibrating with energy and yes, love.

Even the lighting feels softer somehow, which is impossible, and yet I stand by the fact that when four different people are turning on and off a variety of lights, the mood is always comfortable. I normally use the same two lights in every room, which creates shadows in most of the corners and a stale atmosphere.

I've been in a rut, one that includes dinner for one and every streaming service available on the planet.

But now I'm greeted by a wave from Hughes and Dani's warm voice. "Hey! How was the event? You two are home earlier than we expected."

Clapping Crew on the shoulder, I toss my keys on the console table. "This guy pretended to have one too many and shaved about thirty minutes off of our time. I probably should have stuck it out and spoken to more donors but I just wanted to come home."

Something about my tone causes Dani to pause in shaking salt over a bowl of popcorn. She heads toward me, her smile softening. I just stand there and wait, my throat tight, for her to do whatever it is she's about to do. Sometimes when I look at her, I'm incapable of action because she just takes my fucking breath away.

Crew is chattering away about his awesome acting skills as he kicks off his dress shoes and strips his jacket in ten seconds flat before heading straight to the popcorn.

Dani reaches me. She cups my cheeks and rises on her tiptoes to press her lips against mine. I close my eyes, sighing into the kiss, needing her touch, craving her understanding.

When she pulls back, she says, simply, "You miss him."

I know who and what she means. I just nod, unable to speak. It amazes me how in tune with my emotions she is. She knows what I'm thinking and feeling, sometimes before I do.

"It really just sucks, sweetheart," she tells me before kissing me again.

She doesn't try to qualify it with an "at least you have great memories" or "but you're lucky he left you so much money", both of which I've heard. Neither of which make me feel any better.

I've never felt the loss of having my own kids until my grandfather's dementia, and Dani knows the right words to say to me. I'm also pretty damn sure no one has called me sweetheart since I was five years old and I fucking love everything about it, though I will never admit that out loud. Ever.

I kiss her fiercely before brushing my thumb over her bottom lip and staring deep into her eyes. "Thank you," I tell her gruffly.

For her compassion, for her heart, for her passion in bed, and for being the driving force that somehow created this new group dynamic—maybe even a fucking family—for me when I didn't know I needed one.

She smiles and reaches up and loosens the bowtie on my tux. "Come and grab some popcorn and "accidentally" drop some down my cleavage so you can fish it out."

"That sounds like a Crew move," I tell her.

But I do check her out. She's wearing the Racketeers shirt I gave her the night we met. The one that's too small. Her tits are busting out of the V.

God, I fucking love this shirt.

"What's your move?" she asks.

"I'm not telling you," I murmur, nuzzling her earlobe. "But when it happens, you'll know, my dirty little slut."

Danielle laughs softly. "Wait until you see my moves."

I hook my finger in the V of her t-shirt and tug it down so I can see more of her breasts. "I love every move you make."

I love you.

I almost say it, but I can't make the words come out.

"Nathan, do you want a beer?" Michael calls out from the kitchen.

Relieved, I let go of Danielle. "Yes, I would love one."

CHAPTER 24

Crew

SOMEHOW DOC and Nate managed to secure the spots on either side of Dani on the couch. I'm stuck in the armchair across from them. There's an entire ocean of coffee table between me and my girl, while those two have hands all over her. Michael is making inroads on her thigh under her skirt and Nathan has his hand at the base of her neck, massaging her. I'm not jealous. Just envious. I want to touch her, too and it makes me antsy. After bouncing my knee up and down vigorously and shoveling a handful of popcorn in my mouth, I need to take action.

While they're discussing what movie we should watch, I shoot a piece of popcorn at Dani's cleavage. It bounces off her tit and rolls onto her stomach. She picks it up and puts it in her mouth with a smile.

"You missed."

Then she looks at Nathan.

He says, "See? I told you."

She laughs softly and now I wish that she and I had a private joke as well.

"What?" I ask, striving for casual nonchalance. I toss my feet up onto the coffee table to emphasize that I don't care, even though I very much fucking care.

"I told Danielle you would be the one throwing popcorn at her cleavage."

Rubbing my chin, I try not to be insulted and fail miserably. The implication is I'm immature, which I am, in a way. Not immature for my age, because I am only twenty-two. But younger than Michael and Nathan in some key ways. Sure, I've been living on my own since eighteen, playing pro since nineteen, but I have a chaotic, mobile lifestyle being on the road constantly.

I haven't learned how to cook or do my laundry and I don't need to. There's takeout and laundry services in my building. Not to mention the three lovely ladies at the Racketeers who keep my uniforms crisp and clean, my number 17 stitched to perfection. I love those women, they're like a trio of grandmas wishing all of us luck on the ice every game.

"You don't want to get salt and butter on her tits and lick it off?" I ask Nathan. "Because I do."

His eyebrows shoot up. "I wasn't saying it was a bad idea, just not one I would have thought of. We all have our own style."

"Which is what I love about us," Dani tells me.

That is all I need to hear. She's right, of course. She wants each of us for different reasons.

Doc is watching me carefully. "You need to talk this out, McNeill? We should always clear the air if something is on our minds. That's how this needs to work."

I shake my head. "I'm good."

I don't want to say what I'm thinking out loud. I'm not great at expressing my deeper emotions. Happy, proud, excited, celebratory… sure, bring 'em on. Anything else is a little foreign. I've had a lot of opportunities for happy, positive emotions in my life, I can admit that. And when I try to express more complex thoughts and emotions, it comes out a jumbled mess that sometimes makes the situation worse.

I just need to work shit out in my own head, which I'm confident I will.

Hughes studies me for a second, but then he turns to Dani.

"This is the perfect time to share your latest scene with the guys. I'm sure they'd love to hear your writing."

I see what he's trying to do. The writing and love of books is something he and Dani share privately, and now he's offering to share that slice of her with me and Nate.

It makes me feel like a prick for feeling any hint of jealousy. Here Doc is willing to share and I'm throwing popcorn at her to get her attention.

"You don't have to do that," I protest. "That's your thing, the two of you."

"Yes," Nathan agrees. "Only share if you want to, Danielle."

"You don't want to hear my writing?" Dani asks.

Her look of vulnerability shocks me into action.

"What?" I blurt out. "Babe, that's not what I meant."

Now Nathan and I are both falling all over ourselves to reassure her.

"Danielle, that's not what I meant either," he says.

"Of course I want to hear your writing!" I tell her, actually standing up, though I don't know where I'm going. "I just didn't want to interfere with your thing."

"Exactly," Nathan says, taking her by the chin and turning her toward him. "I would love to hear what you've written but I don't want to intrude on what you and Michael have."

"Do you mind?" she asks Michael.

"I think they should be allowed a peek into your creative process as well." He grins. "Besides, you're steadily building a readership on Habanero. I'm not the only one reading it."

"I don't understand," Nathan says.

I'm only half-listening as they both take turns explaining what Habanero is.

Which is why Dani needs all three of us. Nathan looks like he's trying to be supportive, but doesn't entirely grasp the concept.

"You just let random people on the internet read your book for free?" he asks, brow furrowing.

"Yes, to build a readership so eventually I can make money on my writing."

Nathan looks ready to launch into a whole business Q&A session so I jump in. "Can you read it now? We've got the popcorn and everything."

I give her an encouraging smile.

"Yes, it's on my phone." Dani pulls her phone out and swipes on it. She clears her throat and then opens her mouth. But then she abruptly shoves her phone at Michael. "I can't. You read it. Please."

"Sure thing, babe."

Doc has a nice voice and while he does read it with expression and emotion, it's not over-the-top.

"But if you're not a bodyguard, how did you lose your hand?" Divine asked Sturgeon in confusion, staring at her lover anxiously as she pushed her glasses up the bridge of her nose. "Why have you been guarding me?"

She paced around the hotel room, mind swirling with the implications of what Sturgeon had told her. This was all so much bigger than it seemed.

"I lost my hand in an explosion. And I've been guarding you while you were caged because since your birth you were promised to me. I infiltrated your kidnappers and took your virginity so they couldn't."

Divine felt tears prick her eyes and she blinked hard so he wouldn't see how much that hurt her. "It was just to protect me, nothing more?"

All that passion, all that tenderness, was fake?

She'd begged him for his cock and he had given it to her out of duty, nothing more. It was humiliating.

"Your father knew the value of your purity, that's why he kept you locked away all those years. He needed to find the highest bidder to pay back his debts."

"That's impossible. He would never do that. It was for my protec-

tion." Divine couldn't believe the lies that were coming from the tempting mouth of the man she loved.

He was a stranger.

Yet even now, she craved his touch. She wanted him to toss her on the bed and fuck away all the doubt she felt, to make her so crazed with need she would believe anything he said.

"Oh, but he did." Sturgeon raised his hand and tucked her hair behind her ear. "Now your father is dead and tomorrow you'll marry me."

Divine gasped. "My father is dead?"

"Yes, by my own hand."

The story continues for several minutes until Michael pauses and Dani bites her lip, waiting for our reactions.

To be totally honest, I'm not sure what the fuck I just heard.

Was the writing good? I think so. But I don't read stuff like that, so I'm not sure, and I'm also very confused. Why doesn't Divine just get the fuck out of there?

I realize that I am damn lucky that Doc and Boss are here to say the right thing to Dani, because if I open my mouth right now, something stupid is going to fall out.

I clearly don't understand romance novels.

Sturgeon needs a punch in the nuts, and yet, Divine seems all into him. I'm also not sure if the caging was literal or a kink, but at any rate, there were at least three opportunities for sexual innuendos in there and Dani left me hanging in the wind.

Not to mention the line "by my own hand" when the dude's only got one hand. Dani laid down a joke and then never picked it up. It's a more serious style of writing than I expected from her and I don't know what to make of that.

Either that or I'm incapable of being serious unless I'm on the ice, which is very possible.

This is why Cookie & Co. works. Because we back each other up, we make up for each others' shortcomings, we can all step forward with what we're best at and give Dani everything she needs, at all times.

Right now, with my schedule, I can't give her the time and attention she deserves. I'm on the road fifty percent of the time and when I am in town I have practice, PR events, and games. I also can't be the one to critique or praise her writing.

"That's fantastic, Danielle, thank you for sharing with us," Nathan says. "You're so creative. I'm really impressed. How do you come up with the plot?"

Right. The plot. Smart move on Nate's part. That's easy to discuss.

"I don't know. It just sort of pops into my head when I'm lying in bed. Alone," she adds with a grin.

"These twists and turns keep coming, babe," Michael says. "The readers will eat it up."

"The billionaire is hot, huh?" Nathan asks.

"The bossy, dominating guy?" I ask. "That tracks." I walk over to Dani and force my way in between her and the coffee table. I sit on it so I can lean in and kiss her. "You're awesome," I say, simply.

"Thanks, guys. That means a lot to me."

She looks genuinely pleased.

Together, we give her what she needs and that eases my mind.

"Can you read a sex scene?" I ask. "Do you write those?"

"Oh, she writes those," Doc says. "Scorching hot."

Dani blushes. "I have lots of inspiration."

"Maybe we can work on that now," Nathan says, his hand shifting over her and teasing at her clit.

Dani sighs. "I think that sounds like Divine is going to get fucked so good in the next scene I write."

CHAPTER 25

Michael

CREW IS HAVING a hell of a game. That's not unusual, but this is good even for Crew. He's playing hard, but loose. He's having a good time. He seems to have boundless energy. The other team simply can't keep up with him. He scored three times in the first period. He's absolutely on fire.

And I'm just sitting on the end of the bench grinning like an idiot.

I guess living with the guy, falling in love with the same woman, sleeping with the guy—literally—for the past two weeks, has made me a super fan. I laugh to myself. If that won't do it, nothing will.

Crew is fun to watch and easy to cheer for. He has been since day one. Even before he played for the Racketeers, I was a casual fan of his. He's that kind of athlete. Anyone who is a hockey fan has to appreciate the kind of player Crew is—tough, talented, fair, but cocky. He's full of himself, but he can back it all up.

But it's definitely different watching him tonight.

We're sharing something that I've never shared with anyone else.

I've shared a woman before, but it was nothing like this. It was just sex. It wasn't anything like what we have with Dani.

Crew and I are in love with the same woman. We're in a relationship with the same woman. A relationship that will hopefully be long-term. And that means that we're in a relationship with one another. And Nathan.

That makes watching Crew play different now. I feel like I'm watching one of my best friends, or even a brother, play. I'm proud of him.

And a little worried as one of the defenders from the other team, the Dragons, barrels toward him, trying to prevent another point from Crew before the end of the second period.

I get to my feet and lean into the glass to watch. I always worry about our players getting hurt, of course. That's my job. But my stomach is knotted tighter than usual as I watch Crew get smashed against the boards by a guy that easily outweighs him by thirty pounds.

They tussle for a few seconds, then Crew shoves him off, and skates away and I breathe again.

Fuck. Being involved with Crew is going to be tough. Especially when I'm on the bench, right down front for all the people gunning for him, for all the chances he takes, and—

The referees whistle blasts and I shake my head.

And all the stupid shit he does.

Crew turned around and went back after the guy who checked him into the wall. Both players have their gloves off and are swinging hard. And connecting.

Fuck.

Now Crew's bleeding and heading my way.

And grinning.

He stomps into the bench area and down to where I'm already on my feet and reaching for the first aid supplies.

"Damn, I love this game," he declares as he plops in front of me.

"You're an idiot," I tell him, starting to clean the gash on his cheek. I can't tell if it's his nose bleeding or the cut. Or both.

"Nah, I don't even feel it. Did you see her?"

Jesus, of course this is about Dani. "You got hit because you were thinking about her instead of the game?" I ask with a frown, wiping the blood away, pushing a little harder than probably necessary.

"No way. I got hit because I told Travers he needs to get off my ass, I'm off the market and he's not my type anyway."

I huff out a laugh in spite of myself. Justin Travers, the Dragons D-man and one of the best in the league, hates Crew. Crew is the only player to score on him this year.

I apply ointment to his gash. His nose has already stopped bleeding. "So what about Dani?"

"Did you see her?" he repeats. His stupid grin is huge. And genuine.

God, this guy is done for. He is head over heels.

I can't help but smile. Dani deserves that. She's got all of us wrapped around her little finger and, honestly, there is nowhere I'd rather be.

She'll take good care of us. And God knows Crew and Nathan need her. For different reasons, but...yeah. Nathan needs her warmth and happiness. Crew needs her acceptance and the way she blooms for him. He needs to be good for someone. And he really is for her. She's even brighter when he's around. Just like she seems feistier because of Nathan. He brings that sassiness out of her.

It's all gorgeous.

"Doc? Hey," Crew says, snapping his fingers in front of my face. "Did you see Dani?"

I bat his hand away. "I did." She's sitting with Luna tonight. In the same seats she was in the night we met. I'm sure Nathan had something to do with that. They're great seats. Right on the ice.

She's impossible to miss. Even if I wasn't looking for her, which I was. Her gorgeous red hair is down and loose, she's wearing blue jeans that mold to her delicious curves, and she's in a Chicago Racketeers jersey. With MCNEILL and a huge number 17 on the back.

She's not the only one in the arena wearing a jersey with Crew's name and number, of course. But she's the only one making his dick hard because of it. And making him act like he's invincible on the ice.

I love that he's happy and proud and I even like that he's a little possessive of her. That means he's serious about her, I figure. But it's making him do stupid shit like get in a fist fight with a guy bigger and meaner than him.

"I fuckin' love that she's here. It's the first game I've had her in the stands since we've been together."

Yes, I'm very aware of that. I roll my eyes. I'm pretty sure Crew remembers waking up with both of our heads on the same fucking pillow this morning because we're both sleeping with her. Literally sleeping, at least part of the time. In the same bed. And Crew's a cuddler. Not that I'm surprised.

Nathan insists on sleeping with Dani between him and any other male bedmates. Which means Crew and I take turns sleeping on her other side. The other one of us gets the outside of the bed.

There are pros and cons of each position, actually. Up against Dani is a very nice place to spend the night. But the outside makes it easier to get up and out without crawling over another man.

"You need to keep your head in the game and stop getting hit. You can't afford a concussion. You need all the brain cells you've got left. Nathan already tricked you out of..." I glance down the bench, but no one's looking at us. "You know."

The other night, Nathan and Crew had ended up in some argument over hockey stats and Nathan had bet Crew that if Nathan was right, Crew had to sit out sex with Dani and just watch.

Crew had lost.

Crew laughs. "Yeah, yeah, I know. But I just love having her here."

She'd come to the arena with Luna. Crew and I had needed to be here well ahead of game time, of course, and we'd told Nathan that the no-one-on-one dates included not having her to himself in the owner's box. That didn't seem fair. The hockey arena where we all worked and that we all loved should be a level playing field. So to speak.

"She looks fucking amazing with my name on her back," Crew says.

I nod. It's weird. It's not my name she's wearing, but there's something about seeing her in one of our names that even made my blood pump a little harder. We haven't defined our foursome in super specific terms, but she's made it clear that it's all for one and one for all, and her being here tonight, claiming Crew, even if it's only the four of us that really know it, makes me feel possessive of her too.

Besides, I was the only one with enough free time to text her when I'd seen her. Crew was warming up and Nathan was schmoozing, or handing out more VIP tickets, or some other owner-of-the-team crap.

> You look amazing. I hope you have a fantastic time tonight. Can't wait to see you at home.

She'd responded with a selfie of her and Luna in their seats, her giving me a kissy-face.

Then I'd arranged for Sammy, the Malamute mascot, to show up with beers, soft pretzels, and pizza for her and Luna after this period.

"I'm going to make her wear that tonight in bed," Crew says.

My attention snaps back to him. I have his cut closed with a butterfly suture and he's cleaned up, but I can do that shit in my sleep. I've been daydreaming about our girl.

I glance down the bench, but no one seems to have heard him. I suppose even if they had, they wouldn't know that I was going to be in bed *with* them.

"Nathan will not be happy about that."

Crew grins. "I know."

"Doc, any chance of him playing again this century?" Coach barks at me.

"Tonight even," I tell him dryly, clapping Crew on the shoulder. "Get out there and don't be a dumbass. You have to be in one piece for our girl later."

He gives me another goofy, in-love grin and springs up from the bench. "You know it."

He crashes back onto the ice and two minutes later scores again, just before the period ends.

He's going to be impossible to live with now.

But I'm grinning a goofy grin myself. Even Nathan will have to admit that Crew deserves some extra perks with Dani tonight.

And speaking of Dani…

I turn to catch one more glimpse of her as I make my way off the bench and toward the hallway that will lead to the locker rooms for intermission.

Sammy is approaching with beers and food.

And a black…something. And a giant bouquet of… flowers? They look like flowers, but I'm not sure that's what they are. They are on stems, with ribbons, and wrapped in cellophane.

He is barely able to juggle everything and the crowd is murmuring and pointing.

Then suddenly he's on the jumbotron. With Dani. Again.

I freeze, unable to tear myself away.

Dani turns, slowly, almost with trepidation, to face Sammy as the other people in their row scramble out of the way.

The jumbotron gets a close-up of her face, her eyes widening, her cheeks blushing, her mouth falling open.

Sammy sloshes beer and loses a pretzel as he makes his way to her. Then he thrusts everything at her.

She says something that I can't lip read, then starts taking things from his arms. She hands the beers to Luna, takes the pizza slices and remaining pretzel and sets them down on her seat, then she takes the black thing. It's a cardigan sweater.

What the hell?

But realization dawns. I look up at the owner's box. Nathan sent the sweater, and not because he's worried she's cold. He wanted to cover up Crew's name on her jersey. Nice.

I sigh. He is coming around, but I shouldn't expect miracles like Nathan Armstrong changing all his stripes in just a few days.

Dani tosses the sweater onto her seat as well, turning enough that the jumbotron gets a full shot of the back of the jersey she's wearing.

The crowd starts to cheer.

She looks up, startled. She clearly doesn't understand what they're so excited about.

But I think I do.

Sammy thrusts the bouquet of…whatever…at her.

She takes them, then looks toward the Racketeers bench. Toward me.

She smiles and the jumbotron zooms in on what she's holding.

It's a bouquet of cookies.

I look toward the owner's box again. Huh. Was that just a play on her nickname, the one now being used in the group text with all of us, or was that Nathan's way of not-too-subtly reminding her that she's got three boyfriends? Not just the one who's a cocky, hotshot, hockey player?

Either way…that was pretty good.

But when she turns to set the cookies down the jumbotron flashes the Kiss Cam screen and Sammy bends over and taps his cheek as if asking for a kiss. Then the jumbotron operator zooms in on the back of her jersey again and the crowd goes wild.

I shake my head at the owner's box.

The crowd thinks the cookie bouquet is from Crew. They've also obviously remembered who she is. The Kiss Cam is helping. So is Sammy.

Nathan and I just inadvertently helped the Racketeer fans put together that Dani is the Kiss Cam girl from the other night. And in about thirty more seconds, Danielle Larkin is going to be labeled in the press and all over social media as Crew McNeill's girlfriend.

CHAPTER 26

Wade (Sammy the Malamute)

WHAT DID I do wrong now?

I didn't drop her this time. I didn't even touch her. I dropped a pretzel, but geez, is that really a big deal? Carbs just slow you down, anyway.

But according to the muttered, "Goddammit. This is just fucking great. Just. Fucking. Great!" in my earpiece there's a problem.

I think I should head home early tonight. I do not want to go back upstairs, that is for sure.

Mr. Armstrong is a scary motherfucker.

CHAPTER 27

Crew

I HAD the best game of my life tonight.

And now I get to go home. To the apartment where I'm staying with my boss. Who is the biggest jackass I've ever met.

That's not exactly news. I knew Nathan Armstrong was a pompous, stubborn ass before I even signed with the Racketeers. But now, with Dani in the picture and us all having sleepovers, and me keeping a toothbrush and extra Pop Tarts at his place, his assholery affects me even more directly.

"She's nothing more than a fan?" I say as I burst into Nathan's apartment. I throw my duffle to the side, slam the door, and stomp into the living room.

I know he's already here because I texted Michael. I wanted to be sure Nathan was home before I got here.

Michael too, because I can't guarantee I won't treat Armstrong the way I treated Justin Travers tonight.

Nathan is standing by the window with a glass of something, probably scotch, in hand. Michael is sitting on the sofa, his arm around Dani.

She's in sweatpants, a plain blue sweatshirt, and has her legs pulled up on the cushion, hugging them. Her eyes are wide as she watches me.

"Oh, fuck no." I march into the bedroom, rummage through her bag until I find the jersey, *my* jersey, and head back into the living room and straight for my girl.

I reach for the sweatshirt, pull it up and over her head, barely registering the fact she's not wearing anything underneath—okay, that's a lie, I totally register that fact, but we're going to attend to that later—and then pull my jersey over her head and down her body.

I know I still look mad. I am still mad. But I press a kiss to the top of her head and murmur, "You looked fucking gorgeous in my number tonight, sweet girl. I want to see it every game."

She looks up at me with those big green eyes and nods. I run a hand over her hair. Then I stand and face Nathan.

"What the fuck, Armstrong?"

"He was just trying to make it easier on Dani," Michael says calmly. "The media mobbed her on her way out."

"I know. I saw the clips. I don't care," I tell him. I look at Nate again. "You said she's just a fan. She is *not* just a fan. The media asked if she's my girlfriend. You said no." I glare at him. "She *is* my girlfriend."

Nathan finally faces me and speaks. "She's not just *your* girlfriend."

I take a step closer to him. "What's that mean?"

"I mean, she's my girlfriend too and as such, I have a responsibility to protect her. I went down to get her and Luna out of the arena before the game ended, but the media was waiting for her. I feel terrible that I didn't get security involved or take her out the private entrance. I could have just taken them back up to my office until everyone left. But…they saw her. I had to react."

"You reacted badly," I tell him.

He scowls at me. "It's not time for the public to know about our situation, and she wasn't expecting to be mobbed. I got her out of there as quickly and easily as I could. Your ego was the least of my concerns."

"It's not about my ego!" I shove a hand through my hair.

"Goddammit, Nate! I love her! She was wearing my jersey. She was there for me. Everyone saw it and then you decided to downplay it. That wasn't your call!"

"Then who's call was it?" Nathan demands, advancing several steps toward me. "You weren't there. Michael wasn't there. I was. I made a decision for Danielle's best interest. For all of our best interest. Something I would trust either of you to do if I'm not there! I'm sorry you're pissed, but we all made the decision to keep this private. Just because you got all hopped up on adrenaline and testosterone on the ice tonight, doesn't give you the right to change that decision. I'm glad you weren't there now. You would have ruined everything."

"Telling everyone how I feel about Dani would ruin everything?" I ask. "Or would it just ruin you being in control?"

"This isn't about that," Nate denies.

"Bullshit!"

"Okay, that's enough." Michael's deep voice interrupts as he unfolds himself from the couch and comes to stand with us.

Between us.

"You're both right. But," he says, cutting me off when I open my mouth. "Nathan is more right. I know you love her, Crew. We all do. You think I don't want to yell it to the world? Take her home to meet my grandmother? Buy her a goddamned diamond and get down on one knee at the most romantic restaurant in town? Of course, I do. But we can't. Not yet. We care who knows about us," he says. "Nathan's right about that. We decided. And if this is going to work, we have to make decisions as a group, and we have to stand by them."

"Oh my God!"

We all freeze. Then turn as one toward the gorgeous, clearly upset redhead standing by the couch, wearing my jersey. Her hands are on her hips, her cheeks are pink, and she's breathing hard.

"Are you all kidding me right now?"

Michael steps toward her. "What's wrong?"

"What's wrong?" She looks at him like he's just asked the stupidest question she's ever heard.

She takes a deep breath and then moves to stand between all of us. Right in the middle of the little circle we've created.

"I'm your girlfriend?" she asks Nathan. Then she turns to Michael. "And you're talking about diamond rings and getting down on one knee?" Then she turns to me. "And you want to do a news conference about us?"

"Danielle, I–"

"Cookie, I lo–"

"Dani, of cour–"

We all start talking at once, but she holds up her hand in the universal sign for stop. Or, more accurately, the universal sign for I'm not done yet and I'll let you know when it's your turn to talk.

"You're yelling how much you love me, and that you want to be with me, and that you feel protective and want to take care of me, and that you want to tell the world about us, to each other in the middle of the living room," she said. "I was just wondering if you–" She points to Nathan. "Or you–" She points to Michael. "Wanted to maybe share your feelings with *me*?"

None of us dares even open our mouths.

"We talked about all of us having sex together and hanging out and seeing what happens and keeping it private–" She shoots me a look. "But no one has talked about announcing anything on social media or buying any diamond rings." She takes a deep breath and her voice softens. "So, as long as we are doing those things now, I love you all, too."

She looks directly at me. "I've always thought you were cute and fun, but now that I know you better, I love you, Crew. You make me laugh, you make me feel like I make you happy and that makes me feel...special, and amazing. You make me look forward to everything from the small things like making a sandwich to huge things like a European vacation together."

"We will absolutely fucking do that," I say, my voice gruff.

We'd already said the I love yous, but I hadn't realized how much more powerful they would feel in front of other people.

She turns to Michael. "I love you, Michael. You make me feel brilliant. Your praise and approval and partnership in my writing makes me feel confident and like I'm doing something meaningful. You listen to me. You give me your time and attention in a way no one ever has before. I look forward to seeing you every day because the moment you walk in and smile at me, or text me, or just touch my hand, I feel calmer and more steady. You take care of me."

I can tell the man who is always the rock-steady presence wherever he goes, is shaken by this sweet, soft, beautiful woman. He's staring at her like he's never seen anything more amazing in his life. He swallows hard and says, "You are the best part of every one of my days, Dani."

She smiles at him, takes a deep breath, and turns to Nathan. "And I love you, Nathan. You make me feel alive. You make me feel strong because I can stand up to you and make *you* weak."

She gives him a sexy, knowing smile that, holy fuck, is the hottest thing I've maybe ever seen. That kind of confidence on Danielle Larkin is potent.

"You also make me feel protected in a way I've never ever felt before," she continues. "My heart beats faster just thinking about seeing you. And knowing that I can actually distract you, frustrate you, make you laugh, please you, is the most empowering feeling ever."

Nathan is now also staring at her like she is a brand new, stunning, unbelievable being. But he's not smiling. He looks ready to eat her up. "Jesus, Danielle," he manages but it's practically a growl.

But Dani isn't done. She takes a deep breath and looks at all of us again. "So, thank you, for all of these feelings. And thank you for showing me, and each other, that we can have these fights, and then make up and move on, better and closer because of them."

I watch her for a moment. She finally seems finished. I look at the other two men.

"Well guys, it's a good thing we've all fallen for her. One man would never be able to love this girl as much as she deserves to be loved."

Michael smiles at my words, his eyes on Dani. His expression is so full of love and possessiveness, I feel the air around us heat. "You've got a point, McNeill."

Nathan, of course, doesn't say anything, but the heat in the gaze he's got on Danielle is nearly enough to melt her clothes off.

Including my fucking hockey jersey.

So I do the only thing that really can be done after all of that.

I take a step forward, bend, and throw our girl over my shoulder.

She gasps and laughs as I start for the bedroom.

"And now for the best part of fighting," I announce to all of them. "Make up sex."

I can feel the other two men right on my heels. Michael already has his shirt stripped off and Nathan is fully unbuttoned by the time we hit the threshold to the bedroom.

I toss Dani on the bed and yank my shirt off too.

She starts to lift the hem of the jersey, but I say, "No. That stays on."

And when I look at her other two boyfriends, I'm very pleased to see them both nodding.

CHAPTER 28
Dani

MY GUYS SURROUND ME, and I'm hot and tingly, and I can hardly lie still on the bed.

They're all shirtless and I'm trying to take in Michael's broad, hard chest, Crew's six-pack abs and tattoos, and Nathan's sculpted biceps and shoulders at once.

I should feel overwhelmed. I should feel unable to breathe, unable to handle all the sensations and emotions.

But I feel comforted, safe, and happy in a way I never have been before.

Full of anticipation and excitement, yes. Turned on, of course. But this is exactly where I want to be, and I know these men will take care of me, all of me, in every way. They're here for me, because of me. They've accepted everything about the four of us being together, long term, and they're committed. We've fought, and everyone is still here.

And they'll be there for one another too. I can feel that.

We each have a place in this relationship, and we are so damned good together.

They are mine, and there is no place else I'd want to be right now. Or ever.

So no, I don't feel overwhelmed. I feel right.

We've done this before. The hot sex, the dirty, delicious fucking.

But now we're making love. Out loud, together. And God that feels so good.

Crew is the first one undressed. Of course. He's always so eager. He pulls my ass to the end of the mattress, reaches for the top of my sweatpants, and pulls them off in one smooth move.

He's already told me that I'm keeping the jersey on, but he reaches for the hem and pushes it up, exposing my breasts and leaning in to cup one, taking a nipple in his mouth. My hand goes to the back of his head, my fingers tangling in his hair as I arch closer.

"Hughes," Nate says gruffly. "Make our girl hot and ready."

I turn my head to watch Nathan crawling up on the bed beside me. He has a predatory look in his eyes. "I'm already hot and ready," I tell him breathlessly.

His gaze is scorching as it sweeps over my body and Crew teasing my breasts. "Oh, I know, my sweet, dirty girl. You're always ready for us, aren't you?"

I bite my lower lip and nod, moving my legs restlessly on the bed. "Yes, always."

Crew moves to my other side, running one big, rough palm up my inner thigh, parting my legs. "Then let's just let Doc have some fun." He gives me that devastating grin that makes me want to blush, laugh, hug him, and orgasm all at once.

My gaze moves to Michael. He's watching Crew touch me too. I give him a little smile. "Do you want to have some fun, Michael?"

He gives a little half-laugh, half-groan. "Fun is such a mild word to use to describe how all of this feels."

He moves so he's between my legs and sinks to his knees on the carpet at the end of the bed. He places a kiss on my thigh opposite where Crew is still holding me. He rubs his face against my skin, his beard abrading my skin and sending goosebumps skittering.

Nathan stretches out along my side, while Crew settles in on his stomach, lying horizontally across the mattress. He keeps teasing my breasts, while Nathan wraps a hand around my thigh and lifts it to my chest, opening me for Michael. He kisses my neck, then says roughly. "Soak his tongue, Danielle."

A shudder of lust goes through me. Crew lifts my other leg, and he and Nathan hold me open as Michael slips his hands under my ass and then licks over my clit.

"Oh, God," I moan. I'm still holding onto Crew's hair, and I reach up to grasp Nathan's shoulder on the other side.

All of us holding on like this, connected, participating in this one act, rather than each of them doing something different, feels even more intense. It's like they're all a part of Michael licking, sucking, and eating me.

He fucks me with his tongue, then swirls over my clit, then sucks.

Nathan and Crew run their hands over my body, peppering my skin with kisses, squeezing my nipples, caressing my breasts, but they're also watching Michael. Nathan's cock is pressed against my hip, but he's not moving. No one is seeking my mouth, and I'm not touching them except to hold on while Michael drives me out of my mind.

He slips two fingers into me, thrusting deep and steady while he swirls his tongue over my clit, then sucks again.

"My God, you are the most gorgeous fucking thing," Crew tells me, kissing my neck. He sucks on just below my ear as Michael sucks my clit.

I gasp, then whimper.

"Fucking hell, I love your sounds," Crew says. He grasps my chin and turns me to him so he can kiss my lips. He strokes his tongue against mine as he palms my breast, tugging on my nipple with the perfect amount of pressure to send jolts of heat to my pussy.

"That's right," Michael growls from between my legs. "Fuck my fingers."

I hadn't realized I was moving my hips, but I'm bucking up, trying to get closer to his hand, his mouth, something. I need more pressure, more friction.

"Give her another finger, Hughes," Nathan orders.

Michael adds a third, filling and stretching me.

"Oh…yes," I say. My eyes slide shut, and I just feel.

"You're perfect," Nathan tells me, brushing my hair back, then running a hand down my body and resting hot and heavy on my stomach. "Spread open, taking anything we give you, all ours to worship and claim."

I wiggle on the mattress. "Please," I beg. "Please make me come."

"What do you need, Cookie?" Michael asks, but he brushes a finger over my back entrance, and my pussy clamps hard around his fingers. He chuckles darkly.

Clearly, he knows—they all do—exactly how to drive me wild. Sometimes we go hard, and they get right to it, but as different as these guys are, even in the bedroom, they do all have one thing in common…they love to erotically torture me.

"Say it," Michael says as he flicks his tongue lightly—maddeningly—over my clit. "Tell me what you want."

"Make me come, Michael," I beg. "Please."

"Tell me how," he presses. "Tell me how to make you come."

"Y—you know," I say, my voice hitching as Crew sucks on my nipple hard and Nathan drags my hand from his shoulder, up the mattress, stretching it over my hand and holding my wrist there firmly.

"I do," Michael agrees. "But I want to hear you tell me."

I know he does.

But I like to play too.

Crew stretches my other arm over my head, holding my wrist there. Then he pulls the jersey up. I think he's going to strip it over my head, but he stops when it's covering my face.

A makeshift blindfold.

Oh…fuck. I'm in trouble now. They're holding me down,

they've blindfolded me, and they're going to tease me until I'm a begging, writhing, hot, sticky mess.

I love this.

"Just make me feel good," I say in a sweet, innocent voice, using benign words.

I feel Nathan's hand glide down my body. And yes, I can now tell whose hands and whose mouth and whose cocks are touching me, and which ones I'm touching, even blindfolded.

Nathan's mouth is right by my ear. "We all want to be at the arena next time, see you in this jersey, see your pretty lips closing around a soda straw, see you waving sweetly on the jumbotron to all the smiling fans who think Crew has landed himself a shy, nice girl," he says. He flicks his tongue over my nipple. "But then we'll all picture you lying here, tangled up in this jersey, your gorgeous body spread out for three men, using that pretty mouth to beg to be fucked hard until you can't even spell hockey." He tugs on my nipple. "We love knowing that you're the biggest Racketeers fan in those stands because you're a dirty slut with a greedy cunt that needs three cocks to satisfy her."

My pussy clenches, and Michael groans. "That's right. Just like that." Then he gives me a hard firm lick. As he presses a finger into my ass to go along with the three in my pussy.

"Oh my God!"

"Tell him what you want, Danielle," Nathan says, tugging on my nipple harder now.

"I want him to keep fucking both my pussy and my ass like that," I manage.

They all groan, and Michael picks up the pace a little.

I gasp. They might tease me, but they do always give me what I want and need.

I love being able to tell them what I want, all my fantasies, everything I want to try. They *never* make me feel bad about any of it. When they call me greedy or dirty or a slut, it's so hot and yes, even loving. They love the side of me that other people shamed. They've shown me that I *can* have it all and that wanting is normal and so fulfilling when you find the right people to be with.

"Play with my clit, too," I beg. "And suck on my nipples." I turn my head toward Nathan.

His hot, wet mouth is back on my breast, sucking hard.

"Crew, help a friend out," Michael says, his voice husky.

Michael keeps thrusting his fingers in and out, but Crew's finger is now circling my clit. Nathan takes my other nipple between his fingers and tugs, then twists, keeping things just this side of pain.

And seconds later, I come apart.

I'm gasping and crying, my body not my own. It belongs to these men. All of it. Including my heart and soul.

"Good girl," Crew praises as he pulls the jersey back down. Not off. Clearly, they meant it when they said I was keeping it on. "Good fucking girl." Then he kisses me deeply.

Michael stands, gripping his cock as he positions himself at my entrance. "You are everything," he tells me as our gazes lock when Crew pulls back. "Absolutely everything." Then he slides home.

I moan his name as he grips my hips, thrusting deep immediately.

Nathan and Crew are still holding my legs open. This is intense. So hot, so amazing.

"Take him deep, Danielle," Nathan tells me, pulling my leg even wider.

"Yes," I say to…whatever. Everything. All of it.

Crew leans in to kiss me again. Then Nathan. When they move, my eyes lock on Michael's again. He's been staring down at me the entire time, burying himself deep every time, but his rhythm is steady. Just like the man. He fills me completely. In every way.

His fingers dig into my hip, holding me close.

"More," I whisper hoarsely. "Give me everything."

He groans, and his hips start moving faster.

Just like they know me, I know exactly how to get to each of them. I contract my inner muscles, and he gives me a hot look. But then I say, "I love you, Michael."

His eyes slide shut, and he tips his head back, his broad chest expanding with the huge breath he takes in. Bliss. That's what he's feeling. When our gazes meet again, he gives me a smile, then he really starts fucking me. Fast, deep, and hard.

"Come for me, Cookie," he grits out.

"I'm with you," I manage, as heat and need tighten in my pussy.

"Now," he says firmly, reaching for my clit and circling with his thumb.

My sweet romantic is barely holding back. There's tension through his jaw and shoulders. He's waiting for me.

God, they just gave me a breathtaking orgasm. I don't need to come again. I grasp his wrist. "Fill me up, Michael," I tell him.

Crew groans and buries his face against my neck.

I almost grin. He's the one that has the hardest time waiting. It's killing him to not have his cock involved right now. I'm tempted to give him a hand job while Michael's between my legs.

"Not without you," Michael tells me.

These men. Honestly, there's generous, and then there's ridiculous. "I want you to—"

He cuts me off with a quick smack to my ass.

My eyes go round. *Michael* just spanked me? It wasn't hard, at all. It sent jolts of heat and electricity to my core but not an ounce of pain.

But Michael did that?

Even Crew lifts his head.

I feel my pussy grip him.

"I want you to come on my cock, Danielle," Michael says firmly, his hot gaze on mine.

Oh damn, I love firm Michael.

"Be a good girl, Dani," Crew says in my ear. "Get Doc nice and messy." He strokes my side. "And hurry the hell up, because I'm dyin' over here, sweetheart."

I huff out a short laugh, but it doesn't last because Michael starts thrusting harder and faster. "Come with me," he says. It's practically an order.

The heat in his eyes is intense and I feel my orgasm coiling, but it's the love, the look of holy-shit-I-can't-believe-I'm-here-with-you-like-this he's giving me that makes everything in me tighten in anticipation of the release that's coming. I can read what he's feeling clearly. He gives me that look a lot. Sometimes when we're eating breakfast. Sometimes when we're on the couch, and I'm writing, and he's reading. Sometimes when we're just walking down the sidewalk, or brushing our teeth, or when I walk in the door at the end of the day.

And that look is what sets off my orgasm. It's not a sudden explosion. Instead, it feels like he's slowly turning up the flame on a gas burner to the point where every inch of my body is on fire, and I'm gasping and moaning and then combusting.

"Michael! Yes! Oh, yes! Yes!"

"That's my girl," he says, clenching his jaw. "That's fucking it. God, I love you." Then he comes, squeezing my hips hard, filling me up.

He stiffens, and holds me tight as he empties himself in me.

Then finally he pulls out, breathing hard, his eyes on mine as he steps back.

"Get out of my way, Nathan," he says.

Nathan chuckles and moves to the foot of the bed.

Michael is being bossy, and Nathan is chuckling? Is this the twilight zone?

But Michael crawls up beside me, grips my chin, and kisses me hard. It's deep and hot, and he sweeps his tongue into my mouth.

When he pulls back, he says, "You. Are. Everything."

"I love you," I tell him, running my hand over his cheek.

He turns his head and presses a kiss to my palm. "I know, Cookie. And I'm so fucking lucky that's true."

"Okay, enough mushy stuff," Crew says. "Pussy or mouth, Nathan?"

But Crew is already moving up toward my head. We all know what Nathan will say, given the choice. The other two don't always give him a choice, however.

It's clear, though, that right now, Crew is ready to just do something, anything.

But Nathan doesn't say anything at all. He just leans in, kisses next to my belly button, then grasps my hips and flips me to my stomach, before pulling me up onto my knees.

Nathan runs his hand over my ass, as Crew kneels at my head. He strokes my cheeks. "You were a very good girl for Doc," he says, grinning down at me.

I reach for his dick, wrapping my hand around it. "Your turn, hot shot."

"Fuck yessss," he hisses as I stroke him. "I'm not gonna last long, pretty girl."

"Good," I say just before I lick his head.

He moans, tangles his hands in my hair, and guides his cock further into my mouth. "Take me, Dani. I know you can. Swallow me down."

Nathan's fingers dip into my pussy. "You're so gorgeous like this," he murmurs.

I wiggle my ass. I never would have believed Nathan would be willing to go after another man, but he's adjusted to our dynamic surprisingly easily. He only gives me a breath before he thrusts hard, filling my pussy again.

Nathan and Crew find a rhythm, and it's only minutes before they're both coming.

We collapse into a sweaty, sticky, satisfied pile on Nathan's huge bed.

My head is on Crew's chest, my body draped partially over his, Michael is against my back, Nathan lying over the backs of my legs. Michael's arm is under both Crew and I, and I think Nathan's legs are maybe even partially tangled with Michael's.

We're all breathing hard, no one's speaking, but I know we're all thinking essentially the same thing.

I need these people. We are so damned good together.

CHAPTER 29

Nathan

DANIELLE IS at the game tonight, but we all decided she'd join me in the owner's box to keep her off the fucking jumbotron and away from Sammy the Malamute. I specifically told Wade not to come upstairs tonight. But it was via text and honestly, I have no idea if that communication got through. Not because of the wireless service, but because of Wade. That kid is kind of weird.

The weirdest thing tonight, though, is that I feel restless about Danielle being in the box with me.

The four of us have been dating– as strange as it sounds–I can't deny that it's the most accurate way to describe what we're doing–for a few weeks now and I've gotten used to sharing her.

God, what's happened to me? I'm sharing the woman I love with two other men and…I'm happy about it.

Michael and Crew are good for her. Great for her. I love seeing her with them. They give her things I can't. But I'm aware that I can give her things they don't. We are a team, each with our roles, and crazy as it is, it's working.

So having her all to myself tonight, almost hiding her away in my private box tonight during a Racketeers game, seems wrong. The Racketeers are Michael's and Crew's too. They care about the team almost as much–maybe as much–as I do. They know she's here, but it feels wrong that they don't have eyes on her, can't see her cheering and waving and smiling.

She looks gorgeous tonight. She's in a pretty yellow dress with white flowers that hits her at her midthigh, short black boots, and a bright pink sweater. No jersey. Crew said he was okay with that. It would possibly keep the media from noticing her and freaking out.

But I don't know if Crew is really okay with it.

I don't know if he should be okay with it.

She is his girlfriend. He was right about that the night we argued about it. We were all right about our points. We'd talked about it. We'd made a decision. We thought it was important to wait to go public. And it is. I don't think we're ready for what people will say about a relationship between four people. Many won't understand. Many will think it's dirty and just about sex. People will have very unflattering opinions about us, and if we're honest though, we haven't said it out loud, we know that most of that judgment will be toward Danielle.

But why can't Crew claim her? He's the most public figure of the four of us. And he and Danielle are fucking cute together. Hughes and I have no problems with our egos. We wouldn't feel left out or jealous if people thought only Crew was dating her. Not really. We would discuss it and, yeah, Hughes and I would be okay. We know what happens at home. What's in her heart.

That is one thing we never have to wonder about—Danielle Larkin wears her heart on her sleeve and if you are loved by her, you know it.

I smile and run my hand up and down her back. She leans into me, almost instinctively it seems. We're sharing the loveseat set up right in front of the glass overlooking the arena. She's got her legs crossed and her bare thigh is distracting. I want to run my hand up and down the creamy expanse. But I like having my arm around her, hugging her against me. She's a great cuddler.

She suddenly sits up straight, gasping, and leaning forward as

Crew flies down the ice toward the goal. Her eyes don't leave him, even to blink.

But at the last moment, just before he shoots, a defender from the Gators steals the puck, leaving Crew empty-handed.

"Dammit," she murmurs, leaning back again. She's frowning.

I love how into the game she is. She even shushed me earlier when I asked her if she wanted another drink.

I can tell that watching everything from way up here isn't as fun for her as the seats she's had down on the ice previously. She understands more about the game after the last few weeks with Crew and she's itching to be closer to the action.

He's included her when he watches game videos. She's asked him a million questions. Then, the other night, he decided to quiz her and they played strip hockey trivia after dinner. He asked her questions and every time she got one wrong, she had to take a piece of clothing off. Michael and I thought sitting back and watching was going to be a great spectator sport.

In the end it took him nearly an hour, and finally two made-up cheater questions, to get her totally naked.

Not that she minded. We made sure of that. But damn, she did a great job handling those questions.

"Go, Crew," she whispers, again leaning forward as he takes the puck from the Gators and charges down the ice.

The crowd is wild and loud. It's so quiet up here in contrast.

"Go!" She suddenly shoots to her feet and her hands slap the glass. "Go! Come on baby!"

But again, at the last minute, Crew loses the puck. In fact, the player who steals it from him takes it all the way down the ice and… fuck…scores. Just as the buzzer sounds, ending the second period.

"What?" Danielle yells. "Dammit!"

She's so fucking…adorable. Danielle deserves to have some fun with dating a hockey star. Being on social media all into a game like this. Being that girl–the one who landed a guy like Crew. And

Crew is absolutely the type of guy to make it a big, happy, fun, romantic deal. He'd make sure the entire world, including every single puck bunny, knows how he feels about Danielle Larkin.

Instead, she's hiding out way up above the rest of the arena, with me, frowning at the ice below.

"What's wrong with him?" she asks, swinging to face me.

Crew is playing like shit. This is easily the worst game he's had in a Racketeers uniform. Probably the worst he's had in an NHL uniform.

"He's having a bad night," I say vaguely.

"But why?" she asks, worry in her eyes. "He seemed fine when he left today."

I hadn't seen him since this morning, but Danielle had been home with him until he needed to leave for the arena. "Did you talk about anything specific?" I ask.

She shakes her head. "No. We had lunch. We watched some South Park episodes. He was laughing and being Crew."

"Well…" I'm sure I know the problem. But I'm not sure how to solve it. Or rather, I'm not sure that I should. I know exactly how to fix it, but it might be a bad idea.

"What Nathan?" she demands, putting her hands on her hips. "Did you have another fight?"

I hold up my hands. "Not my fault this time," I tell her. Heaven forbid I upset her sweet little puppy. But I smile in spite of myself. I love how Crew is when he's around Danielle. Somehow all of his usual joking, and lack of seriousness, and cockiness is softer around her. When he's making her laugh, and smile, and blush I can't help but like him. A lot.

"So what's going on?"

"You're not down there, where he can see you, wearing his number," I tell her honestly. "He knows you're here, which is great. But…" I sigh. "He wants the world to know."

She frowns and sits down beside me again. "But the world can't know."

I run my hand up and down her back again, needing to touch her. "I think we need to talk about that."

"About what?"

"Maybe you should be Crew's girlfriend publicly."

Her frown deepens. "But I'm not just Crew's girlfriend."

"No. But Michael and I know that. And we're the only ones that really need to know that. You and Crew could have a lot of fun publicly. He could dote all over you. And it would keep the media from speculating. He could just love you out loud the way he wants to. It's so hard for him not to."

Michael and I are older, and calmer, and it's far easier for us to manage our feelings. Calling Crew an extrovert is an understatement. Asking him to hide feelings of any kind, but especially strong feelings like the ones he has for Danielle, is a lot like shaking a bottle of soda and trying to keep all of that effervescence contained.

She smiles, her eyes full of love and happiness, but then she shakes her head. "You two don't need to step aside for Crew's ego. He knows how to play on a team." She gestures toward the game. "He can be a part of this without being the star."

I laugh. He plays with the team but there's no denying he's the fucking star of the Racketeers. I lean over and kiss her cheek. "*You're* the star, Danielle. That's what we're saying. Keeping you up here, hidden away and keeping you at home all the time, not taking you out and wining and dining you, not dressing you up and showing you off, not splashing your gorgeous face all over social media just isn't right. You landed the hottest hockey star in the league. Do you know how many women would be jealous of you?"

She laughs but her cheeks are pink. "I don't need other women to be jealous of me."

She doesn't. I believe her. But I lean in and say in her ear, "But wouldn't it be fun to have everyone know that you're fucking Crew McNeill every night?"

A little shiver dances through her. "I'm fucking Crew McNeill, *and* Michael Hughes, *and* Nathan Armstrong," she says, her voice husky. "Luckiest girl in the world."

"You sure as hell are." I press a kiss against her neck. "And you're doing it very well." Crew is the one who generally fulfills Danielle's need for praise. Michael is the one who's sweet and romantic with her. I'm the one who gets to be filthy and bossy with her. But I certainly don't mind telling her what a good girl she is. "You make us all so damned happy, Danielle." I tug her sweater off her shoulder and kiss the skin along her collar bone.

She gives a sweet little gasp and tips her head back.

"But think about it. You could meet Crew in that back hallway after games with all the other girlfriends and wives." I lean and press another kiss to her throat. She smells so damned good, I just breathe her in for a moment. I rest my hand on her thigh, stroking the soft skin, inching up under the hem of her skirt. "You could give him big, happy, congratulatory kisses when he's all jacked up on adrenaline. He could pick you up and carry you out of there in front of everyone." My hand slides higher. She parts her knees as her breathing quickens. "Everyone would be talking about how hot you are together. Media would catch you making out in restaurants." My fingertips brush her panties. Her hot, wet panties.

"Nathan," she moans softly.

I run my finger up and down over the middle of her panties, brushing over her clit and pressing a little harder on that sweet spot on each stroke. I move my mouth to hover just over hers. "And think about me and Michael, watching it all on social media. Watching Crew get to be the one you claim in public. The one who can dip you back and kiss you on the sidewalk. The one who can rest his hand on your sweet ass when he walks with you. Think about how turned on we'll be by the time you get home." I slip my finger under the edge of her panties. "How ready we'll be to claim you as ours too."

She moans again and parts her thighs further. The pulse point at the base of her throat is thrumming. "You won't be jealous, though," she says. "You know how I feel about you. And you love to watch us."

I slide my finger over her outer folds. "Oh, I do. I really do." I slip my finger into her heat. "I love how wet it makes you when one of us is kissing you, touching you, undressing you, while the others watch."

She whimpers and grasps the edge of the seat cushion. "Nathan!"

"Which means when you get home you'll be dripping." I slide my finger into her. "So wet and hot." I move my finger in and out, swirling over her clit, then thrusting into her again. "You'll be begging for our cocks."

"Nathan!"

Her pussy grips me.

"And we won't let Crew take you first. He'll get to kiss you, touch you, call you sweetheart in public." I move my fingers faster. "That means Michael and I get this sweet pussy, and your tight ass, and your greedy mouth first." I circle her clit and kiss her deeply.

She's panting, but she shakes her head. "But that's three places for three men."

"Nope." I circle her clit faster, then plunge two fingers into her. "If Crew gets your laughter and your smiles and your name linked with his in the papers, then we get this gorgeous body, and your begging, and your orgasms at home."

She's close. I can feel it. She loves the idea of being publicly claimed, as well as what that will do to us at home. She knows that she's got us all on our knees, metaphorically and literally, whenever she wants us there, and that makes her feel powerful.

It should. There are three men who will do absolutely anything for her.

"But don't worry," I tell her, finger fucking her deep and fast. "We'll let Crew finally take you. He'll be so worked up after having you by his side all night, then having to watch us make you scream."

A few months ago, I would have never believed that I would use the image of two other men fucking her with me to get her hot so quickly and send her careening over the edge of a fast, hot orgasm, but now this is my reality and as Danielle's pussy milks my fingers, I fucking love it. I will do anything to make this woman feel like the goddess she is.

"That's it, my sweet, dirty girl. Think about your men taking care of you in every fucking way you need us."

She grasps my wrist and cries out as she comes around my fingers. Then she wraps her arms around my neck and pulls my mouth to hers, kissing me as the ripples of her orgasm fade slowly. I slide my hand from her panties and pull her into my lap, deepening the kiss.

"Best intermission ever," she says against my lips.

I smile. "Good. Now let's get you into a jersey and get you down by the ice so Crew can see his girl and maybe pull this game out in the third period."

The Racketeers are only down by one so it's definitely possible.

She pulls back and gives me a dazzling smile. "Really?"

"Well, I hear his boss is kind of an asshole. I don't want him to be in trouble for playing like shit tonight."

She laughs. "Well, don't tell anyone, but his boss is actually an amazing guy who really likes Crew deep down and wants him to be the best player he can be."

I lift a brow. "Maybe so. But trust me, his boss also wants him to play well because he's being paid a shit ton and he better fucking earn that money."

She pushes up off my lap, but gives me a sassy smile. "Give him a break. He's madly in love for the first time in his life."

And my heart squeezes. I fucking love that she knows that. That she's owning it.

"You're right," I say, standing and catching her hand to pull her back in for one more sweet kiss. "I'll give him a break. That does kind of wreak havoc on a guy like…him."

She grins up at me. Like she knows that I almost said 'me'.

"Thanks. He means a lot to me."

I lean in and kiss the tip of her nose and then escort her down to the same storage room where I got her the T-shirt the first night we met and outfit her with a MCNEILL 17 fan jersey.

Then, against my better judgment, I have Sammy the Malamute escort her to a seat right off the ice. And to be sure Crew sees her, I text Michael.

I've just stepped back into my box when I hear the crowd cheering. I look up at the jumbotron and watch Crew skate to the glass right in front of Danielle with a huge grin on his face. He puts his gloved hand up on the glass and she leans in, putting her hand up on the glass on the other side.

The crowd goes wild and I feel my own huge, stupid, goofy grin.

Yeah, Danielle is now, publicly anyway, Crew McNeill's girlfriend.

That's perfect.

And it stays perfect for the next sixty-three minutes.

Which is long enough for Crew to score two goals, the Racketeers to win the game, Danielle to meet him in the back hallway, and social media to explode with the photo of the two of them with their hands up on the glass looking all lovey-dovey before the start of that third period and then photos of her in his arms, legs wrapped around his waist, kissing him after the game with the headline JUST A FAN MY ASS.

There is also a shot of Danielle kissing Michael in what looks like the hallway outside of the locker room. Probably right before the game. It's a sweet kiss, but definitely more than friendship.

Right next to the photos of her in my owner's box with her head thrown back, my mouth against her neck, and my hand under her skirt. The photo was obviously taken with a telephoto lens, but it's clear what's going on.

Even though the headline reads, WHAT THE PUCK IS GOING ON?

CHAPTER 30

Michael

"WHAT THE FUCK HAPPENED?" I demand as I come through the apartment door.

I know that Crew got Dani out of the arena immediately after the game and that Nathan left directly after they did. They both texted me. I, of course, had already seen the social media shit storm. But I had to stay and do my usual post-game check-ups. And act like I had no idea that Crew and Nathan might be seeing the same woman. Or that I had anything to do with her myself.

But I finally got home and stormed into the living room to find my three...roommates? Lovers? My girlfriend and my two...best friends? Yeah, that last one fits. But we, of course, can't say that in public. And it's starting to be a problem. I never even noticed anyone around us and yet clearly someone snapped a pic of me and Dani kissing. Along with her and Nathan in his box.

Dani is on the couch, between them. The guys have their arms stretched across the back of the couch behind her, and they're sitting close to her, sandwiching her between them, but they're not holding her. No one's holding hands. No one's talking.

She's obviously been crying. Nathan looks like he's ready to murder someone. Crew looks like someone punched him in the gut.

Obviously, they're all handling it really well.

I take a deep breath. Then another. And then do what I do. I pull it together. For all of us.

"So…first step," I say. "Come here."

They all look over at me. Dani gets up immediately. Which is great. But I look at the guys. "You too."

Crew gets up without question, but Nathan frowns.

"Get your ass off the couch and get over here," I tell him.

I stretch out my arms. Dani gets to me first. She wraps her arms around my waist and buries her face in my chest. I feel her shake as she takes a big breath. "Oh my God, Michael."

I pet her head with one hand. "I know. Shh. We'll take care of it." But I look at Crew and beckon him forward with my other hand. "Come on."

He takes a step forward. Then another. Then he lets out a long breath and wraps himself around Dani from behind, reaching his arms around me too, squishing her between us. He rests his chin on her head. "Fuck," he mutters.

I pat his back. "I know, buddy. Great game, by the way. Well, great third period."

He doesn't respond. So I know this is serious.

Finally I meet Nathan's eyes. "You're part of this too."

He shoves a hand through his hair. "Yeah. I'm the one who messed it all up."

I shake my head. "Not what I meant. Get over here."

He takes a step forward but he looks like he's in pain. "I need to fix it."

"How?" I ask him, knowing he doesn't know how or he would have already done it.

"I…" He swallows. "I don't know."

"Come. Here," I say firmly.

I'm still hugging Dani and Crew. Nathan looks at them, then back at me. We share something when our gazes meet. I can't explain it or even put words to it. But I think there's a shared understanding that, because we're the oldest of the group, the ones with "real" jobs–if you can call being a billionaire a real job, which we all know you can't–the ones with more life experience, the ones with a better grip on our emotions, we're supposed to be the ones in charge.

But we're not perfect.

But there are two of us.

If he doesn't know what to do, then that's where I come in.

I know he feels like he's supposed to be able to fix everything, all the time. He's got power, money, influence. Before now, that's all it took.

But he wasn't in love before. He didn't have a family. He didn't have people that depended on him emotionally. His grandfather was able to take care of himself before he got sick. Now Nathan takes care of him as best he can, but Stanford is slipping and any emotional support Nathan is willing to give doesn't register.

We're his family now. We're the ones that need him. We're the ones he feels responsible for.

We're the ones he thinks he failed.

Finally he takes two more steps and wraps his arms around us. He's at my side, half-hugging me, half-hugging Crew, Dani still in the center. Of course. Right where she belongs.

I settle my hand on his shoulder. I feel Crew's hand move to Nathan's back.

And we just stand there, holding each other, breathing for several minutes. Everyone still feeling kind of like shit, but at least acknowledging that we're all in this together.

Dani finally wiggles. "I'm hot," she says, her voice muffled against my shirt.

"Yeah you are," Crew says. He nuzzles her neck, then pulls back.

They're both smiling. Not the big, life-is-great grins they usually wear around one another, but at least they're smiling.

Nathan steps back and pulls in a long breath. "I'm sorry." He's clearly addressing all of us.

Dani reaches out and grabs his hand. "It's not your fault."

"The fucking guy with the fucking zoom lens fucking being a fucking creeper is at fault," Crew says angrily, his brows slamming together.

I, of course, agree. "I'm sorry, too. I shouldn't have kissed you in public." Even though it's starting to piss me off that I can't. "Can you find out who took the photos? Is there any recourse?"

"Possibly," Nathan says. "But it doesn't really matter. The damage is done."

"People finding out that I'm with all of you is not damage," Dani says.

"Cookie," I say softly.

She turns to face me.

"I don't think you realize what this is going to mean. For you."

"I don't care. I'm in love with all of you. Nathan and I talked about me being Crew's girlfriend publicly and that you two didn't care. And sure, that sounded like fun. But it also sounded strange. I love you all. I want to date you all. I don't care what people think."

"You might not feel that way when you actually find out what they think," I say.

"I will. No one matters more than you three."

"Dani–" Crew starts.

"I mean it," she says. "They don't understand. And that's fine. They don't have to."

"What about your mom and dad?" I ask.

"I planned to tell them eventually anyway," she says. "I mean, I can't be in love with you all forever and never tell my parents." Her gaze darts around at the three of us, landing on each of us one at a time. Then she frowns. "Unless…you don't think this is forever."

"That's not what we're saying," I tell her quickly.

She puts her hands on her hips and faces Crew. "What about you? Were you going to tell your mom and dad? About Nathan and Michael?"

He takes a breath. "Yeah. I didn't think they'd find out like this, but I hadn't really thought through how they would hear it."

"And you?" she asks me. "What will your family think?"

My family is pretty open-minded actually. "They'll be fine as long as I'm happy." I bend my knees so I can look directly into her eyes. "And I am happy. This is just fast and now out of our hands."

She nods. "I know. But I don't care."

"They're already calling you a slut," Crew says bluntly, holding up his phone. "And not in the hot sexy way we do. In the insulting, trashy way."

She flinches. "I'm sure they are."

"And they're calling Nathan a creeper," Crew goes on. He sighs. "They're assuming he somehow tricked you into coming up to his box and preyed on you. Some are saying he paid you. Some are saying we've both paid you, like you're a call girl or something. They're taking sides, Dani. They're also wondering who the hell Michael is."

Dani's face is getting whiter, and I step close, wrapping an arm around her. I hate that this is freaking her out, but fuck, she probably needs to hear this.

"And everyone likes Crew better than me," Nathan fills in. "He's the star. He's the one they know best–or think they know. He's in the media. He's the star of the team and the one who's probably getting us the Cup this year." He actually gives Crew a half grin. "He's their darling. They saw you together. They know he's crazy about you. So they're pissed that I would try to steal you from him. Hell, even the ones saying he paid you are turning your story with him into some kind of Pretty Woman remake. As for Michael, they seem to be assuming he is actually your boyfriend and now you're cheating on him with Crew. Which makes sense, because Hughes is boyfriend material."

Damn. It's worse than I thought. Now they have her not just a victim, but a cheater as well.

She looks completely bewildered. "Already?" is her first word. "All of that is out there already?"

"That's social media for you." Crew turns and heaves his phone against the wall. It's drywall so it leaves a dent in the wall and only cracks his screen.

I think he would have rather shattered something.

We're all quiet for a moment.

"It's okay," Nathan finally says.

We all turn to face him.

He nods. "It's okay. I'll take the blame. Let's go with the story that I made a move on her, but she's Crew's girlfriend. She felt like she couldn't say no because it might jeopardize Crew's position with the team."

"No," Dani and I protest at the same time.

"Don't be a dumbass," Crew tells him.

Nathan raises a brow. At all of us. "Let's not forget that I employ two of you." He looks directly at Dani. "And I love you."

She sucks in a little breath. I'm aware that Nathan hasn't actually said those words to her out loud until now.

"I will fire you two if you fight me on this," he says. "And there is no way in hell people are going to label Danielle as anything she's not."

She steps away from me and moves to stand directly in front of Nathan. "They're saying I'm a victim. Of yours. That is absolutely not true and I forbid you to let anyone believe that."

I'm shocked, but the corner of Nathan's mouth twitches. "You forbid it?"

She crosses her arms. "I do."

Crew moves to stand next to her. "You won't have to fire me. I'll quit."

Nathan's brows rise even higher. "You'll quit? I have you locked down in a contract Mr. McNeill. You're not going anywhere."

"I won't let you throw yourself under the bus," Crew argues. "You can't lie for us."

"Nothing can touch me," Nathan says, lifting a shoulder. "I own the team. No one's going to fire me. Thanks to you, fans are going to keep filling the seats, even if they hate me. Actually, with you madly in love and all over Dani on the jumbotron every damned game, we'll probably have sell-outs for the rest of the season. All you have to do to save her reputation is stand up and make a big sappy, public statement about how much you love her and that she's been your sister's best friend since they were in college and you've been slowly falling for her for years. You will also say that you and the team will refuse interview requests from any publication that prints even a hint of scandal about her anywhere, including online. Your teammates will have your back on that." He finally stops and takes a deep breath. Then he focuses on Dani. "And you'll probably need to spend the night at Crew's place for the next couple of months, in case anyone follows you. Just until this story dies down."

She frowns. "You'll spend the night there too?"

"I'll need to buy more forks. And towels," Crew says. "And pillows. And are you guys cool with paper towels or do I need to get cloth napkins like Nathan has? That seems like overkill to me, but I'll do it for you pampered old rich guys."

But Nathan is shaking his head. Just as I expected. "No. Michael and I need to keep a very low profile," he says to Dani. "People will be watching you and Crew. You need to date just him, make it seem like you broke things off with Michael. At least until this blows over and people start finding you two boring."

I roll my eyes. Even if Crew McNeill were to be in a regular relationship with just a woman and no other men, I very much doubt that it would ever be boring. The guy was born to live in the spotlight and social media loves him. He gets splashed all over even when he just combs his hair a new way or wears new shoes.

"I'll quit," Crew declares again, suddenly.

"You. Have. A. Contract," Nathan grits out.

"I mean hockey. I'll quit it all. I'll get into a fight next game, and I'll let the guy clock me, then Doc here will declare me unfit to play the rest of the season. I'll quit playing and get a coaching job somewhere."

Normally, if Crew was going off like this about some crazy idea, I'd think he'd already been hit too hard. But I realize that what I'm witnessing is Crew McNeill being in love and standing up for his family. Our family.

Nathan sighs. "Hughes will never do that."

I move to stand closer to Crew. And I pull Dani in, wrapping my arms around her from behind. "I will do that. And I'll quit too. We can all go somewhere new. I'm not having people assume the worst about Dani."

Crew gives me a surprised, but pleased look. "Yeah," he tells Nathan. "Fuck these fans if they're going to treat us like this. We'll go somewhere else. Be crazy fucking in love out loud. Take our fucking charm, and goddamned talent somewhere else where they'll appreciate us."

Nathan shoves a hand through his hair. "You are not disrupting your lives and turning everything upside down because of this. Just do this my way."

"Listen, Armstrong," Crew tells him. "There is a time and a place for your bossiness. And it's right down there, past that one doorway." He points down the hall toward Nathan's bedroom. "Also, a time and a place for your power and money. And that's basically whenever the mortgage on this penthouse is due and whenever I need a pizza delivery. Otherwise," Crew continues, pinning Nathan with a serious stare. "We're all making these decisions together."

"Nathan," I say, using my best calm, but serious tone. "Crew's right. You can't take this whole thing on yourself, and you can't decide for us how we handle it. We're doing this together. Stop being a stubborn ass and let us help figure this out."

He's looking at the three of us with a hard to read expression. There are a mix of emotions there. He clearly thinks we're a little nuts. And for a guy who has never experienced people willing to sacrifice for him, willing to stand up next to him even when shit hits the fan, who has basically been going it alone for a long damned time, he probably doesn't quite know what to do with all of this.

But the other things I see in his face are hope—hope that we mean all of this, hope that we won't regret any of this tomorrow, or the next day, hope that he's really worth it—and love.

And it's not just love for Dani. It's love for Crew and me too. Love for what the four of us have found together and built.

Finally, he pulls in a long breath.

"Fine. We can talk about options."

I feel Dani sag with relief in my arms and I hear Crew let out a breath.

I nod. "Great." Then I say, "Tomorrow."

Nathan frowns.

"Tomorrow," I repeat. "We all need to think it through, let some of the dust settle, get the adrenaline out of our systems." I kiss the top of Dani's head, then bend and lift her into my arms. "This girl needs a bubble bath and then bed. You both need a drink, and then bed."

I don't wait to see what the guys do. I turn with Dani, who gives zero protest to the idea of a bath or to being carried—I can tell how exhausted she is—and start for the bathroom.

But as I head down the hallway, I hear Crew say to Nathan, "How's it feel to have finally met a guy who is as used to getting his way as you are?"

And Nathan replies, "Let's just be clear about something– I'm the boss in the bedroom and at the arena as long as you are under contract."

And then Crew laughs.

I grin.

We're going to be okay.

CHAPTER 31

Nathan

THIS IS A TERRIBLE IDEA.

I knew that letting Crew come up with the plan was a terrible idea, but I'd gone along with it because Michael and Danielle believed it was the right thing to do. And because I know they helped him with the details.

And because I don't have a better idea.

Other than just letting people think whatever they want to about me.

I'm used to not caring what other people think. I'm used to being regarded as one of "those guys" who can get away with doing whatever I want to. I've had a life filled with privilege and I know it. But there are now three people in my life who I do care about. I care very much what Danielle, Michael, and yes, even Crew think of me.

I not only want them to respect me, but I want them to trust me. I want them to know that I'm here for them and that I believe in them.

That's why I'm here at the Racketeers arena, getting ready to walk down the steps in section one to take my seat with Danielle and Michael and listen to Crew's "spontaneous" press conference.

He'd come to practice today and then posted on all of his

social media channels that he had something to say afterward if anyone wanted to come hear it.

Specifically, he'd said, *I know you've all noticed the adorable redhead I've been hanging out with. Well, I've got something big to tell you all about today. See you at the arena after practice.*

His teammates had shared it. The Racketeers social media account had shared it. Thousands of fans had shared it.

The arena had been opened fifteen minutes ago and it was already full. People were talking, laughing, speculating, the noise almost louder than a pre-game crowd.

Of course, social media was jumping as well.

The leading theory is, obviously, that Crew's going to propose to Danielle.

And honestly? If he does, I won't be surprised. And Michael will owe me two hundred dollars.

Crew is the wild card, the spontaneous one, the fun one who keeps us on our toes.

I will be fine with his big, crazy, impulsive proposal.

I will also, obviously, go directly to a jeweler and spend ten times whatever Crew has spent on a ring.

And then Michael will talk us both into buying something together because Danielle will wear one ring from all of us rather than three separate rings.

He's the reasonable one, and God help us—God help Danielle —if he's not around.

I spot Danielle standing at the top of the stairs that will lead down to the seats Sammy is reserving for us.

I hang back as more people are still filing into the arena. I want to walk straight up to her, wrap her in my arms, dip her back, and kiss her passionately.

And reclaiming my right to do that is what this 'press conference' is all about.

But Crew hasn't spoken yet, and I'd rather not stir anything up before it's time.

Michael is down on the ice, stalling on the bench until it's time for him to take his seat with us.

Finally, Crew walks out onto the ice. He's taken off his skates and is wearing blue jeans and a Racketeers t-shirt with a huge Sammy face on it. He's also got a microphone in hand and one of his big, charming, of-course-I'm-the-reason-you're-all-here grins on his face.

I shake my head. I swear sometimes I'm paying him millions of dollars for that grin as much as I am for his ability with a hockey stick.

Danielle starts down the steps, Michael sees her and moves toward the seats.

So I take a deep breath and follow her down, ignoring all the murmurings that slowly rise in volume as people start to notice us.

Michael meets her at the seats and pulls her in for a hug. The crowd noise gets louder.

Sammy stands up and bows, gesturing toward the seats, then tips his hat. He steps out into the aisle, making a show of giving me as large a berth as possible.

The crowd laughs lightly, but again, the noise of conversation gets even louder because now they realize who I am, and that I'm with Danielle.

Too.

I step into the row, take the seat that puts her between Michael and me, then lean over and kiss her cheek.

The crowd noise now becomes a little less oh-my-gosh-isn't-that-Nathan-Armstrong-what's-he-doing? and a little more that's-Nathan-Armstrong-with-Crew's-girlfriend-that-bastard. Followed with a side of who-the-hell-is-that-other-guy?

Danielle reaches over and takes my hand. I almost resist, but then I take a breath and let her link our fingers. I look over to give her a smile. I want her to know that I'm happy to be here. I really am.

I mean, I'm not. At all.

But I'm happy to be with her. I'll do anything for her.

Even this shit show.

Michael is holding her other hand.

And we are, of course, up on the jumbotron.

I'm going to take that fucking thing out of this fucking arena, I swear.

"Hey, hey, now," Crew says into the microphone, pulling everyone's attention to center ice. "I thought you were all showing up here for *me*." He gives the jumbotron camera a grin and now his face is huge and has everyone's attention.

I let out a breath. My chest is tight. I just want this over with.

"It's okay," Danielle says softly. "Crew's got this." She squeezes my hand.

I can't believe that I'm actually to the point that I'm sharing the woman I love with Crew McNeill, but now I'm also trusting him to solve our PR issue. Love will fuck you up, in the strangest ways possible.

But I blow out a breath and nod. "If he doesn't, we're screwed," I say. Because, honestly, Crew is the best one to do it. If he can't pull this off, no one can.

"I'm so glad to see you all here," Crew says. "That was a very good choice on your part. Everyone got your phone out and stuff? Where are the reporters?"

Crew looks around, and a bunch of people in the front row across from us start waving.

"Oh, good. But I don't know." He turns a three-sixty, addressing the whole arena. "Social media can be even better. And faster. So… you all ready?"

The crowd starts cheering, and it seems that every person in the building lifts up a phone.

He faces the three of us, walks straight for us with one of his big Crew grins, then stops about ten feet from the glass in front of us.

Then he says, "I'm in love. With Danielle Larkin." He points at her.

I look at her. Her cheeks are bright red, her sweet pale skin flushing with the entire arena's attention on her, but also with pleasure.

"That gorgeous woman right there," Crew says. "Who is sitting between, and holding hands with, her other two boyfriends."

Crew pauses, and the entire arena seems to gasp as one.

He nods. "I know. Cool, right?" He grins. "This girl is so amazing, so fascinating, so damned sweet and perfect, that she had three guys fall in love with her all at the same time."

The crowd is murmuring around us, people are literally on the edges of their seats, and phones are up, recording everything.

"And she has such a huge heart, so much love, so much humor, and compassion, and well…" He gives Danielle a wink and his grin grows. "…she's so sexy, that she's actually able to love all three of us at the same time."

Again he gives the crowd a moment to process that and react.

There's laughter, gasping, louder murmuring, and one woman calls out, "Lucky bitch!"

Danielle actually laughs and turns her face to press it against Michael's shoulder.

"So yes, I'm in a relationship. With three other people," Crew says. "They're my family." His tone and his expression suddenly gets serious. "And Chicago…" He blows out a breath. "Fuck, man, I gotta know that you're gonna be cool about it." He glances at the reporters and says, "Sorry about the cussing. Can you just edit that part out?"

People laugh and I realize that damn, the guy's doing it. He's winning them over.

"Anyway, as I was saying, Nathan, Michael, and I all love the Racketeers. This team means the world to all of us. And you all are a part of that. The fans are integral. And you know I love sharing parts of my life with you. From pre-game fun on the plane with my teammates and friends, to trying a new amazing donut place, to thinking about getting a guinea pig and then deciding against it, I've shared a lot with you all outside of this arena. But…"

He does that three-sixty turn thing again, including everyone in the arena.

"If you fuck with my family, I'm gonna stop. All you're gonna get is Crew McNeill, number 17." He shrugs. "I mean, I'll still be MVP and high scorer and all that…"

Lots of laughter again. And another Crew grin.

"But that's all I'm giving ya', Chicago. Just hockey. But if you're cool, the way I know you can be, I'll share my family with you too. Vacation photos, Sunday brunch videos with recipes—Michael is an amazing cook by the way—and I'm ready right here and now to start a who-gives-Dani-the-best-gifts contest against Nate and Michael with you all as the judges."

Cheers erupt in response to that.

I find myself smiling too. That would actually be hilarious. Bring it on, McNeill.

"And trust me," Crew says when the noise dies down a little. "You want to be a part of our family. We're really damn awesome. Fun, and smart, and hilarious, and sexy."

He gets more cheers then.

He grins and looks directly at the three of us.

I look over at Michael. He grins at me. Then we both look down at Danielle.

She's crying.

We both sit forward and lean in.

She shakes her head and smiles. "I'm happy," she assures us. "Really, really happy. He's doing so great."

I sigh and sit back.

But he is.

"So you have a chance here, Chicago," Crew says. "Show us that you're the amazing, fun, open-minded, accepting city I know you are. Follow along with the coolest hockey family ever. And…" He pauses, and his grin is huge on the jumbotron. "Be very jealous of Danielle Larkin."

He winks.

The arena goes crazy.

And…holy hell.

I think Crew just became the MVP of our family too.

Dammit.

But I'm grinning as he drops the mic—literally, and that's probably going to cost me—walks up into the stands, gives me a bro-hug, gives Michael a bro-hug, and then lifts Danielle up, her legs wrapping around his waist, and kisses the hell out of her.

On the jumbotron.

Of course.

Wade (Sammy the Malamute)

Wow.

I did not see that coming.

Mr. Armstrong is in a poly-relationship.

He doesn't seem like the type to share anything, let alone his woman, but I guess he has a whole other side to him.

I mean, he's still scary.

But turns out he's kind of a cool motherfucker, too.

Epilogue

Dani

"CREW IS ON FIRE TONIGHT," Luna says, briefly glancing up from her phone as the crowd roars as he scores again.

"He's been playing so well," I agree, happily watching my boyfriend move up and down the length of the ice, outskating his competition.

"He better be, given how much I pay him," Nathan says on the other side of me.

I turn to my other boyfriend and smile. "You are such a fake grump. Even social media has caught on that you're not as scary as you pretend to be."

It's true. Most of the Racketeer fans have been eating up Crew's promised posts sharing bits and pieces of our lives together with the hashtag #cookieandco. We've gotten tons of support and now there are even signs at the games that read things like, "I want to be Dani," and "why choose?" with photos of Crew, Nathan, and Michael.

I can't believe I'm Dani most days and that I have these three amazing men in my life, loving me.

"I'm very scary," Nathan protests, dressed casually in jeans and a Racketeers T-shirt. He would prefer to be in a suit, but Valerie and I are working on making him more approachable, more a part of the fan base. "Babies and dogs hate me."

I don't believe him. I kiss him softly. "Well, I don't hate you. I love you."

"I love you too," he says, with a warm smile.

Michael shoots me a text from the bench.

> I'll come up for a minute when the period ends.
> Stay in the seats.

With a smile, I respond, then realize I have a text from my mother.

> Jan from the Ladies Guild says her daughter
> says you have a boyfriend. Is he coming with you
> for Christmas?

Um…yeah, I need to figure out a way to tell my parents about my three boyfriends. So far I'm just glad they're not hockey fans and aren't on any social media. I show the text to Luna.

She grins at me. "Merry Christmas, Mom and Dad, here are my three boyfriends! You might want to mention that before you show up with a poinsettia and three men."

"I'm not sure my parents are going to be thrilled about this. What about yours?" I bite my lip. I like Crew and Luna's parents. I would be upset if they weren't supportive of my very public relationship with the guys.

"Oh, they're totally fine with it. In fact, prepare yourself for my mom to get wine drunk and make stocking stuffer and big package jokes to you all night."

I laugh. "I can handle that."

Nathan's hand is on my knee but he doesn't seem to be listening to Luna and I chat. He's focused on the game. I know every W is one step closer to his ultimate dream and cementing his grandfather's legacy.

Luna is back on her phone.

"What are you looking at anyway? You're barely paying attention."

"I'm trying to find three hot guys to have a hookup with. I want to be Dani too."

That makes me blush and laugh. "If that's what you want, I'm sure you can have it. Do you know how many guys in Chicago would jump at the chance to be with a girl like you?"

"I've been practicing abundance meditations every night and releasing my intentions to the universe so I'm reasonably confident. Plus, I'm cute and I make baked goods. Men should appreciate me."

Alexei, the Racketeers defenseman, skates right up to the boards just then and taps the plexiglass, causing us both to jump, and Luna to finally look up from her phone.

He points his stick at her. "You're my ride home tonight."

Well, damn, that was fast. "The universe has delivered," I say with a giggle.

"What?" she asks Alexei, sounding a little bewildered, but mostly intrigued. "I'm giving you a ride home? Um…sure, okay." She shrugs. "Do you like chocolate chip pancakes?"

I snort. I guess she's planning to stay overnight.

But he laughs and shakes his head, and points at her again.

A voice behind us says, "He means me."

We turn and see a guy in his mid-twenties.

"I'm his best friend, and roommate, Cameron." He lifts a brow. "But yes, we both like chocolate chip pancakes."

"Oh, shit, sorry," Luna gives him a weak smile. "Hi." She turns back around. "Well, that's embarrassing," she mutters to me.

"Not as embarrassing as having your butt on the jumbotron," I tell her. Then laugh. "And hey, there's two right there. You only have to collect a third to be like me."

She gives me a shut up look.

The buzzer ends the period.

Crew skates to the bench and then as the players all take the tunnel to the locker room, he leaves the line and leans in to give me a passionate kiss.

The crowd goes wild.

"You're on the KissCam again," Luna says. "Make it count."

Michael appears behind Crew, who slides out of the way for the hot doc to give me his own searing kiss. I'm practically melting from the inside out I'm so happy.

Sure, there have been haters, but for the most part the fans have been amazing in their support, and it means everything to me—to us—that we can be ourselves in public.

"Your turn, Nate," Crew tells him, clapping him on the shoulder.

"I really should outlaw the KissCam," Nathan says dryly.

But then Sammy the Malamute appears behind the guys and holds his paw out for me. I think he means I should kiss him, which I'm not going to do, but it seems like positive PR to take the mascot's outstretched hand and at least play to the crowd. I start to stand.

That's all my grumpy billionaire needs to spur him into action.

"Absolutely not," Nathan says, waving Sammy off. He turns to me. "You're not going anywhere." Then he kisses me, knowing full well we're on the jumbotron.

I love it.

The crowd loves it.

Michael and Crew love it.

And I think Nathan secretly does too.

It's confirmed when the next day the screen saver on his phone is this moment.

The four of us, all together, on the KissCam at the arena.

God, I love hockey.

Want MORE Nathan, Michael and Crew? Read a Puck One Night

Stands BONUS scene at http://subscribepage.io/emmafoxxbonus

Then Dani, Nathan, Michael, and Crew are back in Four Pucking Christmases, another steamy, fun why-choose rom com!

I always imagined bringing my hot, charming, amazing new boyfriend home for Christmas.

And I thought about how great it would be to meet his parents too.

But I never really thought about what that might look like if I was dating *three* men. Together. As in, what it would be like if we were all dating each other.

And now it's here. Our first Christmas. And our first chance to be together...with our families.

Four Christmases in two days.

Where's that spiked eggnog?

About the Author

Emma Foxx is the super fun and sexy pen name for two long-time, bestselling romance authors who decided why have just one hero when you can have three at the same time? (they're not sure what took them so long to figure this out)! Emma writes contemporary romances that will make you laugh (yes, maybe out loud in public) and want more…books (sure, that's what we mean 😉). Find Emma on Instagram, Tik Tok, and Goodreads.

Also by Emma Foxx

Four Pucking Christmases

I always imagined bringing my hot, charming, amazing new boyfriend home for Christmas.

And I thought about how great it would be to meet his parents too.

But I never really thought about what that might look like if I was dating *three* men. Together. As in, what it would be like if we were all dating each other.

And now it's here. Our first Christmas. And our first chance to be together...with our families.

Four Christmases in two days.

Where's that spiked eggnog?

Dani, Nathan, Michael, and Crew are back in* Four Pucking Christmases*, a steamy, fun why-choose rom com! No cheating, a guaranteed HEA, and the guys are all about her.

Printed in Great Britain
by Amazon

50391602R00184